BLOODY FRIDAY

Edmond Gagnon

ISBN 9781-99928-14-4-1

Printed in the United States of America on acid-free paper.

Edmond Gagnon
2014
First Edition

2019
Second Edition

Acknowledgements

I would like to thank my fans and readers. Your invaluable support, feedback, and constructive criticisms have helped me to become a better writer.

Special thanks to the following people:

Beta Readers and Pre-editing:

Doug and Laurie Cowper
Kay Tall
Michael Carter
Donalie Beltran – author of "Murder is a Family Affair"

Proofreader – Sarah Braund

My wife, Cathryn

In remembrance of the victims of Bloody Friday,

Belfast, Ireland

July 21st, 1972

1

Bloody Friday

Megan Doyle was thoroughly enjoying a pint of Guinness at O'Darby's Pub, on her last day in Belfast, Ireland. It was Friday, July 21st, 1972. The pretty Canadian girl was visiting relatives and touring the United Kingdom for six weeks.

Megan's flight home didn't leave until later in the evening, so she thought she'd spend her last afternoon with her new Irish friend, Erin Kelly. The two twenty-year-olds had met a couple days earlier at O'Darby's. They discovered that they had the same taste in beer and men. They hit it off immediately, joking how they could have been life-long friends.

Erin seemed preoccupied to Megan, so she asked if everything was okay. Erin said she'd been scrapping with her boyfriend, Jimmy Flynn. Jimmy was spending a lot of time with other men she didn't approve of, but he said he was going to make it up to her and take her away for the weekend. Erin's face lit up when she told Megan she would be meeting Jimmy when he came to pick her up.

"Just wait till you see how handsome he is. His long black curly hair and those light blue eyes that I fell for. I just can't get enough of him. Damn his boys club."

The girls giggled, sipped their beers, and talked about how Erin might visit Canada some day. Erin had never been anywhere off the island. Up north to Derry, was as far as she'd gone. A weekend away with Jimmy would probably be a short trip up the coast, to an old abandoned cottage he knew about. Jimmy promised Erin he'd take her to America some day. Jimmy made lots of promises.

The girls were a couple of pints into the lazy afternoon when Jimmy Flynn came strutting into O'Darby's. Megan had her back to the door, but Erin's big smile announced Jimmy's arrival.

Erin leapt from her bar stool. "Hello my darlin. I want ya ta meet my friend Megan, from Canada."

Jimmy gave Erin a half hug and kissed her on the forehead.

He brushed his stringy black hair from his eyes and said, "Aye, good ta meet ya. C'mon baby we gotta get goin."

"What? We just ordered another pint. Why don't ya sit and have one Jimmy?"

Jimmy checked his watch, and then he looked around the bar.

"We gotta get ta the cottage before dark baby, but I gotta meet one of the boys over at bus station first. The car's out front, c'mon we gotta go."

"Oh, one of the boys," Erin said, as she looked at Megan and rolled her eyes.

Erin apologized to Megan for cutting their visit short. Jimmy never even said good-bye. He was already out the door.

"Boy, he's all wound up today; I don't know what the big hurry is! It was so lovely ta meet ya Megan, we'll write each other and stay in touch, okay?"

Jimmy was already waiting in the car as the girls hugged and said their farewells. Megan watched out the front window as Erin and Jimmy drove off. She noticed a pay phone near the front door, so she called a taxi to return to her hotel. Erin cancelled their beer order before she left, so Megan thought she'd catch a nap before dinner.

The Bakery

Erin went off on Jimmy as soon as she got into the car.

"That was pretty rude Jimmy. I'll probably never see Megan again."

Jimmy cut Erin off.

"Maybe sooner than ya think baby, ya know how I'm always talkin about taking ya t'America."

Erin went silent, her big brown eyes fixed on Jimmy. She was a tiny thing with a huge heart. And her heart belonged to Jimmy.

"What are ya talkin about Jimmy? America? I thought we were goin up the coast to your secret cottage?"

Jimmy kept checking his mirrors and his watch, as he darted in and out of the thick traffic.

"I wanted ta surprise ya baby. One of the boys set it up. We're getting outa here for good. We've got tickets on an ocean freighter to Boston. We leave tonight."

"But what about my mum or my things? I need to pack Jimmy."

"I took care of it, baby. I packed yer things and left yer mum with a few flagons of single malt. I know it won't last her long, but I told her we were takin an extended vacation. Yer suitcase is in the trunk."

Erin stared at Jimmy is disbelief. *Was it really true?*

She knew she'd never really miss her drunken stepmother. Her real mother died when Erin was quite young, she barely remembered her. Erin's father died a year after marrying his second wife. She was his mirror image; they were both drunks. Erin was closest to her older brother Patrick. He always looked out for her. Patrick eventually left home and joined the military, to get away from his abusive father who liked to use him as a punching bag.

Erin met Jimmy through Patrick. The two boys grew up closer than most brothers. They even had matching shamrock tattoos on the back of their necks. Patrick always thought Erin was too good for Jimmy, even though Jimmy was his best friend. Patrick had a soft spot for Jimmy, who was orphaned as a baby when his parents died in a car wreck. Jimmy had a bad temper and he was a difficult child. He bounced around a few different foster homes, but eventually went off on his own once he was old enough.

Patrick was the only one who could effectively deal with Jimmy's temper, and the trouble it got him into. He eventually gave into their infatuation and gave Jimmy his blessing. Patrick told Jimmy that there was only one condition: If he ever hurt Erin or let anything happen to her, he would never forgive him.

The trip to America had always been a dream that she and Jimmy talked about. Erin was at a loss for words as dozens of memories and new ideas ran through her head. While she was lost in her thoughts, Jimmy wheeled the car into a parking spot across from the bus station.

"I gotta drop somethin off to one of the boys before we go baby. I'll just be a minute."

Jimmy took a satchel across the street to where another man was waiting in an old black car. The two men got into a heated conversation, so Erin jumped behind the wheel of Jimmy's car. She remembered that Megan might still be at O'Darby's and it would be a great time to tell her that she was going to America. Erin yelled out the window to Jimmy, saying she'd be right back. Jimmy looked back in bewilderment, but he nodded and waived her off.

O'Darby's was only a couple blocks away, but Erin couldn't find a parking spot anywhere close. A car pulled out of a spot in front of the bakery at the opposite end of the block from O'Darby's and Erin wheeled in.

Timing is Everything

Megan's taxi pulled up in front of O'Darby's, so she went out the front door to catch her ride. Megan paused for a split second as her foot touched the paved sidewalk. For that split second, she felt stillness in the air. Then she was blasted with a cacophony of sound; breaking glass, a sharp, ear piercing bang, and the roar of what sounded like a speeding train.

Megan was thrown sideways from the shockwave of the explosion at the opposite end of the block. A newspaper box cushioned her fall, as she was thrown to the sidewalk. Megan was dazed. She looked down the street and saw a thick cloud of dark smoke with an orange fireball mushrooming up, and into the blue sky.

A firm hand grabbed Megan by the arm. It was the taxi driver trying to help her up. She felt like she had just awoken from a deep sleep, and was groggy. She could see the taxi driver was talking to her, but she couldn't hear his words. Megan staggered as the taxi driver guided her to his car. Her hearing slowly came back, like someone was turning up the volume. She smelled something burnt in the still air.

The taxi driver said, "C'mon lassie, we need ta get out a here."

Megan tripped over something on the road as she reached for the rear door of the taxi. It was a woman's sandal, spattered with blood. She felt nauseous and weak in the knees as the driver helped her into the back seat of his taxi. Megan could hear everything now; there were people yelling and screaming. She looked out the back window as they drove away. She saw cars on fire and bloodied people wandering about in the street, like zombies. Some rubble and the bloodied woman's sandal lay in the foreground.

The explosion at the bakery shook the ground under Jimmy's feet, two blocks away. He turned around and saw that Erin and his car were gone. He remembered she had said she'd be right back. Jimmy got a sick feeling deep down in his gut. He immediately broke into a sweat, and then started running toward the bakery.

As he rounded the corner by O'Darby's he noticed the fire and thick black smoke at the other end of the block. Just then, Megan's taxi rounded the corner. Megan saw Jimmy, but he didn't notice the taxi. Jimmy stopped at the bloodied sandal in the middle of the road.

It was such a tiny sandal. *Could it be Erin's? No, it can't be.*

Jimmy's feet felt like they weighed fifty pounds each, as he tried to walk to the other end of the block. He felt sick to his stomach, when he recognized what was left of his car, parked near the bakery. There was an empty parking spot directly behind his car; the vehicle that had been parked there was upside down on the other side of the street, in flames. Jimmy saw the driver's side door of his car was open, but he couldn't see anyone inside.

Jimmy forced himself to move closer, but his feet got even heavier. People around him were screaming and crying. Black smoke wafted through the air. It smelled of burnt fuel, flesh and gunpowder. Some people were helping others who were bloodied and injured by the explosion. A man was bent over a woman's torso, feeling her neck for a pulse; he shook his head and walked away.

The woman's face looked familiar, but one side of it was badly burned. The force of the explosion had blown all of her limbs off. It was surreal, but Jimmy's eyes locked onto the dead woman lying there, in the middle of the street. It was Erin. Just then another explosion shook the whole neighborhood; it came from the bus station just two blocks away.

Jimmy fell to his knees. He looked up to the sky and shouted, "Oh my God, what have I done?"

The heart of Belfast was on fire and in chaos. That day became known as "Bloody Friday." The Provisional Irish Republican Army set off nineteen separate bombs in the downtown area in just over an hour. Nine people died and one hundred and thirty were injured. The IRA accomplished their goal that day, the widespread disruption to everyday life in Ireland.

2

Jungle Ghost

On Bloody Friday Patrick Kelly lay prone and silent in a thick and tangled jungle in North Viet Nam, near the Laotian border. He was three days into his mission. Patrick was following a North Vietnamese tax collector from village to village along the Ho Chi Minh trail. He hoped that the tax collector would lead him back to his army base camp.

Patrick had grown accustomed to living in the jungle; it had been his home for the past year while he was assigned to the CIA's Phoenix program. He was originally recruited from his British SAS regiment, to team up with U.S. Special Forces who were carrying out covert operations in North Viet Nam and Laos.

At the time, Britain wouldn't admit to being involved in the Viet Nam war. Although they denied sending troops to fight in the conflict, they secretly supported the United States by helping them ship essential military supplies. They also permitted some of their elite soldiers to volunteer and serve in exchange programs that allowed them to fight in Viet Nam with the Australians. In the infant stages of the conflict the SAS operatives were known as the Jungle Ghosts. They were the elite, the best of the best.

Patrick checked his watch. The early morning sun was almost completely blocked by the thick jungle canopy. The bits that shone through looked like little twinkling lights hung high in the trees. It had rained through the night; the warmth of the morning sun caused the cool and wet jungle floor to steam like a giant sauna. Patrick was oblivious. He was trained to ignore things like heat, cold, rain, thirst, hunger, and even pain. He knew how to sustain himself indefinitely in the jungle, if the situation presented itself. Patrick was thirsty and his canteen was getting near empty. He reached up and took hold of the giant leaf he had been using for shelter.

He folded the leaf to form a trough and let the rain water funnel into his mouth, *I'll save my canteen for later*.

Things were still quiet in the village, so Patrick lay back trying to picture the sky beyond the jungle canopy. He remembered how big the blue sky was, back home in Ireland. His sister Erin would make him and Jimmy sandwiches to take along when they ran off to spend the day along the seashore.

They'd forget about how shitty their lives were, dreaming and talking about traveling to far away places. They'd fill their lungs with salty ocean air and listen to the sound of crashing waves, as they stared off into the big sky, littered with huge puffy clouds. Erin would point out different animal shapes that she saw in the clouds. The boys just laughed at her.

How is my little sister? Patrick wondered.

A pig squealed, jarring Patrick out of his trance. He rolled over and peered through his sniper rifle scope, scanning the village. A naked little boy was chasing the pig and whacking it with a stick. Chickens scattered as the pig nearly trampled them. Patrick aimed his rifle, targeting the pig.

Patrick imagined the smell of bacon frying. *Yum, fried bacon for breakfast with a couple of fresh eggs, sunny side up please.*

Patrick was hungry. He reached in his rucksack settling for his C Rats, hardtack biscuits and jam were the special of the day. He couldn't pack the normal C rations. The cans were too noisy while humping through the jungle and the extra weight slowed him down. Packing light was Patrick's specialty; he opted for high calorie, high energy foods. Patrick loved to pretend he was a gourmet chef. He loaded up his biscuits with processed cheese spread, jam, and chocolate…his own version of campfire s'mores.

It was time for breakfast in the village too. Some of the old women stoked up the fires and started boiling pots of water. It was rice for breakfast. A couple other rug rats joined the naked boy in chasing the village pig around. The little grass village sprouted to life, just as it had every day for the past hundred years. An old man delivered some fresh kindling to the women boiling water.

Where the hell is that tax collector?

Patrick looked at his watch again.

Did the slimy zipper-head sleep in, or did he sneak off before sun-up?

Mixed Emotions

Patrick's year in the program was almost up. He pondered his future while giving the tax collector another hour of beauty sleep. The military had become Patrick's life, but it was a love/hate relationship. He didn't miss his old life, but he missed a few of the people who were in it.

He missed his sister, and yes, his missed his best buddy Jimmy Flynn. It had been about a year since he'd seen either one of them. His annual leave was coming up; he'd have to decide what his next move would be. There was really nothing for him back home.

The jungle heat and humidity made Patrick a bit drowsy, he started to shift his position but froze stiff. A bright green and yellow snake about three feet in length slithered across his legs, just above his boots. He could hear the sound of the snake's skin rubbing his pants as it slithered into the thick jungle grass.

Guess that's why they taught us to tuck our pants in our boots.

Patrick thought about the training job his colonel offered him, and then recalled his previous missions. *I wonder if I'll miss killing people for a living.*

He had accepted the role of assassin as a normal part of his job. *Just like taking out the trash at home, it's not so bad. After all, they are the enemy.*

Some of the other specially trained assassins Patrick worked with just vanished, or dropped out of the program with mental problems. It was jungle-rot to the brain or post traumatic stress disorder. Not everyone was cut out to selectively kill people for a living. *Must have been my loving up-bringing with my Da using me as his personal punching bag.*

Patrick thought back to his first kill. They tell you the first is always the hardest. He was in the best shape of his life, and mentally prepared for the task at hand. What he wasn't prepared for was how difficult it was for his brain to signal his hand…to make his forefinger curl…to squeeze that trigger. That split-second decision and movement lasted an eternity.

He could still visualize it. The bullet he sent from that trigger squeeze travelled almost the same speed as the brain wave, as it penetrated the forehead of his target, another human being. He was no taller than five feet and couldn't have weighed a hundred pounds. He could have been a school teacher before the war, but on the day, he died, he was wearing the uniform of a Colonel in the North Vietnamese Army. He was the enemy.

According to Patrick's briefing, the little Colonel was attending all the villages in the area spreading propaganda, telling the villagers there was a traitor among them. He would select a villager and execute him or her as an example of what would happen to traitors. This was meant to keep the villagers loyal to their cause. The Americans would sometimes visit the same villages, accusing the inhabitants of being VC. Of course, they'd spread *their* propaganda at the same time. Patrick really didn't believe in anyone's politics. It was just a job to him.

The pig squealed again. Patrick peered back into the village, *Shit!*

An enemy patrol entered the village; the soldiers yelled at the villagers, demanding that they come out of their hooches. Patrick could feel his heart beating through his chest and against the jungle floor. His muscles tensed and his asshole puckered as he scanned the village through his rifle scope, *Shit…shit!*

The tax collector used the diversion to sneak out of the opposite side of the village, and into the jungle. Patrick rolled to his knees, and on to his feet, almost in one quick motion. He flanked left around the village, in hopes of picking up the tax collector's trail. He moved through the jungle like a tiger hunting its prey. He stayed low and stopped every hundred yards listening for sounds of his prey. The jungle was silent except for the sound of his own heart pounding in his ears.

Patrick found the tax collector's trail. He picked up his pace in an attempt to catch up, and put some distance between him and the village. Patrick made a quick left turn with the trail; he felt a sharp pain in his right shoulder. He lost his footing and fell forward towards a large tree.

Patrick tried reaching out with his right arm to break his fall, but his arm did not respond. He crashed face-first into the tree. He rolled off it and into some tall grass. Patrick was disoriented, but he recognized the familiar barking sound of an AK 47. He realized he'd been hit in the right shoulder. He instinctively took the rifle into his left hand and scanned the jungle for his shooter. The gunfire stopped. The jungle was silent again.

The sweat from Patrick's forehead ran into his eyes. He wiped it with his shoulder. It was blood coming from a gash on his forehead. Ignoring that injury, Patrick glanced down to the hole in his shoulder. A bullet had passed through it; his collar bone was obviously broken. The sharp pain started to make Patrick feel light-headed, and a bit nauseous.

He did what he was trained to do. He ignored the blood and pain and concentrated on the job at hand. He continued looking for his shooter. Patrick's vision started to blur. It was like he was looking through a tunnel and the black walls were closing in on him. He realized he was about to pass out.

Just as he was about to fall unconscious, a firm hand grabbed Patrick by the back of his rucksack. He came to just enough to look back. He could only see the back of the man who was dragging him through the jungle. He heard more gunfire. Then everything went black.

A Helping Hand

Patrick saw a blinding bright light. It was not the light at the end of the tunnel, he was still alive. Patrick recognized the blue sky. He hadn't seen it in days. He heard water. Patrick realized he was on a boat. He blinked to correct his blurred vision. His nose was filled with a poignant odor, like cat piss. It was emanating from a man who was staring back at him from the bow of the small wooden boat he was in.

The man looked half Asian, half American Indian. He wore a bandana around his head to hold his long black hair in place. The man had steely eyes that looked right through him. The grunts in Nam called it the fifty-yard stare. He was sweaty and shirtless, except for an open, dirty brown vest. A black stone cross hung on a leather string around his neck. He was holding an M16 rifle, which was a good thing.

"You safe now GI." the man said in broken English.

"We take good care of you."

Patrick looked back at the other similar looking, but shorter man operating the small motor at the back of the boat. They were the Degar, or Montagnards (Mountain people in French). They were indigenous of the central highlands in Viet Nam and had a long history of tension with the Vietnamese majority. The U.S. trained many of them to assist in their Special Forces operations along the Ho Chi Minh trail. They were allies with, and fought alongside the Americans. Patrick nodded to the man staring at him, and then the lights went out again.

A bright light and the smell of ether caught Patrick's attention. He opened his eyes and saw people in surgical gowns and masks hovering over him. He was still alive. Patrick just started to comprehend that he was in a hospital, when someone put a mask over his face rendering him unconscious.

News from Home

Patrick coughed to clear his dry throat. He opened his eyes and recognized his Colonel sitting in a chair beside his bed.

"Patty Boy, good to see you again."

The Colonel always called him Patty. He had personally selected Patrick for his unit, and then took him under his wing and treated him like a son.

"The doc was a bit worried about you but I told him it would take more than a bullet to the shoulder and a concussion to kill a tough Irish bastard like you."

Patrick smiled.

"I missed you too sir."

"If you feel up to it, I want to talk to you about that training job and your leave that's coming up at the end of your tour."

Patrick glanced down to his shoulder.

"Guess I won't be back in the boonies for a while."

"No, I highly doubt it son. Listen up now. I gotta give you some bad news from home."

"You know there's nothing back there for me sir, I was planning a visit to see my sister, and then I thought I might take your job offer."

"That's what I gotta tell you about Patty. It's about your sister. There was an accident back home."

"What kind of accident? What are you talking about?"

"There were some bombings at home Patty, your sister was killed by one of the explosions."

Patrick remained silent. He'd seen so much death and destruction during the war. He wasn't sure how he was supposed to feel. A knot formed in his stomach and a warm sensation came over him. He focused on the Colonel's gaze; his eyes started to burn. Tears formed and flowed gently down both cheeks.

Patrick couldn't remember the last time he had cried, or how it felt. He tried to talk, but there were no words; he just sobbed. Years of built up emotions poured out of Patrick like water from a ten-gallon pail. The Colonel put his hand on Patrick's arm and patted him lightly.

"Don't worry son, I'll take care of you. We'll get you home."

3

Boys & Girls

Academics did not come easy for Megan Doyle. She was enrolled in the law program at the University of Windsor, but she struggled just to get a passing grade her first year. Her second year seemed harder than the first; she finally succumbed and dropped out.

Megan's parents couldn't afford to pay her full tuition, so she worked part time jobs to help pay her way through school. She had hoped to get a law degree, then travel Europe some more. It had been five years since her trip to the UK.

Megan wanted to go back to school. She considered the nursing program at St. Clair College, but she seemed to be too busy working her two waitressing jobs. She worked days at a Swiss Chalet restaurant and nights at the college pub. Both jobs were only part time but Megan made good money from her tips.

Her parents liked the fact Megan was self-sufficient, but they would have preferred that she followed up with some sort of career. They said they'd love to have a grandchild some day and they inquired about her love life.

What love life? Megan would always say. She didn't seem to have much time for that. It's not like she didn't get offers or date any men. They just didn't seem to measure up to her expectations; most were too immature for her taste. Megan could have her pick of the litter.

She was attractive with a great personality. She had her Irish mother's good looks and red hair, along with her Scottish father's green eyes and comedic personality. A few light freckles on her nose and her sparkling green eyes lit up her face when she smiled. Megan was no more than five feet tall, but she had all the right curves. She was quick witted and loved to joke with her customers, which is probably why she made such good tips.

Hooking Up

In 1978 Megan's mom received a favor from an old friend who taught up at the nursing college in St. Thomas. She got Megan into nursing school there. Megan found it difficult being back in school but she swore to give it her best shot. Her mom's friend offered her a place to stay and once again, Megan was able to find a part time waitressing job nearby.

One Wednesday night, after a tough day of lectures, Megan joined a bunch of her fellow students for a night out. They went to the Star Lounge; it was where all the girls went to dance and let their hair down.

The Star Lounge also happened to be where all the recruits from the Ontario Police College in Aylmer hung out. Back then, almost all police officers were men. Wednesday was lady's night, so that meant there would be lots of men there too!

Norm Strom had been a police cadet with the Windsor Police Force for a year when they sent him to the police college for the recruit course. He hated the place because of the shitty food and military type regimen.

Nobody told him that being a cop meant he'd have to get out of bed at six in the morning, eat a breakfast that was cooked two hours earlier, and then march to an inspection in full police uniform. Standing at attention for what seemed like an hour, while extremely hung over, was not fun. Norm saw more than one poor bastard pass out and crash to the floor.

One would think that a greasy breakfast would help soak up some of the previous night's booze. Perhaps it was the soggy pancakes that sat for two hours, that didn't sit well with Norm. After Police College, Norm could never look at pancakes again. Of course, being hung over for morning parade wasn't Norm's fault. He was just trying to be one of the boys, to be accepted by his peers.

It only seemed fitting that Norm joined the boys for lady's night at the Star Lounge. He had a steady girlfriend back in Windsor, they were high school sweethearts. He was a loyal boyfriend, but he still liked to check out the local scenery like any other young and horny boy.

Norm and his other cop buddies got to the Star late, it was their last stop. They found an empty table and Norm scoped out the room. There were a lot of young women, but it seemed like most were spoken for. He spotted a cute little redhead a couple of tables over. She wore jeans and a white sweater that accented her shapely form perfectly. Norm didn't waste any time. Although he was there with the boys, he liked to dance and loved pretty girls.

He caught the redhead by surprise.

"Do you want to dance?"

She was caught a bit off guard.

"Uh, I was just leaving the waitress some money for my drink."

Norm pulled a five out of his pocket and threw it on the table.

"Okay, your drink is paid for, now do you want to dance?"

She looked up at Norm and offered her hand.

"Sure, I'm Megan. Let's go."

Megan led Norm by the hand up to the dance floor. It was packed with hot and sweaty bodies, but the timing was perfect. The hard rock song ended and 'Hey Jude' came on.

Norm thought, *Great, it's a long slow song. It will give me a chance to get close and personal with the cute redhead.*

Norm pulled Megan in close. She had to strain her neck to look up at him. There was over a foot in height difference between the two of them. Norm noticed a slight hint of lavender in her perfume. He had a nose for such things.

"I'm Norm. It's really nice to meet you."

"It's nice to meet you too Norm."

Megan smiled at Norm. Her green eyes sparkled, reflecting the colored lights around the disco ball. She was as cute as a button.

Too bad I have a girlfriend back home, Norm thought.

Megan and Norm chatted back and forth about nursing and policing, not really talking about themselves. The song was almost done but neither Norm, nor Megan let up.

"So, what brings you nurses here Megan?"

"Same thing that brings you cops here Norm."

Norm got the hint. It seemed pretty obvious to Norm that Megan was his for the asking.

She said, "Let's go outside and get some air."

Megan was very affectionate. She took Norm by the hand again, leading him outside and into the parking lot. They both stopped walking at the same time, near one corner of the building. Megan turned towards Norm. Her face was like a cameo in the darkness, but her eyes still sparkled, reflecting what little moon light there was.

Megan put her palms on Norm's chest as he pulled her in closer. Their lips met. Norm felt Megan's excitement as she parted her lips to let his moist tongue slip inside. Norm gently caressed the inside of her upper lip with the tip of his tongue.

She greeted his tongue with her own as Norm pulled her in even closer, almost lifting her off the ground. It was a cold night but Norm felt warm. He felt Megan's warmth. He felt a throbbing heart, but he wasn't sure whose it was. The two were as one for that moment.

"C'mon Megan, the bus is leaving" one of her friends shouted as they exited the bar and headed into the parking lot.

Megan looked up at Norm and said, "Meet me Friday? I stay here all weekend."

"I can't," Norm replied. "I have to go home this weekend."

Norm didn't have the heart to tell Megan he had a girlfriend waiting at home. They kissed again, but the honking horn interrupted them.

"Okay, but you don't know what you're missing!"

Norm stood in silence, as he watched Megan run off to catch her ride.

Missed Opportunities

Norm always travelled back to Windsor on the weekends. He couldn't fathom the thought of staying in that hell-hole over the weekend, even if it would be with a hot redhead like Megan. Norm was loyal to his girlfriend, so he went home to see her. It wasn't until sometime later that he found out she was cheating on him while he was away.

The weekend flew by. It was a great sex-filled weekend with his girlfriend, but Norm couldn't help but wonder about Megan on the drive back up to the college. Norm went up to the student lounge for a couple of drinks before turning in for the night. One of his classmates asked him how his weekend was. The poor bastard had to stay in the college for the whole ten weeks because he lived in northern Ontario, about ten hours from the police college.

He greeted Norm with, "I hope you got laid at home."

"Yes, as a matter of fact I did."

"Well, so did your cute little red-headed friend. She spent the whole weekend here at the college. I saw her by the pool. She looked pretty hot in a bikini."

"What was she doing here?"

"She was shacked up with some Toronto cop who's here on the drug course. Pete or Pat…Kelly, I think."

Norm made it clear to everyone he wouldn't get married until he was at least twenty-five, so he had a couple of years to sow his wild oats. He dated a bit, but liked to have at least one woman available for booty calls.

One day at work, Norm spotted a cute girl working in the records department. He asked Sandra out and they went on a few dates. Feeling this girl was pretty special, Norm sent her flowers for Valentines Day. He didn't see Sandra that day; she was working the afternoon shift, while Norm was on days.

Since Sandra was working, and Norm had an itch to scratch, he took out his regular booty call, Laura for the evening. He knew she was a sure thing. In thinking with the wrong head, Norm took Laura to Flannigan's pub in Detroit for late night cocktails. He wished he had a cloaking device when he walked into the bar and saw Sandra there, drinking with some friends.

Apparently, they had gotten off early and went out for drinks after work. Norm hid in the opposite room, near the pool tables. He'd barely gulped his first drink down, when Sandra appeared at his table.

"Hi Norm. I just wanted to thank you for the beautiful flowers you sent me today."

She couldn't have played it more perfectly. Norm turned as red as a fire truck.

"Aren't you going to introduce me to your friend?"

Norm still managed to get lucky that night, but needless to say, Sandra laid down the ground rules after that. She was a solo act. About two years later, Norm married Sandra. It was one month before his twenty-fifth birthday.

4

Black & Bruins

It was the crack of noon by the time Jimmy rolled out of bed. He shuffled to the bathroom, noticing he still had his socks on. The sun beamed through the little bathroom window and reflected off the mirror, blinding Jimmy.

He yanked the shower curtain closed with his right hand as he fumbled for his dick with his left. The boozy smell of his own urine made him wince. Jimmy looked in the mirror as he released the previous night's beer. His eyes looked just like the Hulk's before he turned green.

Jimmy put the coffee pot on, then returned to the bedroom to get dressed. He looked in his dresser drawer for a fresh t-shirt, but the drawer was empty. Jimmy found his pants half under the bed, and turned inside out. The coins from his pocket were scattered all over the floor.

He picked up two different black t-shirts from a pile on the floor and gave them the smell test; the Bruin's one would do. Jimmy grabbed the part bottle of Jameson from the night stand, and then headed back into the kitchen.

The morning newspaper was protruding through the mail slot in his door, so Jimmy grabbed it and threw it on the kitchen table. He took a dirty coffee cup from the sink and rinsed it out with his forefinger and some tap water. The smell of brewing coffee filled the air in the kitchen. It was the only pleasant thing Jimmy enjoyed in the morning.

The black coffee was piping hot. Jimmy spilled some over his shaky hand and he almost dropped the whole cup on the newspaper. He sat down and wiped the spilled coffee off the front page of The Herald with the back of his hand. Jimmy focused on the date. It was July 21st, 1977. *Shite, had it really been five years since Bloody Friday? Five years since he left home where he had killed the only person who ever loved him?*

Jimmy added a shot of Jameson to his coffee. *Better make it a double today.*

Jimmy liked his coffee black, with a shot of Jameson added, to kick-start his day. He also took a shine to ice hockey and the Bruins, since settling in Boston. Jimmy took a sip of coffee and flipped to the sports page.

There was a write-up on the NHL draft and how the Bruin's acquired a future prospect by the name of Ray Bourque. Jimmy couldn't wait for the season to start. He loved the hard-hitting action of hockey better than the football back home.

A fog horn sounded in the harbor. Jimmy glanced out his kitchen window. From his flat in Charlestown and his strategically placed chair, he could almost see the harbor. What were clearly visible were the cranes in the shipyards, where Jimmy learned how to smuggle weapons from the U.S. to Ireland. He took another sip of coffee and sat back in his chair, gazing out the window.

Jimmy remembered the day he left Belfast, like it was yesterday. He could still smell the cordite and burnt fuel in the air. The human carnage was etched in his memory. He still saw Erin's mutilated body lying in the street.

Jimmy had been recruited by the IRA after he beat the shit out of another bloke in a pub. They overheard him defending their cause after the other bloke chastised their ongoing aggressive actions. Jimmy grew up as an underdog, so believing in their cause was his way of actually *belonging* to something greater than himself.

His escape and the trip across the Atlantic on an ocean freighter, was a drunken blur, with the exception of another fight. He had a nice scar over his left eye to remind him of that. The rest of his IRA crew was ecstatic about the havoc they caused on Bloody Friday. Jimmy got into it with one of them over Erin's death. His mate had bragged about the body count, but Jimmy was bitter that Erin was included.

A New Life

The IRA knew there would be hell to pay and a dragnet would be thrown over the city after the carnage they caused on Bloody Friday. They made previous arrangements for many of those involved, to disappear before the authorities hunted them down.

Jimmy was on an ocean freighter and headed to America before the fires stopped burning in Belfast. He was to meet a man by the name of Kevin Flannigan when he arrived in the United States. Jimmy was still mourning Erin's death and he had mixed emotions about starting a new life in America. His leaders told him it was a chance to step up in the organization.

A sharp poke in the ribs woke Jimmy; his ship had arrived in the Port of Boston. His empty whisky bottle fell off the bed and skipped across the steel floor, as he sat up in his bunk. A hulk of a man stood at Jimmy's bed side. He could only see him from his knees to his chest because of the stacked bunk beds.

Jimmy rubbed the sleep from his eyes and poked his head out to see who the hell woke him up. A grey-haired, broad-shouldered man over six feet tall looked down at Jimmy.

"Get yer things together laddie, you'll be comin' with me."

Jimmy wobbled when he stood, he wasn't sure if he was still drunk, or just badly hung over. The smell of diesel oil from the nearby engine room always made him nauseous in the morning. He had slept in his clothes, so Jimmy only had to stuff a few toiletries into his duffle bag and he was ready to go. Jimmy looked around the bunk room and noticed everyone else was gone; his crew was purposely split up and sent off in different directions for their own protection. That way, if one of them was caught, they wouldn't be able to rat on the others.

Kevin Flannigan was waiting for Jimmy at the bottom of the gangplank. He was a grizzly of a man; he grabbed Jimmy's duffle bag with his bear-paw. Flannigan walked across the pier, to a silver Lincoln Towne Car and threw Jimmy's bag in the trunk.

"Get in" was all Flannigan said to Jimmy.

Jimmy looked around his new surroundings. He felt lost. Flannigan drove a few blocks further along the harbor and pulled into a small diner. Jimmy was still in a fog, as Flannigan waved him along. The waitress automatically brought two coffees to the table.

Flannigan tapped the waitress on her arm with his fingertips.

"Bring the whole pot, will ya darlin?"

Jimmy cupped his coffee mug with both hands to steady his grip. He instinctively reached to his pocket for his bottle of Jameson, but Flannigan grabbed his hand.

"Look here Jimmy, this' how it's gonna be. Yer gonna get yer shite together and right quick."

"I know ya caught a tough break back home, but it's done now and ya can't bring her back. Ya gotta move on."

Jimmy took a sip of coffee and dropped his chin to his chest.

Flannigan continued, "Yer gonna be workin for me now lad, and if ya fuck up I'll stuff ya into the cargo hold of one of those ships bound for home. The cops there'll take care of ya."

The waitress returned to the table with the coffee pot as Jimmy was finishing his first cup; it was burning his tongue, but he had to clear the fog before Flannigan slapped him with one of those bear paws.

"This is how it's gonna work Jimmy. Are ya hearin me lad?"

"Aye sir, I hear ya."

"Right then, the damage you and yer lads caused back home gave me an idea. They'll be lookin for some new cars to replace the ones you lads been blowin up. You'll be workin for a friend of mine at his chop shop. He'll be showin ya how to hide guns in the cars to ship back to the lads back home.

Personally, I don't give a shit about the cause back home. The only green that matters to me is the color of the money here in America. We make money on the guns and the cars. It's a win-win situation for everyone. If ya wanna start a new life and have a piece of the pie, ya gotta learn the ropes."

Jimmy gulped down some more coffee and looked into Flannigan's eyes. He had surprisingly gentle, blue eyes, but a solid jaw and the crooked nose of a boxer. His dry voice highlighted his brogue.

"Are ya getting all this Jimmy?"

"Aye Mr. Flannigan."

"Right then. Ya dunt look like ya could keep any food down right now, so finish yer coffee and we'll get ya settled in. I found you a flat just up the road. It's close to the docks and the chop shop. Don't ya worry now; you'll be paying me back later."

Stepping Up

For the next year Jimmy learned all about the Flannigan's gun smuggling operation. He learned how to conceal all kinds of weapons in the cars he shipped back home to the IRA. While the chop shop guys removed or swapped serial numbers, Jimmy hid automatic weapons in doors and rocker panels. The steel guns in the steel cars did not show up on x-rays at customs, and their dogs couldn't sniff them out like drugs.

It was a good system. Jimmy learned to control his drinking, for the most part. It was mostly a day job for him, but there were lots of meetings after hours and socializing to help keep him liquored. Jimmy became Flannigan's right-hand man.

About a year after Jimmy arrived in Boston, he was invited to a party by Flannigan. Jimmy was a bit puzzled. Everyone kept congratulating Flannigan and wishing him well.

"What's going on Mr. Flannigan, are ya goin somewhere?"

"Jimmy, me boy, it's about time ya start callin me Flanny, like everyone else."

"Okay Mr. Flannigan."

"I'll be movin ta Detroit Jimmy."

"Really, but what's gonna happen to the business here?"

"Yer gonna run things here for me son."

Jimmy was speechless. He had come to admire Flannigan, but he knew when to shut up and listen.

"I bought me self a bar in Detroit. It's a perfect place to wash some of the money we're makin from the business. You've proved yourself Jimmy. I'd like ya ta run things here. Can ya handle that for me?"

"Aye, I guess so."

"Ain't no guessin Jimmy, yer in charge here now. The boys back home'll be countin on ya."

"Aye, if you say so Flanny."

"Atta boy Jimmy, now ya got it. Don't worry, I'll be checkin up on ya from time ta time. Now raise yer glass and wish me well."

Jimmy was a bit numbed by the news. He toasted Flanny, then went and sat in a corner by himself. As he sat there in silence, he thought to himself, *here's a chance to make something of myself.*

Shite Happens

Flanny wasn't gone a month when the shite hit the fan; the cops raided the chop shop and seized all the stolen cars. Half of the cars were earmarked for Jimmy. The good thing was that Jimmy wasn't at the shop when it got raided, and he only lost three cars loaded with guns.

The bad thing was that Jimmy now had no other cars to put his guns in and the ship was leaving in less than a week. The boys back home were expecting six cars loaded with sixty guns and ten hand grenades. Jimmy normally packed ten guns into each car. The cars that the cops seized were loaded with the hand grenades.

Jimmy was almost sick to his stomach when he got news of the raid. He wanted to get drunk, but he couldn't let Flanny down. He had to come up with a solution and needed to get a few more cars to ship. He didn't have the cash to replace the confiscated guns; he needed to move fast and he needed some help.

Jimmy had made some valuable connections in Charlestown. He turned to a guy who was involved in everything and anything that was illegal or profitable, a guy named Conner.

Jimmy wasn't sure if Conner was his real name, or his nickname. It could have been short for O'Connor, or it may have been that he was a con man. The word on the street was Conner could talk any woman out of her clothes, or talk any man into buying his stolen designer clothes. He was a thief, con man, drug dealer, and jack of all criminal trades. If anyone could help Jimmy make things right, it would be Conner. Jimmy found Conner at the Shamrock Pub.

"Conner me mucker, da ya fancy a pint?"

"Aye Jimmy boy, I do. Does that mean ya want somethin?"

"I have a problem Conner; the cops raided the chop shop and seized all my cars. I needed them to send ta Belfast."

"I heard a rumor there's more than just cars yer shipping back to the homeland Jimmy. Some say yer runnin guns for the IRA. It's really none a me business Jimmy, but if yer about to ask me to get in bed with ya, I wanna know who I'm sleepin with."

"Fair enough Connor, I hear lots a rumors bout you too!"

"I can only imagine. What is it ya need Jimmy?"

"I need some cars to ship overseas and some quick cash to replace the guns that the cops seized. I can get more guns, but I'm shy on cash to buy em."

"Cars aren't a problem Jimmy, but I'm not a banker. What kinda cash are ya talkin about?"

"I'll need fifty large ta make things right."

"That's a lot a dough Jimmy, but I think I know what you can do ta make it right."

"And what would that be Conner?"

"You gotta make a deal with the devil Jimmy. Ya gotta sell the devil's candy."

"Ya mean dope?"

"Aye Jimmy; I'm talkin cocaine and lots of it."

"Funny ya should mention coke, me mucker back home was askin me bout shippin some over. I wasn't interested at the time."

"Well, I can set ya up with a guy Jimmy, but he's gonna want some cash up front."

"Hmm, that could be a problem; ya think he'd trade up for some guns?"

"I'll talk to him for ya Jimmy. I know someone else who might be able to get ya a couple cars too. See me tamarraw."

"Thanks Conner, I'll owe ya one."

"Aye laddie, ya will for sure. I was just wonderin Jimmy, do ya ever miss home."

Jimmy got up and dropped a ten on the table to cover the beers.

"I can't say I do Conner, although I sometimes wonder bout me mucker Patrick. Heard he joined the army and went to Viet Nam."

"Ya haven't heard from him since?"

"Nah, I'm not sure he'd wanna talk to me anyway. Let me know when ya hear somethin Conner."

Conner came through and set Jimmy up. He was able to deal some guns and a promise, for some coke and cars. He apologized to the boys back home for the temporary shortage of cars and guns, but he told them how the coke could put some extra cash in everyone's pockets.

Jimmy was the man. Over the next couple of years, he became the man to see if you needed to ship anything illegal overseas. Flanny would never knowingly get involved in drug trafficking, but as long as Jimmy kept sending him money, he was happy and didn't ask any questions.

5

A Night to Kill

Midnight shifts in uniform, on patrol could be brutal. Especially when working out of the eastern precinct, where there were fewer calls for service. Although the calls kept him awake, Norm Strom didn't mind the lack of them.

It gave him more time to quietly patrol his district, looking for bad guys; they were out there somewhere, he just had to find them. Sometimes, Norm would shut the cruiser's lights off and patrol in the dark. He called it silent running. He had surprised more than one bad guy using the technique.

Near the end of the second year when Norm and Digger Daniels were partners, Digger got promoted and moved on. Danny Gates moved up the list and became Norm's new partner. Danny and Norm never worked together but they both played baseball one season on the police team.

Norm worked in a busy district and gained a reputation for getting the job done. Danny was no ball of fire, but he seemed keen on working instead of sleeping. He and Norm made a good team.

Hot 'n Sticky Buns

When Norm first got on the job the police cruisers had vinyl bench seats, with no air conditioning. It was almost overwhelming at times. Imagine the kind of heat where you can cook an egg on the pavement. Then imagine wearing long pants, leather boots, an undershirt, a bullet proof vest and another shirt over top of that.

Now picture yourself sitting in a non-air-conditioned car, in the direct sunlight, on hot vinyl seats! Norm remembers it all too well. The sweat ran down his back inside his vest, then down the crack of his ass. It was like sitting in a wet diaper.

Working midnights offered some relief on those hot and sticky days. The newer cruisers came with air conditioning, but Norm still preferred to have the windows down so he could hear what was going on. One of his old beat sergeants had taught him that. On one night, a car with two male passengers rounded a corner in front of Danny and Norm. Norm immediately switched on the roof lights to pull the car over.

"Why are you pulling them over Norm?"

"Cuz they're drinking beer in there."

"How do you know that?"

"Cause the passenger tossed a beer cap out the window."

"And how the fuck do you know it was a beer cap?"

"Cuz it sounded exactly like a beer cap."

"This I gotta see."

Sure enough, when the car pulled over the cops found a half a case of beer sitting between the passenger's feet and each guy had an open bottle. Danny just looked at Norm, grinning and shaking his head in disbelief.

"Ears like a hawk!" Danny exclaimed later.

It could have been a lucky guess, but Norm knew what he heard, and went with it. That was police work.

Tits Up

If there was any action at all on a midnight shift, it usually happened in the first few hours when the drinkers made their way home. It was prime time for arresting impaired drivers. Some of the drunks that made it home would take out their frustrations on their wives. It was also the time for domestic disputes.

On one particularly hot and sticky summer night, Danny and Norm were dispatched to the housing projects on the eastern border of their district. The call was for a stabbing. Norm flashed back to the stabbing call he attended one Christmas Eve where the kid's presents under the tree got spattered with blood. They arrived within a couple of minutes and found an ambulance parked out front. Danny and Norm entered the townhouse and were summoned upstairs by one of the medics.

There was a bedroom directly at the top of the stairs. The medics were bent over someone on the bed. It was a woman. She was naked from the waist up, literally tits up on the bed. Her double D breasts flopped to her sides exposing a half a dozen knife puncture wounds to her chest. Trickles of blood oozed from the wounds. There was a huge puddle of blood under her torso, soaked into the bedding.

"She's dead," said one of the medics.

"Her boyfriend did it," said the other.

"How do you know that?" Danny and Norm asked simultaneously.

"He's the one who called us. He was here when we arrived. Said he couldn't stop the bleeding. He said he was sorry, and then he ran out the door."

Standard procedure for patrol officers who are first on the scene of a homicide is to call their patrol sergeant and the detectives. Danny went outside and used the car radio to make the calls. Norm took out his notebook, drew a diagram of the crime scene, and made note of any evidence. A bloody butcher's knife was lying on the floor beside the bed; it appeared to be the murder weapon.

Norm stood there in eerie silence with the dead woman; the sulfur smell of her blood filled the air. It wasn't Norm's first dead body. She was a plain looking, average sized woman. She appeared to be in her early thirties, much too young to be dead.

Danny and Norm secured the crime scene until the sergeant arrived. They obtained the victim's name from documents found in the house. The neighbor next door said the boyfriend's name was Ian Anderson. Norm recognized the name; he had dealt with him as a juvenile for some minor offences. His father was a longtime asshole and lived only a few blocks away.

Danny and Norm were writing their reports when a detective met them at the scene. He thought that Anderson would try and return to the scene during the night and that they should sit on the place, in case he did. Norm looked at Danny and made a face.

"Why on earth would Anderson come back to the scene of the crime?"

Before the rookie detective could see Norm's face, he piped up.

"With all due respect sir, I have another idea I'd like to run by you."

"What's that Norm?"

"Well sir, I know that Anderson's parents live a few blocks from here and Ian has a kid that lives there with them. I believe that Ian knows he's going to jail for this and he might want to see his kid before he gets arrested."

The detective looked at Norm, and then at the sergeant.

"What do you think Sarge?"

"Why don't you let them go and sit on the old man's place? I can secure the scene here and wait here for forensics."

The sergeant handed Norm his shot gun, and then they headed over to Anderson's parents' house, stopping at a convenience store along the way to pick up some snacks for the stake-out. They found a dark driveway to back into, a few houses down the street from the Anderson's. Norm decided to play it safe and pulled out his steel breast plate from his briefcase. The plate slipped into a pouch in the front of his bullet-proof vest.

Better safe than sorry. He thought.

Danny and Norm sat there in the darkness, gabbing to keep each other awake. They sat there for a few hours.

"Do you really think this guy's gonna show up Norm? It's gonna be light soon. He's gonna see us."

"I dunno. Maybe we should look for another spot."

Norm looked further up the street. "Wait, here comes someone."

A young male appeared out of the darkness, walking toward the cruiser and the Anderson house. The tension in the air was so thick you could have cut it with a knife. The only sound Norm could hear was his own heart beat.

"Shit Norm, he's gonna see us. He's coming right at us."

Norm remained silent; his eyes fixed on the male.

"Fuck! It's Anderson…he doesn't see us."

Anderson walked past the cruiser, not more than a hundred feet from the front bumper. He cut across a couple of lawns and went towards the front door of his parent's house.

Danny and Norm quietly exited their cruiser and snuck up along the front of the houses while approaching Anderson. He knocked on the door. Just as the porch light came on Danny and Norm were in position and grabbed Anderson. He didn't resist at all, but Danny handcuffed him anyway.

Norm turned Anderson around and said, "You're under arrest for murder."

Danny looked at Norm and nodded in satisfaction. It was the first and only time Norm ever got to utter those words. It was very cool.

Double Down

Danny and Norm took Anderson to police headquarters, and jail. Anderson sat in silence the whole ride. Any utterances he made could have been used in evidence against him. He chose to invoke his right to remain silent. That was okay with Norm, it would have meant more reports and a later court appearance.

After all their reports were done, Danny and Norm headed back to the east precinct; their shift was over. It was a good feeling for both cops; a sense of accomplishment, arresting someone for murder shortly after the crime was committed.

It was something that didn't happen too often, only on the one-hour cop shows on television. Danny and Norm were pumped and proud, bragging about their arrest to the other cops in the locker room.

"Hey, you guys will be on the front-page tomorrow." someone remarked.

"Yeah, we're big heroes for sure." Norm replied as he closed his locker.

"See the rest of you heroes tomorrow night."

Norm went home and slept like a baby, at least for about five hours. That's the way it was for Norm when he worked midnights. He couldn't sleep more than four or five hours; it really sucked. Sandra worked steady days, so she was usually gone when Norm got home. He had a quiet house all to himself.

Later that afternoon Norm got out of bed and retrieved the newspaper from the front porch. He took the rolled-up paper and put it on the dining room table while he poured a glass of orange juice.

Well, let's see what the paper has to say about my big bust last night.

Norm opened the rolled-up paper and looked at the front page. The whole front page was laid out with pictures and a write up. It was about a double homicide at a Sikh temple.

"What the…?"

Norm skimmed the front page in disbelief. There were two other people killed in Windsor on the same night. He flipped the page, more of the same story.

But where's our story?

It was on the lower half of page three: "Woman murdered; boyfriend arrested as prime suspect." The news was not front page worthy, obviously not as sensational as the double homicide.

Norm drank his juice and shook his head. *Oh well, shit happens. Sometimes more than once I guess.*

He went about his day, later whipping up some Hamburger Helper for dinner. Sandra arrived home and walked into the kitchen.

"Dinner smells great. I heard you guys had a busy night last night, a double homicide?"

"I had nothing to do with that one. Did you hear about the stabbing on the east side?"

"No, Norm, I didn't hear about that."

That was it, not even fifteen minutes of fame.

6

Shooter

The crowd cheered as the Toronto Police Pipe Band took to the field at Exhibition Stadium. Patrick Kelly and his buddies in the Drug Squad stood up to welcome their compadres in kilts.

It was opening day in 1983. The Blue Jays were taking on their rivals, the New York Yankees. It was a great day for a baseball game. The breeze off Lake Ontario cooled the air in the stands, but the green field glowed in the warm sunshine.

Patrick always got goose bumps when he heard the sound of bag pipe music. It stirred his Celtic blood. The music was one of the few pleasant memories of his childhood. He and Erin would dance a jig to the music whenever they caught an upbeat tune.

He missed his little sister; her sweet face would never fade from his memory. Patrick thought about Jimmy too, he always wondered where the bastard had disappeared to.

After recovering from his war injuries, Patrick instructed for awhile. He missed the action out in the field. He made a short visit back home to look after his sister's affairs, but being there only brought him bad memories. Patrick relentlessly inquired, but no one knew of Jimmy's whereabouts. He wanted answers.

He wanted to confront Jimmy face to face. He felt Jimmy owed him that much. It didn't take a lot of effort for Patrick to find out that Jimmy was involved with the IRA and that he had left the country after Bloody Friday.

Patrick always believed in good over evil, and right over wrong. He viewed his military service as a positive experience, even though it was in a negative environment. He believed that most people were good by nature, and that bad influences led them astray. Patrick evaluated his own life and he thought it needed more purpose.

Green for Blue

The City of Toronto was actively recruiting police officers. Patrick saw a recruiting poster pinned on a bulletin board in the training office. With his colonel's blessing, he seized the opportunity. He got the job and moved to Canada. Patrick was a bit older than most of the police candidates but his military record and maturity led to his hiring. He traded his army green for cop blue.

The transition from soldier to cop was an easy one for Patrick. The police force was a quasi-military organization; his past training in discipline, fitness, and weapons put him on the fast track.

After some seasoning on the streets of downtown Toronto, Patrick joined the Emergency Task Force (ETF) His previous sniper training made him a perfect fit in the elite unit. In some ways Patrick felt like he was still in the military, he had over five thousand brothers in blue in the greater Toronto area.

Whether in a street cop's uniform, or ETF fatigues, Patrick easily caught every woman's eye. He stood six feet tall and was extremely well built. He was a handsome man, with sandy blonde hair and green eyes. Patrick even had a cop moustache, trimmed neatly at the corners of his mouth, as per departmental regulations. When he walked into a room, his demeanor commanded attention. Although Patrick looked as tough as an army poster boy, he was a teddy bear who spoke softly and had a big heart.

What Patrick hated most about the army was that he never really understood how he was helping people. He was told he was fighting for a cause, but he never knew exactly what that meant. As a cop, Patrick actually felt he was doing something good; most people appreciated the job that he did.

Working on the ETF was quite different than patrol. There was no cruising around writing tickets, or looking for bad guys. When his team got a call, it was serious shit! They were called for all high-risk situations. That meant situations like gun calls and hostage incidents. They assisted the Drug Squad when they suspected guns to be involved. The Task Force was also used to hunt down and arrest repeat violent offenders.

Patrick saw lots of action with the ETF. On several occasions he was ordered to take up a position with his sniper rifle, waiting to be given the green light to take someone out. It was a waiting game. Ninety-nine percent of the time he was told to stand down. It was different from his job in the military, there his targets were pre-selected and he had orders to kill on sight.

Flashback

It was one of those steaming hot summer days in Toronto. Patrick was perched on a black tar rooftop, overlooking an alley off Yonge Street. The midday sun baked the roof and Patrick along with it. The smell of the tar wafted up and into his nose. He could feel the heat of the roof burning through his fatigues.

Now I know how a strip of bacon feels.

Patrick looked through his rifle scope, down into the alley, scanning the windows and door of the abandoned building. He covered his entry team down below, as they breached the building. As a sniper, his job wasn't only to shoot and kill. It was to cover the rest of his team, or watch their backs.

Patrick was taught that high ground was the best place to be. It gives the sniper a bird's eye view of the area, while keeping him out of sight. The other team sniper was positioned in a window across Yonge Street, on the opposite side of the building.

Patrick's team disappeared into the building; they were looking for a barricaded gunman who was reportedly shooting at moving cars on Yonge Street. The team was only out of sight for a minute when Patrick heard his sergeant on the radio.

His voice barked loudly, above the sound of the garbage truck in the alley below.

"All units stand down and stand by. All team members report back to the rally point ASAP."

Patrick was a bit puzzled, but he figured his boss must have a good reason to call off the training scenario.

Back at the rally point the team was briefed on a hostage taking only a couple of blocks away. Uniformed cops chased a robbery suspect down into the subway station at Bloor and Yonge. The suspect missed an outgoing train and the cops cornered him on the loading platform. When the cops closed in the suspect pulled a hunting knife and grabbed a young Asian girl as a hostage. The uniformed cops called for back-up and ETF.

The team was already geared up. They only had to swap out their blanks for bullets, the kind that kills. They raced to the subway station and found the uniformed cops already had all the entries and exits locked down. The knife wielding suspect was surrounded, with no way out.

The sergeant gave the order to take up positions. Patrick knew exactly what that meant. Everyone on his team had specific jobs to do. His was to find some high ground and get a bead on the suspect. He was the Alfa sniper and the other was Bravo.

Descending underground didn't leave Patrick many options; he had to settle for a perch in the stairwell. It wasn't the perfect spot, but he had an unobstructed view of the suspect. He wiped the sweat from his brow and peered through his rifle scope.

Patrick surveyed his target; the white male suspect was average sized, but his hostage was a tiny young girl. They both looked terrified, but the man was holding a huge hunting knife across the girl's throat. The long steel blade covered the width of the girl's neck. Patrick scanned up and down for any other threats or weapons; he noticed the poor girl had wet her pink shorts.

"I'm not going back to jail. Back off or I'll kill the bitch."

"Alfa unit, do you have a shot?" asked the sergeant.

"Alfa, that's affirmative."

"Bravo unit, do you have a shot?"

"Bravo, negative."

"All units stand by."

The ETF cops crept slowly closer; some relieved the uniformed cops from their positions. Their job was to save the hostage, and if possible, to talk the suspect down and disarm him. In that situation, if the suspect did not surrender, and it appeared he would harm the hostage, the police would have to use deadly force. The original uniformed cop continually pleaded with the suspect to put the knife down.

All cops know the rules; you can only use deadly force if your life or someone else's life is in imminent danger. They also know the repercussions, that the split-second decision they are forced to make will be judged by everyone else after the fact. That is the job, the one they have sworn to do. All the years of training and preparation come down to that split-second decision. The final choice is ultimately theirs, life or death?

"I swear I'll kill her. I'm getting on the next train out of here."

The man was serious, his intentions were quite clear. He ignored the continual pleas from the uniformed cop. Patrick placed his scope's crosshairs on the suspect's forehead, that's all that was visible from behind his hostage. The agitated man only peeped out from behind his hostage when he shouted at the cops. The Asian girl's pretty face filled Patrick's scope. Tears flowed and her mascara ran down her cheeks.

"Please help me. Let him go…let him go."

Patrick heard the sound of screeching brakes coming from the tunnel behind the suspect; all trains were ordered to stop where they were, and not enter the station. Silence hung heavy in the air; Patrick could hear his own heart beating.

The suspect looked down the tracks.

"What the fuck is going on? Where's the train? I'm getting on that train, or I'm killing the bitch!"

"Alfa, are you still clear?"

"Alfa, that's affirmative."

"Alfa, you have a Green Light."

That was the signal. It was all up to Patrick. If he had a clear shot, he had permission to take it. The decision of life or death was in his hands. It wasn't the first time he had that kind of power.

He started to bend his finger, applying pressure on the trigger. He could feel the adrenaline flowing through his veins. His finger tightened on the trigger. Patrick saw the look of horror on the girl's face. He flashed back to his first kill in Viet Nam. He remembered that same look of horror on a village girl's face when the army colonel's head exploded right beside her. Patrick blinked hard to clear his vision.

"Bring that train up here right now. I'm gonna do it!"

The suspect was so wound up he probably didn't realize he was pressing the knife's blade into the girl's neck.

"That's it. I want that…"

Those were the man's last words. Patrick never heard the shot, but it echoed through the train station. The suspect's knees buckled. He pulled the girl with him as he fell backwards off the platform, out of Patrick's sight. The cops ran over and looked down on to the tracks. The young girl was lying on top of the suspect. Her eyes were bulging and wide open. She took a final gasp for air, and then she lay motionless, frozen in time.

The two uniformed cops jumped down onto the tracks, while the ETF covered them. The suspect was dead from the bullet to his head, but the knife wasn't visible. One of the cops screamed for someone to get an ambulance when he saw the knife. It had plunged into the girl's side and punctured her lung and heart during the fall. She was dead by the time Patrick got to the edge of the platform. He stared down at the dead girl; her horrified eyes stared back at him.

The sergeant put his arm around Patrick's shoulders.

"It's not your fault son. You did your job. You did what you had to do."

The words resonated in Patrick's ears. How many times had he heard those words before?

"You did your job. You did what you had to do."

The adrenaline started draining from Patrick's veins, he felt his knees getting weak and his hands started to tremble.

The sergeant took Patrick's arm.

"C'mon son, let's get you out of here."

Nightmares

A piece of Patrick died with that young Asian girl that fateful day. He never felt like that before. He thought he was justified in killing people during the war. He felt justified in killing the knife wielding man on the subway platform. What Patrick really had a problem with was killing the innocent hostage. All of his years of training and experience didn't prepare him for the guilt and responsibility he felt.

The newspapers and armchair quarterbacks had a field day with the girl's death. All the usual second guessing and stupid opinions came out. Everyone always thinks they have better ideas than those professionally trained to do the job. No one seemed to care that the suspect had threatened, then slashed a clerk at the corner store he robbed. No one seemed to fault him for taking a hostage or the fact that it was his knife that plunged into the girl's side.

The fact is that the public always needs answers, even when there are none. They need closure and want someone to be accountable, or to blame. The suspect was dead so he couldn't answer for his actions. Therefore, the police should be made accountable. That always seems to be the conclusion when the public can't get the answers they seek.

That is the bane of police work.

Patrick took the bad publicity to heart. He had problems sleeping and he started having nightmares. His victims from the war blended in with scenes from the subway platform. He'd never had nightmares after the war; the subway incident seemed to be the trigger.

A psychologist suggested it might be post traumatic stress disorder. Regardless, Patrick was hurting. He took some time off from work and looked up a buddy he hadn't seen in a while. Barry was up fishing at his parent's cottage on Lake Muskoka and he invited Patrick to come up.

Barry and Patrick had walked the beat together in 52 Division when they were rookies. Barry had moved on to the Drug Squad about the time Patrick joined the ETF

"So, do you want to go fishing, or just get drunk Patty?"

Barry was the only guy since his Colonel in Nam who called him Patty.

"Can we do both?"

"Sure, but let's just fish off the dock so we don't fall out of the boat."

It was just what Patrick needed. A distraction and a good drunk. He slept like a baby that night and didn't recall having any nightmares.

Changing Lanes

"Did you sleep well last night Patty boy?"

"Yeah, strangely enough..."

"You were talking to some colonel about making some changes."

"Really, I don't remember. I was sleeping."

"That's funny. Do you remember our conversation last night about you making some changes on the job?"

"No, I was too drunk."

"Hmm, well last night I had you talked into transferring to the Drug Squad."

"Is that so? Did I think it was a good idea?"

"As a matter of fact, you did."

"Well you know what brother Barry? Maybe that's just what I'll do."

On the way home from the cottage, Patrick stopped by his sergeant's house to break the news to him. The sergeant agreed it was probably in Patrick's best interest to make the change.

"You've done your time and you've served the team well Patrick. Nobody will fault you if you move on."

Patrick focused his attention back on the pipe band. The crowd roared as they marched the Blue Jays onto the field. Patrick took a sip of beer and elbowed Barry in the ribs.

"What was that for?"

"Cuz yer an asshole."

Patrick smiled and filed the memories.

7

Fast Cars & Women

While Patrick learned all about drugs and how to take down drug dealers, Jimmy learned how to deal drugs and how to avoid drug cops. They were the best of friends and practically brothers growing up, but their lives took them in completely different directions and they became polar opposites.

The only thing they had left in common was their love of redheads and the matching shamrock tats on the back of their necks. They were both ladies' men, each in their own, very different ways.

Jimmy loved his cars the way he loved his women—fast and easy. He never stopped to realize that he loved Erin. She faded from his memory like the sun setting over the ocean. Jimmy never found the time for, or saw the need for love. Lust was more his speed. He could walk into a bar, make eye contact with an attractive woman, and then end up having her riding his stick shift. Maybe it was his unique blue eyes. Whatever it was, Jimmy had it.

Jimmy drank hard and he played hard. A barmaid once asked Jimmy how he held his liquor.

"By the ears darlin."

When it came to cars, Jimmy liked American-made muscle cars. The bigger the motors the better he liked them. Mustangs, Chargers, Camaros—Jimmy loved them all. Unlike a woman, Jimmy could run his car as fast and hard as he wanted, it responded to his tough demands, and always came back for more.

Jimmy kept up the shipments of guns to keep Flanny happy and in the money. The truth was, Jimmy lost faith in his politics and his buddies back home in the IRA. Jimmy's new party platform was built on drug running. He ran a tight operation from the docks but he smelled a rat in his crew.

A while after the chop shop got busted Customs agents pulled a surprise inspection, checking some of Jimmy's shipping containers. After that, one of his coke shipments was intercepted. Jimmy wrote it off as the cost of doing business, but he felt the heat.

Flanny called Jimmy in the summer of eighty-three and he told Jimmy he should come for a visit. Flanny said he'd take Jimmy to a Tigers game.

"Who are the Tigers?"

"The baseball team Jimmy boy, they're on a winning streak."

Although Jimmy had become an avid hockey fan in Boston, he knew nothing about baseball.

"Sure Flanny, we can do that. It'll be good seeing ya."

Flannigan's Pub

Jimmy parked his bright red, souped-up '78 Firebird directly in front of the fire hydrant outside Flannigan's Pub.

Fuck It, he thought as he glanced at the hydrant and no parking sign.

"What'll ya have?" asked the smiling bartender as Jimmy stepped up to the bar. Flanny shouted from the corner.

"Pour him a Guinness and shot a Jameson Sandy, he's with me. Jimmy me boy, its good ta see ya. How bout them Tigers?"

"It's good ta see you too Flanny."

Flanny gave Jimmy a big bear hug. Jimmy purposely looked over his shoulder, checking Sandy out from head to toe.

"Sandy, this is Jimmy. We go way back."

"Nice to meet you Jimmy."

"Ya look tired Jimmy…ya getting any sleep?"

"I'll get all the sleep I need when I'm dead Flanny. Wait till ya see me tomorrow."

"Why Jimmy?"

"Cuz I get better looking every day."

Both men laughed out loud. Sandy plopped Jimmy's drinks down in front of him and chuckled along with the men. Her eyes were drawn to Jimmy's. She smiled softly.

"Just let me know if there's anything else you need Jimmy."

"You can count on it darlin."

"Are ya done flirtin Jimmy? Hey, do ya like baseball?"

The two men got to drinking and catching up on life. Sandy went back to serving the other patrons, but she did more tidying up than usual down at Jimmy's end of the bar.

Flannigan's was on the west side of downtown Detroit, not too far from the Ambassador Bridge. It was only a five-minute drive across the bridge from Windsor, so lots of Windsor cops crossed the border to Flannigan's after work. Flanny liked having the cops around. Even though he was gun-running, he liked to feel safe in the rough neighborhood.

A few Detroit cops frequented Flannigan's too; one of the regulars was a white cop named Murphy. He liked to have a beer and a burger there on his extended lunch breaks. He was a uniformed sergeant and no one seemed to care that his liquid lunch breaks could last several hours. Murphy didn't talk much. The rumor was that he was the bar's self-appointed security.

Everyone had their own special seat at Flannigan's. The front door led into the main bar room, where the wide horseshoe shaped bar took up the whole far side of the room. There was a juke box immediately to the left of the front door and an old piano to the right.

Swinging doors at the back of the room led to the kitchen, back door and alley. The bathrooms were to the left of the kitchen, off an adjoining room where there were two pool tables. There was an opening in the wall in the back room, allowing bar access.

Flanny's seat at the bar was on the corner closest to the kitchen. Murphy's was at the corner of the bar closest to the front door. That was so he could keep an eye on his cruiser, or just in case he actually had to respond to a call. The left end of the bar was Jake's perch. Jake was a veteran Windsor cop who spent much of his down time with a Gentleman Jack and Coke in front of him. He was on wife number three or four. She was a daytime barmaid there.

The Grinch was another Windsor cop who was almost as regular as Jake. Even though they knew each other well, they sat at opposite ends of the bar, strictly socializing with their glass friends. The Grinch was a good-looking guy and a great street cop, but his shitty outlook on life and heavy drinking kept most women from getting close to him. The Grinch had a red '79 Camaro, almost identical to Jimmy's Firebird.

Burning Rubber

Norm was working the afternoon shift the night Jimmy blew into town across the river. A couple of the guys said they were getting off early and going over to Flannigan's to wash down the polluted air they had inhaled throughout their shift.

That was enough of an excuse for Norm. Flannigan's was a good destination for Windsor cops; they could let their hair down somewhere they didn't work. Besides, the bars in Detroit stayed open an hour longer. And If Flanny was in the mood, even longer than that.

When Norm was hired on the job, he couldn't afford his own car and was only allowed to borrow his mother's on occasion. Being that he was a lowly police cadet, he didn't even have a locker; cadets weren't allowed in the real cop's locker room.

That's just the way it was back then. What that meant for Norm was that he had to change into his uniform at home, and then take two different buses to get to work.

Norm felt more than a little weird walking a block to the bus stop, then waiting at the roadside for the bus in full police uniform. It got a little better when the bus driver put his hand over the coin deposit machine and shook his head. Norm enjoyed the free rides to work, but one day he found that they came at a price.

The busiest stop on Norm's bus route to work was at Kennedy High School. There, dozens of students packed onto the bus. Norm did what he was taught and gave up his seat to an elderly woman carrying her grocery bag.

A huge kid wearing his football jersey got on the bus, immediately causing a ruckus. The bus driver warned him to keep it down and to move back, allowing more people onto the bus. The football player knocked some other kids around, then dragged a nerdy kid out of his seat and sat in it.

The bus driver pulled the bus to the curb and stopped. He asked the football player to give the kid his seat back. The bus went silent. The football player just laughed and remained in the seat. The bus driver looked at Norm.

"I want him off my bus."

The young cop was embarrassed at being centered out, but he felt obliged to do something. He could feel the blood rushing to his face, as all eyes were on him. Norm made his way down the isle to the football player.

"You have to get off the bus now."

"No, I don't, you gonna make me?"

He grabbed the front of the kid's shirt with both hands and pulled. The shirt tore, but the kid didn't budge. He looked right into Norm's eyes as he stood up. He towered over the six-foot-tall police cadet. The kid had at least fifty pounds on him.

"You didn't have to do that."

"Well, you didn't have to be a jerk. Now get off the bus."

"Yes sir."

He put his head down and exited the bus through the side door. The bus driver nodded his head in appreciation and the rest of the bus cheered out loud. His face as red as a tomato, Norm was a hero.

The next day the rookie cop went to a car dealership and bought a brand new 1977 Grand Prix. There would be no more bus rides for Norm. The car cost less than seven thousand dollars back then, just shy of his annual salary. A tank of gas only cost twenty bucks, but when he put the hammer down and opened up that four-barrel carburetor, he could see the gas gauge move.

On the night that Jimmy blew into town, Norm had a buddy's '78 Trans Am. They had traded vehicles for the week. The guy wanted to borrow Norm's pop-up camper but his car didn't have a trailer hitch. The bright yellow Trans Am had four hundred cubic inches of screaming motor under the hood. Norm thought it was a cool trade.

Norm blew through the tunnel so fast that he shook some of the old wall tiles loose. The individual ceiling lights looked like one long stream of light. The car was a rocket ship. Norm stopped in front of an empty parking spot in front of Flannigan's but it was too small.

He cranked the steering wheel hard to the left and punched the accelerator. The tires squealed and spun and kicked up a thick cloud of blue smoke. Norm spun the car around one hundred and eighty degrees and slid into a parking spot on the opposite side of the street.

The blue cloud hung still in the thick and moist summer air. Norm cut a swath by waving his hand, as he neared the front door of Flannigan's. A crowd had gathered at the front door to see what all the commotion was about. He walked through them shaking his head and pretending it wasn't him who caused the ruckus. A guy with stringy black hair and steel blue eyes winked at Norm on his way in the door.

"Nice ride ya got there, laddie."

He gave obligatory nods to Jake and the Grinch. Murphy was there too, but he never left his seat during the commotion. Norm's buddies had a pool game going in the back room, so he joined them there. Sandy had his 7 & 7 waiting for him at the bar window. He grabbed his drink and put a couple of quarters on the pool table, making him next in line for a game.

The smell of burnt rubber drifted into the bar and hung heavy in the air. Norm smiled. The Windsor cops drank and played pool in the back room, oblivious to the fact that they were contributing to the funding of the IRA. Two of their arms dealers were sitting at the bar in the next room.

Norm had the midnight munchies, so he asked Sandy if the kitchen was still open. She said to go ask Flanny and pointed to the kitchen. He checked the kitchen but he didn't see Flanny. The smell of grease and burnt French fries hung in the air.

He heard someone talking outside the rear screen door and could see the front end of Flanny's shiny silver Lincoln Continental. Norm stuck his head out the door.

"You out there Flanny?"

"Huh? Yeah."

Flanny and the black-haired, blue-eyed guy were standing by the open trunk of the car. Flanny had a semi-automatic pistol in his right hand and the other guy was holding what looked like an Uzi.

Flanny looked at Norm.

"Wanna buy a gun?"

"Nope, I was just looking for something to eat."

Norm saw there were more guns in the trunk. He thought nothing of it since he'd seen the bar owner waving guns around before. It was Detroit, everyone carried a gun.

"Sorry Norm, kitchen's closed. Tell Sandy ta pour ya another one on me."

"Sure. Thanks, Flanny."

Last Call

Norm wasn't having any luck on the pool table. He was usually pretty good, but the more he drank, the worse he got. Ol' blue eyes came on the juke box singing 'My little town blues.' That meant it was last call. Anyone who knew the words always sang along. Those who didn't belted out the chorus... New York, New York.

The men always outnumbered the women at Flannigan's so the guys sometimes danced with each other, but only for that song. Flanny was corked from trying to keep up with Jimmy all night. He kicked everyone out and then started to lock up the place.

"Sandy, you finish closin up kay? I'm goin home."

He was slurring heavily and he swayed as he walked over to Jimmy and Sandy at the far corner of the bar. They were almost nose to nose, leaning over the bar and whispering to each other.

"Jimmy, ya make sure she gets ta her car safe, kay?"

Flanny patted Jimmy on the shoulder and gave him a half hug at the same time. He wobbled out the back door.

Sandy went and locked the back door behind Flanny. When she came back in Jimmy was standing by one of the pool tables. He took a hit off his Camel with his left hand as he caressed the table's felt bumper with his right. He exhaled and gently blew the smoke towards Sandy.

"Can I have one of those?"

Sandy was a young and slender woman, with a bit of a pear shape. She had long, strawberry blonde hair, hazel eyes, and milky white skin. She believed in tits for tips. A push up bra and low-cut blouse gave her the perfect amount of cleavage. She moved closer to Jimmy.

"Did you want to play Jimmy?"

"Aye lassie, right here on the table. You can use my stick if ya like."

Sandy took the cigarette that Jimmy just lit, from his mouth. She took a long and slow drag, and then blew a line of smoke from his chest, down to his crotch. She looked back up at Jimmy. His piercing blue eyes looked cat-like in the dimly lit room.

Jimmy grabbed the cigarette from Sandy's hand and he took another pull. He reached back, putting the cigarette on the edge of the table, and then he reached around and grabbed Sandy by the back of her head.

Sandy put both hands on Jimmy's chest when he pulled her in towards him. Their lips had barely met, when Jimmy rammed his tongue deep into Sandy's mouth. He reached down and grabbed her ass with both hands, then lifted her up and onto the edge of the pool table.

When Sandy came up for air, Jimmy whipped her top up and over her head. He buried his face between her breasts and popped the clasp on her bra with a flick of his fingers.

"Wow Jimmy, something tells me you've done that before."

"Nah, yer my first lassie, I promise."

Sandy ran her fingers though Jimmy's shiny black hair. She grabbed it tight with both hands when he pressed her breasts together and bit both nipples at the same time. Sandy started to slip off the edge of the pool table as she reached forward, running one hand down along the hard bulge in the front of Jimmy's pants.

Jimmy kissed Sandy again, this time biting her lower lip. As she came to her feet, she had both hands on Jimmy's crotch. She fumbled for his zipper. Jimmy grabbed Sandy by her shoulders and pushed her down to her knees. Sandy took Jimmy's throbbing cock into her hands, guiding it into her mouth. Jimmy reached behind and grabbed his smoke. He took a drag, and then put it back on the table.

Sandy licked and sucked Jimmy like she was trying to finish an ice cream cone before it melted. Jimmy pumped her mouth, bouncing her head off the pool table. Sandy moaned and chuckled at the same time. He grabbed her behind the head, for better traction and to cushion her head from the pool table.

Jimmy climbed the stairway to heaven.

He envisioned his next move. *He'd spin her around and bend her over the pool table, banging her from behind.*

The excitement was too much. He felt it .... he was coming. He almost pulled Sandy's hair from her head. He didn't care if Sandy wanted it or not. Jimmy held her tight until he melted in her mouth. When he was satisfied, he released his death-grip on Sandy. She looked up, smiled, and wiped a bit of Jimmy's love juice from the corner of her mouth with the back of her hand.

Jimmy grabbed his still burning cigarette from the table and took a drag. Sandy stood up and he handed her the fag. She took a long drag and blew the smoke in Jimmy's face.

"Welcome to Detroit, Jimmy."

"Aye, it's been a pleasure meetin ya Sandy."

8

Motor City vs. Hogtown

Things changed during the eighties in Ireland. Peace talks finally convinced the IRA to stop blowing shit up. There were still some diehards who swore to believe in the cause till the day they died, but for the most part the Catholics and Protestants stopped slaughtering each other like cattle. The lack of bombings and shootings meant less business for arms dealers like Flanny and Jimmy.

Jimmy decided to stay in Detroit. He banged Sandy or whoever else caught his fancy when the mood struck, and he humored Flanny over beer and whiskey. He even got to watch the Tigers win a world series.

To Jimmy's surprise Flanny wasn't all that disappointed with the lack of business overseas. Jimmy came to learn that Flanny was actually making a buck in the bar business and he branched out into the gun business. Jimmy really didn't mind either; his drug business kept him in the green.

Drugs & Guns

Jimmy liked the Motor City. He shared Detroit's love of American-made muscle cars and Coney dogs. When they weren't busy drinking or chasing women, Flanny introduced Jimmy to his local gun contacts.

"Drugs and guns Jimmy, that's where the money's at now. I'm not into the dope, but the guy's sellin it are always lookin for guns."

America was faced with a whole new war after Viet Nam, the war on drugs. Many soldiers got addicted to heroin in

Nam, which created a demand for it when they returned home. Organized street gangs got into dealing heroin on a national level. Then came crack cocaine. It was the new drug of choice, and the new money maker for organized crime gangs.

"It's the niggers here Jimmy, they turn the powder into rock and make more money than the Rockefellers."

Flanny never asked, and Jimmy never said anything to him about his wholesale drug business that he started from the docks in Boston. The business pretty well ran itself; Jimmy was more of a business manager.

New technology like cell phones and pagers allowed the drug dealers to be mobile. These devices also made it harder for the cops to keep tabs. Jimmy always listened intently when Flanny explained the business to him. He was intrigued by the new crack epidemic.

Jimmy thought to himself, *Hmm, maybe it was time for him to branch out.*

Flanny got tired of being a gun dealer by day and bar owner by night. He took advantage of having his old right-hand man at his side again. Jimmy obligingly conducted gun deals for Flanny and he made some new drug connections at the same time. Where heroin was the hard drug of choice in the sixties and seventies, cocaine was the new kid on the block in the eighties.

At first it was just the rich, famous and shameless who were into it. They were the trend setters, so the trend was set. Besides, you could snort the stuff instead of jamming a needle into various parts of your body.

Coke isn't a downer like heroin, it's a party drug. It keeps you going all night, with only a sinus hangover the next day. Powder cocaine can be addictive enough on its own, but then someone learned how to cook it and turn it into crack. It is purified pleasure—like Pop Rocks you can smoke.

Young Guns

In the late seventies a group of street-smart teenagers on Detroit's west side, formed an exclusively African American gang called, Young Boys Incorporated. By the early eighties, YBI virtually controlled the heroin trade in Detroit, and they expanded into other major U.S. cities. The gang split into three crews and one of them sent their lieutenants to Boston during their expansion phase.

The YBI put a completely new obstacle directly in the path of law enforcement. They used boys as young as twelve to pedal their drugs on the street. Young boys gave up their G.I. Joes for the chance to make some easy money. Penalties were lenient if they got arrested, so it was worth the risk. The crew leaders were in their twenties or thirties, well insulated from the long arm of the law.

The new gangs also introduced new gang violence. Fighting for turf now meant torturing and murdering the competition. They invented drive-by shootings.

Jimmy knew of the YBI from Boston. He had helped them broker a shipment of heroin from the docks there. He didn't trust the black men, but seized the opportunity for their green money. He was leery of them when he delivered a load of guns in Detroit for Flanny.

Jimmy hated how they had stupid nicknames, many using letters of the alphabet. There was G, D, C-dog, and other ridiculous handles. He figured it was because of their lack of education and the fact that they couldn't spell.

It was hard for him to swallow, that these young punks were actually bad-ass American gangsters. C-dog, Jimmy's contact for guns, was seventeen years old. Jimmy grimaced.

"Shit, I was still jerkin off to skin magazines at your age."

C-dog wasn't amused.

"Yeah, well try jerkin this off." He checked the action on a sawed-off shot gun that Jimmy had handed him.

From his IRA training, he'd learned how to operate under the radar and how to keep a low profile. That wasn't the case for the YBI. It was all about showing the world how tough and bad they could be. They walked and talked and acted like they didn't give a flying fuck about anyone, or anything. It was about money and power, and for many young black kids, a chance to belong.

Jimmy didn't like C-dog. He didn't like any of the YBI but he saw an opportunity to use their distribution network. Like any other enterprising corporation, the YBI saw how cocaine was replacing heroin as the drug of choice. They were already in the game but had some difficulty acquiring the amount of coke they needed at wholesale prices.

The heroin they dealt was coming from Asia, whereas the cocaine was coming from Colombia, and the YBI needed a new supply chain. Jimmy asked C-dog to meet with his boss to discuss a new franchise opportunity.

C-dog wasn't happy about Jimmy wanting to go over his head but he knew the request had to go up the chain of command. Jimmy was introduced to a lieutenant named Mack. Mack was one of the oldest YBI in Detroit. He was 28 years old.

Mack had a fuck the world attitude, but he put it aside and showed Jimmy respect. He had never finished high school, but Mack did his homework and checked Jimmy out. His connections to the IRA were no secret. Mack respected the power of the organization.

Jimmy's wholesale coke operation consisted of shipping large quantities of coke out of the country. His new brainstorm was to keep some of the coke in the country, and to have the

YBI distribute it for him. Jimmy bragged a bit about his operation in an attempt to impress Mack.

"I like you Jimmy, but we already have suppliers. Why should we buy from you?"

Jimmy eyed Mack up and down. He was surprised by the scars that he had on his arms and bald head.

"Cuz I know what yer wholesale price is Mack, and I can save ya ten percent per brick."

Jimmy almost smiled when he recognized the smell the of Old Spice cologne that Mack was wearing.

"Well if you know that Jimmy, then you know that twenty percent would make it worth my time."

"If ya can handle twenty-five bricks a month, I can go twelve."

"Jimmy, if you can handle fifty bricks a month, I'll give you fifteen."

"Really Mack, I guess I underestimated the YBI"

"You can dis time Jimmy, but it yer last time."

"No problem Mack, we've got a deal."

Hot Commodity

Patrick could not believe the amount of dope on the streets in Toronto. As in Detroit, the eighties brought cocaine and crack cocaine to Toronto. With a new commodity in Hogtown, someone had to step up and deliver it. The Jamaican Posses delivered it big time. They were already into organized crime so drug dealing seemed like a natural progression.

Canada is a big country. The bikers thought they should grab a piece of the pie; the Hells Angels, Outlaws and Rock Machine all got into the coke business. The white stuff that fell from the sky wasn't the only snow blanketing the country.

Pablo Escobar, of Colombia's Medellin Cartel, even put people in place to oversee operations in Toronto and Montreal.

Patrick and the Drug Squad had their work cut out for them. He took some relief in the fact that Canada's gun laws would not permit everyone to carry a gun like in the U.S. In Canada, only the cops and the bad guys carried guns. And with the influx of cocaine and drug dealers, guns were a common denominator. Along with guns, came gun violence. Drive-by shootings put Toronto on par with the big bad U.S. cities.

The Toronto Drug Squad created different units to target specific groups. They were well equipped to handle street level drug dealers, but organized gangs and cartels needed special attention. Special projects taxed manpower, and financial resources even more. Joint Force Operations with the Ontario Provincial Police and Royal Canadian Mounted Police brought in extra manpower and cash.

Patrick's military experience paid off once again. He was seconded to Project Amigo, a JFO (Joint Forces Operation) targeting the Medellin Cartel's operation in Canada. The cartels ran their organizations like the military with a chain of command.

Unlike the military, the cartels simply executed anyone who was disloyal. Patrick was a quick study. He had already become an expert on the Jamaican Posses.

Road Trip

Training is never-ending for cops. Even though Norm completed recruit training at Police College, and years later an advanced training course, there was still in-house training that was conducted in house every year. Besides qualifying with their revolvers and shot guns, officers learned about changes in law and procedure. The Windsor Police used its own officers to teach others. For certain topics, guest lecturers from other police forces would share their areas of expertise.

In 1986 Norm was working in Uniform. IST (In Service Training) was always held in January or February, when calls for service were low and fewer officers were on vacation.

The training was usually boring, but Norm figured it was better than freezing his ass off out on the street. Winters were nasty in Windsor, not for excessive snowfall, but for the damp and cold temperatures. The kind of that makes your body suck your testicles up inside to keep them from freeing.

Patrick wasn't crazy about the ride down the 401 to Windsor in the middle of winter. He'd never been to the city or even heard much about it. That wasn't unusual. Many people from Toronto think the 401 ends in London. Windsor is two hours from London, but only five minutes from Detroit, kind of like a Detroit suburb.

Windsor was Patrick's last stop on his road trip. He was visiting police forces in southern Ontario, lecturing and educating fellow cops on his expertise in organized crime.

Norm managed to beat one of the old veterans to the last empty chair in the back of the class. It was the perfect place to go unnoticed if you nodded off. Breakfast was always the same in class, Tim Horton's coffee and Timbits. The brass probably figured the caffeine and sugar jolt would keep the cops awake in class. Norm never drank coffee and there was no OJ around, so he grabbed a Pepsi from the pop machine and a handful of the sour cream Timbits before he took his seat.

The instructors knew from experience that they should never start the day with the lights down low and a power point presentation; that was simply an invitation for everyone to go back to sleep. Instead, they would do something like show and tell.

They brought in an assortment of seized weapons, to let the cops see what they were facing out on the street. They'd pass the weapons out so the guys could play with them and point them at the instructors. Cops are worse than kids when they get a chance to play with new toys.

The instructor tried to talk over the noise, while the class played cops and robbers with the assortment of weapons. Something whizzed by the instructor's head and stuck in the cork board behind him. Norm had the poison darts, explaining to the guy beside him how he arrested some poor tourist at the border with the Yaqui blow gun he was holding.

Boys will be boys. The old guy loaded the dart in the long wooden tube, pointed it towards the corkboard, and blew. Everyone in class, except for the instructor, laughed out loud. The instructor pulled the dart from the wall and asked everyone to return their toys.

The instructor was so rattled he forgot to introduce his guest speaker. The out-of-town cop took his cue when the instructor nodded at him. The instructor piled all the toys in a stolen shopping cart and wheeled them out of the room.

"Well now, that's a tough act to follow. I'm Patrick Kelly, currently with the Toronto Police Drug Squad. With the exception of the blowgun, the weapons you just saw are only the tip of the iceberg. Drugs and guns are plentiful right here in Canada, and they are coming down the 401 to Windsor."

The room quieted down; Patrick had their attention. Cops liked to have fun like anyone else, but they aren't stupid people. They know when to shut up and listen. Patrick talked about the cocaine pipeline that flowed into Canada from two different directions. One came up from Miami, where the Cartels smuggled coke into the U.S. using a variety of methods.

From there, the coke made its way up through the states, crossing the border into Canada. The newest influx into Canada was coming from Montreal. From there, it worked its way down the 401, through Toronto, and eventually to Windsor.

No one in class dared nod off. They knew Patrick was as serious as a heart attack. He talked about the Jamaican Posses; they were unheard of in Windsor. Norm was floored when Patrick said that per capita, Jamaica was the murder capital of the world. Windsor cops always thought Detroit held that title. Some in the room whispered to each other about changing their winter vacation plans.

Patrick also talked about a new epidemic—crack cocaine. He explained how the drug market had become so lucrative, organized gangs were competing for their piece of the pie. Posses, bikers, and organized youth gangs were all in on the action. Violent crime was on the rise. Addicts would do anything to get their next high, and dealers would do anything to protect their product and turf.

Norm was intrigued. Patrick went on to talk about his undercover work and some of the projects he'd been involved in. Norm was inspired. He decided right there and then that he'd apply for the drug squad when there was an opening.

After class, Norm personally thanked Patrick for the lecture and said he'd love the chance to chat with him some more.

"I'm staying in town tonight. Maybe you can show me the sights here?"

Familiar Faces

Norm's buddy Jesse was in the same training class. He told Norm in the workout room that he liked the drug lecture. Norm said he was taking the Toronto cop out on the town and that Jesse should come. Norm was happy when Jesse agreed; Jesse had given up drinking, so he could be the designated driver.

Jesse and Norm picked up Patrick at his hotel after dinner. They took him around town to different bars that they worked at while off-duty. It was all part of a grand plan; knowing the owners and bartenders meant free drinks. Patrick was impressed with the free booze and hot women in Windsor.

"What's this I hear about the Windsor Ballet, Norm?"

"Funny you should ask, Patrick. That's where we're heading next."

The boys went downtown to the Million Dollar Saloon. Jesse and Norm knew the two brothers who owned the place and they introduced them to Patrick. The owners were always good to the cops. It paid off when they needed their services.

Patrick grinned from ear to ear as he sipped on his free Jack & Coke, watching nude women parading all around him. He lit his free cigar with his free MDS lighter. He blew the smoke in the air as he held up a pink MDS monogrammed thong the owners gave him.

"No matter what everyone says, you Windsor cops are alright."

After more free drinks and a couple of lap dances, Norm figured Patrick was ready for Detroit. Jesse took the scenic route along Riverside Drive and over the Ambassador Bridge so Patrick could enjoy the scenery. He was impressed by the Detroit skyline but happier with the pink thong. When the U.S. customs officer asked if the boys were *packing,* Patrick was confused and slurring pretty good.

"They *want* us to bring our guns over here?"

Norm was drinking heavily too, so it was good that Jesse was the one packing. Not all, but most of the Windsor cops carried their guns across the border. It helped to even the odds. Besides, the customs officers and Detroit cops thought they were nuts if they didn't.

Flannigan's was packed and Norm and Patrick were pretty well pissed when they rolled in. Like the good buddy he was, Jesse steered the wobblers to a half-empty table in the back corner. While Jesse introduced Patrick to a few of the boys, Norm went to the bar for drinks.

Flanny's stepson Sean was working behind the bar with a hot little redhead. Sean was always friendly to women in the bar, but he really didn't like cops much. The only time he smiled was when he was waiting on a woman.

The Grinch was in his usual spot at the bar. He nodded. Norm wedged in between the Grinch and another guy so he could order from the redhead.

"Who's the new hottie behind the bar, Grinch?"

He apparently said it loud enough that she heard the question.

"I'm Megan, what can I get you?"

Norm ordered a 7 & 7, with a Jack & Coke for Patrick, and a ginger ale for Jesse. He eyed Megan up and down when she turned and walked away.

"Don't even think about it, Storm, she's doing Jimmy Irish."

The Grinch always called folks by their first name, followed with whatever else rolled off his tongue. Megan returned with the drinks for Norm. Something about her looked familiar. Norm never forgot a face, even if he *was* seeing two of them.

"You look kinda familiar Megan. Do I know you?"

"I don't think so. I'm not from here."

Norm shrugged it off and delivered the drinks. Patrick had his eyes on Megan.

"Thanks, Stormy, who's the hot redhead you were talking to? I love redheads. Do you think I should give her my pink thong?"

"No, I don't think she'd appreciate it."

"She looks familiar."

"No, I tried that one Patrick. She's apparently doing Jimmy, Flanny's buddy."

"Flanjee who?"

"Never mind Patrick, she's taken. There's the guy over there."

Patrick turned to look. Flanny and Jimmy went out the kitchen door. Only the back of their heads was visible over the crowd.

"Well do ya think Jamfee would mind if I gave his girlfriend my pink thong?"

"Probably Patrick, you should take it home with you."

The Toronto cop's grin was wider than his face. He fiddled with the thong like it was a new Christmas toy. Jesse said the bus was leaving. It was time for Coney dogs. As they left, Flanny waved at Norm from the back alley. Jimmy was standing in the shadows; a cloud of cigarette smoke hung over his silhouette.

9

Irony

Megan had struggled but she graduated from nursing school. She returned to Windsor with her crisp new diploma, only to find there were no jobs to be had. The good news was that they were crying for qualified nurses in Detroit. Megan was hired on the spot by Detroit Receiving Hospital. They even helped her file the paperwork for her green card, allowing her to work in the U.S. Americans didn't like Canadians taking their jobs, but they didn't have enough qualified people available.

Commuting and working across the border wasn't a problem for Megan; the job paid well and her check was in U.S. dollars. The greenback was worth about forty percent more than the Canadian dollar at the time.

She couldn't believe her windfall. She was proud to wear her nurse's uniform and she looked forward to going to work everyday. Like every other nurse she worked with, she dreamed of marrying a doctor someday.

Life in the Trenches

The hospital routinely put new nurses in the trenches, attending to the emergency rooms. Working in the ER's in downtown Detroit was like being in a MASH unit in Viet Nam. On any given night they could be bombarded with people who'd been shot, stabbed, or injured in traffic accidents.

On Megan's first night shift in the ER she froze at the sight of a thirteen-year-old boy with a sucking chest wound.

He'd been shot by a rival gang member. The sounds of him gasping for air sent chills down her spine. The attending doctor got directly in her face.

He sarcastically welcomed her to ER and told her to get her shit together. She instinctively removed the field dressing from the boy's chest and slapped her bare hand over the bubbling and bloody wound until someone handed her the proper bandage to stop the air from escaping from the boy's lung.

Another nurse pushed Megan aside as she shoved an I.V. into the boy's arm. Everyone was talking at the same time but Megan heard someone shout, 'flat line' and she took a step back.

She could see everything that was happening but her tunnel vision made the boy and his gurney look like they were shrinking in the distance. She was mesmerized by all the blood, it was everywhere. The doctor and nurses' voices sounded like they were fading away.

Megan stared at the blood all over her hands and her new scrubs. Her mouth dropped open when she saw the boy jolted from the table by the electrical shock from the paddles. Her hearing started to come back.

She had a flashback to Bloody Friday in Belfast. She remembered the explosion that almost took her life and the bloody sandal on the street. The room came back into focus, the doctor called out the time of death. A nurse handed Megan the boy's belongings and told her to bag them.

Her innocence was lost forever that night in the ER. It was the real world, the hard results of life on the street. She chalked the experience up to being part of her job. After all, she was a nurse and it was her job to help people. It was the people that she wondered about while she laid awake in bed that night, the whys and the hows of it all.

Looking for Love in all the Wrong Places

About two weeks later, Megan worked another night shift with the same doctor who got in her face. She had seen Dr. Morris since, but tried to avoid him for fear of being yelled at again. Megan was busy patching up an elderly woman who had been in a traffic accident, when Dr. Morris checked in on the patient. He looked over Megan's work and the woman's chart.

"I see you've managed to get your shit together."

Megan was surprised and she blushed.

"Yes Doctor, thank you."

"Everything looks good here Megan, can you see me back at the nursing station when you're finished here?"

She thought, "What's the matter now? He said I had my shit together."

Megan checked on another patient before she got back to the nursing station. Dr. Morris sat there drinking a coffee, doing his notes. Dr. Morris was a young intern, not much older than Megan. He was of average height and build but he wore his black hair combed back and longer than most doctors. Dr. Morris looked up at Megan and smiled. His dark brown eyes and gentle smile were the bait.

"I've been watching you Megan; you're good at what you do!"

He threw his line into the water.

"I'd like a chance to get to know you better, how bout dinner on one of your nights off?"

Megan bit and took the bait.

Without hesitation she answered, "Sure that would be nice."

He caught the fish.

"Great, I'll give you a call."

"Okay, do you want my number?"

"I'm a doctor, I'm sure I can find it around here somewhere."

Megan heard someone scoff. The head nurse looked up from her desk at Megan, rolling her eyes and shaking her head.

She met her Dr. McDreamy a few nights later for dinner. By the time her entrée came she was bored. Dr. Morris was easy to look at but he was arrogant; he only talked about himself and how he wanted to be a cardiovascular surgeon.

Megan nodded in agreement so much she thought she better put her chin in her hand, before someone mistook her for a bobblehead. Watching the other meals go by her table was more interesting than the doctor.

After dinner Dr. Morris offered to drive her home. When she told him she had her own car and that she lived in Windsor, he raised his eyebrows and grimaced. Against Megan's better judgment, she let him talk her into a nightcap at a bar around the corner, in Greektown. One drink turned into a few. The next thing Megan knew she was naked in the good doctor's apartment.

His good looks, hard body, and Sambuca got her hot and horny. She may have been bored earlier, but her loins came alive when he kissed her and grabbed her by the cheeks of her ass. He ground his crotch into hers, and then pushed her back onto the bed. The scent of him and his musky cologne got her even more hot and wet.

Megan reached down for Dr. Morris's cock but he was already slipping it inside her. She broke free from his lip-lock and gasped for air. He pumped her hard and twice as fast as she was panting. The good doctor got off as quick as he got in.

She continued thrusting her hips, wanting more, but he lay on top of her like over-cooked fettuccini. He was content. Her Dr. McDreamy turned out to be Dr. McDud.

He rolled over and looked at his watch.

"Shit, I'm on shift in a couple of hours. I gotta get some sleep. I'll call you later. You can let yourself out."

Megan lay there for a minute in disbelief. It wasn't her first wham-bam-thank-you-ma'am, but for some reason she thought it would be different.

Doctor, Dentist, doorman…are they all the same?

The next day in the locker room at work, one of the other nurses asked, "So how was your date with Dr. Morris?"

"Okay, he said he'd call me."

"Uh-huh, another hit and run," she replied walking away.

Megan looked at another nurse and asked, "What does she mean by that?"

"Don't worry about it honey, we've all been there. They hit you, and then run off to their next rotation. By the way, Dr. Morris has been transferred to cardiology."

Turn of Events

Megan was embarrassed, but it didn't shatter her dream of marrying a doctor someday. Over the next few years, after a few more interns and a couple of residents, she finally gave up on her dream. She almost took the one relationship with a resident seriously, until she got pregnant and he told her to abort the baby.

The young nurse struggled with the final decision, she wasn't sure if she could handle her career and a new baby all on her own. Her parents said they would help, but her father was showing early signs of Alzheimer's and she didn't want to overburden her mother.

Megan took a week off to have the abortion, and then visit her parents at their cottage in Northern Ontario. As if the abortion wasn't traumatic enough, she got into a bad car accident on the way home from the cottage and suffered severe whiplash that resulted in nerve damage to her neck.

Her vacation evolved into a long-term sick leave. Painkillers, muscle relaxers, and therapy helped her eventually get back to work. After eighteen months she still had only limited neck movement.

The hospital treated Megan well, allowing her to work restricted or light duty jobs. She still needed strong pain killers just to get her through the day. The range of her neck movements got better over time but the pain never went away.

Her doctor thought that she had grown immune to her medication so he changed it. They disagreed on the changes even though Megan said she was still in pain. Her doctor warned her of the possibility of addiction, but she only wanted to live pain free.

Working in pain every day gave her pause. Not knowing it would change her life forever, while delivering pain meds to one of her patients, Megan pocketed some pills. It wasn't long before she was taking pills from other patients. The cancer ward was the perfect place for her to get the type that worked for her.

She thought everything was fine, the head nurse called her into her office. Apparently, a few of Megan's patients had complained about receiving different doses from different nurses.

The head nurse searched her locker and found Dilaudid and Fentanyl in one of Megan's pockets. Her prescription was for Morphine Sulfate. She was suspended on the spot and told she should seek help if there was a problem.

Admitting she had a problem was not an option for Megan. She tried her doctor again but he was worried about addiction. She told him he was wrong.

Later that night, she found herself drunk in a downtown Windsor bar, asking a guy she just met if he had any pain meds. She thought it was just asking for a favor, not actually trying to buy illegal drugs.

Megan struck out in the bar. A few days later she called a girlfriend whose husband was on heavy pain killers. She asked if she could bum a few pills, and went to visit her friend.

She was introduced to her friend's weed dealer; her husband said it helped him stomach his medication. When Megan refused the weed, the dealer said he could hook her up with Dilaudid.

The hospital left several messages on Megan's answering machine asking if she was ready to come back to work. They told her she'd have to pass blood and urine tests before she could return. She received a deadline, but missed it and was suspended indefinitely without pay.

Megan did her best to buy and borrow pills to support her habit. She lied to her parents, telling them she was laid off, and growing more distant while she tried to hide her habit. Her former pried and confidence was shaken to the core, her failed relationships and drug habit were responsible for her new-found low self-esteem.

Happy New Year!

It was a lousy Christmas and New Year for Megan in 1986. She was almost thirty-five years old with no man, children, or job to brag about. She had been depressed for some time. One night in early January, her girlfriend Lisa stopped by. Megan wasn't in the mood, but Lisa insisted they needed a night out.

"I can't afford to go out."

"Don't worry about it, I'll buy the first round. Then we'll let guys buy drinks for us, you know, like the old days. So put something sexy on and let's go."

It took some more coaxing, but Megan agreed to go out. The two girls hit a few bars and got a few free drinks. They bailed when guys got too pushy, or too close. Megan started to feel the alcohol.

"Let's go to Detroit, I miss it over there."

The girls strutted through the front doors of Flannigan's and nestled up to the bar.

"Hey girls, I'm Sean, I run the place. What are ya having? The first one's on me."

The girls ordered a drink and Sean delivered them. Sean ignored Lisa and stared at Megan.

"And what might yer name be, red?"

"I'm Megan and this is my friend Lisa."

"Well it's nice to meet you, Megan. Are you from around here?"

"I live in Windsor but I work at Detroit Receiving Hospital."

"Is that so? Are you a nurse?"

"Yes, I am, but I'm laid off right now and looking for work."

"Really, it just so happens we're looking for a bartender."

"Thanks Sean, but I don't know anything about bartending."

"Not to worry Megan, we have on the job training. I can teach you personally."

Megan looked at Lisa, then back at Sean.

"Really? I guess I could give it a try."

"Great Megan, come in day after tomorrow and I'll get you started."

"Can you believe that Lisa? I can really use the job."

"Uh, can you believe that hunk over there?"

Lisa pointed to a good-looking guy in tight jeans and a black crew neck sweater. He was bent over, putting some coins in the Juke box.

"I love his hair, and look at those blue angel eyes."

Megan looked over, but Flanny stepped in front of her and introduced himself to both girls.

"I hear you'll be workin for us, Megan."

Lisa interrupted.

"Who's the hot guy over there with the black hair and blue angel eyes?"

"Oh, that's me mucker, Jimmy Irish."

Right on cue, Jimmy swaggered over to the bar to where Flanny was standing with the girls. He locked his eyes on Megan, checking her out from head to toe like he was buying a new car. He could never resist a red-head.

Jimmy's hard life was starting to show in the wrinkles around his eyes, and graying side burns. That didn't matter. It was like Megan was drawn toward an eternal light. His eyes were babe magnets and she couldn't resist the gravitational pull.

"Jimmy, this is Megan. She's gonna be workin for us."

"Is that a fact," Jimmy said directly to Megan as he maneuvered around Flanny and wedged himself between the two of them.

"Jimmy, this is my friend Lisa."

Lisa and Flanny no longer existed. The bar wasn't crowded, but Jimmy and Megan pressed together like two dogs in heat.

"Jimmy Irish huh, what kind of name is that?"

"It just means I'm from Ireland darlin, ya know…the green island near England?"

"Yes, I know Jimmy, I've been there."

"Is that so, Mo Chuisle?"

"Are you trying to impress me with your Gaelic, Jimmy? I was nearly killed in Belfast, on Bloody Friday."

Jimmy remained silent.

"Yeah, I was at a pub with a friend I met there. Ellen, Erica…I can't remember. Anyway, when I left the pub a car bomb exploded and knocked me on my ass. I was lucky I wasn't any closer."

The color in Jimmy's face faded, his blue eyes watered.

"Were you there, Jimmy?"

Jimmy pounded back what was left of his whiskey.

"No, I was living in Boston when that happened. C'mon Megan, let me show ya how to handle a pool stick."

Megan picked up her drink and followed him to the pool table. With his back to her, he pinched the top of his nose and wiped the corners of his eyes. Flanny didn't miss a beat. As soon as Jimmy and Megan walked away, he put the moves on Lisa.

"Sean, set this pretty lass and me up with a couple more drinks, will ya?"

10

Twins

Being members of the largest organized street gang in the world didn't mean that cops were exempt from becoming victims of crime. There were all sorts of bushwhackers who got a boner just thinking about nailing a cop in some way.

That is why some cops carry their guns when they are off duty. Actually, cops are never really *off-duty*. They are morally obligated by their duty to respond whenever they witness a crime taking place.

One night after Norm finished working an off-duty job at the Canada Tavern, he found three of the four tires on his car slashed. He had also had three of his homes broken into over the years. His buddy Jesse's car was completely trashed in the downtown police parking lot.

Windsor is a big, but small city where it's very easy for cops to run into the people they've arrested. That is one of the reasons the Windsor cops chose to drink in Detroit, and why many of them chose to live outside the city.

There will always be bad asses who want to prove how tough they are. In a Windsor bar one night, a steroid abusing muscle head eyed up an off-duty Windsor cop, who was minding his own business, playing pool with some friends.

The muscle head practically sexually assaulted the cop's lady friend, just to get in the cop's face. He eventually forced the off-duty cop into a fight or flight scenario. The cop was about half the muscle head's size but he felt obliged to protect the woman's honor. The cop got the living shit kicked out of him that night.

That same muscle head later became one of Windsor's biggest cocaine dealers and he affiliated himself with the Hell's Angels. Instead of continuing to pick on cops, he learned how to keep a low profile and avoid them all together. A sudden onslaught of traffic tickets after he assaulted the cop might have helped to wizen him up.

In Toronto, Patrick Kelly noticed he was being followed around the Eaton Center one day by a couple of members of a Jamaican posse. One of them recognized Patrick. He had busted him for drug trafficking a while back. Patrick ducked into a clothing store and dialed up his own posse. Within minutes the boys in blue were all over the Jamaicans like flies on shit.

Gone but Not Forgotten

Whether he was working or not, Patrick often thought about his sister Erin and how much he missed her. He also thought about Jimmy Flynn. He used his police resources and contacts, trying to locate Jimmy over the years. He seemed to have disappeared from the face of the earth on Bloody Friday. Patrick learned that Jimmy fled Ireland that fateful day, probably heading to America.

Patrick developed a lot of great police contacts. He reached out to one of them at Customs and Immigration. The agent told Patrick that they had some dated information on an Irish guy named Jimmy Flannigan who they thought was running guns out of Boston for the IRA. That caught Patrick's attention. He followed up the tip by calling the Boston Police.

The Boston police said they suspected that Jimmy Flannigan was tied to a chop shop that they raided on the docks, but they didn't have any grounds to arrest him. The Boston detective said they had an informant who helped them take down the chop shop, and later a shipment of stolen cars headed for Ireland. By the time they got enough information together to put surveillance on Jimmy Flannigan, he had disappeared.

There was one useful piece of information that would later prove to be very important to Patrick. The Boston detective told him that a man named Kevin Flannigan had sponsored Jimmy Flannigan in coming to the U.S., saying Jimmy was his nephew.

It was obvious to Patrick that Jimmy entered the U.S. with fake identification. The Boston police had information that Kevin Flannigan was involved in the chop shop too, but he had also disappeared. Their informant vanished mysteriously after the two busts; the police figured the gun runners made him vanish.

Rivals

Jimmy never really thought about Patrick, Erin, or his past in Belfast. He was too busy banging American women and selling guns and drugs. Business was business as far as Jimmy was concerned. He sold his guns and drugs to whomever had the money.

Another gang from Chicago called the Latin Counts saw the potential for further drug profits in Detroit and decided to expand their operation. There was a large Mexican or Latino population on Detroit's west side, so it was easy for the Counts to move into and recruit from the area.

The Counts instantly became rivals of the YBI as they fought and killed each other for their piece of the pie. Jimmy could care less about the blacks or the browns; he only cared about the green.

Sometimes the gangs fought amongst themselves. A disagreement in the upper ranks of the YBI caused Jimmy's contact Mack to break out on his own. He took a group of his disciples and formed the Mack Boys Gang. Mack expected Jimmy to stay loyal to him but Jimmy wouldn't go for exclusivity.

Mack was a smart businessman. He had seen too much useless slaughter between the YBI and the Latin Counts. He no longer had the manpower to war with the Counts so he brokered a deal with Jesus, the leader of the Counts. Mack told Jesus that there was enough business for the both of them.

Jesus was young and ambitious but he had difficulty getting established on the west side of Detroit. He was outgunned by the YBI. Mack was able to seal the deal by offering to supply the Counts with guns.

Jimmy was now indirectly supplying his guns to two rival gangs. As far as the YBI was concerned, they had an exclusive relationship with Jimmy and they were not impressed. The YBI thought Jimmy should be reminded about his loyalty to them.

Carjacked

Flannigan's was busier than usual, when Norm and Jesse showed up about two drinks before last call. Sean was working the bar by himself. Norm ordered a 7 & 7 and asked where the hot red-headed barmaid was.

Sean rolled his eyes.

"Megan and Jimmy Flanders are quite an item now, who knows where they are."

"Who's Jimmy Flanders?"

"You know him Norm, the Irish guy who always hangs out with Flanny."

"Oh, that guy. He always seems to be banging your female staff."

"Tell me about it."

Norm took his drink, and joined Jesse where he had just set a fresh rack on the pool table. While Jesse broke, Norm noticed Flanny by the kitchen doors in a heated conversation with Murphy. Flanny was quite animated and it sounded like he was telling Murphy off. Norm was curious. He stuck his head in the bar window.

"Hey Sean, what's going on over there?"

"The old man's pissed. Someone stole his Lincoln from out back."

"No surprise in this neighborhood. He's insured ain't he?"

"Yeah, but that's not what he's pissed about. As usual, he had a trunk full of guns. I don't think the insurance company covers those."

Sean actually smiled when he made the wisecrack, he never really approved of Flanny's antics.

"Order for last call now Norm, it looks like we'll be closing up early."

Jesse and Norm got another two games in while Norm polished off the four drinks he ordered for last call.

"Coney's Norm?"

"For sure, brother."

Norm gave the Grinch a pat on the shoulder as he walked by. He was carrying on a private conversation with his drink, but that wasn't unusual.

"Take it easy Grinch."

Jesse and Norm did their Coney run, and then headed back home. There were a couple of weird things about Lafayette Coney Island and their Coney dogs. The first thing you noticed was how delicious they were after you'd been drinking all night. Another oddity was that the American Coney Island was right next door, but hardly anyone ever went there. The clincher was how awful your clothes reeked of Coney dogs the next morning when your sense of smell returned.

The next day at work the Grinch was the topic of conversation. Apparently, he had some difficulty getting home after closing Flannigan's. The story was that he got rear-ended at a stop light, in his 1979 red Camaro. Even the drunken Grinch knew better than to stop or get out of his car at that time of night in that neighborhood, but he noticed a flashing red light in the vehicle behind him.

The Grinch got his wallet badge in hand and waited for the cops to come to his door. Before he realized what was happening, two black guys pulled him from his car, threw him to the pavement, and one put a gun to his head. The Grinch fumbled for his own gun, but it was knocked from his hand on his way to the pavement.

"You crossed us white boy. Now ya gotta die."

The Grinch saw his life flash before his eyes. He felt the pressure of the gun barrel on the back of his head.

Click, click. The sound was larger than life. It was that sound that gave him life.

"Fuck, this gun's a piece a shit."

The shooter kicked the Grinch in the ribs and grabbed his gun off the road.

"I'll cap ya with yer own gun, fucker."

The other guy picked up the Grinch's wallet from the road.

"Wait, this guy's a fuckin cop. It ain't him. We ain't killin no cop."

The shooter used the Grinch's gun to pistol whip him, knocking him unconscious. They took off in the Grinch's Camaro, leaving him bleeding on the road in front of their abandoned stolen car. Obviously the two gang bangers didn't know the difference between a red Firebird and a red Camaro.

Somehow, the Grinch managed to stumble into a Detroit Police precinct that was only a few blocks away. He identified himself as a cop, so the DPD called Windsor. The on-duty Inspector from Windsor went to the Detroit precinct and asked to see the Grinch. He found the poor bastard in a holding tank, beaten, bloodied, and still drunk.

The Inspector tore a strip off the desk Sergeant's ass.

"You'd never treat one of your own like this. I want this man out of that cage and cleaned up immediately."

The Grinch recovered and he wrote the whole experience off to bad luck. The Detroit cops wrote it off as a simple car jacking. The Grinch eventually got his car back; he never knew it was a case of mistaken identity. Jimmy Flynn knew.

The two gang bangers disappeared shortly after that. They were never seen, or heard from again.

11

Narcs

Jesse got transferred to the Drug Squad before Norm, but that wasn't unusual. The brass always favored Jesse, probably because they were afraid of him. Norm got on the police force first, but when he tried to get the Christmas holidays off to represent Windsor in a European water polo tournament, they just laughed at him.

Jesse got on the job about a year later. When he asked for time off to play AKO football, they asked if he needed a ride there.

When Norm joined Jesse in the Drug Squad, they found themselves on opposite shifts, no doubt it was done on purpose by their boss Teflon Tim. It was probably a good thing for two reasons: first, the two high school buddies easily got into trouble when they worked together.

Second, they had two completely different working styles. Jesse was a balls-to-the-wall, heart breaker and life taker kind of cop. Norm was more laid back and methodical in his approach. Regardless, they remained the best of friends.

Jesse and Norm hung out more off the job than on. They invested in real estate and flipped houses. They used the extra money to take their wives on vacations. Their ideas of family also differed. Jesse's wife loved kids so they had three of them.

Sandra never wanted kids and that was fine by Norm. He practically raised his five siblings. Having a marriage without kids, meant Norm and Sandra could spend all of their money on themselves.

On one sunny summer day, the two amigos worked the same shift because of a manpower shortage that week. Blackjack typed up a search warrant for a weed dealer on the west side of town.

Tanker was the sergeant that day and Bongo was the fifth man on the team. The two of them did a comedy routine that rivaled Billy Crystal and Robin Williams. They babbled on to each other like two old Jewish guys, in the back of the plain clothes van on the way to the target's house.

How could anyone suspect these two comedians to be cops when they got out of the van yakking gibberish to each other? Besides that, the squad dressed down to blend in. Bongo had long grey hair and a handlebar mustache. He favored a worn jean jacket. Blackjack had his head shaved completely bald. He sported a light goatee and wore a biker type leather jacket.

Jesse had his long hair combed back and a neatly trimmed beard. He liked his Levi jacket and sneakers. The undercover holsters were not designed to be concealed under such clothes, so Jesse always stuffed his pistol into the waistband of the back of his pants.

Norm trimmed his shaggy beard into a goatee, and let his hair grow long in the back. He had an assortment of undercover duds to choose from. On that day he chose a Hiram Walker work shirt his dad had given him.

You would think that five big guys dressed like street punks might look suspicious climbing out of a minivan in any neighborhood. If not, you would definitely think something was up when you saw those guys wielding guns, with one of them carrying a battering ram.

Nonetheless, Norm was always amazed that nobody ever called the police to report such a sight. There was one exception. Norm gave some of the other guys in the squad some of the Hiram Walker shirts his dad had given him. The shirts were perfect cover for the team while doing surveillance on a coke dealer in an industrial area near the whiskey distillery.

The team swarmed the dealer in his car, taking him down at a busy intersection during rush hour.

The dispatcher made the following broadcast over the radio: "Is there a plain clothes unit around the Hiram Walker distillery?"

There wasn't always time to notify the dispatcher when a quick decision had to be made in making an arrest. The drug squad responded to the dispatcher, confirming their location.

The dispatcher replied, "Okay, a citizen reported that there was bunch of Hiram Walker men running around there with guns."

"Uh…yes dispatch. Sorry, that was us."

Smashed and Busted

The wooden door on the lower half of the duplex looked pretty weak so Blackjack kicked it in with his size twelve shoe. Once again, no one called the police. The upper unit was vacant and as it turned out, the suspect wasn't home down below. Tanker told Jesse and Norm to watch the front in case the suspect returned home. The rest of the team searched the apartment and kept an eye on the back door.

Jesse found a spot for him and Norm up against the building next door, on the front sidewalk. His gun fell out of his waistband and clunked on the sidewalk when he sat down.

"Jesse, you dropped something."

"Ah shit. Hey Norm, why don't you go across the street and grab us something to drink? I'll hold the fort."

The day dragged on while the two old buddies contemplated life and easier ways to make a buck. They sat for what seemed like an eternity; the store owner across the street started to look at them suspiciously.

"My ass is getting sore, Jesse. I'm going inside to see what's up."

"Alright, I'll scope out another spot."

Norm went into the apartment and saw the other guys sitting around the kitchen table sharing a bottle of whiskey.

"Hey Storm, you want a drink?" Bongo slurred his words.

Norm laughed.

"What the fuck are you guys doing?"

"We're checking to see if there's any dope in this bottle. We haven't found any yet."

"How long are we gonna wait for this guy?"

Norm no sooner finished his question when he heard a strange voice in the room.

"What the fuck are you guys doing in my house?"

Norm saw the suspect closing the sliding patio door behind him. The three cops at the kitchen table didn't budge.

Bongo held up a pair of handcuffs.

"Yer under arrest."

The suspect sported a puzzled look on his face. Then he saw Bongo reach for his gun on the table by the bottle of whiskey. He turned to head back out the door, but before he could open it Blackjack hit him with a flying tackle. Their momentum sent the two of them smashing through the glass patio door, down the steps, and on to the back lawn.

Blackjack lost his grip when they hit the ground; the suspect rolled up on to his feet and ran out the back yard.

Tanker yelled to Norm, "Get Jesse and head him off!"

Bongo followed the other two men out the back door; he stopped to brush the glass off Blackjack.

"Are you okay? You're covered in blood."

"Never mind me, it's not my blood. Get that bastard."

Jesse heard the commotion, ran down the side of the house, and was hot on the heels of the suspect. He ran into a dead-end alley and then tried to climb over a wooden fence. Two hundred and twenty-five pounds of speeding Jesse slammed into the guy on the fence.

The impact was too much for the rickety fence. It collapsed under Jesse and the suspect. The back yard looked like it was hit by a tornado when Norm got there. Jesse emerged from a pile of kindling that was once the fence. He had a big shit-eating grin on his face and the suspect in hand.

Ice Cream

The suspect was injured too badly to take into the cop shop. He had a deep gash on his upper left arm, so the squad stopped at the hospital first. Because the guy was in police custody, the doctor quickly attended to him.

The squad had only recovered a minimal amount of weed in the apartment so Tanker explained how he would only be charged with simple possession. Tanker was smooth. He told the guy how the cops were only doing their job and that the city would pay for the damage to both his doors.

Bongo had the munchies and said he was hungry. Norm commented how it was such a lovely day, that perhaps they should all stop for ice cream.

The suspect piped up.

"Wow, I'd love an ice cream."

Everyone chuckled. The chuckles turned to laughs when Jesse wheeled the van into a Baskin-Robbins. Everybody ordered double scoops of their favorite flavor. The suspect was handcuffed in front because of his injury. He looked like a kid on Christmas morning when Norm handed him an ice cream cone.

"Don't worry buddy, it's on us," Tanker said, while patting him on his good shoulder.

"Really, you guys are all right."

Norm was riding shot gun while Jesse drove. He licked the drips around the edge of his cone—held in one hand while he drove with the other. The scoop dislodged and fell from the cone. Jesse pulled his hand from the wheel and tried to juggle the mushy scoop of ice cream, but he fumbled the ball and fell out the window.

The look on his face was priceless. Like a kindergarten kid who just got scolded by his teacher. Everyone in the van, including the suspect, howled with laughter. Jesse looked back at the suspect and scowled.

"What? Don't look at me. You can't have mine."

Norm laughed so hard he cried. It's one of those stories that he recalls from time to time and laughs out loud. Jesse never thought it was very funny.

A Message

During all the commotion, Norm forgot about a message on his pager. It was a long-distance number, so he waited until he got back to the station to check it. There was also a message from Patrick Kelly on Norm's phone.

He wanted to know the name of the Irish pub that Norm took him to in Detroit when he was down for the lecture. He said he was interested in Kevin and Jimmy Flannigan. Norm was puzzled. It would have to wait until he came in to work the next day.

12

Crack Kills

Day shifts were usually quiet in the Drug Squad. The bad guys didn't get out of bed until the crack of noon. Norm looked at the flashing message light on his phone when he sat down at his desk. Not a morning person, he liked to ease into his day slowly. Norm cracked open a Pepsi and turned on the radio behind his desk for background music.

"Hey, who's been fucking with my radio again, putting this country shit on?"

Teflon Tim poked his head out of his office door.

"What's the matter with country?"

"All that whiny shit's gonna ruin my radio."

"Yeah, well that rock and roll's gonna ruin your brain."

Someone called out from the peanut gallery.

"Don't worry boss, his minds already gone."

The bantering went on, but Norm ignored it and got a fresh scratch pad ready to answer his phone messages. The first message was from Patrick Kelly playing phone tag, and the second was from a detective Myers of the Detroit Police.

"Hmm, wonder what the hell he wants?"

The last message was from the drug prosecutor, who wanted to know if Norm could testify as an expert witness in an upcoming drug trial. That meant some more research and paperwork, but that was what day shifts were for.

Norm made Patrick Kelly his first call.

"Patrick? It's Norm. We've been playing phone tag. Guess you're it."

"Hey Norm, thanks for getting back to me. I know how busy you small city cops are. You're probably sitting there eating your Cheerios."

"Close buddy, a Pepsi and a sugar-free date turnover."

"Great, breakfast of champions and drug cops, eh?"

"What can I do for you brother? Are you looking for someone? I didn't write the names down from your message."

"Yeah Norm, I'm working on something here. I'm interested in Kevin and Jimmy Flannigan; I think they're hanging their hats in Detroit. Hey, what was the name of that bar you took me to over there?"

"You mean Flannigan's Pub? The owner is Kevin Flannigan. Now that I think about it, he has a buddy named Jimmy Flanders that's banging one of his barmaids. It could be the same guy. How the hell are two guys in Detroit connected to drugs in Toronto?"

"I'm not sure yet Norm. It's something I'm working on. Do you have any connections over there?"

"FBI, Border Patrol, Customs & Immigration, DEA…shit, now that I think of it, I don't think I've ever dealt with anyone in the DPD directly. I can reach out for you though. I'm sure someone here knows someone there."

"Thanks Norm. I'll owe you a beer."

"Make it a case and you've got a deal."

"Hey, that's graft, ain't it?"

"No, not when it's between cops. I'll see what I can do and get back to you."

Cracker Jack

Norm checked the second message again, then called detective Myers in Detroit.

"Homicide, Meyers here."

"Good morning detective Meyers, It's Norm Strom over in Windsor."

"Hey Norm, are you still in the Drug Squad there?"

"Yes sir, I am. What can I do for you detective?"

"You know a guy by the name of James Acker, from Windsor? We found him with one of your business cards in his pocket."

"Yeah, Cracker Jack. He's one of my rats."

"Well, one of our drug cops blew poor Cracker Jack out of his socks during a drug raid on the west side. We're not sure of the level of his involvement yet. Listen, I'm up to my ass in alligators here. Do have some time to come over here?"

"Sure detective, how bout this afternoon some time?"

"I'm downtown for most of the day; shall we say 1 pm at Lafayette Coney Island? I'm buying."

"Sounds good to me, I'll see you there."

"Just look for the fat bald black guy wearing a gun."

"Okay..."

"See you at 1 pm Norm."

Norm told Teflon Tim that poor old Cracker Jack was in drug heaven and that DPD wanted to talk to him. Norm thought he could maybe kill two birds with one stone and ask Detective Meyers about the Flannigans. All the other guys had court appearances and Jesse was pissed off he'd miss out on Coney dogs, one of his favorites.

"Don't worry, brother, I'll bring you back a couple."

Meyers looked just like his description. He resembled the uniformed cop in the first Die Hard movie, the guy who loved Twinkies. He sat with a clean-cut white guy in an expensive suit, who looked more like a fashion model than a cop.

"You must be Norm Strom. I'm Bill Meyers and this is Al Thomas from Internal Affairs."

"Oh yeah, something I did over here?"

"Don't worry Norm. We're working on some things together. Since Acker was shot by a cop, IA is automatically involved. We just want to pick your brain about James Acker and his friends."

"I'm not sure what I can tell you. He's a crack head informant of mine. He calls from time to time, setting up crack dealers for me. He works for cash. He did mention once that he had a cousin in Detroit and that he bought crack here before it was popular in Windsor."

Norm ordered lunch.

"I'll have one of each, chili and cheese only with a milk."

He used the proper Coney lingo. Meyers raised his eyebrows.

"You've been here before, huh? What's with the milk?"

"Hey, can I throw a couple of names at you guys while I'm here?"

"Sure, go ahead Norm."

The dogs and drinks were delivered quicker than any fast food joint, and the men dug in. Norm couldn't help but notice how different the place looked in daylight, while he was sober.

He took a break between Coney dogs.

"Jimmy Flannigan aka Jimmy Flanders, or Kevin Flannigan, from Flannigan's pub?"

Both men looked wide-eyed at Norm and stopped chewing. Al Thomas washed his mouthful of food down with a Schlitz beer and leaned over the table closer to Norm.

"What do you want with those two guys?" asked Meyers.

Both men were all ears. It was like he'd just asked who killed JFK.

"I know them from the pub. A Toronto drug cop reached out to me, asking about them."

"And what's his interest?"

"I don't know. It's something he's looking into. Maybe you guys should talk."

Thomas chirped in.

"Maybe we should."

"C'mon guys, I'm just a drug cop from Windsor who bought information from a dead crack head."

"Okay Norm, relax. We all want to trust each other here, but there are cops involved on our side of the border, from what we know so far."

Right under Your Nose

Bill Meyers sat back in his chair and poked the remainder of his fully loaded Coney dog. A gob of chili and mustard leaked from the corner of his mouth. He caught it with a napkin before it spilled onto his wrinkly white shirt. Al Thomas took another sip of his cola.

Meyers continued, "The guys you mentioned, the Flannigans? We have information they're tied to the IRA and they run guns for them from here to Ireland. The old man's been using his bar as a front for years. We know some of you Windsor cops drink there but we're more concerned about one of our own."

"You mean Murphy?"

Bill Meyers gestured to the waiter for another round of dogs. He'd already devoured two.

Thomas replied, "Yes Norm. I can't get into specifics, but Murphy is on a short leash. He's working both sides of the fence. He's free police security for Flanny, but he is accountable to us. His drinking has gotten him in a jackpot, so now he's *our* rat."

Thomas stopped talking as a uniformed traffic cop walked by the table with a take-out brown bag. The Detroit cops all nodded to each other in acknowledgement.

"As I was saying Norm, we have a pretty good idea of what's been going on at Flanny's pub. We haven't had anyone to make a positive ID yet, but we think that Jimmy whoever, is really Jimmy Flynn from Ireland. He's wanted by Interpol in relation to some bombings in Belfast. Boston police were also looking into his activities, but he disappeared before they could nail him down."

"Holy shit guys, all this has been going on under our noses at Flanny's? I did see him with a trunk full of weapons once, but I just figured him for a gun nut."

"That's only the half of it, Norm. We believe Jimmy's been selling guns and coke to the YBI"

"Okay, I'm losing you Al. Where does Cracker Jack fit into all this?"

"We don't think he's a player, just in the wrong place at the wrong time. He was with his cousin who is YBI when our guy capped him. This is all about gangs, guns and drugs."

Bill Meyers nodded in agreement. Al Thomas caught the waiter's attention, and pointed to a piece of coconut cream pie.

"There's not too much more I can tell you guys. I don't get over to Flanny's much anymore, now that we have our own social club. Actually, I heard he was closing down."

"Yeah, we're not sure if he's on to us or not. He's probably moving because of the neighborhood and gang activity there."

"Did you guys know the trunk of Flanny's Lincoln was full of guns when it got ripped off? Murphy was there."

Meyers looked at Thomas as he shoveled the last fork full of pie into his mouth. Thomas motioned for Meyers to wipe the whipped cream from the corner of his mouth.

"No, he must have *forgotten* to tell us that. Flanny just opened a fancy new place downtown. He's called it Paddy's Tap & Grill."

"Should I steer clear of the place?"

"That's totally up to you Norm. We can always use more eyes and ears there. Besides, Flanny thinks all you Windsor cops are just a bunch of hick-town drunks."

Meyers was just polishing off his beer when he choked on it. Both men laughed.

"Yeah, and our guys are a bunch of saints."

Thomas leaned in toward Norm again.

"Anyway Norm, we'd appreciated it if you can keep this under your hat. It's an ongoing investigation."

"No problem. I understand completely."

"And by the way Norm, if you think you can arrange it, I'd like to talk to your cop buddy in Toronto. He's got me curious."

"No problem Al. I'll reach out and work on that for you."

Norm tried to hand the waiter some money for his lunch but Meyers beat him to the draw. The waiter had a puzzled look on his face. Meyers rolled his eyes toward Thomas and the light bulb went on. The waiter nodded and took the cash.

Norm just smiled, figuring that Meyers usually got freebies there. Norm thanked Meyers for lunch and the three cops swapped business cards before they parted company.

Norm shook his head on the walk to his car. He really did feel like a dumb hick- town cop. Flannigan's was always a comfortable place to let your hair down and get drunk. All those cops there with all that shit going on right under their noses.

Norm wanted to put up a huge banner in the cop shop locker room, but he knew better. It was just another secret he had to file away.

13

Shadows

Jimmy and Megan got on as well as you could expect for a drunk and a junkie. They came from completely different backgrounds, but they were heading in the same direction. Jimmy was scarred from childhood, so it was doubtful he could ever really love someone.

He was physically attracted to Megan and she kept him amused, which was good enough for Jimmy. After Erin, he was never really loyal to any one woman. He wasn't sure if he was slowing down in his old age or if Megan was growing on him.

Megan was brought up in a loving family, but her overbearing mother always thought Megan could do better, in everything she did. Her mother was not a happy woman and was never satisfied with Megan's decisions.

Alzheimer's put her father into a nursing home, where he later died. The lack of support from her mother eventually pushed Megan away, and under Jimmy's spell. The doctors she tried to land never paid her half the attention that Jimmy did. He was so intense.

Jimmy never had money until he got involved with running guns for Flanny, so it was no surprise he didn't manage his money well. He drank the best whiskey, ate in the best restaurants and crashed a few of the muscle cars he owned.

Jimmy also chipped away at the profit from his drug business when he started using his own product. He kept Megan happy, treating her with a steady supply of coke to powder her nose. When Megan was happy, she kept Jimmy happy. The arrangement seemed to work.

Lights in the Mirror

It was closing time, on Saturday night at Paddy's Tap & Grill. Flanny shut off the lights and waved to Jimmy and Megan on their way out the front door.

"Can we go to my place tonight Jimmy? I'd like to check my mail and water the plants."

Jimmy rolled his eyes.

"Aye, we can do that."

Megan kept an apartment in downtown Windsor, although she rarely spent any time there. She told people that she and Jimmy lived together, but he never acknowledged it. They walked across the street and got into Jimmy's candy-apple-red '93 Mustang Shelby Cobra.

Jimmy fired up the engine, revving it twice before putting it in gear. The after-market exhaust pipes rumbled and echoed off the glass storefronts on the empty street.

Megan was fiddling with the radio when Jimmy turned onto Michigan Avenue. He reached up and adjusted his rearview mirror; a set of headlights had followed him around the last two turns.

"Fuck me."

"What's the matter Jimmy?"

"We have a shadow."

"Cops?"

"If it was the cops, they woulda stopped me when I rolled through that last red light. Hang on, I'm gonna see if I can lose em."

Jimmy accelerated and made two quick right turns. The headlights were still in his mirror.

"Can you see who it is?"

"No, I can't, a black SUV with tinted windows. There still on us."

Jimmy put the hammer down. His cobra jet engine roared. The tires squealed and spun as the ass end of the car fishtailed all over the road. Jimmy was only a few blocks from the tunnel to Canada, but he didn't want to tip his hand. He bolted north on Woodward, then hung two hard lefts. He gained on the SUV in the turns so he did two more hard rights, and then ducked into an alley.

Just when Jimmy thought he'd lost them, the SUV stopped at the mouth of the alley.

"Shite. Who is this guy? He drives like a cop."

Jimmy hammered it down the alley and then made more turns to gain on the SUV. He flew by the Coney shops on Lafayette, and hung a right on Randolph. A cop car passed Jimmy, going in the opposite direction. They put on their roof lights and made a u-turn. The SUV flew around the corner at the same time and nearly broadsided the cop car. The cops cut off the SUV, forcing it to the curb.

Jimmy never let up off the gas. He watched the cops and the SUV fade away in his rearview mirror. He turned left on W. Jefferson and then wheeled into the tunnel to Windsor.

"What the fuck was that all about?"

"I dunno darlin, but I'm glad we're stayin at yer place tonight."

Jacked Up

The streets were deserted in Windsor as Jimmy and Megan exited the tunnel. Just to be safe, Jimmy did a few more heat checks before pulling into the driveway of Megan's duplex on Church Street.

Edna Stern, who lived across the street, was up getting a glass of milk because she couldn't sleep. She noticed the car lights in Megan's driveway, and peered out her window. Edna was the self-appointed neighborhood watch captain. She copied the American license plate down on a pad she kept on the coffee table, just like Norm Strom had instructed her to do.

"Megan, you got any blow?"

"Just a few lines...don't you want to get some sleep?"

"I'll sleep when I'm fuckin dead and buried. Besides I'm still jacked up from that car chase. I wonder who that fucker was."

"I'll have to make a call Jimmy. I need money."

Jimmy and Megan knew better than to bring drugs back and forth across the border. Megan had her own connections in Windsor. She made a call, while Jimmy inhaled the two fat lines she had laid out.

"Thanks, a lot. You couldn't save one for me?"

"Sorry darlin...didn't know you wanted any. You shoulda said somethin."

"Yer so selfish, sometimes I wonder if you love me at all."

"Ah, you know I do baby."

Building a Case

Norm never took the job home with him, but he couldn't help wondering about his conversation with the Detroit police, Cracker Jack, and Patrick Kelly's curiosity with the Flannigans in Detroit. Norm played it over in his mind, making a mental note to call Patrick first thing Monday morning.

A can of Pepsi and a sugar-free apple turnover were sitting on Norm's desk when he walked into the office. Teflon Tim mumbled good morning as Norm walked by his office door. Blackjack was already in, sitting at his desk.

"Did you shit the bed?"

"No, but I had a wet dream about your wife. C'mon Storm, grab your pop and breakfast. We gotta go meet Fat Fiona."

"Why do you need me? Afraid she might try to take advantage of you?"

"Not quite. I know how much you like looking at her big fat titties."

Norm made a face and stuck his finger down his throat like he was gagging and going to throw up.

"Alright, let me check my voicemail first."

Norm checked his phone; there was a message.

"Hello Officer Strom. This is Edna Stern, the neighborhood watch captain over on Church Street. I've been writing down license plates like you asked. You know, in case they're drug dealers. Anyway, there was an American car at that girl's house across the street.

She was with a man. I think he's her boyfriend, but he always has different cars. It's that duplex at 540 Church I told you about. The plate number is 395 AXR. I just know something is going on there."

"Jesus Christ, Norm. Are you on the sex hotline again?"

"Hold your horses, I'm coming."

Fat Fiona was Blackjack's rat at the time. He did his due diligence and followed her all over the city one night while she was out dealing. When the timing was right, he jumped her and choked her to prevent her from swallowing the crack she had concealed in her mouth. It wasn't a whole lot of crack, but enough that she was afraid of losing her kid to the Children's Aid society.

She was a master at staying one step ahead of the cops and she knew exactly how to play both sides of the fence. Sometimes you need a rat to catch a rat.

Instead of taking her chances in court, she worked her patch and called Blackjack just often enough to keep the other drug cops off her back. She also started hiding the crack up her twat; she knew the cops couldn't and wouldn't look in there.

Blackjack wheeled into a Mac's Milk parking lot near Fat Fiona's house and she climbed into the back of the van. She gave Norm the evil eye.

"You've seen Storm before. Don't worry, he's cool."

Fiona rambled on about the usual Detroit crack dealers...this nigger, that nigger. Funny thing was, Fiona was half black herself and most of her friends were black. Blackjack turned onto Wyandotte Street West.

"Turn down Church Street. I'll show you a house I dropped off to late Saturday night. Slow down, it's right there...number 540, upstairs."

Norm jotted the house number down for Blackjack while he drove past the duplex.

"Yeah, some redheaded chick named Megan. She used to be into Dilaudid, but now she calls me for two or three eight balls of blow at a time."

"Not rock, like the rest of your customers?"

"No, she likes the powder."

Blackjack asked Fiona for more details. Norm raised his eyebrows; a light went on. He hadn't written it down, but he was sure it was the same address that Edna Stern had called him about. He kept it to himself. Fiona went on to tell them that Megan was banging some Irish guy from the states.

To put icing on the cake, Fiona added, "One time I was there Megan was all spooked about someone watching her. She showed me a gun."

Norm and Blackjack looked over at each other. They were both grinning.

14

Search Warrant

Back at the cop shop, Norm told Blackjack about the information he'd gotten from Edna Stern. He sat back in his desk chair.

"With Fat Fiona and your nosy neighbor's info, I think I've got enough for a search warrant."

"I agree, go for it."

Norm sat down at his own desk. He looked at the phone, and then flipped through his notebook. His wheels were turning. He had to call Patrick about the Detroit cops, but should he update them first? No. Norm picked up the phone and called Patrick.

"Drug Enforcement, Patrick Kelly."

"Hey ya limey bastard, how's it hangin?"

"Hey Norm, busted any grade schoolers smokin up on recess?"

"No, I've been too busy fielding calls from gay guys looking for Stormy Normie. Did you give my number to the gay hotline?"

"Not me, it sounds like something one of your homies would do. What can I do ya for?"

"Well sir, let me tell you about a conversation I had with the Detroit Police."

"Yeah, I'm listening."

Norm went on to tell Patrick about the Flannigans, their gun running business, how Jimmy changed his name and keeps moving to stay one step ahead of the law. He left out the part about the Internal Affairs investigation in Detroit. There was only silence on the other end of the phone.

"Patrick, are you hearing me? Are you still there?"

"Yeah, I hear you."

Patrick's tone changed. He got really quiet.

"Can I trust you Norm, I mean really trust you?"

"Sure brother, what's up?"

"The guy you know as Jimmy Flannigan, aka Jimmy Flanders, is really Jimmy Flynn from Belfast Ireland."

"Sounds like you know the guy?"

"You could say that. We grew up together. Once upon a time he was my best friend. We even have matching shamrock tattoos."

Norm listened quietly, trying to piece it all together.

"I've been looking for Jimmy Flynn for over twenty years Norm. He killed my little sister."

Patrick sounded like he was reliving his past; he went back in time and told Norm how he had introduced Jimmy to his sister and how he had made him promise he'd take care of her. He got a bit choked up. He went on to tell Norm about Bloody Friday, what Jimmy did, and how his sister was killed. Norm didn't interrupt. He let Patrick continue and get it all off his chest.

"Let me ask you something, Norm. Not cop to cop, man to man. Have you ever wanted to kill someone?"

"No, can't say that I have. I've thought about the possibility, but never had a reason. I can't relate to your pain."

"She was my sister, and he was my best friend. He promised me, can you understand that?"

"I'm trying. Is there anything I can do?"

"I don't' know, keep tabs on him for now, I guess. He needs to pay for what he's done. I want to look him right in the eyes and tell him that. I'd like to…well, there's lots of things I'd like to do to him."

"Maybe you'll get a chance real soon—one of the guy's in my squad is working on a search warrant for Jimmy's girlfriend's apartment, in Windsor. We hope to execute it later today."

"That's great. Keep me in the loop will ya? And I'd appreciate it if you keep our conversation between the two of us."

"No problem. Take it easy man."

Knock Knock

Blackjack was no slouch; he banged away at the keyboard like a woodpecker on a dead tree. If he was to get the warrant signed that day, he'd have to have it done by 3 pm. Norm's stomach growled so loudly that Blackjack stopped typing.

"Storm, I can't hear myself think over your stomach growling. Why don't you go and get us something to eat?"

"Sounds like a great idea, how's a chicken Caesar from La Guardia sound to you?"

"Great, but only if you're buying."

"Sure, anything for you."

"Yeah, that's because I'll be making you some overtime today."

Norm smiled, and then headed out to pick up a late lunch.

Blackjack got the warrant signed, briefed the rest of the squad and then hit Megan Doyle's front door before you could say, "Police—Search Warrant."

Megan had her purse and keys in hand and was almost hit by the front door as the cops barged in. She probably wet her pants, but it didn't show. Blackjack arrested her and explained the search warrant. A female uniformed officer strip-searched Megan, while the Drug Squad searched her apartment.

Megan was tightlipped, but wide-eyed as the cops fumbled and searched through her personal things. Blackjack told her they'd make less of a mess if she just told them where her stash was.

She hesitated for a second, but then pointed to a cookie jar on the kitchen counter. Norm emptied the contents of the cookie jar. A plastic baggie containing about two eight balls (one quarter of an ounce) of cocaine fell out, along with an old credit card and a rolled-up U.S. twenty-dollar bill.

"Anything else?" Norm asked.

Just as Megan answered no, one of the other guys came into the kitchen with a pill bottle from her medicine cabinet. He handed the bottle to Norm who was the squad's pill expert.

Norm looked at Megan.

"Whose Dilaudid and Percocet?"

"They're mine. Can't you read the prescription?"

"Yes, I can. It's expired, and it's for only twenty Percs. There are at least a dozen Dillies in here."

"I just put them all in one bottle. I need them for pain."

She went on to tell Blackjack about her car accident and the injuries that she had to be medicated for. Norm heard some chuckling coming from the bedroom. When he walked in, one of the guys was flipping through some naughty Polaroid's of Megan showing off her fellatio skills. He grabbed a handful of the pictures and noticed a familiar looking guy in one of the pictures. He went back out into the kitchen to see Megan.

"Who's the guy in this picture?"

"Hey, you can't look at those."

"I don't care about his big dick. I just want to know who he is."

"He's my boyfriend, Jimmy."

Norm glanced over at Blackjack.

"Jimmy who?"

"Jimmy Flanders. He lives in Detroit. He's got nothing to do with this."

Blackjack took the picture from Norm and looked at it.

"Shit Norm, he's got you beat."

Megan was more teary-eyed than angry.

"You guys are assholes."

A horn sounded out front of the apartment. Norm looked out the window and saw the paddy wagon parked at the curb. He glanced across the street. Sure enough, old Edna Stern was peeking through her curtains. He gave her a little wave but she didn't respond.

Norm smiled at Megan.

"Your ride is here, princess."

Spilling the Beans

In the interview room, back at the station, Norm let Blackjack run the interrogation. That was the unwritten rule, the guy who did the warrant was given the opportunity to try and get the accused to roll over and supply information. Blackjack laid out the ground rules to Megan but she didn't bite. She was offered a lawyer, but she said she didn't need one because she had done nothing wrong. The drugs were for her personal use.

Blackjack slid his chair closer to Megan, but he kept his tone soft.

"Let me explain exactly what is going to happen to you Megan."

She sat back in her chair, folded her arms in front of her and rolled her eyes.

"You had enough cocaine and un-prescribed pills in your possession that we are charging you with possession of narcotics, for the purpose of trafficking."

"But I…"

"Let me finish Megan. You also had a small amount of weed and the phone numbers of known crack dealers, not to mention that we know all about your boyfriend and what he's up to."

A good investigator never shows his hand and should listen more than he talks. Blackjack said just enough about Jimmy to get Megan thinking. She obviously knew more than she let on.

"I told you Jimmy's got nothing to do with this, it's all mine. He just stays over once in a while."

Blackjack moved in even closer, his knees were almost touching Megan's near the corner of the table. He never changed his tone.

"Again, please let me finish, Megan. If you don't cooperate with us, you will have a criminal record and never be able to cross the border again. You'll never get your job back. We'll make sure that your Jimmy can't come to Canada. You can call him right now and say goodbye if you like."

While Blackjack explained the facts of life to Megan, Norm sat and watched her intently. It was his job to watch her body language and takes notes. Her crossed arms dropped to her lap and her bright green eyes got red around the edges as they started to well up. She did her best to remain tightlipped and hold her composure. He looked over to Norm. That was his cue to step in if he wanted to.

He was just about to speak when it hit him like a slap in the face.

"You don't remember me do you Megan?"

Megan wiped a tear from the corner of her left eye and looked at Norm. He never forgot a face, even one that showed each and every hard day of living. Her eyes had lost their sparkle and the wrinkles around their edges were getting thick.

Her light freckles turned to age spots and her red hair showed flecks of grey.

"You said you worked in the States, right?"

"Yeah, why, did you drink at Flannigan's with all the other cops?"

"Yes, Megan, but when I first saw you there, I asked you if you remembered me. You dismissed me at the time. I remember you from way before that, back when you went to Nursing College in St. Thomas."

Megan sniffled and looked at him. Her eyes then rolled up to the left, while she was accessed her memory.

Her scrunched face showed puzzlement.

"I don't remember you."

It wasn't important that she remember; Norm was just trying to make a connection, trying to get her to open up. He went on to talk about her nursing career and how he knew she lost her job in the states because of her drug habit. That did it. Megan looked down to the floor and her flowing tears turned into sobs. He moved in closer this time.

"We can help you, but you have to help us first. You have to give up Jimmy. Did you know he's an IRA terrorist wanted for murder in his own country?'

Megan sat up, wide-eyed with tears still flowing. Norm had her full attention so he laid all his cards on the table.

"His real name is Jimmy Flynn. He never told you about the bombings and how he killed his girlfriend, Erin Kelly, did he?"

"You don't know what you're talking about. Jimmy was in Boston when that happened. I was the one in Belfast."

A look of horror came over her face.

"What did you say that girl's name was?"

"Erin Kelly, his girlfriend and his best friend's sister. He left Belfast the day she died, and moved to Boston."

Megan shook her head.

"It can't be. I met her that day, but forgot her name. She had a boyfriend…no, it can't be."

"It sounds like you know Jimmy better than you thought. You must know about the guns and drugs."

Megan shook her head again and put her face in her hands. She got really quiet. Blackjack looked over at Norm and shrugged. He nodded back.

"Okay, if you can't give us Jimmy, then you'll have to give us something else, someone he deals with maybe."

"I can never give Jimmy up. I love him. Why don't you go after that Flanny bastard? He's been selling guns for years. When he wasn't grabbing my ass, he was selling guns in the kitchen and in the back alley."

"Well, that's a start, but Flanny lives in the states. Would you be willing to work with the cops there?"

"I don't know…what's in it for me?"

"It all depends on what you can do for us. You're just a little fish. We want the big fish. I can't promise you anything, but there is a possibility you could walk away from this, if you play your cards right."

"I wouldn't have to go to jail or give up my green card?"

"It depends on how much you can help. Are you on the team?"

"I don't know. I'll let you know."

Norm looked at Blackjack and then slid his business card across the table to Megan.

"Call me."

15

The Good Samaritan

Personal relationships can be complicated. For Patrick Kelly, that seemed to be the case, in every case. From his drunken abusive father, to the death of his sister, and the betrayal of his best friend, things were always complicated.

Patrick loved women and they loved him. He blamed his shortcomings and failed relationships on the luck of the Irish. Of course, Patrick was the author of his own misfortune in most cases. It didn't help that he was never in one place long enough to cement any intimate relationships.

It was on one of the worst hang-over days of his life, when he met a woman who he thought might be the one. It was on his ride home from the Windsor road trip, where he met Norm Strom.

Patrick was grateful for Norm's hospitality and friendship but not for the terrible hangover he was saddled with for the drive home. As fate would have it on that lonely day on the 401, someone else's bad luck was a blessing in disguise for Patrick.

A snowstorm caught Patrick by surprise before he was even out of the city limits. His badly bloodshot eyes impaired his vision even more. The dragging sound of his windshield wipers vibrated in his aching head. Patrick couldn't fathom the idea of breakfast but he had downed two coffees before leaving his hotel.

He wasn't even out of Windsor, when he realized he had to pee. The service center in Tilbury had a Tim Horton's so he could answer the call of nature and grab a real coffee there.

"Yes." Patrick said out loud when he saw the sign that said three kilometers to the service station.

He had just gotten in the curb lane and was slowing down, when he noticed a car broken down on the shoulder of the road. Patrick looked over as he passed by the car; the hood was up and a woman was standing in front of the car. She only had a light jacket on and she was trying to hold on to her dress which was blowing up in the wind. Patrick hit the brakes.

Shit. I can't let her stand out there like that.

He stopped further up the shoulder, and then reversed his car back towards the woman. She waved frantically as Patrick got out of his car.

"What's the problem, Ma'am?"

"I don't know, it's a rental car. It just died and won't start."

"Do you mind if I give it a try?"

"Not at all, go ahead."

Patrick tried the ignition. The engine turned over, but it only chugged and stalled.

"Do you think you can fix it?"

"No, I doubt it, but there's a service center just up the road. I can drop you off there, and you can call the rental company."

"That would be great. Thank you very much."

The cold air refreshed Patrick a bit, but he had to pee so bad he could taste it.

"I'm Maureen Spence," said the woman as she settled into her seat and buckled her seat belt.

"Patrick Kelly. Where were you headed, Maureen?'

"Home to Burlington. Damn it's freezing out there, thanks again."

Patrick pulled off the highway, and into the service center.

"I was heading into Timmy's for a coffee. It's better for you to wait in there for a tow truck or replacement car."

Patrick made a beeline for the men's room as soon as he got through the doors.

"Thanks again, Patrick. It was nice to meet you."

He couldn't stop or wait.

"No problem. You're welcome."

After relieving his bladder of his two previous coffees, he headed over to the Timmy's counter. He looked into the lobby and saw her on the telephone. The line up for service was long; it was a good thing he hit the pisser first. Patrick stepped up to the cashier to place his order.

"Can I at least buy you a coffee for your kindness?"

She caught him off guard.

"Oh yeah, sure. Thank you."

"It's the least I can do. The rental company is backed up with the weather. They said it would be at least two hours, so I guess I'm stuck here."

Patrick was planning on taking his coffee and hitting the road, but it seemed like she wanted company. *Maybe the distraction of an attractive female would help him to ignore his lingering hangover.*

"That sucks. I hope you weren't in a hurry?"

"Not to get home, but I did have an appointment in London at the liquor store on Wellington."

"An appointment at the liquor store? That's different."

Maureen chuckled.

"Yes, it does sound funny. I sell wine. My territory is from Windsor to Toronto."

She went on to tell Patrick about her job. He listened, but he was completely distracted by her beauty. She had wavy auburn hair down to her shoulders and smoky brown eyes, what he liked to call bedroom eyes. The cold air outside gave her cheeks a rosy glow and her smile was right out of a Colgate commercial. Maureen was well-spoken and intelligent.

Wow, he thought, almost saying it out loud.

"So, can I ask what you do, Patrick?"

"Uh, I'm a cop in Toronto."

"Really, that's commendable."

He blushed and cleared his throat.

"Did I say something wrong?"

"No, not at all. It's just that whenever I tell someone I'm a cop, they want to tell me about a traffic ticket they got or some cop who gave them a hard time. I guess you caught me by surprise. But thank you."

"I'm sorry. I have the utmost respect for what you guys do. I don't think you get enough credit or money for what you do every day."

"Thanks. I wish more people felt like that".

He felt funny. Patrick got warm and tingly all over. He forgot about his hangover. He thought about it and realized it wasn't the coffee. It was the beautiful woman sitting across from him. He couldn't remember the last time he met anyone that made him feel that way. He took a deep breath to savor the moment and caught the light scent of the rose pedals in her perfume.

Maureen looked at her watch.

"God, it's going to be a long day."

"Listen Maureen, I have an idea. I really hate to see you waiting around here all day for a tow truck when you have other places to be. I was thinking..."

It was almost like she knew what Patrick was going to say. She smiled.

"Yes, you were thinking?"

"Well, what if I give you a lift up the 401 home? You could tell the rental company to pick up their car and stick it where the sun doesn't shine."

"Really, I suppose I could cancel my appointment in London. Are you sure? That's a very kind offer."

"I insist. Don't cancel your appointment though. That liquor store is only a few minutes off the highway. Burlington is on my way home from there."

"Hmm, well I guess it would be okay, since you insist."

Her smile lit up the room.

The ride home was a blur. Patrick and Maureen talked and got along like they'd known each other for years. They discussed their work, wine, politics, and even their past failed relationships. Patrick was smitten to say the least.

He exited the highway on Wellington Road so Maureen could keep her appointment at the liquor store. She cut her meeting short so that she wouldn't hold Patrick up.

He was actually sad to arrive in Burlington. Maureen lived in a high-rise apartment building on Elgin just off the QEW and not too far from the lakefront.

An awkward silence came over both of them when they pulled up in front of Maureen's building. Patrick couldn't let this beautiful woman walk out of his life. He had to make a move. It was now or never.

"I was thinking..."

"Oh-oh, there you go thinking again. I was thinking took. The answer is yes, we should see each other again."

Before Patrick could respond, she handed him her business card and a bottle of wine she had picked up at the liquor store.

"Call me any time. My home number is on the back of my card. I am home most evenings. The wine is a token of my appreciation for the ride."

"I'd love to call you. I will."

"Thanks again. You're my knight in shining armor. Call me when you get home so I know you made it safely."

"I will. Good night."

16

"Murphy's Law"

It's a funny thing with cops and the long arm of the law. As many of them have said before, "There's more than one way to skin a cat."

Johnny Law even found a way to take down a notorious gangster like Al Capone. Most criminals consider charges of tax evasion a joke, but it meant prison for Capone, and his imprisonment became a death sentence. He fought the law, but the law won.

The only laws that guys like Jimmy Flynn and Kevin Flannigan believed in were the laws of averages and chance. Flanny taught Jimmy that you make your own luck, first by making good decisions, and then by making good money. It's too bad Flanny didn't practice what he preached. The bar business is a terrible place to make money, especially if you run it like Flanny.

Kevin Flannigan was his own worst enemy. He had a bookkeeper, but he rarely kept track of anything, including receipts. On some nights, he drank or gave away more liquor than he sold. He'd often stuff cash into his pockets instead of the cash register.

Death and Taxes

It seemed ironic when Flanny preached about the two certainties in life: death and taxes. The irony lay in the fact that Flanny lived every day like it was his last. He smoked like a chimney, drank like a fish and ate like a bear. He didn't age well; he always looked pale and God only knows what kind of shape his liver was in. Even Flanny's women started to look as battered and worn as he did.

Jimmy and Megan paid Flanny a late-night visit at Paddy's after dinner one night. They thought it was strange when they found the front door locked. Jimmy used his own key to get in the back door.

They found Flanny alone inside. He was drunk and passed out at the bar with a smoldering cigarette between his fingers on one hand. Megan went and put a pot of coffee on while Jimmy shook Flanny, trying to wake him.

Flanny came around quicker than expected; he was probably more tired than drunk. He got angrier and louder, the more he came around. Megan knew when to keep her distance and this seemed like one of those times. She put down a coffee for Flanny and a scotch for Jimmy, and then turned on the TV in the corner. An episode of Cops was on. They were doing a drug raid at a crack house.

Megan looked back at Jimmy. She'd kept her own drug raid a secret; she never told him. The show's theme song, Bad Boys resonated in her ears. She kept the volume down low so she could hear Flanny and Jimmy. Flanny was really pissed about something. She finally pieced his incoherent words together. He was in trouble for not paying his taxes. They were taking his bar away.

"They say all good things must come to an end Jimmy, but I say Fuck'em all. I ain't goin down without a fight."

"What are ya gonna do?"

"Fuck it; they can have this place. The rent's too high anyway. I'll open another place."

"Can ya afford that? Don't take this the wrong way, but ya haven't been selling much hardware lately and ya ain't lookin too well."

Megan's ears perked up as she tuned into their conversation.

"Fuck you Jimmy, I can keep up ta ya in drink any day and I still fuck like a porn star. You took most of my business from the gang bangers."

"I've only done what ya've asked me ta do, Flanny."

"Aye, maybe yer right, I'm gettin too old for this shite. Lucy has a little place near Tiger Stadium, maybe I'll go in with her."

"I didn't know ya were that serious about her. Ain't that bar a shite hole?"

"Aye, but it's my kind a shite hole. Besides, it's in her name. I can be a silent partner."

Flanny was slurring; he winked at Jimmy.

"C'mon over here Megan. Let's toast to my next adventure."

Megan switched off the T.V., and then went behind the bar where Jimmy was and poured them all a double shot of Jameson. Old Duke, Flanny's dog, perked up. The blood hound was sleeping at his feet, but he could smell Jameson a mile away.

"Give Old Duke a wee nip too, will ya darlin?"

Cheers!

"C'mon you two, raise yer glass with me."

Just as they clinked their glasses and exclaimed, Slainte! the front windows exploded. Broken glass and bullets flew into the bar. Flanny dropped to the floor covering Old Duke. Jimmy and Megan took cover behind the bar. Booze bottles and the mirror behind them shattered, pieces of broken glass and alcohol rained down on them.

Jimmy rolled over to one corner of the bar and peeked around the corner. He saw muzzle flashes coming from the back window of a black SUV that was driving by. The loud banging of the shots fired was followed by the tinkling of broken glass bouncing off the floor.

When the shooting stopped Jimmy looked out the gaping holes where the front windows had been. A wisp of gun smoke hung in the air over the street. The shooters were long gone.

Megan was too scared to scream, she'd wet herself. Flanny moaned. Jimmy crawled around the front of the bar. He got up and looked out the windows, then ran back to Flanny. He was bleeding from a shoulder wound, all over his dog.

"Flanny, yer hit."

"Nah, I'm alright. I think they hit Duke though, he's covered in blood."

"It's yer blood Flanny. Ya got hit in the shoulder. I'll call an ambulance."

"Don't worry bout me. The cops'll be here in a minute. You gotta get outa here before they come."

"Are you sure?"

"Aye Jimmy. You and Megan gotta get outa here. No use you getting involved."

"If ya say so. I'll check in on ya later."

Megan was still curled up on the floor behind the bar, scared stiff and shaking like a leaf. She was soaked in alcohol and urine and covered with broken glass.

"C'mon, we gotta get outa here."

Megan didn't respond. Jimmy tried to brush the broken glass off her. He heard sirens getting close.

"C'mon baby, we gotta go."

He picked her up like a baby and carried her out the back door to where he was parked.

As Jimmy drove away, he saw flashing lights coming closer. He held his composure and turned the corner, losing sight of the cops.

Megan snapped, "What the fuck Jimmy…what's going on, someone just tried to kill us?"

"I don't know. It looked like that black SUV again. It might be one of the gangs."

"Might, Jimmy? Why the fuck are they trying to kill us? Look at me. I'm soaked in booze, covered in glass and I pissed myself."

Reality set in, Megan sobbed. Jimmy headed east, toward his flat near the Eastern Market.

"No Jimmy, take me home…to my home."

He turned and headed toward the river. He looked over his shoulder. Sirens wailed in the distance. Jimmy took Megan home and shut the car off in her driveway.

"I need to be alone. I don't know what the fuck happened tonight, and I don't know what the fuck is going on with us."

"C'mon darlin, we'll have a drink, do a few lines. You'll be fine."

Megan got out of the car.

"Not tonight, Jimmy, go find another party. I've had it."

The Irish gangster's temper flared.

"Fine then, be a bitch. I'll find another bitch who wants to party."

Megan slammed the car door.

"Whatever."

Jimmy fired up the engine, slammed the gear shift into reverse and smoked the tires leaving the driveway. He yanked the shifter into first and hammered the accelerator.

He yelled out the window, "fuck you bitch!" and sped away, down Church Street.

Hot Breakfast

Jimmy blew the stop sign at Wyandotte Street when he flew around the corner off Church. A Windsor Police cruiser pulled up right behind him with the roof lights on.

"Fuck! What now?"

He pulled over and a cop came to his window.

"Can I see your license, ownership and insurance please?"

"Is there a problem, officer?"

"Yes, you're speeding and you blew the stop sign back there…"

"I'm sorry officer; I just had a fight with my girlfriend."

"Have you been drinking tonight, sir?"

"I had a couple with dinner, a while ago."

"You smell like someone poured booze all over you. Can you step out of the car please?"

"I told you I had a fight with my girlfriend. She threw a drink on me."

"Can you put your hands behind your back sir?"

"Why, what's going on?"

"You are under arrest for impaired driving. It is my duty to inform you that you have the right to…"

"Yeah, yeah, I know my rights. Save your breath, I'm not drunk. You're making a mistake."

Jimmy got a free ride to the cop shop in the *paddy* wagon. How fitting. He failed the breathalyzer, blowing over the legal limit for alcohol in his system. He didn't bother to call a lawyer since he knew he'd get out of jail in the morning. A long night on a cold cement slab made Jimmy more than a bit cranky by morning.

He took a disliking to the jail guard who seemed to enjoy slamming the cell doors all night long, when he put people into their cells. Jimmy voiced his displeasure by calling the guard by various terms of endearment like cocksucker and motherfucker.

At breakfast he sat and watched as everyone else around him get fed first.

"What the fuck is up? Where's my breakfast you bastard?"

When everyone else was done eating, the guard came to Jimmy's cell and politely asked, "And what would you like for breakfast, sir?"

Jimmy changed his tone.

"A coffee would be nice, with some eggs maybe?"

"I'll see what I can do for you, sir."

Two minutes later the guard returned with a mushy cheeseburger and carton of milk.

"Hey, where the fuck is my coffee and eggs?"

"I'm sorry, sir, but this isn't the Holiday Inn. This is what you get."

Jimmy grumbled when the guard slid his food under the glass door.

"Ah go fuck yer self."

He opened the cheeseburger and took a bite.

"Ahhh!"

He screamed in agony. The piping hot cheese stuck to the roof of his mouth. The burger had been micro-waved on high for about ten minutes.

Jimmy ripped open the carton of milk and took a big gulp to relieve the pain.

"Ahh! You fuckin bastard!"

The milk was like scalding coffee. The jail guard's deep belly laugh echoed through the cell block.

"Enjoy your breakfast, sir."

Jimmy learned an important lesson that morning. You don't fuck with cops in their house.

17

Rats

Norm tried to make a habit of checking the overnight arrest sheets at the start of his shift each day. It was helpful to see who'd been arrested, especially if it was one of his rats, or someone he was investigating. He grabbed his morning Pepsi from the fridge and one of the clipboards that hung on the wall beside it.

Norm spotted Jesse's name on the board with the departmental orders; he was being transferred from Drugs to the Morality Squad. It was a move in the right direction for Jesse, the next step before promotion. Norm wasn't sure when his day would come, but for the time being, he was happy in the Drug Squad.

Norm put his Pepsi down on the clipboard, after laying it on his desk. As he grabbed the phone to check his messages, he spilled the pop all over the overnight arrest sheet. His listened to his messages on the speaker and looked for a napkin in his desk drawer to clean up the mess. He eyed up a chocolate bar he had hidden under the napkins, but he figured he'd save that for later.

The first phone message was from Megan Doyle. It seemed she wanted to join the team. Norm was pleasantly surprised. The second message was from Bill Meyers. He wanted Norm to call him about a shooting at Flanny's bar in Detroit.

The third message was from Norm's mom. She always called on his birthday. He had forgotten about it. Birthdays were never really a big deal for him. His mother disagreed.

Norm knew what was coming, so he turned off the speaker. Sure enough, mom was playing her piano, belting out Happy Birthday. Granted, Norm's mom could sing. She had cut a country record way back in her day, but Norm hated the birthday song.

It was lame. He never sang it at others' birthday parties, and demanded that it never be sang at his. He could never bring himself to tell his mom that. She lived in Calgary at the time, but Norm knew she would give him a smack on the back of the head the next time she saw him.

Team Player

Norm liked to hear good news first thing in the morning, so he called Megan first. He wiped the spilled pop off the arrest sheet as the phone rang. Just as Megan answered, Norm spotted the name Jimmy Flanders on the arrest sheet.

He held back a chuckle when she answered her phone.

"Good morning Megan, it's Norm Strom."

"Hi Norm, I was wondering if we can get together and talk. Something's happened and I'm scared."

Norm couldn't resist.

"You mean with Jimmy getting busted for Impaired Driving last night?"

"What? No, I didn't know about that. We had a fight; he didn't stay here last night."

"What was the fight about?"

"We got shot at in Detroit last night, at Flanny's bar. I can't take it anymore."

"Holy shit, was anybody hurt?"

"I'm not sure. I was a mess. I think Flanny got shot."

"Wow. I'll have to talk to the cops in Detroit and see what's up. I've got some other things to take care of. How bout I call you back later today?"

"Okay. I'm so fed up. I need your help."

"Alright, I'll get back to you later. Take care."

New Boss, Same as the Old Boss

"Detroit Homicide, Myers here."

"Hey Bill, its Norm Strom in Windsor. I heard Flanny's bar got shot up last night and he might have taken a bullet."

"That's only the half of it. It's been a crazy couple of days over here. Flanny took one in the shoulder, but unfortunately, he'll live. Funny thing is the first cops on the scene said he was laughing his ass off when they found him. Something about the IRS taking his bar so he wouldn't have to pay for the damage."

"Any truth to that?"

"I dunno. I haven't had any time to look into it. We're up to our necks in dead gang bangers."

"I'll bet you're all broken up about that too."

"It's all the paperwork that's killing me. I could give a rat's ass about those punks. Thing is, Norm, there's a power struggle going on. A few of the leaders got capped. Out with the old and in with the new, you know?"

"You should move to Windsor; we don't allow that shit here."

Bill laughed out loud.

"I guess it's back-page news that Jimmy got busted for impaired driving here last night, and his woman wants to join our team. It seems she wasn't too happy about getting shot at last night."

"She was at Flanny's last night?"

"Yeah, her and Jimmy."

"Shit, I think the YBI is out to whack Jimmy. They've known for a while that he's been selling guns to the Latin Counts through the Mack Boys. The YBI took out Mack, who had an alliance with the Counts. The Counts retaliated and took out one of the lieutenants from the YBI. A couple of others got caught in the cross fire."

"Sounds like all that police work is cutting into your beer drinking time?"

Bill laughed out loud.

"Yeah, I think I may have lost a couple pounds. Oh, our man Murphy says Flanny's gonna keep a low profile and put some money into his girlfriend's bar. Wanda's Whiskey Well or something like that. So, what about Jimmy's girlfriend? Can she help us?"

"I'm gonna see her later today. I'm not sure how much she knows, but she sounds willing."

"Good, let me know how you make out. I think we're getting somewhere with all this shit. Two more things I forgot to tell you…about a guy named Connor, from Boston. It seems he got in a pinch there and rolled over on Jimmy. Between him and a rat we have in the YBI, we might just be able to put a case together."

"Wow, sounds great, Bill. You better get back to work then and get something to eat; I can hear your stomach growling over the phone."

"Yeah, nice talking to you too, Norm. Let me know how you make out with Jimmy's woman."

"You bet. Catch ya later."

Cry Me a River

Everyone has a sob story and Megan was no different. She was terrified that Jimmy might catch wind of what she was up to, so she met Norm in a supermarket parking lot downtown. He told her she'd be safe in the back seat, behind the tinted windows. She shed so many tears telling her tale of woe, he thought about going into the store for a roll of paper towels.

When Megan finished crying about what a shitty hand she had been dealt, Norm asked her what she wanted to do, to make things better. She didn't want to go to jail and knew she needed help for her drug problem.

He told her he could get her into a drug rehab program and maybe, just maybe, he could talk to a cop buddy in Detroit, whose wife was head nurse at Detroit Receiving Hospital.

"Really Norm, you would do that for me?"

"Sure, I'd love to help you, Megan, but you have to help me first."

"I don't know what I can tell you, Jimmy scares me. He has a crazy temper."

"It's simple. You need to be my eyes and ears. Like I told you before, it's out of my jurisdiction so you'd be helping the Detroit cops. I want you to meet my buddy, Bill Meyers. He's a really nice guy."

"So, if I help you guys, I won't have to go to jail?"

"I told you Megan. If you help us, we'll help you. That, I can promise."

"Jimmy doesn't usually tell me his business, but he thinks I'm stupid. I've been with him lots of times when he meets guys for business and I've seen guns in the car. I know where he keeps them at his place…and cash too."

"See Megan, you know more than you think. I'm gonna call Detroit so I can introduce you to Bill Meyers. In the mean time, you'll have to make up with Jimmy."

"That won't be a problem; it won't be the first time."

"Great, call me tomorrow. I don't want to call you if Jimmy's around."

"Okay Norm, I'll do that."

18

Drug Wars

For drug cops everywhere, fighting the war on drugs is like using a bucket of water to put out a forest fire. Arresting drug dealers is like fighting Medusa with a sword, you cut off one head, and two more appear.

In their day, crime organizations like the Mafia and the Mob were respected and feared for their brutality and power. When the drug cartels entered the scene, they made the others look like glee clubs.

The cartels took brutality and torture to a new level. Where the Mafia would kill and bury their victims, the cartels would publicly display the severed heads of their victims. Where the mob would bribe cops and politicians, the cartels simply executed them.

Instead of threatening your immediate family, the cartels kidnapped and/or executed the whole family tree. There is no end in sight to their brutality, all done in the name of loyalty. The simple truth is if you mess with the cartels, you sign your own death warrant.

Although the drug cartels have taken terrorism to new levels, law enforcement has endured, and refuses to give up the battle. It would seem apparent that they will never win the war, but they strive to win every small battle that they possibly can. Fighting the war on drugs has cost billions of dollars and thousands of lives.

Cartels in Canada

Most Canadians go to sleep at night feeling safer than their U.S. neighbors. They think that gun control and less violence on the street makes their country a safer place to live. For the most part, they are correct. The downside is that the same things that make Canadians feel safer, is what lures organized crime into their country.

There is less law enforcement and Canada's vast borders are easier to breach. The largest unprotected border in the world and free trade creates huge opportunities for drug traffickers. With those opportunities, comes fortune.

Like major U.S. cities, Montreal and Toronto became easy targets for organized crime. The cartels moved into those cities, taking advantage of already established shipping and trade routes. They moved cocaine across Canada and the U.S. just like any other commodity.

Once the City of Toronto realized the Medellin Cartel had established itself there, they put together Project Amigo. Targeting an international drug cartel is an arduous task.

After being seconded to the project, it was Patrick's job to attack from the street level. That meant starting at the bottom of the totem pole. Drug cops made buys on the street, finding out who the low-level dealers were.

When an undercover cop got established on the street, he could pose as a dealer and buy from higher level dealers. Once the identity of the higher-level dealers was revealed, surveillance and wire taps were implemented. It was like putting together a jigsaw puzzle, one piece at a time.

If the situation warranted it, the drug cops arrested low level players and rolled them over to become their informants. Those informants, police agents, and undercover cops all added to the mountain of intelligence information gathered on cartel players. Patrick loved the work and thrived in the environment.

Visitors

Teflon Tim called Storm and Blackjack into his office. His training budget was approved so he told the two narcs they were going to Toronto for an Expert Witness seminar. The Toronto Police were hosting the seminar, to better educate drug cops on how to testify as expert witnesses in court. Once qualified as an expert in court, you can give opinion evidence.

The boys were happy. It meant a few days in the big city, and no doubt there would be some partying involved. Blackjack and Storm had never gone away anywhere together, but they had shared more than a few cocktails in the past. Norm dropped a dime to Patrick, warning him of his pending arrival.

The Windsor cops started off with a bang. They arrived in time for a late afternoon snack and a few beers. Norm thought it would be a good idea if they had a little nap, then dinner. He had no doubt that they'd be out late, and class started bright and early. Blackjack agreed, but first he hung all his dress clothes so they wouldn't get wrinkled.

After his nap, Norm took a shit, shave, and shower, and was ready to go. Blackjack moved his hung clothes into the bathroom and turned the shower on.

"The hot steam gets the wrinkles out," he said on the way out the door.

Norm rolled his eyes.

"Uh-huh, I'll have to remember that."

They hit the road, scoping out restaurants downtown. A steakhouse fit the tab, since a portion of their meals was covered by the company. The bars were just coming to life when the boys left the restaurant. Norm checked in with Patrick, but he was tied up at work. He promised to hook up with them after class the next day. The Windsor men bar-hopped around downtown, trying not to stick out like old guys.

Someone yelled out last call and Blackjack looked mortified.

"Holy shit, we gotta get up in the morning."

"Bet yer glad we had that nap now, eh?"

Both men had had lots to drink, but Norm was mystified when he found their hotel room completely fogged-in.

"What the fuck, brother? The shower's been on all night."

Norm open windows while Blackjack retrieved his clothes. The room was like a sauna, the ceiling so wet it dripped.

Blackjack came out of the bathroom smiling.

"See, the wrinkles are all gone."

"You fucking idiot, now I gotta sleep in a rain forest."

Morning came too soon. The nap, dinner, and late-night munchies weren't enough to curtail the hangover. Police headquarters was only a few blocks away, so the boys walked there. The fresh air helped a bit, but Blackjack headed right for the coffee when they arrived in class. Norm found a Pepsi to wash down a few Timbits.

The emcee laid out the agenda. His opening remarks brought on applause; there would be no test at the end of the seminar. That meant that hangovers, sleeping in class, and a general lack of attention would be acceptable.

The seminar was excellent. Crown prosecutors, defense lawyers, qualified expert witnesses, and even a Judge gave lectures. They put on a mock trial to show how it all came together. One Toronto cop listed his qualifications as an expert witness. Surprisingly, he had only been qualified once in opiates.

Norm reached around and gave himself a pat on the back. He had been qualified on three separate occasions in Dilaudid, an opiate used for terminal cancer patients. That meant Norm was the only other cop south of Toronto qualified as an expert in opiates.

Patrick met the boys on their last break, near the end of class.

"Shit Norm, did you have a liquid lunch? You guys reek of booze."

"That's from last night, ya Limey. Hey Patrick, I want you to meet Blackjack. The late-night drinking was his fault."

"Good to meet you. Nice shirt, did you have it steam cleaned?"

Blackjack eyed Patrick like he had two heads.

"Just fucking with you; Norm ratted you out. I hope you guys have some steam left for tonight?"

Norm asked, "So what's the game plan?"

"Well, Normie, I'm good to go as soon as you kids get out of school. I'll meet ya in the front lobby."

"Can we stop at our hotel first, Blackjack needs to change his shorts. I think he shit them in class."

Patrick laughed as he walked away.

"Whatever. I'll see you guys shortly."

Tales over Cocktails

They started at The Devil's Advocate. Norm had been there once before, it's where he got hooked on Rickard's Red draught beer.

"So, Norm, what's my old pal Jimmy been up to?"

The Windsor cops brought Patrick up to speed on the warrant at Megan's house and how she had become a team player. Norm also told him about Jimmy's woes and how someone was literally gunning for him in Detroit.

"That don't surprise me. He's got enemies all over. A DEA agent working the project with me says someone in Boston rolled over on Jimmy's operation there. Lost a whole load of coke. He's gotta owe someone serious cash."

"I heard that, Paddy. My buddy in Detroit told me the same thing. They figure Jimmy's in shit with the gangs and they might be who are after him."

"You know I still wanna look that fucker in the eyes and…well, you know what I wanna do."

Blackjack didn't know the whole story between Patrick and Jimmy and Norm changed the subject.

"So, what can you tell us about your project Paddy? Did you catch Pablo Escobar yet?"

"No shit, you guys, you wouldn't believe how deep rooted the cartel is here and how much dope they're putting on the street. I can't get into details, but chances are if you're buying coke on the street here or in Windsor, it's probably from the cartel. Even the bikers are buying from them. They control the market."

"Sounds pretty heavy. Do you think Jimmy is tied in to them?"

"I don't know. The guy's been a ghost for over twenty years. I can't say it would surprise me. Being connected to the

IRA can open a lot of doors. Hey, to change the subject again, I'd like you to meet my new sweetheart."

"Does that mean we're going to a gay bar?"

"Fuck you and the horse you rode in on…this could be *the one*."

"*The one* that's blind and deaf, so she can't see your ugly mug or hear your bullshit."

"You found one gullible enough to marry you, Norm."

"Okay, I surrender."

The men grabbed a bite to eat and had a few more beers at a bar on King Street. Blackjack nodded to a couple of women walking in the front door.

"Wow, look at the rack on that redhead."

Patrick smiled.

"She's taken boys, but I think the other one's up for grabs. Too bad your both married."

The women walked up to their table. The redhead planted a big sloppy kiss on Patrick. She turned and offered her hand to Norm.

"You must be Norm. I'm Maureen and this is my friend Karen. She's single, but I heard you're happily married."

"Hey Karen, Blackjack…I'm married too, but would like to buy you ladies a drink."

Karen looked at Maureen.

She grabbed Patrick's hand.

"Maybe just one. We don't want to intrude on boy's night, and we already have tickets for a show down the street."

Norm eyed at Maureen.

"I hear that you come to Windsor for work. You'll have to look me up when you come down. You know, when you're not with Patrick."

Norm winked at her. Patrick shook his head and chuckled.

"Maybe I'll do that, Norm. I'd like to meet your wife too..."

Maureen winked at him. Blackjack jumped in.

"A threesome, Norm. Aren't you lucky?"

Patrick interjected.

"That's enough you guys. You're lucky your wives aren't here."

"You're right Paddy; looks like you're the lucky guy here."

Maureen smiled and lit up the room.

19

Humpty Dumpty

To say the least, Jimmy wasn't impressed by his night in the slammer. He was pretty-well used to getting his own way. He was lucky that he had a wad of cash on him when he was arrested and was able to make bail.

Megan probably wouldn't have bailed him out and Flanny was out of commission. That thought made him realize that he didn't have many true friends. Jimmy had to take a taxi to the police impound lot to retrieve his car.

No wonder the cops arrested me, he thought when he climbed in. His car reeked of booze. There were still pieces of broken glass on the front seat, that had fallen from his and Megan's clothes.

Shite, I wonder how Flanny is?

Jimmy drove across the border and stopped across the street from Flanny's bar. Someone was nailing boards up over the broken windows and sweeping up the glass from the sidewalk. Bullet holes and chips in the brick were still visible.

Damn, reminds me of Belfast, back in the day.

He headed to Flanny's apartment, but neither he or Old Duke were there. He thought he'd try the nearest hospital; maybe Flanny would still be there. Jimmy wasn't sure, but he thought he picked up a tail after leaving the bar. He lost site of the van just before he got to Detroit Receiving Hospital.

Sure enough, Flanny was still laid up in the hospital.

"Good ta see ya Jimmy me boy, looks like ya slept in yer clothes."

"Somethin like that. I haven't been home yet, I'll tell ya later. How you doin? Ya look like ya got shot."

"Always with the wisecracks, I'm doin just fine, thanks. The bullet fractured my collar bone. Other than that, I could use a drink."

Jimmy instinctively pulled a mickey of whiskey from his pocket.

"I hit the liquor store before I came up, figured you'd be thirsty."

"Ahh, yer too good ta me. Hey, while we're alone I gotta tell ya…the cops asked me a lot of questions. Some about you."

"Why the fuck did they ask about me?"

"Somethin's up Jimmy. It was like they already knew the answers and were trying ta get a rise outa me."

"Shite, that's all I need. If ya don't need anything else Flanny, I wanna go home and take a shower."

"Aye, that ya should. Ya smell like a distillery."

Jimmy did a couple of heat checks when he left the hospital. He didn't notice anyone following him, so he went home.

No Delivery

Jimmy parked in the meat market's parking lot across the alley from his apartment, like he usually did when he was being careful. He slipped through a hole in the wooden fence at the back of his building and climbed the old wooden stairs.

Just before he got to the top, he heard someone on the stairs below him. He looked back over his shoulder and saw a young black kid he didn't recognize. Jimmy turned back around and reached for the door.

The door opened before he could grab the handle, another black kid was standing there pointing a gun at Jimmy's head. It was Silky, the YBI lieutenant Jimmy had been dealing with since Mack split from the gang. If not for the gun, Silky would not scare anyone. He was light skinned, possibly mulatto.

He should have been called Skinny. He didn't weigh more than one hundred and thirty pounds and was six feet tall. He had a buzz cut with the letters YBI shaved into the back of his head. He wore a thick gold chain around his neck with the letter "S" hanging on it.

"Hey Jimmy, c'mon in. Bout time ya got home."

"What the fuck Silky, ya scared the shit out a me."

"I'll say. Ya smell like it, let's go inside and talk."

As soon as Jimmy unlocked his apartment door, the younger gang banger pushed him inside, and up against the wall. He began patting him down.

"I ain't packin Silky, what the fuck's goin on?"

"I oughta bust a cap in yo ass right now."

"Yeah, like yer boys tried last night?"

"What you talkin bout?"

"Ya tryin ta tell me yer boys didn't shoot up Flanny's place last night?"

"I'll tell ya this, Jimmy, yer man didn't show up with the twenty-five bricks you owe us. The boys are pissed at ya, but I told em we couldn't get the stuff if you was dead."

"This is the first I'm hearin bout it, I swear. I spent the night in jail over in Windsor."

"That's yo problem. What you gonna do bout the coke you owe us?

"Ya gotta give me a few days. I'll get it for ya. I gotta make some calls and see what's goin on."

"I'm only letting ya live cuz we want yer stuff, Jimmy. There's a late fee by the way, twenty per cent per day. Don't let us down. My boy Lil Mikey here needs ta pass his probation, I'm sure he wouldn't mind cappin yo Irish ass."

"Does this mean yer boys will stop followin and shootin at me?"

"I don't know what yer talkin bout, Jimmy. I think yer seein ghosts. Don't make me look bad, call me."

"Sure, Silky, no problem"

Missing Links

Jimmy thought to himself, *what the fuck is happening to me?* He checked his phone messages as soon as the gang bangers left. The only message was from Megan. No surprise there, he always told his guys not to talk on the phone. Megan's message was an apology for her behavior, she wanted to make up.

Stupid bitch, she can just wait.

He made a call to his guy in Boston. There was no answer. He called Conner. No answer there either.

Where the fuck is everyone?

Jimmy reached out to his buddy in Boston who ran the chop shop.

"What the fuck's goin on out there, Bruno? I can't get hold of anyone."

"Didn't you hear, Conner got busted and disappeared. Word on the street is he's working for the cops."

"Fuck. That explains a lot."

"The heat's on, hope you have some shade to hide in."

"I wish it were that easy, Bruno. Thanks man."

"Later. Keep your head down."

"Fuck me, I need ta clear my head and think this through."

Jimmy peeled off his rancid clothes and jumped in the shower. The phone rang again. He stuck his head out from the curtain and listened to his machine. It was Megan again, pleading for him to call her.

Not now bitch.

He turned up the hot water and inhaled the steam. He went over everything in his head, there were rats and cops and gang bangers all over his ass.

There's got ta be a way outa this.

Jimmy took another deep breath. He turned down the hot water; he had an idea that might work.

Jesus was already waiting in his low rider, behind the old Fisher auto body plant. He looked like your typical Latino gang banger, loaded with tattoos.

Jesus was small-framed, but muscular. He always wore a white wife beater shirt that accentuated his physique. His greasy black hair was cropped over his ears, where he wore heavy gold hoops. Jesus also wore a gold chain with his namesake hanging from it. He had perfect teeth, except for one gold tooth.

"What up Jimmy Irish? Got new toys for my boys?"

"You bet Jesus, but I wanna get paid in coke instead of cash."

"What you talkin bout?"

"I want twenty-five kilos of coke in exchange for a load of automatic weapons. I'll even throw in a couple of grenade launchers."

"I like the hardware, but there's no way I can handle that kinda weight."

"Can you hook me up with your supplier?"

"Maybe, but there'd be a commission involved."

"Whatever it takes, Jesus, I'm in a jam."

"What you gonna do with that kinda powder? You gonna sell it to the niggers?"

"That's the best part of the deal. I can tell ya where the deal's goin down and you can use yer new toys to steal the shit back. As long as I get my money, you can take the niggers down if it makes ya happy."

"Yeah, that would make me *very* happy. I gotta tell you though, my people are serious players. Chicanos from south of the border, if you know what I mean. You fuck with them and they'll cut yer balls off and feed em to ya."

"I think I get the picture. Can you set it up?"

"I'll see what I can do."

Jimmy stayed in his car after Jesus left.

Hmm, that's one problem solved.

The other problem hadn't bit him in the ass quite yet. He still owed a load of cash to his supplier in Boston, from when his courier got busted. They would consider it his debt, since the courier took delivery of it. The dope and money were never in the same place at the same time. He knew they'd be expecting payment, regardless of the lost product.

Jimmy had the cash to pay them, but he'd need it to buy the new stuff from the Latin Counts. He couldn't go back to his Boston supplier; he'd have to come up with double the cash. Besides, they'd treat him like cancer, knowing his organization had been breached by the cops.

He nodded to himself. *The deal with Jesus was the only way to go. Fuck me. I need a drink and a piece of ass.*

Jimmy stopped at the nearest watering hole and ordered a double shot of Jameson. He downed it and waved at the bartender to hit him again. He pulled a quarter from his pocket and put it in the pay phone.

"Megan me darlin, it's Jimmy. I miss ya."

"I miss you too Jimmy. You're just calling cuz you're horny."

"No, I really I did miss ya baby. But yeah, I wanna bang ya like a screen door in a hurricane."

20

Man with a Plan

"Under Siege 2" with Steven Segal was just released and playing at the movie theatre. Jesse and Norm both loved action movies, so they took their wives to the show. The movie hadn't been on for twenty minutes when Norm's pager went off. It was on vibrate; he wasn't one of those rude people who let their pager or cell phone ring out loud during the show. He ignored the page.

Ten minutes later it went off again. This time he looked at the number on the display, but he didn't recognize it. It soon went off a third time. Having a pager of his own, Jesse knew why Norm was fidgeting in his seat.

"Gee, you're popular tonight."

Figuring the calls were work related and probably important, Norm left the theatre to answer them. He went to the pay phone in the lobby. The messages were from Megan, she wanted him to call her at home right away.

You always had to carry a pocket full of quarters in the pager days; it took one to retrieve your messages, then another to return each call. Norm used his last quarter to retrieve Megan's message. He had spent the others on popcorn.

After waiting in line and then getting a funny look and change from the pimply-faced teenager at the concession stand, he returned Megan's call. She was out of breath when she answered the phone.

"I was already out the door when I heard the phone ring. Jimmy wants to see me. I don't know what to do Norm, what should I do?"

"Take a breath Megan. Like I told you before, don't ask any questions that are out of the ordinary. Just watch and listen, you're my eyes and ears. I need names, times, places… whatever information you can gather."

"Okay, I'll call you when I can."

Ducks in a Row

Norm didn't get ten feet from the pay phone when his pager went off again. It looked like a Detroit number.

"Hmm, must be Bill Meyers. I wonder what the hell he wants. Damn! I'm missing half the show."

Having only two quarters left, he wondered, *is this gonna be enough to call the states?"*

It was back to the pimply-faced kid for more change. There was no line but the kid looked at Norm like he was from another planet.

"What's the problem kid, you never played the pay phone like a slot machine?"

Norm heard the rumbling sound of shit blowing up inside the theatre. *Sounds like I'm missing a good movie. The things I do for work. I'll need a raise just to pay for all these phone calls!*

Bill Meyers answered on the first ring.

"Were ya sitting on the phone?"

"No, but I've been on it all day. Hey Norm, hope I didn't interrupt your dinner?"

"No, I'm at the movies watching Segal kick some ass…or at least I was."

"Shit, sorry man, that's supposed to be a good movie."

"Yeah, so I hear. I'll have to ask the wife when she comes out. What's up mister?"

Bill paused for a few seconds. Norm could hear paper shuffling and other voices in the background.

"What's up? Sounds like you've got a party going on."

"Things are happening here. I'm just trying to get all my ducks in a row; we're hoping to move on Jimmy in the next couple of days. Have you heard anything from his woman?"

"I just got off the phone with her. She's on her way to his place as we speak. She's nervous, but she knows what we need."

"Good. Our guy in the YBI says Jimmy owes them a shipment of coke and they expect it in the next couple of days. I checked with Boston PD and they confirmed popping his guy with a shipment. The rat who rolled on him wouldn't give up Jimmy's supplier. It's still a mystery."

"Jimmy's not making any friends, is he? Hey, do you remember my buddy in the Toronto Drug Squad?

"Vaguely. We never talked to him."

"Well, he's been busy too. He's working a secret task force thing, looking into the cartels, but he's got a personal interest in Jimmy. I know he'd love to be in on the take-down."

"I have no problem keeping you in the loop, Norm. You can bring your buddy and popcorn too for all I care. Just remember you're only observers on this side of the border."

"I appreciate it. I'll let you know the minute I hear from Megan."

Get Out of Dodge

Jimmy wasn't the same guy when Megan showed up at his apartment. Sure, the fast and hard sex was the same, but he was more distant than usual.

"What's up Jimmy, where are you at?"

"I got a lot goin on darlin, business stuff, ya know?"

"No, I don't. Not that I ever cared, but you never talk about your business."

"It's for yer own good. The less ya know, the better."

"Are we gonna be okay? I'm scared after what happened at Flanny's."

"I got a plan baby, don't you worry. I been thinking it might be time to get outa Dodge, time to move on."

"Move where, are you taking me?"

"Well, that's part of my plan. I was thinking about Canada. Does your mom still have that place up north?"

"Yeah, but it's been vacant for years. She stopped going after dad died. She never talks about it."

"That would be a perfect place for us to lay low. Would you like that?"

"I don't know, Jimmy. I still wonder about us."

"What's there ta wonder about? Ya know we're good for each other."

"It's just that sometimes I feel like I don't know who you are."

"What are ya talkin about, what da ya want ta know?"

Megan hesitated, but she looked him in the eyes and went for it.

"You never told me about your girlfriend Erin, and what happened to her in Belfast"

"What are ya talkin about? Where'd ya get that name?"

"I went back though my old travel journals. I couldn't remember her name, but I was with Erin the day she died… and so were you. If we're gonna be together, I want you to be honest with me"

Jimmy went silent. His eyes glazed over.

"That was a very long time ago and they were different times. I was so young."

She listened as Jimmy opened up. He told her everything. How he grew up with Erin's brother, and met her through him. How they planned on leaving Belfast, for America. How the plan came together and then went so terribly wrong. He fought hard to hold his tears as twenty-three years of pent up emotion spilled out.

He went on to explain how he got involved with the IRA and how he did things for them when he moved to America. Jimmy felt justified in his illegal activities, because of the raw deal he was dealt in life. At the time, he truly believed in the cause. He told Megan how Flanny took him under his wing, teaching him the business.

That's what he called it, *the business*. He never once admitted to gun smuggling, or drug dealing. It was all just business to Jimmy.

"I've gotten myself into a jam here baby. I need to take care of a few things, and then we can to blow this town."

"I really appreciate your honesty, Jimmy, but this is all very sudden. When would we have to leave?"

"Probably Friday. I'll know for sure tomorrow."

"You mean this Friday? Today's Wednesday."

"Ya, baby. If ya wanna be with me, that's the way it is. Ya know I love ya. I've never told anyone these things before. I hope I can trust ya."

"Oh Jimmy…you've never said that to me before. You know I love you too."

"I know ya love me baby, but can I trust ya? Yer gonna have to stick to me like glue until we leave town. It's not safe for ya ta be alone."

"You know you can. I'll be good and stay out of your way."

The Set Up

The next morning Jesus called Jimmy.

"Meet me at the same place. We need to go over the details of our business arrangement."

He took Megan with him to the meet. He couldn't chance leaving her alone with all that was going on.

"Stay in the car while I go talk to this guy."

He got into the car with Jesus.

"Who's the bitch?"

"She's my girlfriend. She's cool. I have to keep an eye on her; someone's been gunning for me lately."

"Maybe you need to take a vacation—get out a town for a while."

"Aye, I've been thinkin that."

"Anyway, this is the deal, Jimmy. My friends from the south can help you out but they want all the automatic weapons you told me about. You get your coke and I get the two grenade launchers as my commission on the deal. Then I get to take the coke back like you said. You can keep the money."

"That coke and those weapons are worth a lot more on the street."

"I know, but remember you came to me and asked for help. This is your ticket out—take it or leave it. You can use the cash for your extended vacation."

"I'll take the deal. When?"

"Right here tomorrow morning. We'll do it inside at 10:00 am. My boys will hide when we're done and wait for the niggers. Then we'll take back what's rightfully ours."

"I hope yer gonna give me some time ta get out a there."

"Don't worry. We won't hit 'em till ya leave."

"Okay. I'll set it up."

Jimmy never liked the gang bangers. He thought, *why not let them kill each other while I make off with the cash and blow this town?*

He knew he'd have to suck up to Flanny for the grenade launchers he had hidden away for a rainy day. He figured Flanny wouldn't mind after what happened to him. He was going to have to give up his own stash of guns to make the deal work.

The next stop was Flanny's new watering hole, the Whiskey Well. Flanny and Wanda sat at one end of the small bar, a small cloud of smoke hung over their heads. There were only two other regulars in the bar. One man had the head-bobs; he was ready to go down for the count. The other was fixated on a small TV screen behind the bar.

Jimmy took pause when he walked into the bar. He looked at Flanny sitting there. He had aged forty years in the past twenty. He was no longer the hulk of a man that rescued Jimmy from the ship that day in Boston. He looked smaller and frailer than ever before. His dry voice now crackled when he spoke.

"Hey, there's my favorite lad. How're ya doin, Jimmy?"

"Honestly, I'm tired. I need a vacation."

"Aye, I figured ya might wanna lay low for a while with what's been going on around here."

"I'm thinkin of an extended vacation with Megan, maybe up in Canada, where they worry more about bears than gang bangers."

"That's probably a good idea, Jimmy. I wish I could help ya but I've got my own problems. The fuckin government owns me now."

"I appreciate the offer. I was thinking bout a different kind a goin away present."

"Just ask, son. If the government ain't got it, you can have it."

"Ya still got the heavy artillery stashed away for a rainy day?"

"Aye, I surely do."

"Well, it's raining and I need a big fuckin umbrella. I might a come here with a whimper, but I'm gonna go out with a bang."

"What's mine is yers, Jimmy. You know the combination to the warehouse, take what you need."

"Thanks, Flanny. You know you've been like a father to me. I'm gonna miss ya."

"Aye, I'll miss ya too. Maybe we'll come up and visit for Thanksgiving."

"That would be great. I gotta call the Young Boys and tell em we're on for tomorrow."

"Okay, give them black bastards my love."

Jimmy dropped a dime to Silky.

"I have your product. I can deliver tomorrow. Bring my money."

"Why? We never deal like that."

"Cuz I don't trust anyone right now. We meet on neutral turf."

"Gimme the time and place. We'll be there."

"In the old Fisher plant at 10:30 am."

Saying Goodbye

"It's all set, Flanny. I've set the stage for Young Boys Inc and Latin Counts to do some ethnic cleansing."

"That's a dangerous game yer playin lad. Do ya think ya can pull it off?"

"With a little luck of the Irish."

Both men laughed out loud. Megan sat as quiet as a mouse while the two men conversed. She pretended she wasn't paying attention, but she was horrified by what she heard. She was torn between doing the right thing and whatever it was that Jimmy was about to get her into. She asked Jimmy if she could borrow his cell phone.

"Who the hell ya gonna call?"

"I wanna call my mom and tell her I'm okay. I haven't talked to her in a while and who knows what will happen tomorrow."

Jimmy rolled his eyes, but handed her the phone.

"Go ahead, and tell her you'll be seeing her soon…that we'll need the cottage keys."

Megan lit up a smoke, and then took the phone outside. She called Norm Strom.

"Hey, its Megan. I need your help. Jimmy's meeting some gang bangers tomorrow to sell guns, but he's talking about a war or something. I don't know what to do. Je wants to do this deal and then take off up north, to my mom's cottage."

"Okay, that sounds pretty important. Tell me everything you know about when and where it's going down. I'll need to pass on the information to Detroit."

Megan blurted out everything she could remember.

"Okay, I gotta go. He's giving me the evil eye. Promise me, Norm, you'll make sure nothing happens to Jimmy, I love him."

"I'll do my best."

She went back into the bar and handed Jimmy his phone. She couldn't look him in the eye. He didn't pay her any attention. Him and Flanny were pounding back double Jameson's.

Megan didn't feel like getting drunk, she wasn't sure what she felt. *Was she a Judas? Did she do the right thing? What was going to happen to her and Jimmy?*

"Are we gonna eat soon, Jimmy? I'm starving."

"Aye, darlin, just one more shot with Flanny. Have one with us. We won't be seeing him for a while."

The old friends had three more shots, but eventually said their farewells. Flanny gave his countryman the same bear hug he did when he first arrived in Detroit. Jimmy knew he'd miss the old man, but things would be a lot worse if he stayed in Detroit. Besides, if his plan worked out, it was best he get as far away from Detroit as he possibly could.

The Blue Team

Norm called Bill Meyers as soon as he got off the phone with Megan.

"We heard from our rat too, Norm. He told us about the dope exchange but he didn't mention anything about guns or a gang war. It sounds like there might be more to Jimmy's plan than he told the YBI. Our Drug Squad will be running the show, but I'm involved because of the murders."

"Does that mean my buddy and I are still invited as spectators?"

"It's gonna be too tight to get you in close, but I'll find you a spot near the action and give you a radio. You can roll in once we have things under control."

"Thanks, Bill. I'll see you bright and early."

Norm got on the phone to Patrick.

"Yo, brother, how fast can you get your ass down to Windsor? The shit's hittin the fan. Jimmy's goin down tomorrow morning."

"I'm packing a bag as we speak. I'll have to call Doctor Fridayov and take a sick day. Is my bedroom available?"

"Yeah, I think the wife's cleaned the sheets after your last visit. And like that hotel commercial says, we'll leave a light on for you."

"I've been waiting a long time for this. I'll see you in a few hours."

21

Bloody Friday Redux

The porch light was on, just like Norm joked it would be. Patrick saw his buddy in the Florida room window, waving him in as he walked to the front door. Even though they lived almost four hours away from each other, the two men had become good friends.

"I don't know if I'll be able to sleep tonight, Norm, I'm all geeked up about tomorrow. I brought my old sniper rifle, so I can pick off Jimmy at first sight."

Norm grinned and raised his eyebrows in wonderment.

"Just shittin you."

"Asshole. Let's have a night cap, it'll help you sleep."

The Briefing – July 21st, 1995, 8:00 am

Driving into the parking lot behind Detroit Police H.Q. was like going back in time. The building was an architectural gem in its day, but decades of aging and neglect had taken its toll. The fleet of police cars looked like they belonged in an auction yard.

Taking in the prehistoric-looking station, Patrick turned to Norm.

"Will you look at this place? I feel like I'm in an old black and white movie."

"That's nothing, wait till you see inside."

The two Canadian cops flashed their badges and asked for Bill Meyers at the front desk. Without looking up, the old desk sergeant pointed them to the stairs. Patrick was dumbfounded. Norm knew exactly what he was looking at. Detectives worked on ancient computers, with green or yellow screens. There were walls of cabinets where paper reports were still filed manually. Even finger prints had to be searched by hand. The poor bastards were living in the dark ages.

Bill Meyers was at the back of the huge room. He waved the Canucks into an outer room where the briefing was being held.

"C'mon in guys. We're about to start."

Norm and Patrick grabbed seats at the back of the room. There were about a dozen plain clothes and four uniformed cops chatting and drinking coffee. Norm had seen a lot more men used for similar take downs, but the group looked capable.

Some cops slipped bullet-proof vests on, while others checked their weapons and ammunition. Patrick nodded toward a cop in the corner with a high-powered sniper rifle. Stern faces reflected the tension in the air.

Instinctively, Patrick pulled his pistol from his shoulder holster and popped the magazine out. Bill Meyers looked to the back of the room. Norm grinned and shrugged his shoulders. He knew they had no authority in the states, but he went along and checked his weapon too. Butterflies danced in his stomach.

Norm whispered, "Hey sniper boy, how many extra mags did you bring?"

Patrick smiled.

"Aren't you nervous?"

"Not really, Normie, it doesn't usually hit me until I've got someone in my sights. Desensitized over the years, is my guess."

A couple of the brass wearing lots of egg yoke on their shoulders walked into the room. Bill Meyers addressed the group and made the necessary introductions. He briefed the group on the background of the investigation, which included drug and gun dealing, and a few murders.

Aside from the Detroit cops and the two Canadians, there were two DEA agents in the group. They were interested in the cocaine pipeline and the distribution network. At the center of the whole investigation was Jimmy Flynn.

Bill Meyers introduced the Drug Squad Sergeant. He pointed to a roughly-drawn map on the chalk board. The plan was to watch Jimmy exchange his cocaine for cash, and then arrest everyone before they exited the old factory. The sniper would cover the main entrance from the water tower. The four uniforms would be hiding nearby, for back-up and to grab stragglers who might escape.

The sergeant thanked the DEA for the loan of their camera equipment. It was being installed in the abandoned factory as he spoke. Hopefully, it would capture the transaction, while all the cops were hidden out of sight.

The deal with the YBI was scheduled to go down at 10:30 a.m. so the sergeant told everyone he wanted them in place no later than 9:30 a.m. Once he gave the signal, everyone was to move in and surround Jimmy and the YBI. Surprise was key since the targets would undoubtedly be armed.

The group was shown the layout of the six storey abandoned factory. The building was vacant, but fenced in. The front gate was broken, allowing access to the service road and building. There were vehicle entrances at the front and back, allowing entry to the ground floor of the building.

Factory style windows covered much of the exterior of the building, but most had the glass smashed out. Gang graffiti covered both the inside and outside walls.

After the briefing, Bill Meyers waved Norm and Patrick up to the front of the room. He handed them a radio.

"I couldn't say anything in front of the boss. He'd have my head if he knew you guys were involved. He eyed Patrick.

"You must be the Toronto cop."

"Oh, sorry, Bill. This is my buddy, Patrick."

"Pleased to meet you. I understand that you and Jimmy Flynn have some history?"

"Yeah, you could say that. It's good to meet you too. And thanks for inviting us along."

"Alright you guys…you see the map? This is where I want you."

Meyers pointed to a spot on the roadway leading to the factory entrance.

"You can plug in here, behind the big garbage bins. You won't be able to see the action inside, so that's why I'm giving you the radio. You'll be in a good position to give me a heads up if anyone else shows up for the party. I have some concerns over Megan's information."

"No problem, Bill. The Canucks have your back."

"Thanks, Norm, I know I don't have to tell you that if something can go wrong, it usually does."

The Stakeout

Even though drug dealers are never on time, Norm liked to get set up early. Patrick popped into a 7-11, grabbed a coffee for himself, and a Pepsi for Norm. He tossed him a granola bar when he got back in the car.

"Did you look across the street at the Coney joint? I can't believe people eat that shit for first thing in the morning."

"Breakfast of champions. What have you got in the bag, Paddy boy?"

"Sunflower seeds. They keep me busy while I'm sitting on the edge of my seat, waiting for shit to happen."

"Don't forget to roll the window down. I'm not cleaning up your mess."

"Nag, nag, nag."

Norm drove around the factory area once, checking out the neighborhood and looking at the ways in and out. Once around was the limit. Twice would look suspicious, if someone was watching. He drove down the laneway and backed the car in behind the dumpsters like Meyers told him.

"It stinks here and I can't see shit."

"You want some cheese with that whine?"

Patrick was right. It did stink, like there was a rotting corpse in the garbage bin. The heat made it worse. The mercury was stopped in the low nineties, and it wasn't even nine in the morning yet.

The good news was that the car had air conditioning. The bad news was that Norm had to shut the engine off to remain quiet and undetected. Patrick spit his seed shells at the garbage bin, trying to make them to stick. Norm did a radio check to see if anyone else was set up yet. The drug sergeant responded.

"Team leader here. I read you loud and clear."

Hurry-up and wait. That was the way it was in the drug business. Norm had to relieve himself of the sixteen ounces of pop he'd consumed, so he went for a pee while things were quiet.

At the back of the car he discovered the origin of the horrible smell. It looked like the rotting carcass of a small dog. He kicked it closer to the pile of garbage and pulled a piece of old carpet over it to mask the odor.

Patrick gawked at Norm when he got back in the car.

"Christ, you roll in something fresh?"

"Not quite, but there *is* something dead back there."

"Speaking of dead, how's your sex life? Can you still get it up, now that you're over the hill?"

"Ha-ha, that's not the problem. Getting the wife to do something with it when it's up is the challenge."

"That's why I'm not married."

"Are you back to jerking off in the shower, or is Maureen still in the picture?"

"Honestly, Norm, I think she's the one. We were supposed to spend the weekend together. I think she wants to move in with me."

"It's the same as being married, buddy."

"Yeah-yeah. Damn it's hot. I can feel sweat running down the crack of my ass."

"That's good, it'll keep your balls cool. Hey, I know you've been waiting a long time for this. You're not going to do anything stupid, are you?"

Patrick smiled.

"I dunno, I hope not. Fuck, it's hot."

"You said that. It *is* the middle of July."

"I know, it's my birthday."

"You're shittin me. You never said anything about that."

"I stopped counting birthdays the day my sister died. It was twenty-three years ago today. They called it Bloody Friday back home. It was hot just like today and I remember it like it was yesterday. I was on a mission in Nam…took one in the shoulder that day."

"You've never talked about that stuff before. It sounds like…hey, this could be our boy coming in."

"How do you know that?"

"Looks like a '93 or '94 Mustang. Jimmy likes muscle cars."

The black Mustang GT slowed down at the entrance road, but then continued on and turned at the next corner.

"Nope, looks like you were wrong."

The radio crackled. It was Bill Meyers.

"Heads up everyone, eyes on the black Mustang. It looks like he's doing a heat check. He's on his second loop around the block."

Sure enough, the Mustang appeared again. This time it turned onto the entrance road and headed towards the front of the factory, out of their sight. Patrick gazed through the binoculars.

"Can you see who's in the Mustang?"

"No, the windows are tinted."

There was another radio transmission

"Eyes on the Mustang. Anyone got a visual on the driver?"

"No, the windows are too dark."

Bill Meyers came on the radio.

"That's not the car we have for the target. I'll run the plate."

A moment later someone else radioed.

"The Mustang is in the factory. We see him on the camera. He's driving around, checking things out. Okay, he's stopping in the middle, facing the main entrance door. We can't see who is in the car."

Meyers replied, "Okay, we have confirmation. The car belongs to our target. All units stand by."

The cops all stayed hidden. The minutes ticked by like hours. Patrick checked his weapon again. Norm's butterflies made another appearance. They really flapped their wings, as if trying to escape.

"Heads up everyone. We have two low riders coming in, an old Chevy and a Plymouth. Multiple targets visible in both vehicles. It looks like the Counts, not the Boys."

The Chevy circled the Mustang giving it a wide berth. The Plymouth split off to the right and made a bigger circle, tracing the inside wall of the factory. The Chevy hesitated behind the Mustang until the Plymouth caught up and stopped about two car lengths away, facing the driver's door. Jimmy got out and waved. The Chevy completed its circle and stopped facing his Mustang.

The Exchange

He stood behind his open door. Jesus emerged from the passenger side of the Chevy and flashed a hand sign to Jimmy. He never understood that gang shite. He looked over at the Plymouth.

"What's with the extra soldiers? You ready for war?"

Jesus walked toward him.

"We just wanna to make sure you get off safely for yer vacation."

Jimmy walked to the rear of his car and opened the trunk. Jesus joined him and looked inside.

"There's enough here to start yer own little war."

Jesus looked over the weapons and picked up an assault rifle.

"Very nice, but where's the heavy artillery?"

Jimmy nodded to the back seat.

"In there."

Jesus moved around to the side of the car and looked in. He saw Megan. She sat still as a rock, staring straight ahead. Jesus smiled at Jimmy, then waved his soldier over from his car. He retrieved two black duffle bags from the trunk and brought them to Jimmy's car.

The Latin Count unzipped both bags, grabbed a brick of cocaine, and handed it to Jimmy.

"All units stand by. The exchange is on. It looks like guns for coke. We don't see any cash. When the deal's done we move in."

Bill Meyers made a frantic call to his informant. The YBI were supposed to be meeting Jimmy, not the Latin Counts. It was a critical point, but the main target was there with illegal guns and drugs. The cops watched and waited.

While Jimmy counted the bricks of coke, Jesus held up two guns so that his soldiers in the Plymouth could see them. He told his driver to bring the Chevy around and load up the weapons.

Once the guns were out of his trunk, Jimmy put the two duffle bags in. Then he took the two grenade launchers from the back seat and handed one to Jesus. He looked it over, then turned and pointed it at his soldiers in the other vehicle.

"Wonder what this would do to that car?"

"Oh, it'll do the trick, Jesus."

He handed the weapons to his soldier and told him to put them in the back seat of the Chevy.

He turned back to shake Jimmy's hand.

"I guess this is it. We'll hide close by while you deal with the niggers, then we'll take them by surprise."

The Takedown

"All units move in. Go, Go, Go!"

The cops emerged from the stairwells, charging towards Jimmy and Jesus. Norm and Patrick watched in anticipation as police cruisers sped down the road, heading for the factory's entrance and exit. The bad guys saw the cops stampeding towards them and ran back to their cars.

The Latin Counts in the Plymouth raced to the front entrance but one of the cruisers cut them off. They turned around and headed to the back entrance. Jimmy and Jesus tried to escape by following in their cars, but the second cruiser blocked the back exit.

The gang bangers in the Plymouth fired automatic weapons at the police cruiser, forcing the two cops to bail out and take cover. Drug cops advanced from behind. They shot at the Latin Counts and blasted out the back window of their car. A banger fired at the cops out the broken window. A police bullet caught his right eye, killing him instantly.

More police bullets rained in the back window, forcing the other Count in the back seat to bail out of his side of the car. He fired wildly at the drug cops who took cover behind the cement support pillars. The Count emptied his gun's magazine.

Chips of cement exploded in the air. He left himself exposed while trying to change his mag. A cop emerged from cover and shot the Count twice in the chest.

The two Latins in the front seat exchanged gunfire with two uniformed cops who had taken up positions behind their open doors.

One screamed, "Die, mother fuckers!" as bullets from their automatic weapons made Swiss cheese of the police car. Two drug cops snuck up behind the Counts, shot and killed them both on the spot.

One of the cops answered, "Not today boys."

All four of the Latin Counts that were in the Plymouth lay dead.

Jimmy was like a rat trapped in a maze. He drove around in circles, shooting wildly out his window at the cops. They returned fire, blasting holes in Jimmy's windshield and driver's door.

The flying glass and thumping sound of the bullets hitting the car sent Megan into a fetal position, under the dashboard.

She screamed at Jimmy to stop but it was doubtful he could hear her over the noise. The cops in the second cruiser left the front entrance and boxed Jimmy's car into a corner.

Norm and Patrick heard the gunfire. Eyes widened and hearts pounded while they sat on the edge of their seat in anticipation. Norm tightened his grip on the steering wheel. He looked over sweat streaming down the side of his buddy's face.

Voices on the radio were excited and loud. It only added to their frustration. Then Norm saw a Cadillac and a Land Rover turn onto the factory road. He tried to warn the cops in the factory, but he couldn't break through the heavy radio traffic.

With no way out, Jesus had his driver stop their Chevy. The cops moved in on him, but he wasn't ready to give up. One of the drug cops yelled out when the Cadillac and Land Rover full of the YBI rolled into the factory through the unprotected entrance. They were unaware of what was happening inside.

They thought it was a set up so they drove in a big circle, shooting out the windows scattering the cops. Gunfire echoed off the walls of the cavernous room, sounding like a vicious thunderstorm.

Patrick offered his friend a Clint Eastwood glare. It was time to join the party. Norm gunned it towards the factory entrance. The YBI had the cops pinned down with heavy gunfire. Bullets and cement chips flew through the cloud of dust that hung like a thick fog, in the air.

The Land Rover and Cadillac bolted to the front entrance. Just as they got there, Norm wheeled his car in. They hit the Land Rover head on, crushing the frontends of both vehicles and block the entrance. Norm's head bounced off the door pillar and he was knocked unconscious.

The driver of the Land Rover was ejected half way through the front windshield. Silky jumped from the passenger door and sprayed the front of Norm's car with bullets. A few smashed through the windshield, narrowly missing Norm. He was slumped over in his seat.

Patrick ducked and fired a few rounds from his window. He pulled Norm's gun from its holster, kicked open his door, and took cover behind it. He exchanged gunfire with the gangsters in the Cadillac. One of his bullets hit the driver in the chest and killed him. During the exchange of gunfire, Patrick was hit in the right ankle and he fell to the pavement.

The police sniper on the water tower watched the action through the broken factory windows. He never had a clear shot at anyone inside the factory until Silky left himself exposed at the front entrance. He never knew what hit him. The large caliber bullet took most of head clean off and he collapsed into a pool of his own blood.

The passenger in the left rear of the Cadillac jumped out and closed in on Patrick, who was on the ground and exposed. Just when he got a bead on him the sniper took out the banger with another head shot. He hit the pavement like a bag of wet cement.

The two remaining passengers tried to make a run for it. The guy from the front seat tried to climb over the wrecked cars blocking the entrance. His escape was cut short by a third kill shot from the sniper. He was laid out over the car like a bloody hood ornament.

Bill Meyers and two other cops exchanged shots with the last standing member of the YBI. At least a dozen rounds took him down and finished him off.

During the confusion Jimmy bailed out of his car, leaving Megan behind. He ran to one of the stairwells and fired at the cops to keep them behind cover while he made his escape.

Megan couldn't believe Jimmy left her behind. She was too scared to stay in the car so she ran after him.

Patrick recognized his old friend as he tried to make his escape. He wiped sweat and dust from his eyes. It was a long shot, but he took aim at Jimmy. He squeezed off a shot that caught him in the ass, just before he disappeared into the stairwell.

While the cops were distracted, Jesus used the opportunity and attempted to escape. He told his driver to ram the cars blocking the rear exit and break through. When he reversed the car, he slammed into Megan. She flew through the air and crashed into a cement pillar, collapsing like a rag doll.

Before Jesus' driver could change direction, police bullet pierced the windshield and struck him in the neck and killed him. Jesus pushed the dead man out the door and slid behind the wheel.

Police bullets riddled his car. He reached into the back seat and grabbed the grenade launcher. He got out of the car and aimed at the cruiser blocking his exit. A round caught him in the left knee as he fired the weapon.

The stray grenade hit the Plymouth, causing it to explode in flames. Pieces of metal and body parts from his own soldiers flew everywhere. Another bullet hit Jesus in the right shoulder, knocking him to the ground. He reached out, trying to grab the driver's gun but a police boot stepped on his hand.

He looked up at the cop who was crushing his hand. The hot muzzle of an automatic rifle pressed against his temple told Jesus the game was over.

When the gunfire subsided, Patrick made a bee-line for the stairwell where Jimmy disappeared. He ignored the bleeding and pain in his right ankle while he hobbled across the room. By the time he got to the stairwell, his old friend was half way up the stairs.

Jimmy saw he was being pursued and fired a few shots down the stairwell. The bullets ricocheted near Patrick but he continued up the stairs.

As he ambled up the stairs, he remembered chasing Jimmy when they played cops and robbers as kids. Those were good memories. Hearing about the death of his sister Erin were not.

His emotions ran wild as he neared the top of the stairwell. He pushed the rooftop door open and Jimmy fired two shots into the opening. Patrick honed in on the sound of his gun. It clicked on an empty chamber when he tried to fire another round.

Patrick stepped onto the open roof and saw Jimmy duck behind a brick knee wall. He'd left a blood trail leading to it. Patrick had no cover, but he knew Jimmy was wounded and out of ammunition. He hobbled toward him.

"Show yourself, Jimmy, it's over. Are ya gonna make me come over there and get you?"

Jimmy was scared shitless. There was no place to run and he didn't want to go to jail. His heart pounded as heavy footsteps approached.

"C'mon, Jimmy, I've waited a long time for this."

The brogue sounded vaguely familiar. Like a voice from his past, back home.

Fuck it; I ain't goin down without a fight. Jimmy pulled out his back-up pistol and saw there was one round left in it.

I better make it count, he thought.

Patrick walked closer to him. He felt no pain or anger, only loss—of an old friend and a sister. The Toronto cop stopped in front of the knee wall, his gun hanging at his side.

He leaned forward to see over the wall.

"Jimmy, I just wanna…"

He saw a man peering over the wall. Jimmy swung his gun up and fired. In that moment, he thought he recognized an old familiar face. In that same split-second Bill Meyers emerged from the other stairwell. Instinctively, he fired twice at Jimmy. One of the bullets caught him in the right shoulder.

No one will ever know if it was the impact of the bullet to his shoulder that caused Jimmy's gun to go off, or if he squeezed the trigger himself. That bullet struck Patrick point blank, in the face. Both men collapsed, each on their own side of the knee wall.

Bill Meyers charged forward.

"Give it up Jimmy, it's all over."

He kicked aside the gun that Jimmy had dropped. He handcuffed him, and then looked over the wall to check on Patrick. He lay there motionless, his face covered in blood.

Norm dreamt that he was caught in rain storm. He heard thunder and felt warm rain running down his face. When he woke up, he saw the aftermath of the storm through the broken windshield. The smell of gunpowder hung in the air.

It was quiet, except for the faint voices of the cops he saw milling about. He was wet from the rain, but it wasn't raining. Blood ran down the side of his face from a huge gash on the side of his forehead. Coming to his senses, he reached for his gun. It was gone.

The Windsor cop crawled over broken glass and climbed out of his crumpled and bullet riddled car. It was no dream. There was a bloodied body sticking out of the windshield of the Land Rover, and others on the ground near by. He tripped over someone's leg getting out of the car.

A DEA agent helped steady him as he got to his feet. Norm looked down to see whose leg he tripped over.

"Where's Patrick?"

His head hurt and everything appeared shrouded in fog. It was steam bellowing from the car's busted radiator.

"Where's Bill Meyers?"

The agent pointed to the stairwell.

"They're up top."

Norm made his way to the roof and saw Meyers holding Jimmy, in handcuffs. A body lay near their feet. The man had been shot in the face. Norm recognized the gun in the man's hand—it was his. His jaw dropped; the man was Patrick.

Bill Meyers cleared his throat.

"I'm sorry Norm…your friend is dead. He took out a few gang bangers before Jimmy shot him."

He'd seen many dead people during his career, but never someone that close to him. He felt nauseous. As Norm stood in silence, one of the uniformed cops came up to Meyers and told him an ambulance was on the way for the girl.

Wide-eyed, Jimmy turned to the cop.

"You mean Megan? What happened to her?"

Meyers replied, "After you ran and left her, she got hit by a car. She's busted up pretty bad…we're not sure if she'll make it."

Jimmy was silent. The news and blood loss from his wounds wobbled his legs. He looked at Norm, standing over Patrick's body.

"Do I know you?"

"Not really Jimmy, we used to drink at the same watering hole. You know this guy though."

He pointed down to Patrick.

"Who, the dead cop? Why would I know him?"

Norm knelt down beside Patrick. He gently rolled his head to one side and wiped the blood from his neck with his hand until the shamrock tattoo appeared. He looked up at Jimmy.

"Recognize him now?"

His eyes got as big as saucers, and then he took half a step back, nearly collapsing. Meyers held him up.

"No, it's not…it can't be him."

"I'm afraid so. It's your best friend, Patrick Kelly. He waited twenty-three years for this reunion and you killed him."

Jimmy stuttered and mumbled. He could only repeat the same words.

"No, it can't be."

He couldn't remember the last time he cried, but as the faces and years flashed through his mind, tears dripped from his eyes and streamed down his face. His knees buckled and his bodyweight pulled him from Meyers grasp.

Jimmy knelt over Patrick's body sobbing. He threw his head back and looked to the sky.

"Oh my God…. not again."

The End

Epilogue

Life does not always work out the way we'd like it to. For Jimmy Flynn it didn't matter because he never really had a plan. He lived hard and he played hard. People around him died hard.

In the end, he had no more than he started with. As it turned out, it wasn't the end for Jimmy. He never knew who the mysterious black SUV's belonged to, but the cops did.

His supplier in Boston was a direct pipeline to the Medellin Drug Cartel. They tracked him after the drug bust in Boston. After that, it was a race between the Cartel and the cops to see who could get Jimmy first. The Cartel's loss of drugs and weapons in Detroit ensured that he was a dead man.

The DEA sat Jimmy down and offered him a deal. He jumped at the offer and gave up his connections to the Cartel. To avoid extradition to Ireland he also gave up his IRA connections in Belfast. He told the cops everything he knew about the YBI and Latin Counts. The only person he refused to rat on was Flanny.

For his cooperation and his own safety, Jimmy entered the Witness Protection Program. The location top secret, but Bill Meyers later told Norm he heard through the grapevine that he was working at a gun and knife store, somewhere in the south.

Patrick Kelly never got to face his old friend, although his death stare would haunt Jimmy forever. His body was taken back to Toronto, where he was given a full police funeral. Over two thousand police officers from across Canada and the U.S. attended his funeral. Even his old army Colonel attended.

Maureen Spence was devastated. She was planning on moving in with Patrick, and had a surprise for him. She was pregnant and later gave birth to a healthy baby girl with red hair and green eyes. She called the baby Patricia and asked Norm Strom to be her godfather.

Megan Doyle survived her injuries, but slipped into a coma. Although she was never charged with anything, the cops kept her under guard at Detroit Receiving Hospital where she'd once worked. After one month of police protection, they transferred her to Hotel Dieu Hospital in Windsor, where her mother was her only protection.

Feeling partially responsible for her demise, Norm Strom checked in on her every day. Two months after Megan was admitted to the hospital, her mother had a stroke and died. Megan never recovered and died one week after her mother.

Jesus Martinez survived his gunshot wounds and was sent to prison in Jackson, Michigan for drug and gun trafficking. To gain respect there, he shanked and killed the highest ranking YBI gang member. They retaliated by beating Jesus to death during a staged prisoner uprising. In the aftermath his body was found with over forty stab wounds.

Silky James died from a police bullet. It was his destiny. Almost all gang members die by violence, or end up in jail. The YBI blamed the Latin Counts more than the cops for Silky's death. It gave them a reason to seek revenge and add to the body count of wasted young lives.

Kevin (Flanny) Flannigan reneged on his back taxes and had to file for bankruptcy. A few months after Jimmy's arrest, Wanda found him slumped over on his barstool, dead of a massive heart attack. A bottle of Jameson sat on the bar in front of him, like a personalized tombstone. Old Duke was curled up, asleep at his feet.

Bill Meyers was never able to close the book on most of the gang murders he investigated. He received commendations from the DEA and his own department for his part in the arrest of Jimmy Flynn. His efforts in the war on drugs had no lasting effect. New players quickly took the place of old ones. After the dust settled, he took a desk job and then early retirement. He was hired as the chief of security at Tiger Stadium.

Norm (Storm) Strom stayed with the Windsor Police. He eventually got promoted to the rank of Detective and became an Arson Investigator. He remained friends with Jesse James. On their days off they often took in Tiger games, courtesy of Bill Meyers.

Norm found Arson Investigation to be challenging. It was easy to prove how and where a fire started, and even that it was intentionally set. Most difficult was proving who set the fire. He investigated a string of factory fires, but was stumped as to who was responsible. It seemed they'd been torched for insurance money.

*Be sure to read "**Torch**," the third book in Edmond Gagnon's Norm Strom crime series. Here's a preview…*

Torch - Chapter 1

Eagle on Fire

They say that your first time is the best. If we are talking about getting high on crack cocaine, I would have to agree. Although I have never really known exactly who *they* are, if we are talking about arson, they're wrong.

Like any other apprentice I started with small jobs, honing my skills, watching and learning each time. Being drunk and bored were the only two reasons that I needed to set my first fire.

It was only a garbage bin, but there was something about watching it burn that excited me. After that, I set fire to a small shed. It was like I could feel my own blood rushing through my veins, rinsing away the boredom.

My first orgasmic experience was watching a fire that I had set. It was an abandoned house that the neighborhood kids used as a hangout. My curiosity overcame my good sense as I gathered old magazines and small cardboard boxes, stacking them in a corner in the empty living room.

Using my lighter, I lit the dry paper and cardboard. The orange flames quickly consumed the refuse. The fire called out to me; it wanted more. I placed a broken wooden chair over the fire and looked around to see what else I could burn.

I found an old wooden stepladder in the kitchen. When I returned to the living room the fire cried out to me like a hungry kitten. I fed it the ladder.

At first the wood turned black, but then yellow flames appeared, like they emerged from a cocoon. In search of nourishment, the new hatchlings lapped at the peeling wall paper. A light gust of wind entered through a broken window.

The hungry tentacles reminded me of a giant octopus. It looked at me and smiled, as it reached across the wall and up towards the ceiling.

The wood in the fire cracked and shot sparks across the carpeted floor. It sounded like words dancing in my head. The glowing embers warmed my soul. The monster's heat forced me back a few steps, but I stayed in the room and watched with amazement.

The flames grew like Jack's beanstalk, pushing their way through the ceiling and into the attic. The papered ceiling turned as black as a twilight sky. Then little fingers and flaming hands appeared and crawled across the room.

Thick grey smoke gathered in the air. The monster's body heat backed me into the kitchen. I laughed out loud when a fiery hand poked through the kitchen wall at the light switch.

The monster taunted me…look what I can do. Another hand poked through the wall under the kitchen cupboards. Then another reached through the doorway from the living room. I was scared, but never felt so alive. I retreated to the back door as the kitchen filled with acrid black smoke.

I couldn't believe my eyes when I got outside and looked back at the house. The monster used its fiery-hot fists to punch through the roof and reaching for its distant relatives, those burning spheres in the distant sky.

I was and silhouetted by the monster's light so I took cover in bushes at the back of the property. I heard sirens in the distance, but my eyes were glued to the monster and we weren't going anywhere.

The orange and red glow gave me a euphoric feeling. The hand-like flames tickled my loins, arousing me sexually. My excitement grew with the raging inferno. I lurked there in the shadows, masturbating. I was spiritually connected to the fire.

The reaching flames were like the fingers on my hand. It was my hand that created the fire and my hand that was master of my own passion. My climax came as flames leaped high into the night sky. In that surreal moment, I felt free.

My name is Johnny Eagle and I am an arsonist. I am also an accomplished thief, con-artist and a drug addict. I like the high that I get from smoking crack, but I *love* the high I get from watching a raging fire.

The Reservation on Walpole Island is where I grew up. My persistent childhood nightmares prompted my mother to take me to the tribal medicine man. He smoked his pipe and waved the smoke all around my head. I don't remember the experience, but my mother said I shared the old man's vision.

Like my namesake, he said I was an eagle in the spirit world; a hunter and bird of prey, but to some, a sign of hope and freedom. Apparently, my spirit was conflicted, that it would have to fight for its own survival, while constantly being pursued by the wolf. He saw the eagle being drawn to the gates of hell and then narrowly escaping with its wings on fire.

He called me, Eagle on Fire.

Life on the reservation was mundane. That, and the constant abuse from my father, drove me to leave the island at the age of fifteen. About five years later, I found myself living on the street in Windsor, Ontario. It is a lunch bucket town; being an aboriginal didn't make my life any easier. My mother always suggested to me that someday I could become an artist, just like her. We would both work for the government, drawing welfare.

Getting money from the government was easy while living on the reservation. The white man felt guilty for stealing our land so he let us live on the reservation for free. They kept us happy with tax-free booze and cigarettes.

In the big city, the government expected me to go to school or work for a living. To get a welfare check I would have to prove that I was unable to work. I would also need a permanent address if wanted a check mailed to me. I managed to get some part time work as a roofer, but I found it a lot easier just to steal what I wanted.

Fire for Hire

One day, after boosting an armload of meat from a local grocery store, I visited my fence to trade him the meat for drugs or cash. He offered me a beer and we smoked a big fatty. While we were discussing my next score, my fence asked if I'd be interested in a torch job. He didn't know about my fascination with fire; he had caught my interest even before he said the job paid five hundred bucks.

A set of license plates from a neighbor's car found their way onto my old pickup truck. I slowed down as I drove past the target, a motorcycle repair shop on Tecumseh Road in Windsor's east end.

Even though it was three in the morning I wanted to make sure that there was no one around who might see me. The shop was in complete darkness, but there was a car coming toward me from the opposite direction. After it passed me by, I turned around in a gas station parking lot and headed back to the repair shop.

Using the quiet time of night and darkness to my advantage, I wheeled into the driveway at the motorcycle repair shop. I drove around to the back of the building and backed in at the far end of the parking lot. With the engine off and the window down, I sat perfectly still, watching and listening.

It was so quiet I could hear the snowflakes landing all around me. As my plan played over and over in my head, I watched my breath roll out the window like I'd just exhaled smoke from a cigarette. I felt my heart pounding in my temples and perspiration gathering on my brow.

Exiting my truck, I pulled the five-gallon gas can out of the back. I looked down and saw my footprints in the fresh snow. That would be a problem; I'd have to obscure them somehow on my retreat from the garage.

The moon was full in the clear night sky; it was like someone was pointing a giant spotlight directly down on me. In my opinion it wasn't the best time for the job, but the guy who was paying said the shop had to be torched on that specific night. A promise of five hundred bucks was all the convincing I needed.

Butterflies fluttered in my stomach as I walked up to the bay door at the back of the shop. Looking through the windows, I could see that all was quiet inside. The bay door consisted of rows of wooden panels, with one row of windows in the middle, at eye level.

I figured that the wood would make less noise than the glass so I used the heel of my boot to kick in one of the bottom wooden panels. The brittle wood gave way easily, leaving a square hole just big enough for me to crawl through.

A dog barked in the distance; it must have heard the noise. I stood still for at least a minute, waiting to see if the barking would arouse anyone's attention. I took another peek around the side of the building towards Tecumseh Road to check for cops. It was the only direction they could come from since there was nothing but a huge field behind the garage.

The sweat from my brow was about to drip into my eyes so I wiped it with my coat sleeve. Crawling in through the hole, my baggy winter parka bunched up and I got stuck. Cursing under my breath, I backed out and peeled off my parka. After crawling back in, I stayed crouched down and checked the front windows for cops.

The owner of the shop wanted the fire to look accidental so I had assured him that is how it would look. I stood quietly in the garage looking around at the assortment of motorcycles in various states of repair. The only sound came from the motor of a portable space heater that the owner had purposely left on. I took a few deep breaths to calm my nerves. The smell of motor fuels and lubricants filled my nostrils and made my nose twitch.

All the right ingredients for a nice fire, I thought to myself.

I kicked over the space heater and then poured gasoline all around it and on to the motorcycles. The shop owner had said he wanted all of his records destroyed in the fire so I made sure I soaked his office desk and file cabinets with gasoline. Pausing at the office door I admired Miss January on the Playboy calendar and rubbed her titties for good luck.

Suddenly, flashing red lights reflected off the front windows sending me scurrying into a corner to hide. An ambulance raced by, heading east on Tecumseh Road. I almost pissed my pants and I cursed out loud.

I splashed more gasoline around the shop, and poured a trail leading to the back door. That would be my exit. I placed the empty gas can in the corner, making it look like it belonged there. Then I carefully placed the broken wooden panel back into the bay door, hoping the fire would disguise my forced entry.

The rear pedestrian door was locked, but the panic bar would allow me to exit there. I could then close the door and it would lock behind me as I left.

Standing just outside the back door, I smiled and admired my handiwork. The smell of gasoline fumes was intoxicating. God, how I loved that smell. Fishing through my pockets for my cigarette lighter, I realized it was in my parka. The door almost slammed shut and locked behind me when I reached for my coat.

Cursing again, I took a couple deeper breaths to regain my composure. A flashback of all the other fires I had set made me feel giddy. It was great getting paid for something that I loved to do for free. The anticipation was exhilarating; I couldn't wait to watch the place burn.

One more look for the cops and then I flicked my Bic. That is the last thing I remember from that night.

Some time later, I woke up in the hospital with a splitting headache and pain radiating down the whole left side of my body. The doctor told me I had suffered a concussion, along with second and third degree burns on the left side of my face, neck and arm. A cop that was standing at the back of my room told me that I was lucky to be alive.

He said that the gas explosion blew me backwards about sixty feet from the garage, where I landed in a big snow pile. Apparently, the snow cushioned my landing and extinguished my burning clothes.

The cop explained to me how the garage had filled up with highly combustible gasoline fumes after I poured the gas all over inside. My lighter ignited the fumes and created an explosion that instantly blew me clear across the parking lot. He was right, I was lucky to be alive.

The cop arrested me for Arson. It wouldn't be the last time that cop arrested me.

About the Author

Edmond Gagnon is a retired police detective from the City of Windsor, Ontario which lies directly across the border from Detroit, Michigan.

Ed began his police career as a rookie cop walking a beat. He evolved from a respected street cop into a seasoned detective investigating crimes like murder, rape, robbery, drugs, prostitution, fraud and arson. As a criminal investigator he learned the art of writing a good story. It was *the story* after all, that convicted the criminals.

Upon his retirement Ed travelled extensively, writing about his adventures and misadventures. He put together a collection of fun travel stories, and then published his first book called, **A Casual Traveler**. Ed wrote the book so that he might share his travel experiences with his family and friends. His readers complimented his writing style, saying that he made them feel like they were right there with him.

After writing A Casual Traveler, Ed realized he had caught the writing bug. He wanted to share some of his police stories from his thirty-one-year career. Police informants helped Ed with many of his investigations. He wanted to tell their stories, showing the real value of informants to the police. He created his Norm Strom crime series and wrote, **Rat** - A Cop's Secret Weapon.

Bloody Friday soon followed, as well as the titles listed on the next page.

Other books by Edmond Gagnon

A Casual Traveler

Rat - A Cops Secret Weapon

Torch – Fire for Hire

Finding Hope

Border City Chronicles

All These Crooked Streets

Four – A Paranormal Thriller

All of Edmond Gagnon's Books can be purchased through major sellers and via his website.

Website and Blog:
www.edmondgagnon.com

9 781999 281441

so Father would be in a good mood to look at the tool chest plans.

He ran to the kitchen, got some coals from the stove, and then went to the shop to start the fire. While he was waiting for the coals to start the kindling, he went outside and got in enough wood for the day. The crispness of the morning air bit at his face, but he quickly worked so that he wouldn't notice. He got back upstairs just as Father was sitting down to eat.

"Good morning, Son," Father said. "Did you get the fire started?"

"Yes, Father and I got enough wood in for the day."

"That's good because we have a lot of work to do today, but let's eat first."

As usual, the aroma of Mother's morning feast filled the room. Father enjoyed breakfast almost as much as he enjoyed the mornings. Hans didn't enjoy the morning, but he couldn't resist the smell of eggs, ham, and fresh rolls making their way from the kitchen.

"Father," Hans started cautiously, "could we talk for a little while before we go down to the shop this morning?"

"Well," Father quickly replied, "as a matter of fact, that was what I was planning on doing."

Father's willingness to linger over breakfast surprised Hans because Father always liked to get right to work in the morning. Father figured that they could visit while they worked, which Hans always enjoyed. They had spent many hours in the shop, working side by side and talking about everything from their work to Hans's dreams. Father never said a lot but patiently listened as Hans would spin a tale of the future and what he was going to do.

Father never spoiled Hans's dreams and plans by replying to them with experience and reason. He always listened with an understanding heart. Father was always the first to hear of Hans's ideas, except for the tool chest he was planning to spring on him this morning. It was supposed to be a surprise, and Hans now wondered if Father had found his plans.

"May I get something from my room first?" Hans asked.

"Of course," Father replied.

Hans quickly ran to his room and got the plans out of the corner. His hands trembled as he went over everything in his mind to double-check that they were complete. He took them back into the kitchen and laid them on his chair. He then started helping Mother clear the table, and Father watched with a chuckle. Father knew that something big was coming by the way Hans was acting. He thought that this would work out well because he also had something very important to discuss. As soon as the table was cleared, Hans picked up his plans and sat down. He couldn't hold his excitement any longer.

"Father," Hans began, "I only have two months left of my apprenticeship, and then I will be a journeyman. I want to go to the city and build furniture in one of the big shops, but I will need to supply my tools. I have most of the tools already, but I don't have a place to keep them. I have been working on some plans for a tool chest that I would like to show you. I think that I can complete the chest in my last two months, and it would be a perfect learning project for me. I'll need your help on some parts, but when I'm finished, I'll have much more experience."

"Well, Hans," Father said, "let's see these plans of yours."

Hans quickly unrolled his plans and laid them out on the table. He placed the main drawing of the tool chest right in front of Father. He was excited to see what his father thought because he had done his best work on these plans. He kept watching Father's face to see his reaction. Frederick looked at the master drawing and then began to look over the others. Finally, he looked at the list of materials and costs.

"Hans," Father said, "it will take me a few days to study these plans, but they look perfect. Before we decide to build this, I want to talk about some changes for your training schedule."

"Is there something wrong with the plans?" Hans asked. "I know it's a difficult project, but I believe I can build it. I have saved enough money to buy the wood and fasteners. I don't mind reworking the plans at night if there is something wrong with them."

"Hans, Hans," Father interrupted, "the plans look fine, but I have something different to speak to you about."

"Oh," Hans sheepishly replied.

"You have two months left on your apprenticeship. As you know, at the end of that time you will be a journeyman, and that means you can go and work in any shop you want. It also means that you can work in the city as you have always dreamed of. As your supervising craftsman, I can shorten or lengthen your apprenticeship as I choose. I have decided to add some time to your training."

"But Father," Hans protested, "I have done all that you asked of me and more."

"Hear me out, Son. It is not just my responsibility to teach you about furniture making, but as your father, I have a responsibility to teach you about much more."

"What more could there be, Father?" Hans asked.

"Hans, there are many things that you will face in the city shops that you have never faced here in our village. I have to be sure that your heart is ready for the things that you will face. I have spent the last seven years training your hands, but I must be sure that the training of your heart is also complete."

"Father, what are you saying?"

"I have arranged for you to spend the next seven months in seven different city workshops. I wrote to the craftsmen at these shops, and they will each take you as an apprentice for a month. At the end of this time, you will return here and complete your final two months in my shop. I thought that you would be excited to go to the city and work in the big shops."

"Not like this, Father," Hans said in shock at what he was hearing, "I wanted to go to the city as a journeyman, not an apprentice. Besides, all of my friends will finish their apprenticeships this winter. If I go away for seven months and return here to finish, I won't be done until next fall. I already know as much or more than most journeymen. Why are you doing this to me?"

"Because I love you, Hans."

"No, Father," Hans shouted. "You're doing this to me so that I will get discouraged and not finish. You're jealous because I want to go to the city and make something of myself instead of wasting away in this village as you have."

"Hans!" Mother exclaimed. "Your father is a great craftsman, and he loves you. How could you say this to him?"

"Because it's true, Mother!"

"I'm sorry that you feel this way, Son," his father said softly. "I truly believe that it is best. I will help you pack for your journey today. You have arrangements for travel tomorrow."

"Just like that, Father? I have no say in this? Fine, I'll prove to you that it won't make me quit! I will finish my journey and come home for my certificate."

Father took a long breath and said quietly, "Hans, it is for you that I do this. I hope that you know that my only motive is love."

"I cannot believe that, Father," Hans said as he gathered up his drawings and went to his room. Mother was softly crying, and Father got up to hold her.

Hans could not believe Father was doing this to him. He had always thought of his father as a friend, and now he had turned on Hans. As he sat on his bed, tears of anger began to run down his cheeks. Father was not going to take his dream away. He would do what he must to get his journeyman's papers, and then he would be gone to the city for good. Never in his life could he have imagined such a betrayal from Father.

Father helped Hans that day to gather his belongings. They had to pack his clothes and tools together in one bag. Hans did not talk to Father once. When Father asked him if he thought that he should take one tool or another, Hans would shrug his shoulders. He wanted Father to feel his anger and pain. He knew that he could hurt Father by not talking to him, and it was only fair since Father had delayed his plans by almost a year.

That night, Father went over Hans's itinerary with him. He had written out the names of the towns, the location of the shops, the craftsmen's names, and how he would travel there. As usual, Father had taken care of every detail. Hans still had nothing to say but just sat and listened unemotionally as Father talked.

"I will take you to the pick-up place in the morning," Father said just as Hans was going to bed.

"Fine," Hans replied as he went to his room.

"I love you, Hans," Father said as Hans closed the door to his room. Hans did not respond.

Very early the next morning, Hans awoke before anyone else. He got dressed and sat down to write a note. When he was finished, he picked up his bag and started to leave. Just as he was taking a last look at his room, he saw his plans on the floor where he had flung them the night before. He picked them up and carried them outside. As he crept away from the house, he threw the plans behind the woodpile and started for the road.

An hour later, Hans's father awoke and slowly sat up on the side of the bed. He so hoped that Hans's anger would have eased by this morning and that they could have a proper farewell. As he made his way to Hans's room, he started to knock on the door and found the note Hans had written hanging there.

The Decision

Father took the note off of Hans's bedroom door and read it slowly.

Dear Father,

By the time you find this, I will be gone. You said that I have to become a man before you will give me my journeyman's papers. Only a boy would have his father escort him to the crossroads. I thought I had worked hard enough for you to respect me and see me as a man, but I was wrong. I will not go on this journey because I want to, but because you have forced me into it. As you have requested, I will write of my progress to fulfill your requirements. Please tell Mother goodbye.

Hans

Frederick clutched the note to his chest as his heart broke. Father had not wanted to part this way with Hans. He knew that it would be hard for Hans to accept the delay, but Frederick had hoped that the chance to visit the cities would make it bearable. He would have to tell Elsa, who was now starting to scurry around the kitchen, about the note. Frederick fought to hold back the tears as he slowly walked to tell her.

"Is Hans up already?" Elsa asked with excitement.

"He's gone, Elsa, our Hans got up early and left. I found this note on his door." Frederick handed the note to his wife and waited for her to read it.

"How can he be gone already? He did not even say goodbye." Her voice was starting to crack as she held the note close.

"He is almost a man now. We must love him enough to let him make his own decisions, even if it hurts us," Frederick said as he took her in his arms and they quietly wept together.

Hans cursed the cold as he made his way out to the main road, which was an hour's walk from home. His father had made arrangements for him to catch a ride with Thomas, the freight hauler, to the town of Amare. The air was still and cold, and the only sound that Hans heard was the snow crunching under his feet as he walked. He had stopped on the covered bridge as he left town just long enough to vow never to come back and live. He did not want to waste his life in a small village as Father had. He would make furniture one day for nobles and kings, not butchers and farmers.

When he reached the main road, he was so cold that he could barely feel his feet. Since he had left early to avoid seeing Father, Hans would have to wait for almost an hour before Thomas arrived. He gathered up some brush and started a small fire to warm himself while he waited.

The heat felt good, and the feeling in his feet began to return. As he stared blankly into the fire, he could not understand why Father had sent him off. Had he not worked hard enough? Was he not progressing as he should? Hans just wanted the next seven months to be over.

All his plans for arriving in the city with his journeyman's papers were gone. Now he would show up and be just like all the other apprentices, a nothing. He would only be another glorified errand boy to the craftsmen.

As he sat on his bag next to the fire, he heard the sound of a wagon coming. This time in the morning, it could only be Thomas. He got up, kicked the snow onto the fire, and waited.

Thomas and his team were easy to spot. He had a matched pair of black shires that stood 18 hands high. Thomas was a big man at six-foot-five inches, and he was hard to miss sitting on his wagon. He was a jovial and soft-spoken man who was easy to like. He pulled the wagon right up to where Hans stood and stopped.

"Where's your Father?" Thomas asked.

"I came by myself this morning," Hans replied curtly.

"Well, better get in, we've got a long day ahead of us. If we hurry, we will make Amare by nightfall. Just throw your bag in the back somewhere, and we're off."

Hans did as Thomas said and climbed up on the wagon. He was glad that there was a moose hide to throw over his legs so that he didn't get a chill. As he huddled his hands under the blanket, he noticed that Thomas did not even have on gloves. He was a burly man who would scare you if you didn't know how gentle he was. His beard was full of ice crystals from his breath, but he still had a twinkle in his eye as they rode along.

"So your father says that you're going on quite a trip for the next several months," Thomas said.

"I guess so," Hans sarcastically replied.

"You don't sound very excited about it. I would think that a young fella like you would be just bitin' at the bit to go to the city and see the sights."

"Not like this."

"I suppose the King's carriage would have been more to your liking?"

"No," Hans replied, "I'm not talking about your wagon. I was hoping to go after I had completed my apprenticeship so I could make a name for myself and stay."

"Well, maybe your father figured that this would give you a chance to see where you wanted to go without being stuck somewhere."

"No, he just wanted to make my life miserable."

"No kiddin'," Thomas said as he lifted his eyebrows and tilted his head back to get a good look at Hans's face. "How do you figure?"

For the next several hours, Hans told the whole story to Thomas. He couldn't hold back all his anger and disappointment. Thomas quietly sat and listened as Hans shared all the frustration he felt and how he believed Father did not want him to have all his dreams. It wasn't like Hans to run Father down, but he was so hurt that Father had not even given him a say in the matter. Finally, about mid-afternoon, Hans had finished, and they just rode along in silence for the next hour.

"You know, Son," Thomas finally said, "I get to meet a lot of people haulin' this old freight. Now and then, I get a chance like this to do a little listening to other folks' problems. Do you really think that your father wants to ruin your life and keep you in Crescere?"

"I can't think of any other reason he would be making me do this. I'll never be able to go back as a journeyman and get any respect. No matter how hard I work, they will always think of me as an apprentice."

"I guess that I have known your father since before you were born. In fact, just after I got married to the missis, I bought our first piece of furniture from Frederick. We've had that table for over twenty years now, and it is just as solid as the day I bought it. I don't guess I have ever known a better furniture builder."

"I know Father's good. That's why I don't understand why he never went to the city and became a rich man."

"Well, there is more to life than being rich. Your father is the type of person that no amount of money can buy. There are kings that would give all they own to have what your father has."

"And what is that?"

"A good heart, Hans, a good heart. Occasionally, your father has me haul some freight for him. I always know that it is him waiting for me because he comes out in that little two-wheeled cart of his and parks right at the road where I picked you up today.

He always gets there early and has a fire and a pot of coffee ready. He knows how long a day can be on the road, and I sure appreciate the thought. While we drink our coffee, we sit and visit. Do you want to guess about what?"

"His furniture? Your horses? I don't know."

"You, Hans, your father always tells me about you."

"Why?"

"Because he loves you, boy."

"Well, I know that. I mean, he is my father, and he is supposed to love me."

"No, Hans, it ain't like that. Is that really what you think?"

"Well, sure. Fathers are supposed to love their sons and all that. That's why he took me on as an apprentice, because I was his son. That's why he feels he has to drive my dreams out of me because he knows what's best and 'loves' me."

"You know, Hans," Thomas slowly began, "I used to think the same as you. When my kids were younger, I loved them out of duty, just like you were sayin', but your father taught me a better way of loving them."

"How did my father teach you?"

"Well, you see, I used to be a very hard man. I grew up with a tough father who believed that us kids were just free labor, and he was going to get every ounce out of us. If we didn't work or if our work wasn't up to Father's standards, then we got a good whippin'. Now I'm not saying that a kid doesn't need correctin' sometimes, but my father did it because he was inconvenienced and he was cruel about it. It wasn't because he cared how we turned out. Your father was the first man I ever respected and looked up to that could talk about loving his kid. For a long time, I just thought that he was bent on spoiling you, but the more I listened to him, the more I realized that he was using his love to shape you into a better person."

Hans could see that Thomas was very serious about what he was saying, so he decided to just listen for a change.

"I think that the hardest thing I ever did in my life was hug my kids and tell them that I loved them. I thought they ought to know it 'cause I was their father, but Frederick convinced me I needed to tell them. He told me I should tell them so that they knew without a doubt that I loved them. One day, they would need someone to turn to when things got rough, and I wanted to be that person. I did pretty well until one day my two boys left my new harnesses out in the rain after I had told them to put them away for me."

"What did you do?" Hans asked.

"Well, I didn't find out until early the next morning when I went out to leave for a run. It was a good thing I had to leave that morning, and also that your father had some freight for me to pick up. Just like usual, he was waiting there with the coffee. I was about as mad as I ever remember being. I had saved up for a year to buy those harnesses, and I was furious with my boys. If it wasn't for your father, I might have hung on the King's gallows for whippin' those two boys when I got home. Your father helped me see things better."

"What did he say?"

"Well, he listened for half an hour while I fussed and fumed, and then he asked me a couple of questions. First, he asked me if I wanted to punish the boys for the financial loss they had caused me, or if I wanted to teach them a lesson. I said I wanted to teach them to fear me if they did wrong, and I was serious. Frederick told me that if I motivated them through fear, then they would only be motivated as long as the fear was present. When the boys grew up and were away from me, they would no longer have a reason to be responsible. He said that I should teach them something useful instead of just punishing them. Punishment, according to him, was easy to dish out, but discipline took thought, love, and courage to carry out."

"So what did you do?" Hans asked.

"Well, your father helped me work out a plan. The first part was for me to work that day on getting over my anger so I could put the boy's best interests ahead of my own. Then I was to figure out what was wrong with what the boys did in a way they could understand. In other words, I had a responsibility to teach the boys that money does not just fall out of the sky and that I was building a business that one day would be theirs. Finally, I had to treat them like people with minds that could understand things instead of like a critter who only has to learn to obey.

"So when I got home, I called the boys in, and we had a nice long talk about what they had done. I explained how things were, and they had never realized how long I saved for those harnesses. That shocked me. I don't know why I thought they should have known, but I did. Then they weren't able to play with their friends until they had oiled every inch of those harnesses. They realized it was such hard work that they even offered to help me sometimes after that. The boys still did childish things, but I learned to teach them instead of punishing them. I think the last thing your father said to me that day changed my life more than anything since."

"What did he say?" Hans was almost speechless now.

"He asked me if I just loved my boys when it felt like it or if I had a real love for them. I didn't know what he was talking about until he explained it to me. He said that most people love with their emotions, and when the feeling is gone, so is the love. He said that nobody is always lovable and feelings will come and go, but real love is a decision. Frederick told me we have to make a decision to love others because it is the only kind of love that will take us through the tough times. I began to use what he said, not just with the boys, but with my wife and others. It changed my life, Hans, and I have your father to thank."

"Wow, I never knew Father knew all that stuff. I mean, I know he is smart, but I just never heard it put that way."

"There's a lot about Frederick that you may not know," Thomas said.

"I feel like such a fool for the way I left. I'm still upset with Father, but I should have given him the benefit of the doubt. He has never done anything to harm me before, and that's why I can't understand why he did this. I wish I could go back and make things right."

Thomas' heart went out to Hans because he knew how close he was to his father. "Frederick taught me that we can never go back, but we can always choose to go forward. You still love your father with your feelings as any boy does, but you are almost a man, Hans, and you must have a more mature kind of love. Always treat the ones you love as though it were the last time you would see them. We know that we will one day say goodbye forever to those we love, but we don't know when that will be."

The city of Amare was in sight now as the sun was setting over the ocean. Hans could see the masts of the merchant ships in the harbor as the sun faded out of sight. He was glad to get off the wagon. Thomas dropped him off at the inn, and they said their goodbyes. Hans would spend the night in Amare and depart by carriage in the morning. His room was small, but the bed was warm and soft. As tired as he was, he couldn't sleep as he thought about Father and what Thomas had told him.

The next morning, Hans purchased his ticket for the three-day trip to Pax, which was southeast of Amare. There were two merchant salesmen on the journey with him, and he kept to himself as they talked their trades. Hans had never traveled before, and he was amazed at the towns and villages he saw. Each night, they would stop in a different city, and Hans would stay up as late as he could to watch the town from his window in the inn. Pax was very deep in the King's forest, and the whole last day was spent driving through the trees. These were different trees from what they had at home. Father had shown Hans drawings in books of the different kinds of trees, and he tried to name them.

Late in the afternoon of the third day, the carriage was winding through the forest when they rode into a large clearing. At that moment, bandits attacked with fury.

Sink Or Swim

Zzzzzzip-thud, Zzzzzzip-thud

"What was that?" Hans asked the merchants as he stuck his head out the window of the carriage to look. Just as he did, he heard another zzzzzzip-thud right next to his head. He looked out of the corner of his eye to see an arrow just inches from his head.

"Ah!" Hans exclaimed as he pulled his head back in the carriage.

"Look," said one of the merchants, "there, three hooded riders with crossbows coming out of the woods!"

At that moment, the driver cracked the whip and yelled to the horses.

The carriage lunged forward, and Hans was thrown back, hitting his head. "Get down on the floor!" Yelled the other merchant.

"Why?" Asked Hans.

Zzzzzzip-thud. Another arrow hit the back of the carriage and came through, nicking Hans in the arm.

"Don't worry; I know why," Hans exclaimed as he dove to join the other two on the floor.

The carriage was bouncing violently as the driver tried to outrun the bandits. Hans and the other two were thrown from side to side as each tried to find something to hang onto. Limbs were striking the carriage as the driver swerved to block the bandits who were trying to get in front of the carriage and stop the horses. Hans was sure that they were all going to die. He thought about his parents and how he had not even said goodbye.

As Hans looked up and out the window of the carriage, he saw several riders go by in the opposite direction. The next thing he knew, the carriage was slowing down to a stop.

"Oh no," one of the merchants said," they've caught us, and we are all going to die."

"Are you all right in there?" a voice called out.

Hans got up to look out and saw one of the king's soldiers. He couldn't believe it.

He had never seen a soldier in armor before. The soldiers' horses bore the emblem of the king, and the soldiers sat like giants in their saddles. All Hans could do was look at him with his mouth open and nod his head.

"We've been patrolling this road for two weeks trying to catch these thieves," the soldier said. "With any luck, they will be in the king's dungeon tonight." With that, the soldier took off to join the pursuit.

The driver stepped down from the carriage and came to the door.

"You might as well get out for a while. I ran the horses pretty hard, and I want to let them rest and cool off before we go into Pax. It shouldn't take long. Are you sure you're all right?" the driver asked.

"I hope they find those murdering thieves and hang them," one of the merchants said.

"I would be more than glad to furnish the rope," the other added.

"That was the most exciting thing I have ever seen in my life," Hans said as he looked back to see the chase.

"Well, I'm glad someone enjoyed it," the older merchant replied, but was obviously annoyed.

Hans walked to the front of the carriage as the driver was unhooking the team. The horses were all lathered up from running and were still breathing hard. The driver unhooked them and began to walk them around. The two merchants went over to a fallen tree and sat down to continue their small talk where they had left off. Hans walked up to the road where the hill crested to see what he could. There in the valley before him was the city of Pax.

"Wow," he half-whispered as he beheld the sight of the largest city he had ever seen. The smoking chimneys seemed to number in the thousands. There was a great river that ran through the middle of town with several different bridges crossing it. As he stood there, he tried to imagine where he would be working in the city. Before he knew it, the carriage pulled up next to him, and it was time to go.

It was just about nightfall when they reached the station. Hans had to hurry to the furniture shop before everyone else went home. Father had sent him with specific directions, which led Hans right to the shop as the head craftsman was locking the door.

"Excuse me, sir," Hans cried out. "My name is Hans, son of Craftsman Frederick of Crescere."

"Ah, yes," the craftsman replied. "We were expecting you today, but not this late."

"Forgive me, sir, but we had trouble on the road."

"Well, you're here now. Come in, and I will show you where to stay."

The craftsman led Hans by a lamp to the back of a vast building and up a short flight of stairs.

"It's been years since our apprentices have stayed here, but your father asked if we could allow you to stay. I'm afraid that the old apprentice quarters have been turned into storage rooms. You'll have to make a place for yourself in here. If you move a few things around, I think you can find the bed. Sleep well because tomorrow will be a long day."

"Yes, sir. Thank you, sir."

The head craftsman left the lamp and started down the stairs. Halfway down, he stopped and said. "By the way, you will be working under a craftsman named Peter. Be ready and in the shop at sunrise."

Hans had trouble sleeping that night as he tried to imagine what the shop looked like and the grand projects he would see. He hoped that his skill would show, so he could work at a journeyman's level. He wondered what this man named Peter was like and if they would get along. At 5:30, Hans awoke and quickly ate some biscuits and cheese leftover from the trip. At 6:00 a.m., as the sun was rising, he was in the shop.

All the workers were coming in as Hans stood there. The shop was larger than any building in his hometown. He couldn't believe the number of benches and tools he saw. As well as he could tell, there were almost forty workers in the shop. It was easy to tell which workers were the apprentices because they were scurrying about and getting things ready for the day. Several boys were attending to the fires, while the rest of them were dusting off the workbenches and laying out the tools.

"You must be Hans," a gruff voice called out. "Yes, sir, I am," Hans replied, a little intimidated.

"I'm Peter, and you will be working with me for the next month. Let's get started."

Peter was a stocky man, about the same age as Hans' father. He had a graying beard and long hair. His features were rough and weathered, and he led Hans to a workbench without saying another word. Hans had expected that the craftsmen would be short with him. His father had warned him that the craftsmen in the big shops had little time to guide the apprentices. These shops had a lot of work to do, and it was the responsibility of the apprentice to observe and learn what he could. Hans was not worried, though, because he had learned many skills from his father.

"You just take today and get to know the shop, and tomorrow I will give you some specific tasks," Peter said as he started right in on the chairs he was building.

Hans kept quiet and tried to keep up with Peter when he needed something. He had to fend for himself when Peter needed another tool because everyone else in the shop was too busy for him to ask them for directions. It was a day filled with confusion and anxiety for Hans. Still, he was determined to earn Peter's trust within a couple of days so he could get some hands-on experience. Before Hans knew it, the day was over, and the workers were preparing to leave. Peter had said very little to Hans all day, and as he started to go, he turned to him.

"Tell me before I go why you want to be a furniture maker," Peter said.

"Because one day I will make great furniture for the King and his nobles. That is why I am so excited to have the chance to work in a real shop like this one. Most of my experience has been to make furniture for working people, but now I can learn to make great furniture."

"You don't say," Peter said as he crossed his arms. "Then tomorrow I will begin to teach you how to be the greatest of furniture makers."

Peter turned without another word and left. Hans was so excited! Peter had already recognized his potential, and he would be able to start on some real work tomorrow. He barely slept a wink that night because he was so excited. He began to think of plans for pieces of furniture that he could build while he was there. The next morning, Hans was in the shop long before the others arrived. He saw Peter come in with the other craftsmen. They all stepped inside the front door and talked for a few moments. Perhaps, Hans thought, Peter was telling them what a talented apprentice he was and how he would do great things. Hans waited anxiously for Peter to come over to the workbench.

"Are you ready to become a great woodworker, Hans?" Peter asked as he walked up.

"Yes, sir!" Hans replied with a smile.

"Good, I want you to sharpen all the wood planes in the shop."

"OK," Hans replied," I should be done by noon."

"I don't think you understand, Hans. We have close to a hundred planes in this shop. I have talked to the other craftsmen, and they will have their apprentices bring the planes they need to be sharpened to the bench in the back of the shop where you will sharpen them."

"How many need sharpening?" Hans asked.

"Well, each craftsman will have at least two a day that will need to be honed."

"That's forty planes a day," Hans complained.

"That's some pretty good figuring, Hans. I guess you also figured out that you better get started," Peter said and turned to his work without another word.

Hans wasn't sure what was going on, but he made his way to the small workbench in the back of the shop. Some of the other apprentices were already bringing dull planes to the table. Each one laid them down and looked at Hans with a smirk on their face. Hans wasn't sure how much he liked this. It was the responsibility of each apprentice to sharpen the planes of his craftsman or journeyman. This was precisely why he did not want to come to the city as an apprentice. He was just the low man who was going to get all the dirty jobs.

Angrily, he took the first plane apart and started sharpening it. By the time he started on the third plane, the end of the table was covered with dull planes. His hands were already beginning to ache from holding the steel blades against the oil stone. He was reassembling the last plane when Peter announced that it was quitting time. Hans's hands were black from the oil and steel, and his fingers were numb from honing. He fell into bed, exhausted from the lack of sleep and hours of standing in the same place.

The next morning, Hans was not so quick to get down to the shop. He was hoping that the previous day had just been some cruel initiation, and today he would be told that it was over. He knew this was not true when he arrived at the shop and saw some planes already sitting on his table. He had just started taking the first one apart when Peter walked over to him.

"Hans," Peter started, "the last four planes that you sharpened yesterday were not done right. I want you to start today by redoing those. The last plane you sharpen each day should be as good as the first one. When you do poor work, it reflects badly on me, and I don't like that. If you can't keep up, then I would rather you stay after everyone else has gone to finish rather than do poor work. And don't just put the planes back together; adjust them as well. The craftsmen should be able to pick up a freshly sharpened plane and go to work without having to check the adjustment."

"Yes, sir," Hans replied angrily.

Peter slapped him on the back as he walked away. It was meant to be a gesture of encouragement, but it just annoyed Hans. He spent the rest of the day and a couple of hours after work at his bench. Peter left without saying a word to him. He spent every day sharpening planes. By the end of the week, none had been returned, and he was happy to finish the last one by quitting time on Saturday night. Peter, who had not said a word to him since Wednesday, came over to his table.

"Hans, tomorrow is Sunday, and I will come by at 10 o'clock. You're welcome to come to my home and stay for lunch. I'm sure you are ready for a good home-cooked meal."

"Yes, sir," Hans replied. He didn't know how to take the invitation. He wasn't sure if this was an act of hospitality, pity, obligation, or another order. Either way, Hans thought, it was a free meal. Try as he might, he was not able to get the black oil stains out of his hands that night. He figured that Peter knew he had tried.

The next morning, he put on his one set of good clothes and was outside when Peter arrived. They walked back to Peter's home, which was a few blocks from the furniture shop. Even though Peter did not say much to Hans, it was different to see him with his family.

Peter played with his children before lunch and even joked with them. This sure wasn't the man who had exiled Hans to the sharpening table at the back of the shop.

The meal was terrific, and Hans thanked Peter's wife several times for having him.

As soon as lunch was over, Peter offered to walk back to the shop with Hans. He figured that this was a nice way of telling him that it was time for him to leave. He wasn't sure why Peter had gone with him because he never said a word until they arrived at the shop and stopped outside.

"Hans," Peter finally said, "do you know how to swim?"

"Yes, sir, I do," Hans replied, completely puzzled.

"Well, if you want to be a great furniture craftsman, then you'd better learn how to swim in this business, or you'll never survive," Peter said, turned, and walked away.

Hans just stood and watched him walk away. He raised his hands in exasperation and went into the shop. He had no idea what Peter meant by him swimming, but he really didn't care. All he wanted to do was get out of that shop. He had three more weeks, and it couldn't pass quickly enough for Hans. He spent the rest of the day taking care of his personal chores.

The first order of business was to get his clothes washed since they were covered with oil and metal shavings. He went to the well located at the back of the shop to fetch some water. It had been so cold that a layer of ice had formed at the bottom of the well. He filled the well bucket with rocks and dropped it in three times before the ice broke. Next, he found a tub in the shop and washed his clothes as best he could. Finally, he went to the market and got some food to keep in his room for the week.

Monday morning came too soon for Hans, and it found him back at his little table sharpening planes. By now, the other apprentices were feeling sorry for him, and they no longer smirked when they brought planes to Hans's table. Some would even pat him on the back and apologize for bringing another one.

Peter, as usual, had nothing to say to Hans unless it was in the form of a directive about the work he was doing. His hands were getting stronger, and no longer ached except for an occasional cramp. He had learned to switch off which arm he used, and the week was a little more tolerable.

On Saturday night, Peter again "informed" him about lunch on Sunday. The day went the same as the Sunday before. As they walked to Peter's home, Hans wondered if Peter's children knew what a jerk he was at the shop. He figured if they knew what he was really like, then they would run away from home. Again, after lunch, Peter offered to walk Hans back, and yet nothing was said until they got to the shop.

"Have you thought about what I said last week, Hans?" Peter asked.

"About what, sir?"

"About swimming?"

"May I speak openly, sir?" Hans asked, growing quite frustrated.

"I wish you would, for a change. I thought the only thing you knew how to say was 'yes, sir. ' I was beginning to wonder if you had a mind of your own."

"What in the world does swimming have to do with furniture building?"

"Tell me about when you swam for the first time, Hans."

"Why? It doesn't have anything to do with building furniture!"

"Tell me about the first time you swam, Hans," Peter said with a sternness in his voice that Hans dared not challenge.

"Well, it was nothing spectacular. I was six or seven years old, and I had gone with some other boys to the swimming hole about half a mile from town. We had been there for a while, and the older boys threw me in."

"What happened then?"

"I almost drowned, and then I learned to swim."

"No, Hans, be specific. What happened just after they pushed you in?"

"Well, I was scared 'cause I didn't know how to swim, and I kicked and fought to get some air. The other boys were yelling at me, and I figured out how to swim," Hans said, shrugging his shoulders and still failing to see the relevance.

"What did they yell to you? Do you remember exactly what they were yelling?"

"They told me to quit fighting the water."

"That's what I thought," Peter said, and he walked away.

"I'm gonna go crazy talking to that man for another two weeks," Hans thought to himself. He was glad that Peter didn't talk much because what he did say was just gibberish to Hans. He took the rest of the day getting ready for the week ahead.

Monday arrived with a pile of dull planes on the table, and Hans almost worked mechanically for the next six days. By now, he had earned the respect of the other apprentices. Many confided in him that they would have quit after the first week of sharpening planes. Hans was resigned to his fate and just shrugged it off.

He was starting to be haunted by Peter's obsession with swimming. He just could not figure out what it had to do with furniture building. The only thing that Hans was swimming in was honing oil. Saturday came a little quicker this week, and Hans got ready for his Sunday morning visit with Peter's family.

As usual, Peter walked Hans back to the shop after lunch. At the front door, Peter spoke up.

"You hate sharpening planes, don't you, Hans?"

"Sir, I think that hate is too mild a word."

"Good, I hoped that you would hate it 'cause it was the dirtiest job I could think of in the shop."

"Am I to thank you now?"

"You're drowning at that table, Hans, and you only have one week left to learn how to swim," Peter said as he turned to walk away.

That was it! Hans was fed up with all this swimming talk.

"Peter!" Hans yelled, "Would you please just tell me what you want from me?" Peter just kept walking.

"Peter!" Hans yelled, now furious and frustrated. "Peter, would you finish a conversation with me just once? Peter!"

Without turning around, Peter just waved at Hans and kept walking. Hans was livid. He was so mad that he almost broke the glass out of the front door when he slammed it. Just one more week and he would be out of there. He would show Peter.

The next morning, he was at his table before any of the other apprentices were in the shop. When the first plane showed up, he immediately disassembled it and started sharpening it. He did not even look toward Peter's workbench; he just kept up with the sharpening as fast as he could.

At the end of the day, Hans went right up to Peter and asked, "Any complaints today?"

"Haven't heard any," Peter responded, a bit surprised by Hans's confrontation. Without a word, Hans turned and walked away.

The next morning, on Tuesday, Hans got down to the shop early and gathered the dull planes. By the time the workers got there, Hans had half of the planes sharpened. No one was talking to Hans because it was evident that he was on a mission. On Wednesday, he took things one step further.

That morning, he not only gathered up the dull planes, but when he finished sharpening each one, he returned them to the craftsman who owned them. He had sharpened the planes enough times to learn the mark on the tools that told whose it was. He still did not look at Peter, but Peter was watching him and smiling.

On Thursday, Hans not only arrived at his table early, but he was actually looking forward to the day. He had a spring in his step, and he even whistled some while he worked. The different craftsmen would thank Hans when he brought a plane back, everyone, that is, except Peter. Some of the craftsmen even sent their apprentices back to watch how Hans was sharpening the planes. He had grown very proud of his work and decided that if he were going to do the dirtiest job in the shop, then he would be the best he could at it.

Friday and Saturday flew by, and once again, Sunday found him at Peter's for lunch.

After lunch, came the customary walk back to the shop; only this time, Peter spoke as soon as they got to the street.

"So tomorrow you leave for Patientia."

"Yes, sir, I leave first thing."

"You did well this week, Hans."

"Thank you, sir."

"I was sure relieved to see you swim. I was worried about you for a while. I didn't know if you would make it."

"Sir, may I please ask what all this talk about swimming has to do with me sharpening planes?"

"Hans, we have twenty apprentices in our shop, and every one of them wants to build furniture for the King. At least ten of those young men quit the program every year. Of those that start, only a handful ever finish the full seven years, and even fewer make it from journeyman to craftsman."

"Why do so many quit?"

"Cause they can't swim."

"What does that mean?"

"Hans, the only thing that kept you from drowning when you were a boy was the fact that you made peace. You made it with yourself to relax enough to float to the top so you could breathe. Few men in this life ever make peace with themselves and believe in the talents they have. Most young men in our shop are so unsure of themselves that they wage a constant war to prove something to themselves and others."

"When you got here, you knew, and I knew, from the first day that you had great woodworking skills. That isn't enough, but it did help you survive. You knew that if you had to be confined to sharpening planes, you had to make peace with your situation and do the best job possible. You see, most men drown in their situations because they cannot make peace with it. They think that the way out is fighting instead of making peace and floating to the top.

"Much in the same way that you had made peace with the water. Fighting the water only makes things worse, but once you have made peace with it, you can get somewhere. Most think that peace means you give up; but in reality, peace, in a person's heart with himself and his circumstance, is the most powerful thing in the world.

"You see, Hans, a person must make peace with the opportunities that he is given. Some men jump into opportunities, and others are thrown in. Either way, if they're not willing to make peace with the hard work that opportunity presents, then they're doomed to drown in failure. I had to teach you to make peace with the dirtiest and lowest job in the shop if you were to one day make furniture for kings."

With that, they had arrived at the shop.

"Peter, thank you for everything. I'm sorry that I was so stubborn and ungrateful."

Peter just nodded and turned to walk home. Hans figured he should have known that a fond farewell was a bit much to ask of Peter. That afternoon, Hans did his laundry and got ready to leave the next morning.

At first light, he went to the station and bought his ticket for

Patientia. The carriage was on time, and he loaded his bag and got aboard. Just as they were about to leave, Peter appeared at the window of the carriage. Without a word, he handed Hans a package. The driver called to the horses, and the carriage took off. As they drove off, Peter called out to Hans.

"Please tell Frederick that I said hello!"

Hans stuck his head out the window as they drove away.

"You know my father!? How do you know Father? Peter! How do you know Father?"

Peter turned without a word and walked away.

A Very Fishy Job

Hans sat back in his seat and settled in for the three-day journey to Patientia. He had forgotten about the package that Peter gave him as he watched the city of Pax fade in the distance. He wanted to take a nap but remembered the promise he made Father to write at the end of each month. Since his paper was in his bag on top of the carriage, he decided to take a nap and get into his bag at the lunch stop. Hans slept soundly as they bounced along the road, and before he knew it, the carriage stopped for lunch. As planned, he reached into his bag and started writing to Father.

Hans was not about to tell Father that he spent every day for a month sharpening planes. Even though he had learned much from Peter, the method wasn't anything to brag about.

Dear Father,

As you requested, I am writing you concerning my progress. After a scare with robbers on the trip to Pax, I arrived
safely. Please tell Mother not to worry, because the king's
soldiers captured the thieves, and we should not have any
more trouble. One of my travel companions told me thieves
were rare in our country, and it was just an isolated occur-

rence.

I began my duties at the furniture shop on the following morning. I was assigned to a man named Peter. He was not a very talkative person, but I did learn much from him. With his instruction, I was able to sharpen my skills daily.

I am now en route to Patientia and will write you again at the end of the month. Please tell Mother I love her.

Hans

He was still not ready to make peace with Father. Even though he had learned the importance of making peace with himself, Hans was not sure that he had successfully accomplished it.

Thankfully, the trip to Patientia was uneventful. The entire trip was through the forest, and after a while, the trees all began to look the same. They arrived in Patientia on the afternoon of the third day, and Hans had time to get food and supplies before going to the furniture shop. As he walked slowly through the streets, he was intrigued by the vendors and shops. He couldn't believe all that was available for the asking. In his home of Crescere, there was only one store, and the selection was very limited. He sat by a fountain for a time and listened to a minstrel band before making his way to the shop.

Hans arrived at the shop about half an hour before quitting time, and the workers were just starting to put away their tools. Hans walked in the front door, and the little bell attached to it dinged. A man at the first workbench waved and said hello.

"I'll be with you in a minute, young man," he said with a smile.

The shop was half the size of the one in Pax, and it was much better lit from dormer windows in the roof. The pace seemed to be slower, and the pieces that they were building were much nicer. The atmosphere was more of a handcrafted shop instead of a production shop. Hans was excited to be there.

"May I help you?" the gentleman inquired as he walked over to Hans.

"Yes, sir," Hans replied, extending his hand, "I am Hans, son of the craftsman Frederick from Crescere."

"Ah, yes, we have been expecting you. Was your journey a good one?"

"Yes, sir, it was very good," Hans replied, already liking this shop much better.

"We are always glad to have a talented apprentice in our shop. As you can see, we specialize in fine furnishings, and although the shop is small, we take pride in the work we do. You will be working with a craftsman named Johann. He is one of our most talented and gifted craftsmen. Follow me and I will introduce you to him."

Hans followed the kindly gentleman to the back corner of the shop. The workers at the tables each nodded and said hello to Hans as he walked by. In the back of the shop, a man was working on a beautiful walnut dresser. The man was humming while he worked and had not noticed them as they walked up. His workbench sat under two big windows that looked out upon the forest. The evening sun was shining through the windows and highlighting the sawdust in the air.

"Johann," the old man called as he touched the worker's shoulder.

"Yes," Johann replied as he turned and looked at him with a smile. He was a man in his early fifties with eyes that crinkled when he smiled. He wore spectacles that were down on the end of his nose. He looked over to see Hans with the other man.

"This is the young man named Hans that we have been expecting.

I thought you would like to meet him."

"Of course," Johann said as he held out his hand to Hans. "It is a pleasure to finally meet you. I have heard many good things about you, and I am looking forward to helping with your training."

"Thank you, sir," Hans said as he returned the handshake.

"Well, good," said the old man. "Why don't we get you settled in for the night, and then you can get started in the morning?"

He led Hans to a little building in the back with a small, but nicely decorated room. "I hope that you will be comfortable here. I have to apologize about the flowered curtains. My wife felt obliged to decorate when she found out that you were coming. I told her that you would be more concerned with a good bed than curtains, but she insisted."

"It is quite nice, sir. Please thank your wife for her thoughtfulness."

"Well, we do not have live-in apprentices often. Since we are a small specialty shop, our young men come from local families. It just seems to work better for us because we know the boys and can choose the ones we think will last for the seven years. We used to have boys from all over the country come to apprentice, but it was so hard for a boy of 11 or 12 to be away from home. Make yourself at home, and we will see you at seven in the morning."

Hans thought this must be a dream. Everyone was so nice, and he had a real room for a change. He really didn't mind the curtains because they reminded him of home and his mother. He got settled in and had a good night's sleep.

Hans was used to getting up at 5 a.m., so it was hard for him to sleep in. He was in the shop before anyone else, and he took the opportunity to look at the piece Johann was building.

This had to be some of the most beautiful work Hans had ever seen. The dresser was six feet long, and each of its drawers had intricate carvings. The legs were of the finest design, and the top had been planed to perfection. As Hans was running his hands over the piece, Johann walked up.

"Do you like it?" Johann asked.

"Oh yes, sir. It is one of the finest pieces I have ever had the privilege of seeing."

"I've been working on it for six months now. What do you say we get started?"

"Yes, sir."

"Hey, call me Johann. Every time you say 'sir', I start looking for the owner."

"Yes, sir, I mean, Johann."

"That's better," he said with a wink and a pat on the back. "Tell me, Hans, are you good at sharpening a plane?"

"Oh no," Hans thought to himself, "I knew that this was too good to be true. What is it with planes and the new guy?"

"Yes, I have some experience in sharpening."

"Great, would you please put a fresh edge on this plane. The only thing I have to do is edge the top, and we will be ready for the final steps. You'll find the oil stone on the bench over there, and I'll do a few other little tasks while you sharpen. Oh, and be careful with the oil, it can really stain your hands."

"Yes, sir, I mean, Johann, I know."

Hans laughed to himself as he took the plane apart and began to sharpen it. In half an hour, he had it reassembled and adjusted. He presented it to Johann, who had just finished what he was doing. Johann looked at the bottom of the plane through his spectacles and then looked back at Hans.

"Hans, that is about the best job of sharpening and adjusting I have ever seen. Looks like you've spent some serious time at the oil stone before."

"Yes," Hans replied, "let's just say that I have received some concentrated instruction in plane sharpening."

Hans watched as Johann began to plane the top edge of the dresser. He was amazed at the softness of his touch and how he focused on what he was doing. The edge he was putting on the dresser was very delicate, and he worked patiently to make it perfectly uniform. In an hour, the top was finished, and Johann handed the plane to Hans to put away.

"What do you think, Hans?" Johann asked, "Will it be good enough for a nobleman's castle?"

"It's beautiful, Johann," Hans replied in amazement at the finished top crowning the dresser with grace and delicacy.

"Well, now that it is built, the real work begins. Would you please fetch that red bucket in the back of the shop for me?"

Hans quickly went to the back and found the large red bucket with a lid. He really enjoyed working with Johann. His manner was gentle, and he visited with Hans while they worked. His way of working with Hans was different from most craftsmen.

"Should I take the lid off?" Hans asked.

"Let's wait until we have to," Johann replied. "I want to explain to you what we will be doing first. We are now going to do the most important work on this piece. This is going to make the difference between a good piece of furniture and a great one. We are going to smooth the piece."

"Johann, has that bucket got in it what I think is in it?"

"To the educated talker, it is shagreen, but to us common folk, it is just plain old dogfish skins." Then Johann said softly, "Watch how fast everyone else moves their projects to the far end of the shop when we open this bucket."

"Can I go with them?" Hans asked, turning up his nose and cringing at what was to come. At home, he had always done this job outside or at least opened a window.

"Afraid not. Come on, it's not that bad after the third or fourth day."

"The third or fourth day?"

"Grab a skin and let's get started. I want to start with the inside first, and when it is perfectly smooth, we can start on the outside."

"Why are we doing the inside? I've never heard of anyone doing the inside of a dresser. I thought Father was being silly to have me smooth the underside of his tables."

"Hans, this will go in the bedroom of a nobleman's daughter. A noble woman of wealth has many fine silk .... well, you know. How would she feel if they were to snag on the inside of our dresser?"

Out came the dogfish skins, and sure enough, the workers started moving their projects to the other end of the shop. The sharpening bench was starting to look very good to Hans, but then he figured he could stand anything for a couple of days. He tried to remember that he should make peace with his work.

Though the skins were very abrasive, the walnut smoothed down slowly. It was Wednesday of the following week before Johann was satisfied with the inside of the dresser.

After spending more than a week working with the dogfish skins, the other workers would not even go near Hans and Johann. Their hands, hair, and clothes all smelled of dried fish. Hans was growing very impatient with Johann and his obsession with perfection. He no longer seemed like such a nice guy to Hans, though he still acted cheery and friendly.

The daily routine became Hans wanting to move on, and Johann making him work more on a piece or section of the dresser. Each time Hans felt a place was smooth enough, Johann would pull out a silk scarf and run it across the piece, and it would snag.

"Hans," Johann finally asked, "do you know what the most dangerous words a craftsman can say are? Good enough," Johann said. "Good enough, in craftsmen's terms, means that you are settling for less than your best. The word you want to train yourself to say is 'perfect'."

"There's no such thing as perfect. Besides, what's wrong with 'good enough'. Some things are good enough the way they are. Not everything has to be perfect," Hans interjected.

"Good enough for what or whom?"

"I don't know. Good enough for whatever you are doing."

"Hans, most men and craftsmen do things' good enough', but a maker of furniture for kings has standards that set him above the others, no matter who he is working for, be it a pauper or prince. By striving for perfection, you will always do a better job than you thought you could."

The end of the second week came, and the only parts of the dresser that were done were the inside, the back, and the bottom. Now began the difficult process of smoothing the intricate carvings on the front of the drawers. Hans was getting sick of this job.

Everything he ate now tasted like fish, and no matter how hard he tried, he could not get the smell out of his clothes. Even so, his dream of being a great craftsman caused him to do better. On Sunday, he had managed to find a merchant who had a small silk handkerchief that he could afford. When he thought Johann was not looking, he would take it out and check where he was working before asking Johann. When a piece was perfectly smooth, Johann would pat Hans on the back and wink.

Time was running out, and Hans was afraid that he would not be able to see the piece completed and varnished. He had never dreamed it would take all month to prepare the dresser for varnishing. He had resigned himself to the fact that his entire time would be spent smoothing. Then, on his next-to-last day, Johann asked him if he would return to the shop after he had eaten his supper. Hans did as he was asked, and Johann was waiting for him when he arrived.

"Hans, you have done a wonderful job. I think we are ready to varnish this."

"Are you sure?" Hans asked, afraid to rush a job now that he had invested so much time in it.

"I am glad you asked. I want you to take that silk handkerchief you have hidden in your pocket and go over every inch of the dresser. If you find just one place that it snags, we will go home and smooth more tomorrow."

Hans did as he was instructed. He carefully removed all the drawers and checked the inside. Then he went over every crack, crevice, and carving of the outside. Finally, he looked at Johann and checked the back and the bottom of the dresser. When he finished, he turned to see Johann smiling like a child at Christmas.

"Well?"

"I can't find a single snag."

"Marvelous! Now I want you to get every oil lamp you can find and turn them up as high as they will go. I will get the rags and the varnish and start applying the finish."

"OK, but why are we doing it at night? Wouldn't it be better to do it in the daylight?"

"The lighting would be better, Hans, but the air would be full of sawdust from the other workers. This way we will be sure to get a finish that is perfect and not just good enough."

"I never thought of that. I'd hate to waste all our hard work now."

"That's the spirit, Hans! Let's get started."

Deep into the night, they worked on the dresser. They took great care that every detail of the carvings received an even coat of varnish. Hans watched with wide-eyed amazement as Johann worked. It was evident that he loved being a craftsman and putting his very self into his furniture. By midnight, they had finished varnishing. They were both exhausted, but pleased to be done. They cleaned up and called it a night.

"Hans, it will take many more coats, but I am very happy that we got the first one on. Sleep fast tonight. Morning will be here soon."

The next morning, Hans skipped breakfast and slept as long as he could. Just before seven o'clock, he dragged himself out of bed and stumbled into his clothes. It was nice to smell varnish on his hands, even though the fish smell still came through. He went into the shop and found all of the workers crowded around their workbench. The way they were murmuring, he was worried that something had happened to the dresser. Hans made his way through the workers, and then he saw what they were talking about.

Hans just stood silent beside Johann and looked. Never had he seen a more beautiful piece of furniture. The morning sun made it come to life. After endless days of smoothing the dresser, he had lost its beauty in the work. But now it was a different piece.

"Almost takes your breath away, doesn't it, Hans?" Johann asked.

"Uh-huh," was all he could reply as he stood there with his mouth open.

All the days of endless smoothing and awful fish smell suddenly disappeared for Hans. He knew that even one less day of work would not have produced this result.

"Listen, Hans, we really can't work on it today because it is still tacky. I think we should go for a walk."

"Are you sure? What will the owner say?"

"I think it will be all right. Come, let's go."

With that, they left the shop. Though there was still snow on the ground, it was a beautiful day filled with sunshine. They walked through the town and discussed many things. Hans told about his home, family, and youth. Johann said little as Hans went on about the places and people that he loved. He shared his dreams and fears.

Occasionally, Johann would interrupt just long enough to point out a place or building of interest. Finally, as they made their way back to the shop, Johann spoke.

"Hans, what have you learned this month?"

"Well, I learned a lot about smoothing and that I hate the smell of fish."

Johann laughed. "Is that all?"

"I guess so. Did I miss something?"

"You did not miss the lesson I gave you, but perhaps you missed its meaning."

"What meaning?" Hans asked curiously.

"Tell me something. If you had been in charge of the dresser, would you have taken so long to smooth it out?"

"No. I would have probably spent three or four days on it at the most."

"Why, Hans?"

"Mainly because I hate the smell of those skins. I guess that I hate the job of smoothing, too."

"Why?"

"I don't know. It always seems to go so slow, and you don't see any real results. It's a necessary evil of building furniture."

"I have known very few men who liked to smooth a piece of furniture. They are so excited about what they have built that they want to hurry up and varnish it."

"Yeah, that's exactly how I feel. I mean, you are so close after the construction phase to seeing your work come to life that it just seems like the smoothing just stands in your way."

"After seeing our dresser this morning, are you glad that we spent the whole month working on it?"

"Of course, who wouldn't be?"

"The sad thing, Hans, is many never see their furniture come to life like our dresser because they never have the patience to smooth it properly."

"Patience? It seems like perseverance is a better word."

"No, Hans, it is patience. More men have lost out on greatness because of a lack of patience than any other virtue. Men who were not geniuses, of great talent, or didn't have a golden opportunity have become great in their trade with the tool of patience."

"But I always thought that patience was just the absence of drive or desire in a man."

"That is what most people think, but they are wrong. Patience is the ultimate display of self-discipline. It takes great courage and strength to be patient. We could have varnished the dresser two weeks ago, but we would have done it at the cost of greatness. Between every dream and its reality is a road wrought with frustration and hard work. Many start the journey, but only the patient finishes."

"Why, Johann? Why do so many quit along the way?"

"Because they lose sight of the destination. When I was an apprentice, I was taught the importance of knowing what your creation will look like when it is done properly. Most men can only see the work of today and not the destination of tomorrow. Mind you, it is not just in making furniture that a man needs patience."

"You mean other trades?"

"No, I mean other areas of your life."

"Like what?"

"Well, one day you will meet a young girl and marry. Everything will be marvelous for the first couple of weeks, and then you will realize that you have married a stranger. If you do not have the destination of a long, happy marriage in your mind, you may quit because of the work that it takes for two people to learn to share their lives.

One day that girl will give you children. They will be darling and cute right up to the point where they learn to talk. Then you find out they have a mind of their own. You must have patience to see them through to the dream you have for them to grow into happy and productive adults. The sorrow I have seen is when parents give up on their children before the journey is over. Life takes patience, Hans."

"How do I learn this, Johann?"

"By using both sets of eyes that God gave you."

"What?"

"God gave you the eyes in your head to see what you are doing with your hands that it may be done well. He also gave you eyes in your mind to see the end of the journey, so you do not grow tired of what your other eyes see you doing. Some call it faith, others a dream, and some a vision, but it is the ability to see clearly in your mind the completion of the task that God has given you to do this day."

By now, they had returned to the shop, and the other workers were just leaving. Each one shook Hans's hand, wished him well, and congratulated him on the beauty of the dresser. Hans beamed with pride and occasionally looked at Johann. His look told Johann that he was grateful for his patient instruction and the privilege to share in such a magnificent accomplishment. Johann would just wink and smile each time Hans looked at him.

The two said their farewells, and after everyone had left, Hans ate his supper in the shop. He just sat and looked at the dresser as the sun slowly sank. As the horizon turned pink and purple, the dresser reflected the colors of the wood. Hans could not move or say a word; he just sat and watched until the light was gone.

Early the next morning, Hans went to the station and purchased his ticket for Genus, which was four days away. He loaded up, and as the stage drove out of town, it passed by the furniture shop. As they drove by, Johann came running alongside the carriage.

"Hans! Hans, wait, I have forgotten something ."

Looking Further

As the carriage drove away, Hans heard the sound of someone running on the cobblestones. The steps were fast and uneven as though the runner was about to fall. He looked back to see Johann running as fast as he could to catch the carriage, but he was running out of steam. He was huffing and puffing to the point that he was no longer able to talk. Without a word, Johann reached up and handed Hans a package just before the carriage went around a corner.

Hans watched Johann stop and bend over, gasping for air. Hans looked at the package, and on it was written a note asking him to tell Father hello from Johann. Hans could not figure out how these people knew his father because he never remembered Father leaving their village to go further than the main road. He shrugged it off and took out his paper, and began a letter to Father.

Dear Father,

I am on my way to the port city of Genus. I am doing well. I really enjoyed the shop at Patientia. It was smaller than the first one, but they produced very fine work. I was able to help a man named Johann finish his work on a dresser for a nobleman. It is exactly the kind of work that I would

like to do. He was able to help me smooth out some of my
rough edges. Please tell Mother that I love her and that I
have gotten her a very nice silk handkerchief.

Hans

At the end of the first day, they had driven out of the forest onto the plains. Hans missed the trees but enjoyed being able to see for miles. By the third day, winter assaulted them. The North wind began to blow with anger as though it was punishing them for leaving the safety of the forest. Like a relentless army, the dirt and the snow invaded every crack and crevice of the carriage. The carriage was rocking back and forth so hard that the driver could hardly keep it on the road.

Hans did not know how the driver even knew where the road was since the ground blizzard had turned the scenery into a sea of blinding white. It was strange to see the snow blowing so hard with blue skies above. On two separate occasions, the carriage had to stop because snowdrifts had blocked the road.

Hans and the others would help the driver clear a path by digging with anything they could find. The snow and wind stung them as they dug for hours, trying to make enough of a pathway for the carriage to get through. Finally, by the fourth day, the wind had died down, and they were nearing the sea.

Genus was one of the largest port cities in the country, and Hans had always dreamed of seeing it. As they descended from the plains to the city, he could see the masts of all the sailing ships in the harbor. They reminded Hans of a dead forest because there were so many masts sticking up. He tried several times to count how many ships there were, but the masts all ran together, and he would lose count at thirty to thirty-five. The majority of the country's goods flowed through here, and it was rare for the port to be closed because of ice.

Hans closed his eyes and breathed deeply as the smell of the salt water rose up the hill and greeted them. He was glad to be close to the sea and away from the bitter cold of the interior. His feet began to bounce uncontrollably with excitement as he strained to see more of the city. He had a feeling that this would be one of the most exciting towns on his journey. His anticipation of the city was so overwhelming that it had made him forget about the shop where he would be working.

The road took them south of the city and along the docks. Hans looked awestruck at all the great ships and the massive amounts of cargo being loaded onto them. All of the sailors were yelling and motioning as the freight was being lifted high onto the ships. The groaning of the dock men and the straining of their muscles under the heavy loads blended with the creaking of ropes and the crackling of the tackles into a symphony of motion and sound.

Hans wanted to stop time as the sights and sounds excited all of his senses, and he wondered if one day it would be his furniture being loaded onto one of these great ships. The sailor's life seemed so rugged and exciting that for a moment, he wondered if it might be a better life than that of a craftsman. Then he remembered the smell of the fish hides back in Patientia, and he thought that a ship may smell fishy all the time.

The carriage turned into the city and passed the market where the merchants were selling goods from all over the world. The orderly symphony of the docks was quickly replaced by the confusion of the merchants calling out to the shoppers as they tried to lure them to their goods. Sellers and buyers were arguing as butcher's cleavers continuously slammed against their tables like an unofficial auctioneer's gavel signifying the closing of all the negotiations.

Children cried as they impatiently waited for their mothers to buy their daily provisions while stray dogs darted in and out of the tables, hoping to find a discarded treasure to eat. Hans could not take it in fast enough, and he determined that every day he had off work would be spent in the market. He had managed to save a small amount of money, and perhaps he could find a treasure to take home.

The carriage arrived at the station, and Hans departed on foot to find the furniture shop. The shop was hidden deep within the city, and Hans had to walk a long way to get to it. His path took him past noisy taverns and dilapidated buildings. The interior of the city blocked out the sky and took on a character of its own. He had seen taverns in most of the towns he had been in, but not so many.

The streets assumed an eerie life of their own as the smell of stale beer and the blood of countless fights assaulted him. Just then, a fight from one of the taverns spilled out onto the street, and if it had not been for quick footwork, Hans would have gone down with the brawlers. He found himself a bit scared and did not stay to watch, but quickly made his way out of this man-made bedlam. Fortunately, Father's directions led him right to the front door of the furniture shop, and he quickly went in to escape the streets.

"What do you want?" a gruff voice asked. Hans was so startled by the man that he just stood there.

"Well, speak up or get out. I've got work to do."

"I am Hans, son of Frederick the craftsman."

"Who?"

"Hans."

"Oh, you're that apprentice kid from Crescere."

"Yes, sir," Hans replied sheepishly.

"The man you want is back there," he said as he yelled out, "Hey,

Rafael, that kid you've been expecting is here." Without another word, the man went back to work.

Hans looked back to the center of the shop to see a middle-aged man of slight build coming toward him. The shop was a beehive of activity as people yelled at each other while working at their benches. It was poorly lit and messy. Sawdust, wood shavings, and scraps of lumber lay everywhere. Hans was startled by all of this and was only brought back to reality by a kind voice.

"Hans?" The man asked. "I have been expecting you. My name is Rafael and I will be working with you this month. I am very glad to meet you," the man said as he extended his hand to Hans.

"It's nice to meet you, too," Hans said, quite relieved to find a friendly face.

"I want you to come and meet the other two apprentices who work for me. Since we market our furniture all over the world, we are a very busy shop. Each craftsman has from two to five apprentices and a couple of journeymen working under him," Rafael said as he led Hans to their work area.

The group that Rafael oversaw worked in the middle of the shop. Patterns and jigs were hanging from the ceiling, and Hans had to be careful not to hit his head on some of them. The floor was covered with sawdust, and tools were strewn all over the benches. He quickly figured out that there was no wasted time or motion in this shop, and he would have to be on his toes. Unlike shops that worked at a slower pace, these fast-paced shops demanded that an apprentice work his hardest because there were plenty of eager replacements wanting to take his place.

"Boys, come here," Rafael called out, and the two that Hans had assumed were the apprentices came running. "I want you to meet someone who will be working with you. Hans, this is Franz and Martin. Hans comes from out of town, and I want you two to show him the ropes. Now let's start cleaning up for the day."

As Rafael turned to go back to his work, Martin hastily wiped his hand off on his pants and extended it to Hans with a smile.

"It's nice to meet you, Hans," Martin said. "You will like working for Rafael; he is a fair man."

Hans then extended his hand to Franz, who just stood there and glared at him.

"Don't expect me to babysit you. I don't know what you did to get into this shop, but you'd better carry your weight. Just stay out of my way," Franz said with obvious annoyance.

Hans was taken aback by this sudden and unprovoked hostility.

Franz turned to start cleaning up, and Martin placed his hand on Hans's shoulder.

"Don't mind him," Martin said. "He was born with a chip on his shoulder. I just stay out of his way, and I would advise you to do the same."

Hans pitched in with Martin for clean up and tried not to get in the way. He thought it would look good to Rafael if he jumped right in and helped. The younger apprentices started picking up the wood scraps from the floor. They carefully set aside those big enough to reuse and hauled the rest out the back of the shop.

Others started picking up the tools on the benches and returned them to their proper tool chests. The remainder swept the floor and hauled out bushel baskets of sawdust. By closing time, the floor was spotless and all the benches were cleared of tools. As everyone was leaving, Rafael came over to Hans and Martin.

"Martin," Rafael began, "would you be so good as to show Hans to the apprentice quarters and help him get settled in?"

"Yes, sir," Martin replied sheepishly. It was obvious that he was intimidated by Rafael.

"We'll see you boys bright and early tomorrow," Rafael said as he turned to go. Martin and Hans put their brooms away on the rack, and Hans picked up his bag.

Martin led him upstairs to a large room with two rows of cots. It was just an attic with a floor that was covered with dust from the shop below. There was a walkway down the middle and a window at each end of the room. There wasn't a ceiling in the room, just the bare rafters that left enough room down the middle to stand up.

"You can bunk next to me," Martin said as they stood at the top of the stairs looking at the room. "Just put your bag on one of the beds at the end of the room on the right, and we'll go wash up before we eat."

Hans did as Martin said and followed him outside to a well house where all the other boys were washing up. They waited their turn and made their way up to a large waist high-water trough. It felt good to get the road dust washed off, and Hans was feeling much better as he went back to their room. He and Martin made small talk as they walked between the beds to the far end. Hans began to scan the beds for his duffel bag, but he couldn't find it.

"Martin, do you see my bag anywhere? I know that I left it right down here."

"No, I don't see it," Martin said as he looked around the room.

"You don't mean that ugly old brown duffel bag, do you?"

Hans turned to see who was talking to him. On the bed where he had laid his duffel was Franz. He was propped up on one elbow and looking very smug.

"What did you do with my bag?" Hans asked.

"Well, whoever's bag it was, it was on my bed and it took a flying trip across the room."

"Hey, is this it?" one of the other boys called from the other end of the room, holding up Hans's duffel.

"You threw my bag to the other end of the room?" Hans asked Franz as the tension in his voice began to rise.

"Hey, it was on my bed. If you don't want it thrown around, then you better not put it here again," Franz said as he lay back and put his hands behind his head.

"My tools were in that bag, and you could have broken them. Was it too much for you to just set it on another bed?" Hans felt his jaw tighten and his pulse quicken. "Listen, I don't know what your problem is..."

Before Hans could finish, Franz shot up off his bunk and grabbed Hans by the collar and got right in his face.

"You listen to me, boy. You think you can just come in here and do what you want cause your father owns his own shop. Well, that don't mean nothing around here, and it sure don't mean nothing to me. You stay out of my way. Understand?"

Hans had had all he wanted of this guy, and he pushed him back. Franz came back in an instant and took a swing at Hans. Without thinking, Hans ducked the punch and came back up to look at Franz face to face. Both boys stood there stunned; Franz that he had not landed the punch, and Hans that things had escalated so fast. The hesitation they both had was just enough to allow them each to think. Franz hoped that he had made his point clear, but he was still taken aback by the quick duck. Hans realized that this was no way to make a good impression on his first day.

Hans looked out of the corner of his eye at Martin, who shook his head and motioned with his hands to just let it go. Hans just raised his hands to Franz and backed off. Franz backed up and flopped down on his bunk as he glared at Hans. The room was utterly silent, as all the other boys waited to see what would happen. As soon as they realized that the fight was over, they slowly started murmuring and went back to their beds.

The empty bunk next to Martin was also right next to Franz. Martin traded places with Hans and took the one next to Franz as a precaution. Hans was furious that night as he tossed and turned for hours. He lay there and wondered why Father had made him go on this ridiculous journey. By now, he would have been done with his apprenticeship had he stayed home. What he wouldn't give to be here as a journeyman so he could put Franz in his place.

The next morning, Hans kept his distance, but he noticed Franz's glare each time their eyes happened to meet. He was glad that the work group was large enough that they each worked at a different bench. By mid-morning, he had forgotten all about the friction with Franz and was focusing on his work. He was working with two journeymen on a buffet, and he was enjoying the project very much. At night, he spent his time talking to Martin and the other boys. It wasn't hard to avoid Franz because he pretty much kept to himself. The other boys also seemed to avoid him, even though they respected him when contact was unavoidable.

The week went well until Saturday afternoon. Hans had been asked to go out back and select a board from the stacks for some trim work. He was carefully sorting through the boards for just the right one when he looked up and found the right one about four boards down from the top. As he was setting the top boards off, he looked up to see the stack falling. He tried to get out of the way, but he was not quick enough. The boards knocked him to the ground, and one caught him right in the face, bloodying his nose. Still lying under a dozen boards and trying to get his wits about him, he looked to the end of the stack to see Franz standing there with a grin.

"Have a little accident, pretty boy?" Franz asked. "You should be more careful. You could get hurt real bad around here."

Hans went to jump up, but as he did, pain shot through his leg. One of the boards had caught him in the shin, and he couldn't get up. Franz just laughed and walked back to the shop. Hans lay there and rubbed his leg for a few minutes until he could get up and walk it off. He limped back into the shop, carrying the board, knowing that after work, he would have to go out and re-stack the wood. He figured that would give him plenty of time to plan his revenge.

After they cleaned the shop, he went out to start stacking the wood. Martin noticed what he was doing and came over to help.

"What happened?" Martin asked.

"It seems that Franz helped the stack fall over on me. You just wait, though, when I get back to the room, there will be some answering to do. I've had all I can stand from that guy. Win or lose, I'm not gonna put up with any more of his guff."

"Well, you're gonna have to wait until Monday if you want to even the score with Franz."

"No, Martin, today is the day. We are gonna settle this thing once and for all."

"That's what I'm trying to tell you, Hans. Franz is gone and won't be back until Monday morning."

"What are you talking about?"

"Since his family lives in the city, he goes home from Saturday night until Monday morning. All of the boys from town do the same thing."

"You mean that I don't have to look at his ugly face until Monday?"

"That's right," Martin said, raising his eyebrows and smiling.

One whole day without Franz was all Hans needed to hear to take the thunder out of his rage. He just began to laugh as they stacked the rest of the boards. As soon as they were finished, they washed up and went to their bunk room. The atmosphere was very relaxed on this night, and the other boys were laughing and playing around. Hans wasn't sure if the light heartiness was due to Franz being gone or the fact that they all had tomorrow off. He and Martin decided to go ahead and do their laundry so they could spend the whole next day at the market.

The following morning, they arose early and ate breakfast at a bakery on the way to the market. Hans was glad that Martin was going with him because he wasn't sure of what to see first. Martin had been to the market many times and knew all the best places to go.

Hans was amazed at how Martin would barter with the merchants and get great deals. Hans didn't buy anything, but looked to get some gift ideas for Mother. All too soon, the day was coming to an end, and it was time to get back to the shop for a good night's sleep.

As Hans lay in bed that night, he began to think about Franz and how he would handle the next day. He wanted to make things very clear to Franz as soon in the day as he could, but he knew he would have to be careful. Saturday night, he was ready to go out behind the shop and slug it out with Franz, but that would not be the way to handle it in the shop. He decided to wait for the right moment, hoping it would come.

The next morning, Hans dreaded the prospect of having to go back to the shop and face Franz. Franz was about his size, but Hans wasn't sure that he could take him in a fight. Each Monday, Rafael had the practice of rotating the apprentices so they could work with a different group of journeymen on different projects. That morning, he was assigned to a bench right next to Franz. He kept track of where Franz was at all times to the point that he was occasionally distracted from his own work. He was irritated because Franz acted like nothing had happened on Saturday.

Just before lunch, Hans got the opportunity he had been looking for. He had been at the sharpening bench working on a chisel and was returning to his bench when he noticed Franz bent over, picking something up. Franz had not noticed Hans coming toward him. Hans held the chisel out waist high and walked right up to Franz as he stood up. Franz froze just halfway up when he saw the razor-sharp chisel less than an inch from his face. Suddenly, Franz's expression showed that he remembered the score that needed to be settled.

As Franz looked up at Hans, Hans just glared down at him.

"You're right, Franz, accidents can happen around here, to EV-ERYONE," Hans said, and returned to his bench without another word. For the rest of the day, Franz was visibly shaken, but by Tuesday, he had gotten over it.

He no longer made any flagrant attacks on Hans, but for the next two weeks, he still managed to get his jabs in. It was just little things like purposely bumping into Hans or dropping something as he was handing it to him. Hans decided that he was only there for a month, and since he wasn't entirely sure he could take Franz, he would just let it slide and settle for an occasional glare at Franz. Hans had felt that he had found a way to manage the situation until Saturday of the third week.

It was at the end of the day, and Rafael had told them to clean up. They were the last group to start the clean-up, and only two brooms were left. Martin had already gotten one broom, and Hans was closest to the rack to get the last one. As he reached for it, he felt an elbow slam into his side. The blow sent him flying away from the rack, and as he fell, his head went right into the side of the wood stove. As his head hit the side of the cast iron stove, he felt a stinging pain as it burned his ear. He flinched away from the stove and grabbed his ear as he looked up and saw Franz walking away with the last broom.

Hans exploded. He sprang to his feet and took off in the direction of Franz. He didn't think of the consequences of a fight in the shop, nor did he consider winning or losing. He only wanted to tear Franz apart and deal with the repercussions later. Halfway to Franz, an arm swept around his waist and picked him completely off the floor. He spun his head around to see who was so arrogant as to rob him of his vengeance, and he looked right into the face of Rafael.

Even though Rafael was not a large man, he was incredibly strong. With his arm still around Hans's waist, he slung him under his arm like a sack of feed and took him right out the back door of the shop. Hans uselessly struggled and kicked all the way outside until Rafael set him down.

"Come on, Hans, let's tend to that ear," Rafael said.

As Rafael started for the well house, Hans bolted for the door of the shop. Rafael caught him before he got far and carried him out to the well house, where he firmly sat him down.

"Stay!" Rafael commanded as Hans stewed.

Rafael drew some fresh, cool water and soaked a rag in it. Hans flinched in pain as Rafael pressed the rag against his ear.

"Just hold that there for a while and listen to me," Rafael said. "Here's the deal I will make with you. I saw what Franz did and has been doing ever since you got here. The problem is that I don't think you really want to fight him. Now ..."

"You just let me back in that shop and I'll show you how bad I want to clean his plow," Hans snapped.

"Hans, you just give it until Monday, and if you still want to fight him, then I'll bring you both out back and let you have at it."

"Why wait till Monday? Bring him out here now, and I'll take care of it."

"Well, Hans, I could do that, but you don't know enough to fight him."

"What do you mean? I've done just fine in my share of fights. I'm mad enough right now that I could whip the whole shop."

"You just stay right where you are until closing and keep that rag on your ear. I'll be back to get you after he has left for the day," Rafael said and went back into the shop.

Hans would have his revenge. Even though he had been raised by his father not to fight, there was only so much that a person could or should have to take. His ear stung, his head had a knot coming up, and his side was sore. He thought that Monday might be better so that he could heal a little.

Before long, Rafael returned and removed the rag to check his ear.

"Well, it's going to be sore for a while, but I don't think that there is any permanent damage. Can you walk?"

"Yes," Hans replied, a lot calmer now.

"Good, follow me."

"Where are we going?"

"You'll see," Rafael replied as he helped Hans up. They went down the alley to the main street and headed north. They walked through a part of town that Hans had not seen yet. Like most of the city, every other building was a tavern. It always seemed that as the evening wore on, the streets grew alive and became a different place as the brawlers and drunks took over the streets.

As darkness fell, Hans walked close to Rafael, and they continued through town. He was glad to be with an adult, as the buildings and homes looked worse. The streets narrowed and became like caverns beneath the buildings. Soon, they were approaching the edge of town. There were fewer people now, and Hans could see that they were following a figure about a hundred yards in front of them.

On the outskirts of town, the homes thinned out, and the streets gave way to open fields with scattered shacks. They followed for about another half mile, and then Rafael grabbed Hans's arm and stopped him.

"This is far enough," Rafael said softly.

"What are we doing here?" Hans asked.

"Just watch, Hans," Rafael said as he pointed to the figure they had been following.

The figure approached one of the shanties where a man was sitting on a stool in front of it. They had not gotten close enough to make out who it was in the dark, but they could hear them.

"It's about time you got your sorry self here," the man sitting on the stool said. His speech was slurred, and he was obviously drunk as he tried to get up. "Did you get paid today?" he asked.

"Yes, sir," the figure replied. Hans knew the voice instantly; it was Franz.

"Let's have it," the man said as he put his hand out. Franz pulled out a small pouch that contained his meager apprentice's pay.

"Hey, this isn't your full pay," the man growled.

"This was the week that we were required to buy a tool, Father. Each month we are to buy one tool so that when I am a journeyman I will have what I need," Franz said apologetically.

"You stupid brat," the man yelled, grabbing Franz by the collar. "I send you there to earn money, not to spend it."

"But Father," Franz started.

The man slapped Franz across the face, jerking his head around.

"Don't sass me, boy." He slapped him again. "You tell that boss of yours that your family needs that money. Now get in the house!" With that, the man threw Franz towards the door and kicked him. "You're worthless just like your mother."

Hans just stood there in the darkness with his mouth open. He had never seen anything like this in his life. Animals treated their young better than this man did. Rafael broke the silence.

"Seen enough?" he asked.

"Yes, can we go now?" Hans said, turning away from the sight.

They started back into town and walked in silence. Hans didn't know if he wanted to cry or throw up. The image of Franz being humiliated like that kept running through his mind again and again. He just wanted to go back to the shop and wash the awful scene away. He no longer thought about his pain, just the inhumanity of the night. Finally, Hans spoke.

"How did you know about that?"

"I worked with Franz's father years ago in the shop. I watched him as he began to drink more and more until he lost his position there. He got to where he had to borrow tools all the time because he had sold all of his to buy more ale and wine."

"Why does someone like that even have kids?" Hans asked.

"Oh, it wasn't always like that. I remember when Franz was a little boy. I remember that he was the joy of his father's life. Then, as the drink took over, he became an annoyance. I saw him hit Franz the first time when he was about eight. His father used to feel bad about it, so he drank more and more until he felt nothing."

"So how did Franz ever get on at the shop?"

"I took him on, hoping that I could help him create a better life. Sometimes I think that there is hope, and then days like today make me wonder."

The rest of the way back to the shop, the two were silent. Neither could believe that anyone would have to live in such a way as Franz. Hans spent the next day reliving the horror of what had happened. Martin kept asking him what was wrong as they walked through the market, but Hans remained silent and sometimes did not even hear Martin's queries.

That night, he lay awake, wondering how he should act towards Franz the next day. He knew that he could not say anything about what he had seen or Franz would know that they had followed him. Hans now understood why Franz resented the fact that his father owned his own shop.

The next morning, he was still unsure how to act and very nervous about seeing Franz. He was already in the shop getting the tools out when Franz arrived.

"I'll bet you're glad this is your last week. I know that I am," Franz said as he arrived at his bench.

"Yeah, next week I'll be in Bonum," Hans said in passing as he kept getting out tools for the journeymen.

"Good riddance," Franz muttered under his breath.

The week wasn't any different than the others except that Hans did not react when Franz was rude. He tried to be as nice as he could, but his tolerance just met with more resistance. He had never known anyone so angry in his life.

He thought about how he could change things between him and Franz, but the week ended before he could think of anything. There had just been too much that had happened between them, and no matter what he tried, he could not overcome Franz's resentment. At quitting time on Saturday, he followed Franz outside the shop to talk to him as he left.

"Franz, wait," Hans called out as he ran to catch up to him. "I wanted to give you something."

"Leave me alone, pretty boy," Franz said as he kept walking.

"Please wait," Hans pleaded.

"What?" Franz snapped.

"I wanted to give you something before I leave tomorrow," Hans said as he handed a small pouch to Franz.

"What's this?" Franz asked defiantly as he opened the pouch. Inside was the amount of money that the apprentices were to use for their tools each month. "What is this for, pretty boy?"

"Well, I wasn't very nice to you this month, and I guess that it's my way of saying I'm sorry."

"Rafael talked to you, didn't he?"

"No."

"I don't need your pity or charity, pretty boy. You can keep your stupid money," Franz said as he threw the pouch back at Hans and walked away.

Hans felt his face become flushed, and the nerves in his stomach were so bad that he could not even mutter a word as Franz walked away. He was embarrassed by his self-righteous attempt to make things better for Franz. He had hoped to be some kind of saint and rescue Franz from his situation. Instead, he had only managed to alienate him more.

He had never felt so helpless and awkward in his life. For the first time on his journey, he wished that he could stay just a little longer and make things right, but he couldn't. The next day, he had a ticket for the trip to Bonum. He had failed.

Bonum was also a port city, much smaller than Genus, which was just across the bay to the South. Hans was scheduled to catch a ship the next morning. He spent the night packing his bag and saying goodbye to the other boys. He went to bed and tried to sleep, but all he could think about was Franz and how isolated he was. He saw the sight of Franz's father beating and kicking him, and he thought of his own father. For the first time since he had left home, he deeply missed Father.

The next morning, as he was leaving the shop to go to the docks, Rafael walked up to him.

"Looks like you're all ready to leave us, Hans," Rafael said with a smile and a pat on the back.

"Yes, sir, I have to catch a ship to Bonum."

"I know, I'm headed there today also. It seems that we have some furniture being carried over, and the head craftsman wants me to see it safely to the freight hauler in Bonum. We have had some trouble with shipments being damaged on the ship, and this is a very important customer."

Hans wasn't necessarily looking forward to company on the ride, but at least he would know someone. They made their way to the docks and watched as the crates containing the furniture were hoisted onto the ship. By mid-morning, they were ready to leave and boarded for the four-hour trip. Hans was somewhat excited because he had never been on any kind of ship before. He made his way to the front and leaned against the railing.

From there, he could watch the bow cut through the water, and behind him, he could see the sailors manning the sails. The smell of the saltwater spray coming off the front of the ship made him forget the events of the past month, and he closed his eyes, taking in all the strange new sensations. As he enjoyed the spray and the sun on his face, he was interrupted by a voice.

"There you are, Hans. I've been looking for you." Hans turned to see Rafael standing behind him. "I'll bet that you have had a lot on your mind this week."

"Yes, sir", Hans said as Rafael leaned on the railing next to him.

"I have something that I want to give you," Rafael said, holding out a small package.

"What is it?" Hans asked as he took it.

"Open it and see."

Hans began to unwrap the package with a smile of excitement. Inside the brown paper was a small cylinder with glass ends. Hans asked, "What is it?"

"It is a ship captain's telescope. Here, let me show you how it works." Rafael said as he took it and pulled at both ends. The telescope made two distinct clicks as it was pulled to its full length. "Here, Hans, put the small end up to your eye and point the other end at the crow's nest. Like this." Rafael demonstrated how to use the telescope.

Hans took the strange-looking little device and used it like Rafael had. As he looked through it, he smiled and removed it from his eye to be sure that he was really looking at something a long way off.

"That's amazing! Thank you very much," Hans said as he took

another look around the ship through the telescope.

"Hans, I want you to always remember what you learned here when you look at that telescope."

"I don't understand. What does a telescope have to do with furniture making?"

"It doesn't have anything to do with furniture building, Hans. It has to do with Franz."

"Oh, I had almost forgotten that. I tried to do something nice for him yesterday, and it was a total fiasco. I just decided that you can't be nice to someone like that."

"Quite the contrary, Hans. The thing that people need the most, they usually deserve the least. Franz is the kind of boy who takes a lot of kindness."

"Well, I'll admit that I feel sorry for him, but he doesn't have to act like a bully to everyone else."

"No, you're right, and no one has to show him kindness either. But that does not mean that one CANNOT show him kindness."

"I tried, Rafael. Really, I did."

"Hans, what you gave to Franz was pity, which is the lowest form of kindness."

"Well, I didn't know that he had such a hard life at home or what his father was like. Maybe if you had told me sooner, I would have had a chance to be kinder to him and make friends."

"It shouldn't have mattered."

"Of course it would have. I'm not so insensitive to treat someone like Franz like he deserves."

"Hans, you didn't treat him differently until you knew why he needed our kindness. There are a lot of people like Franz in this world, and you can't follow everyone around to find out what makes them so bitter and angry. No, Hans, true kindness is that which we give to others without their deserving. You see, deserving has nothing to do with true kindness."

"I don't understand, Rafael," Hans said, puzzled at why he was getting this lecture when Franz was the problem.

"Tell me something, Hans, how did you feel this week compared to the three weeks prior?"

"I don't know. I guess that I wasn't so mad about how Franz acted toward me. I mean, I understood that he was mad and embarrassed about his father, so I didn't take it personally."

"That's right, Hans. You have learned a great lesson. Kindness is something that we choose to give to all people, and not just those who deserve it. In reality, no man deserves it, but all men need it. You cannot change another person, nor can you make them accept your kindness, but you can still give it. It will take something very special or tragic in Franz's life to open his heart, but it is our kindness that begins to prepare the way. That's what the telescope will remind you of."

"What?"

"That sometimes we need to use kindness to see beyond what our eyes show us in another man. There are events in a man's life that shape him for better or worse, and we cannot always see those things. We must use kindness to see beyond the outward appearance to where we treat all men kindly. We also need to use the telescope to remind us to look deep into our own hearts and see our motives. Usually, we are only kind to those who return our kindness. If we truly possess kindness that is pure, then we will give it to all, deserving or not."

Hans knew that Rafael was right. He had treated Martin well because he was nice to Hans, but he had treated Franz just like his father had. Hans wanted to beat Franz just like his father had done.

"Hans, never give men what they deserve; give them what you have decided to give them. A real man does not live by his feelings, but rather by his decisions. Hey, let me see that telescope."

Rafael took the telescope and looked far out to the horizon. He handed the telescope back to Hans and pointed into the distance.

"Look that way, Hans, and tell me what you see."

"Is that Bonum?" Hans said with a laugh. "How far away are we?"

"About twelve miles, we should be there in an hour."

As the town neared, Hans continued to use the telescope to survey the city. The heart of the city ran along the front of the bay with houses going up the hill inland. As they were approaching the dock, he could see the ladies beating their rugs on the front porches of the homes on the hill. From the dock, he could even tell the time on the clock tower five blocks away.

The ship docked, and he stayed with Rafael to watch the workers unload. Hans was looking out across the bay when he thought he saw another ship coming in. He pulled out the telescope and was trying to find the ship when he heard a voice screaming at him.

"HANS!"

He looked around and froze in terror.

A Generous Soul

Suddenly, everything seemed to be moving in slow motion for Hans. As he looked around, all the faces that he could see were pale and silent. He knew from the way they were looking at him and backing away that something very bad was about to happen... to him. Just then, out of the corner of his eye, he saw Rafael lunging at him. Rafael hit him with the force of a raging bull, and the two of them were thrown onto a pile of fishing nets just as a large crate crashed onto the dock where Hans had been standing. Hans just lay there, wide-eyed, as the people screamed and tried to get out of the way of the flying debris. Rafael got up first and then helped Hans, who had still not closed his mouth.

"Well, now I know what has been happening to our furniture. I'm just glad I came along to take care of the furniture maker."

"I could have been killed," Hans stammered.

"No, Hans, you WERE almost killed. Just stand here out of the way and look up often. Our furniture is coming off the ship as soon as they fix the rigging that just broke. Afterwards, we'll get some lunch and I will take you over and introduce you to Sebastian, the man you will be working with here."

Hans just shook his head yes because he was in shock. He was still somewhat shaky on his feet, so Rafael propped him up against a post and went to watch the unloading. The dock workers seemed unaffected by the accident, as though it was commonplace, and Hans didn't notice that Rafael was yelling at the dock foreman about the rigging. With much arguing and fussing, the furniture was unloaded and safely in the wagons after about an hour. Hans was still leaning on the dock post when Rafael came over to him.

"You ready to go?" Rafael asked.

"I think so," Hans replied as Rafael took his arm and led him off the docks. "I think that was about the scariest thing that ever happened to me."

"Life is very scary sometimes, Hans. Just remember that you felt what Franz feels every Saturday night when he goes home. After a while, a man like Franz has to turn off all his feelings just to survive." They walked through the city, which was just a quarter of the size of Genus. Hans was glad for the slower pace and less crowded streets. Genus had been an adventure, but not very pleasing for him. He decided that when he came back to the city for good, it would be to a smaller town like Bonum, which was more to his liking. They found a small cafe for lunch, and Rafael insisted on paying. By the time lunch was over, Hans's nerves had calmed down enough that he was no longer shaking.

They walked to the South end of town, where there were neat but humble houses. They stopped at a small home with a well-kept yard and walked up the lane. They stepped up to the door, and Rafael knocked. After waiting for a few moments, a little gray-haired woman answered the door. As soon as she saw Rafael, she stepped out and hugged him.

"Rafael, you rascal, I didn't know that you were coming by. Come in and sit down," she said as she ushered him in.

"Now, Millie, I can't stay 'cause I have to catch a boat home in just a little while," Rafael protested.

"Oh, what a shame, have you eaten anything?"

"Yes, we ate in town 'cause you don't need to be spending your time in the kitchen, and I knew that you would if we had shown up without eating first."

With that, Millie playfully slapped Rafael on the arm and gave him another hug. Just then, an older man slowly walked into the room. His face was all aglow as he made his way to Rafael. He had a twinkle in his eye that made Hans ignore his age. The old man took Rafael into his arms without a word spoken as though he were a long-lost son who had come home.

"Sebastian, this is..." Rafael started with his introduction.

"This is Hans, son of Frederick. I would know this boy from across town cause he is the spitting image of his father," Sebastian said as he took Hans into his arms for a big hug.

Hans was startled by the old man's gesture, but he was also unable to resist his genuine affection. Hans half-heartily returned the hug and said hello.

"We have been so looking forward to your stay, Hans," Sebastian started. "You will be staying with Millie and me this month. She has a room all ready for you upstairs. Can I take your bag?"

"No, sir, that's OK," Hans said, feeling like he was missing something.

"Would you like something to eat, Hans?" Millie asked, "It wouldn't take me long to make something, and I'm sure that a growing young man like you could always eat."

"No, thank you, ma'am."

"Let's show you to your room, young man," Sebastian said as

he took Hans's bag.

Hans looked back at Rafael as Rafael gave him a wink to assure him that it was all right. They went upstairs to a beautifully decorated small room. Millie had followed them to see Hans's reaction to the room and make sure that it met his approval. Realizing this, Hans smiled and nodded as Millie beamed with pride. He placed his bag at the foot of the bed and waited for someone to break the silence.

"Well," Rafael finally said, "I have a boat to catch."

"Oh, Rafael, I wish that you didn't have to rush off," Millie pleaded.

"Now, Millie, I'll be back next month and bring the wife. I promise you that we will stay for a couple of days."

"I'll hold you to that, Rafael," Millie said as she patted him on the back and followed him to the door.

As Rafael was leaving, Hans began to fear being smothered by these two sweet old people. "Hey Rafael," Hans called out, "I'll walk you to the dock. That is if it's OK with you," he said, looking to Sebastian and Millie for approval.

"Sure, go ahead," Sebastian said with a smile and a wave since Hans was already halfway to the street.

When they were a safe distance from the house, Hans spoke up. "They sure are a loving old couple, aren't they?"

"A little much for you, Hans?" Rafael asked with a laugh.

"Well," Hans hesitated as he tried to find words which did not make him seem ungrateful for the hospitality he was shown. "I just haven't been around old people much, and I'm not sure how to take them."

"Don't let their old bodies fool you, Hans. Those are two of the youngest hearts you will ever find," Rafael said as he put his arm on

Hans's shoulder.

"You seem to know them pretty well. How does he know what Father looks like?"

"I wouldn't be alive today if it wasn't for those two," Rafael said turning serious. "You see, I grew up like Franz. My father was a drunk, and I had no mother. When I was about thirteen, my father finally drank himself to death, and I was left on my own. I was angry, scared and desperate. One thing led to another, and before I knew it, I had a very serious run-in with the king's soldiers. They were talking about sending me to prison, and that's when I first met Sebastian. He was good friends with the captain of the guard, and he offered to take me in and teach me woodworking."

"What did their kids think about that?" Hans asked.

"They never had any kids of their own. I took him up on his offer because I figured I could get out of going to prison. My plan was to take this gullible old man for all he was worth and then strike out on my own."

"So why didn't you?" Hans asked as he tried to imagine this kind man being like Franz.

"Everyone I had known in my life answered my anger with more anger. I had become a very good fighter, Hans, but there was no weapon I had to combat the love that Sebastian and Millie gave me. They saw something in me that I didn't, and they just kept believing in me until I was able to do it for myself. They are the only real parents I ever knew. This will be the pinnacle of your trip, Hans. Many people can teach you how to live, but Sebastian can teach you how to be alive."

They arrived at the dock just in time for Rafael to get aboard the ship. He had to run to get on before the gangplank was taken up. Hans stayed on the dock and waited as they set sail. Rafael found a place on the railing where he could wave to Hans. As they waved to each other, Rafael cupped his hands around his mouth and called out to Hans.

"Please give Frederick my greetings!"

There it was again, Hans thought, as he cringed at not knowing how these people all knew Father. He stomped his foot as he turned to go back to Sebastian's. He resolved that he would remember to ask Sebastian about this before the month was out. He took his time walking through town because he still wasn't anxious to get back. If he was lucky, Sebastian and Millie would go to bed early, and he would have time to write Father before he went to sleep.

As he feared, Sebastian and Millie were awaiting his return. Even though it had only been a couple of hours, Millie had to give him another hug. He accepted their invitation to sit down and visit with them. They wanted to know all about his journey and what he had seen and learned. Sebastian laughed until he cried when Hans related his experience with the fish skins. Evidently, it hadn't been long enough ago for Hans to find it humorous. He politely smiled as Sebastian laughed and Millie shook her head as if to apologize for his behavior. They were particularly interested in the men that Hans had worked with and how they were doing.

The evening passed quickly, despite Millie's frequent interruptions to run to the kitchen and check on supper. She prepared a feast for the three of them. Hans feared that he would never get his plate emptied because as soon as he got close, Millie piled it high again. Finally, Hans gave up and had to leave half a plate of food. After visiting around the kitchen table for a bit longer, Hans excused himself and went to his room to write to Father. He got ready for bed and climbed in with his paper, pen and ink to write.

Dear Father,

Genus was an interesting town. The work there was very hard and fast-paced. I had the chance to work with many different journeymen and a craftsman named Rafael. I would like for my furniture to be on the great ships one day. From Genus, I could send my furniture all over the world. I don't think I would like to live there because it's a very big city. I am now in Bonum. I am staying with a very old couple. They are nice, but they like to hug a lot. Tell Mother that I think I've found someone who can cook almost as good as she does.

Hans

Hans was glad to have a room to himself and quickly fell asleep. Morning came too soon, and Hans was slow to wake up when Sebastian called. He arrived downstairs to find Millie smiling and fixing up another mountain of food. He hoped that the walk to the shop was long enough for him to work off breakfast and wake up. As soon as they had finished eating, Sebastian kissed Millie goodbye, Hans got his hug from her with the added bonus of a kiss on the cheek, and they were off.

As they walked through town, the sun was just rising. Sebastian seemed to drink in the morning as if it were the first one he had ever seen. Hans felt like he was intruding on some special occasion. He was amazed at the old man's love for life as they sauntered along. Hans had to slow himself down so that he did not run off and leave Sebastian behind. Finally, he decided that it was safe to interrupt.

"Have you worked at this shop for a long time?" Hans asked.

"Oh, I don't just work at the shop, Hans, I own it. Or rather, I did own it, up until several months ago. I have sold the shop and I am working there to help the new owner until he knows what he is doing. Millie and I have decided that we should take some time for ourselves while we still have it."

"You own the shop?! That's exciting because I want to own my own shop one day," Hans said as he skipped to get alongside Sebastian.

"And so you shall, Hans," Sebastian said as he looked at Hans with a twinkle in his eye.

Hans pulled his shoulders back and held his head high. He could tell that Sebastian was serious about what he said. To his surprise, someone wasn't treating him like a starry-eyed kid. For the first time in a long while, Hans was excited to get to work. They went into the heart of town and entered a medium-sized shop. Inside, Hans saw one of the warmest and neatest shops that he had ever seen. The shop looked just like Sebastian acted, warm and sincere. All the workers were in a group, and the man in the middle was addressing them. Hans and Sebastian quietly walked over and joined them as the man spoke.

"Gentlemen, I want you to start being more careful with your lumber. I have noticed that there is a lot of waste. I want you to take your plans home at night before you start a new project, and work carefully on your cutting. I have figured that we have about 5% waste, and I would like that to be reduced to 2%," the man said.

Hans looked over at Sebastian. The old man just hung his head in deep thought and placed his hands in his pockets. It was clear to Hans that he didn't really agree with the man speaking to him. His eyebrows were wrinkled up like he was trying to decide if he should say something or not. Hans waited, but Sebastian never said a word. The man finished, and everyone started back to their workbenches. Sebastian spoke up.

"Hey everyone, I would like you to meet Hans from Crescere. He will be working with me, and I'd like you to help him anyway you can."

Everyone came over and shook Hans's hand, welcoming him. He and Sebastian made their way to the back of the shop, where his bench was located. On it was a very intricately carved mantle in process. Hans marveled at the fine detail of the carvings and the scenes that they depicted. The two uprights, which would hold the mantle, were of walnut and cherry. The mantle itself was of a solid slab of cherry. The cherry centers of the uprights and the mantle itself received the intricate carvings. Hans studied it and ran his hands over the figures.

"This will be my last project in the shop," Sebastian said as he watched Hans admire his work.

"Who is it for?" Hans asked as he continued to touch it.

"It's for Millie. She always joked that she would know we had succeeded when we had a carved mantle for her parlor room. It's far richer than our humble home, but she deserves it. That sweet woman made my life a success from the moment I saw her. I don't know why I have waited so long to let her know," Sebastian said with the look of a young man who had fallen in love for the first time. Realizing he was getting too sentimental for Hans, he quickly raised his eyebrows and smiled.

"What would you like me to do?" Hans asked, not thinking he would be qualified to do much but watch and sharpen tools.

"Well, Hans, I have a very special project for you. I have a wonderful slab of cherry all cut out for another mantle in the kitchen. I want to have a harvest scene on the front of it, and you are going to carve it for me."

"But, Sebastian, I have done very little carving. I am not qualified to do this."

"Hans, learning means that you have to trust your teacher. Do you trust me?" Sebastian asked.

What was Hans to say to this great master craftsman? Even though he knew he could never make a carving worthy of Sebastian's talent, he also knew that he could not dispute his ability and experience as a teacher.

"Don't worry, son," Sebastian said as he patted Hans on the back, "I'll guide you through each step and before you know it, you will be an excellent carver. I'll draw the scene out and get you started."

Everything seemed so easy for Sebastian. He took joy in his work and didn't take anything too seriously. Working next to him was a joy for Hans. He would often catch himself looking at the excitement in the old man's face instead of what he was showing Hans. Never had he seen someone so excited about his work. Besides an occasional interruption from the new owner to ask a question, the two were left alone to work and talk.

"Sebastian, where did you learn to carve so well?" Hans asked after lunch.

"Well, when I was a little boy and the King's grandfather ruled our country, my father was the King's carver. I grew up in my father's shop, watching him for as far back as I can remember. By the time I was your age, I had already become a very experienced carver. When I met Millie and had to strike out on my own, my father already had the job I wanted, so I opened my own shop. Unfortunately, there wasn't enough carving work for common people to make a living, so I started making furniture. It was a silly idea since I knew nothing about furniture. I could carve you the most beautiful chair, but it would fall apart the first time you sat on it," Sebastian was laughing as he recalled his early days. "Finally, after almost starving to death, my father arranged for me to spend six months with a furniture maker friend of his. In time, I was able to start a meager business that grew into this."

"Did you ever wish that you could have carved for the King after your father passed on?"

"Oh, sometimes I thought about it, but I decided that life was about today and not tomorrow. Besides, by then I had several journeymen working for me and I felt an obligation to them."

Hans realized that there was more talent in this man than anyone would ever really know. It was so easy to talk to him, and before Hans knew it, the day was over.

Sebastian stayed for a while after everyone else had left and talked to the new owner. Hans just quietly waited in the back of the shop so as not to eavesdrop on what seemed like a very serious conversation. As they were about to leave, Sebastian asked Hans to carry a stack of boards home for him. He thought it strange to take rough-sawn boards home from the shop, but he willingly obliged, and they were off.

Millie was waiting at the door when they arrived home, and she gave each of them a hug and a kiss. Hans had never seen a cuter couple in his life. They reminded him of the newlyweds who had moved in next door to his parents a few months ago. Trying to eat all the food that she had prepared was the hardest work he had done all day. Not that the food was bad; there was just so much of it. He figured she must have started cooking the minute they had left that morning. Just as he was finishing his last plate full, Millie struck the final blow.

"I hope you like cobbler because I just made a fresh one. I saved the cream from this morning's milk and had it out in the snow to chill for you. Do you want more than two scoops, Hans?"

Hans just rolled his eyes as Sebastian laughed and shook his head. "Millie, this boy came to town as a passenger. If you keep feeding him like this, he'll leave as freight."

"Now, Sebastian, I'm just taking care of him like his mother would. He's still a growing boy, and you two work hard at that shop all day," she said as she placed the third scoop of cobbler in Hans's bowl.

By the time Hans had finished off his cobbler and refused seconds as politely as he could, he wondered if he would be able to make it to his room. Unfortunately, Sebastian had other plans.

"I'm headed to the shop for a little while, would you like to come with me?" he asked Hans.

"We're going all the way back to the shop now?" Hans asked, surprised.

"No, no. I have a little shop out back. I have a very important project that I am working on, and I thought that you might like to help."

"Sure," said Hans, knowing that if he didn't do something to work off supper, he would never get to sleep.

In the back of the house was a one-room shop. Just like the shop in the city, it was warm and neat. There was a single bench in the middle of the shop, and on it were the boards they had brought home. Sebastian must have started the fire and lit the lamps while Hans was getting washed up for supper. There was also a table close to completion in the corner.

"I come out here in the evening and work a little while so that Millie's good cooking doesn't make me as big as a barn," Sebastian said, patting his belly. "I am finishing up on that table and wondered if you would use these boards to make two benches for it. It's for a very important customer and I need help getting it done on time."

"I would be glad to help," Hans said as he surveyed the shop for the tools he would need. He began planing the boards as they visited and Sebastian worked on the table. In a couple of hours, it was evident that the long day had been too much for Sebastian, and they called it a night. When they went into the house, Hans had to eat one more bowl of cobbler before Millie would let him go to bed.

The days went smoothly as Sebastian guided Hans through each step of carving the mantle. The gifted craftsman knew just what needed to be removed, how much, and where. Hans was amazed at how the carving was starting to take shape, and he couldn't believe he was doing it. He noticed, as the week wore on, that Sebastian was preoccupied with the activities of the new owner. He would watch as the man made his way around the shop and talked to each person several times a day. Hans could tell by the expressions on the faces of the journeymen and apprentices that the owner was reprimanding them for something. Occasionally, Sebastian would just shake his head and go back to work.

On Saturday night, they waited for all the workers to leave, and then Sebastian spoke to the owner. Hans could not hear what they were saying, but he could tell that the gentle old man was very upset. He wasn't scolding the new owner, but he was very serious about what he was saying. They talked for half an hour, and then Sebastian just shrugged his shoulders and walked out the door. Hans quickly left and caught up to him.

"Are you all right, Sebastian?" Hans asked with great concern.

"Yes, son, I am fine. I'm sorry that you had to see me get so upset back there. Perhaps I should never have agreed to stay on because it disturbs me so."

"Why, is there a problem?" Hans asked out of genuine care and wasn't trying to pry.

"I do not want to say anything bad about the man, Hans. He and I just have some very different ideas about how a business should be run. I have sold the shop to him and it is his now. I guess that it is just very hard to let go sometimes."

"Is he doing something bad?"

"Not if you mean dishonest. He is an honest man, but he just has things turned around."

"In what way?"

"He is an excellent businessman, but anything can be taken too far. Lately, he has been getting on the workers about wasting things. They use too much honing oil, too much hide glue, and too much lumber. I know that I did not train them to be the most efficient workers, but they are good men. He is going to alienate them, and he cannot see that the alienation will cost him much more than the materials. He wants to cut everything to the bone, and it will kill the shop. Every man should learn to handle his money wisely, but only a fool would put money ahead of people. But enough of this, we should conserve our strength for Millie's feast."

The two of them laughed and walked home. Hans was getting to where he looked forward to Millie's hug and kiss on the cheek at the end of the day. Her cheerful smile seemed to wipe the day's troubles away at the doorstep. Hans was amazed at how Sebastian could leave the problems of the day behind and enjoy his wife. After supper, the two of them went out to work in the shop.

The old man just worked on his table and visited with Hans. Not once did he check up on what Hans was doing with the benches. Hans felt like the old man treated him as an equal, and he treasured the feeling. The small one-room shop in the back seemed to be a sanctuary for Sebastian, as he could work without the pressures or worries of a commercial shop.

The next two weeks went quickly for Hans. The mantle he was

carving was coming along very well. As well as it looked, Hans couldn't believe that he had actually done the carving. Both mantles were just about ready for finishing, and Hans felt he might get to see them completed before he left. The carvings would not have to be smoothed like a piece of furniture, and the following week, he thought that the final oil could be applied.

Sebastian tried to ignore the new owner's activities as best he could. On two occasions, workers followed him home to complain, but he refused to say anything negative about the owner. He would encourage them in his gentle manner and send them off feeling better. Hans had come to regard being around Sebastian as an honor. He was learning much more from the old man than just how to carve.

It was Thursday of the last week when they went out to the shop after supper and checked the finish on the table and benches. The finish was still a little tacky, so they decided to build a nice, warm fire to help it dry.

"I think tomorrow we can deliver these, Hans. It's been fun, hasn't it?"

"Yes, it has. I wish that working with my father were this fun. You have treated me like a man, and Father treats me like a boy."

"Do I sense a little resentment, Hans?"

"No, a lot. Why does he have to be like that? Just like this trip. I have enjoyed it, but why couldn't he have let me finish my apprenticeship first? If you had been my teacher, I'll bet that you would have let me finish first."

"Oh, Hans, you cannot compare me to your father. Being a father is the hardest job in the world. I'm your friend, and that's different from your father, who is your parent. I never had to punish you for misbehaving or had to scold you for staying out with your friends too late. I have grown very fond of you, but you must never forget that no one can ever love you like your father."

"Then why does he do these things to me? He treats me like I know nothing. He has never just turned me loose on a project like you did."

"Hans, would you do me a favor? I'm going to go to bed now. Would you mind staying with the fire for a little while longer and stoking it when it starts to get low? That way, we will be sure that the finish is dry tomorrow."

"Yes, sir", Hans replied, realizing that Sebastian would never say anything bad to him about Father.

As he slowly got up to go into the house, Sebastian took something out of his tool chest and handed it to Hans.

"Something for you to read while you wait for the fire." He placed a piece of paper in Hans's hand and said good night.

He laid the piece of paper down and sat there thinking about Father. As the fire began to burn down, Hans came out of his daze and stoked it. Remembering the paper, he picked it up to glance over it before he went inside for the night. It only took reading the first few lines for Hans to sit down and read it all.

Hans took the letter and read each word carefully. He could not believe what he was reading. As he sat by the fire, each word cut deeply into his heart, and he read it again to be sure he had understood exactly what Father was saying.

Dear Sebastian,

I hope this letter finds you and Millie well. I think of you both often and hope to see you again, but I'm afraid it will be impossible this year. I have a great favor to ask of you. I

have given considerable thought to your counsel regarding
my son, Hans. I have decided that you are right in suggest-
ing that he undergo a training journey before completing
his apprenticeship. His skill at making furniture amazes me
daily. Even though he is my son, I have never seen someone
so talented and gifted at woodworking. I have labored hard
to watch his fundamentals so that he will get the most out
of his journey. He is very gifted, but I am afraid that I have
taken him as far as I can. One day, he will far surpass my
skills, and already it is hard to keep up with him. He will be
leaving next month and will be with you during the fourth
month. Please care for him and teach him all that you can in
one short month. I trust you, old friend, to take this wonderful young man and help him to become the craftsman
that he can be one day. Please give Millie a hug for me.
Regards,
Frederick

The tears welled up in Hans's eyes, and his throat went tight.
All this time, he had admired Sebastian and scorned his father when
it was Sebastian's idea. The hot tears began to run down his cheeks
as he reread the words his father had written about him. He didn't
know how long he had sat there rereading the words, but the fire had
burned down again. He gently placed more logs on the fire, turned
out the lamp and went into the house.

The next day at work, Sebastian could sense Hans's turmoil. Hans
wasn't mad at him, but he was shaken deep in his heart for how he
had treated Father when he left. Not much was said between him and

Sebastian. That evening, as they walked home, the gentle old master placed his arm on Hans's shoulder.

"I'm sorry if I hurt you, Hans. I didn't know how else to respond to you last night. You have come to mean as much to me as your father did, and I wanted you to know how very much your father loves you."

Hans could feel the tears coming back, and it made him angry.

"Sebastian, I just want to ask you one question, and I want an honest answer."

"Fair enough, Hans."

"How do you and the other men know Father?"

"Long before you were born, your father and the others were all apprentices in my shop at the same time. It was probably the happiest time of my and Millie's lives. The shop was growing fast, and we became like a family. Every night, the boys would come over to the house for supper, and Millie would fix one of her feasts. I was their teacher and they were our family." Sebastian looked to see how Hans was doing and reached over to squeeze his shoulder before he continued.

"Your father was the best of all of them, Hans. Like you, working with wood came very naturally to him. It was all I could do to keep up with him. I could have signed him off as a journeyman two years early, but it would not have been fair to him."

"Like he held me back... not to mention with your help. Why?"

"Greatness, undisciplined, is wasted talent, Hans. You have been given a great gift in your ability to build furniture, and you must care for that, and those who love you must help. I'll admit that having you come here was a bit selfish on my part. I looked forward to having a second-generation craftsman at my side who was like family. Your hands are skilled and know all they need to make you a great craftsman, but your heart must be ready. That is why we all agreed to help you complete your training, because we know that skill alone is not enough."

They walked the rest of the way in silence. Hans could tell that Sebastian understood and knew his pain. He wasn't angry, just humbled by his father's words. How could a great craftsman like Father believe in him so much? Millie read the despair in the faces of her two men, and never had a hug been so tender and understanding as she held Hans. She gently took his face in her hands and assured him that everything would be all right. It was a two-hug night.

After supper, Millie did not bring dessert out as usual.

"You two have a very important delivery to make, don't you? I'll save dessert until you get home so we can celebrate," she said.

Sebastian and Hans forgot the troubles of the day, and both lit up at the thought of delivering their table and benches. Hans hooked the horse to the cart as Sebastian wiped down the furniture. They gently loaded the pieces, and Millie brought out blankets to cover them, keeping them from getting scratched on the road. Hans thought it a bit strange to be delivering the furniture this late at night, but he was too excited to worry about it.

This was a VERY important customer, and Hans was anxious to be seen with Sebastian. He hoped that this might be a good contact for the future. Once loaded, they headed into the city and down the narrow streets. After turning down several streets, they pulled up in front of a run down building and stopped. Hans figured that it must be a warehouse for the customer.

There was a sign above the door, but it was too dark to see. Sebastian climbed out of the wagon and started removing the blankets from the load.

"Let's set it off right here, Hans. Be as quiet as you can."

Hans lent a hand, and soon the furniture was unloaded. Sebastian then asked him to take the cart around the corner at the end of the street and come back. This all seemed strange to Hans, but he did as he was asked, and Sebastian was anxiously waiting for him when he got back to the front door.

"You're young and strong, Hans. You knock on the door and do it like you are trying to wake up the dead."

Hans looked at him, puzzled, and reared back to thump the large wooden doors as hard as he could. The hard door stung his knuckles as he rapped on it several times. With that, Sebastian grabbed his arm and said, "RUN!"

"What?" Hans asked as Sebastian dragged him down the street toward the cart.

Sebastian was laughing and running so fast that Hans could hardly keep up. Hans kept looking back to see who or what they were running from. They got to the cart and climbed in. Sebastian didn't call to the horse, but he just slapped the reins on its back three times, and the horse bolted. Hans almost fell over the seat when they took off, and he thought that the old man had lost his mind. Sebastian was laughing and rocking in his seat like a kid who had just pulled a nasty prank on someone. He just laughed and kept slapping Hans on the knee until they were halfway home, and he slowed the horse to a walk.

"Sebastian, have you lost your mind? What was that all about?"

"That, young man, was your lesson for this month. Fun wasn't it?"

"Fun? I almost fell and broke my neck. Do you realize that we just left a month's work setting in the middle of the street?"

"Right where I wanted to," Sebastian replied as he let out a chuckle.

"Could you let me in on the joke?"

"Did you see what that place was? It was the town orphanage.

They came into the shop last month and priced a table and benches that they needed very badly. The new shop owner gave them a price that they could never afford. They have come to me for years, and I always told them that I would get around to it, but I acted too busy to build their stuff. Then I would build it at home and give it to them. That's your lesson."

"What, to act crazy and give my work away?"

"If need be, to keep you a great craftsman."

"It seems like it will keep me a broke craftsman."

"Hans, have you ever seen a stagnant pond?"

"Sure, there are several around Crescere."

"Tell me what they are like."

"Well, they stink, they have scum on them, and no one wants to go around them, not even the livestock," Hans said, wrinkling up his nose at the thought of it.

"Hans, a man's heart is much like a pond. You have been given a great gift in your ability to work with wood. If you keep that to yourself and never let it flow freely out of you, you will become a stagnant pond just like the man I sold the shop to. There is nothing wrong with making money, but it can't become more important than anything else."

"You're saying that I should make time for good deeds."

"No, I am saying that you should give back from what you have been given. Many people sit around making excuses for why they do not help others, all the while using the talents they have for their own benefit. Goodness is not just about giving money; it's about giving of who we are and what we have. Everyone has something of themselves that they can give. Places like the orphanage need money, but they need others to give of themselves, too."

"So why couldn't we have let them know who gave it to them?"

"What would have happened then?"

"They probably would have been very grateful for your goodness and thanked you."

"Exactly, and when you start doing that, you begin to love the praise more than just doing a good thing for your neighbor. The greater your talent, Hans, the more important it is that you give to others out of the goodness of your heart and hands."

Hans was beginning to understand. This was what kept Sebastian young. He never forgot that he was part of a much bigger world and that he had to play his part every day of his life. Now that he thought about it, the night was quite fun.

They arrived home, unhitched the horse and rubbed him down. They went inside to enjoy a wonderful treat of cake, laughing and telling Millie about their adventure.

Over the last two days, they finished the mantles and presented them to Millie on Saturday night. She didn't say much; she just cried and kept hugging each of them. Hans helped hang the mantles in place as Millie watched every step. She waited on Hans and Sebastian at supper as though they were kings, and to her, they were. Even though Hans was tired that night, he wanted to write his father. After Sebastian and Millie went to bed, Hans went to his room and began his letter.

Dear Father,

I have had a wonderful month with Millie and Sebastian. I have never seen such a spry old couple. I have learned a great deal from them about the kind of person I should be, and I am beginning to understand why you sent me away.

Please forgive me for leaving the way I did; it was wrong.
Sebastian told me that it was his idea and that he used to
be your teacher. Thank you for allowing me to learn from
this man and for your faith in me. I have acted like a spoiled
boy, and I know that I have hurt you and Mother. I am now
excited to finish my journey and come home to you. Thank
you for loving me enough to send me away for a time.
  Love,

  Hans

He slept better that night than he had since he left home. Even
though he missed his parents, he felt reconnected and very close to
them. All the anger he had felt toward Father was gone, and he regained
the sense of friendship that they had shared for so long. He did not
need to be awakened the next morning because he was now excited to
continue his journey and return home. Millie had her usual feast for
breakfast, and as he got ready to go, she handed him two bags of food.

"Now you take this," she began, "because I know that you won't
eat right on your trip to Amicitia." Millie's eyes filled with tears as she
gave Hans a hug, then turned to go back into the house so he would
not see her crying.

With a smile, a wink and a pat on the back, he and Sebastian
took off for the station. They arrived just as the carriage was ready to
leave. Sebastian had been carrying a small package, which he handed
to Hans. He began to untie the string around it when Sebastian placed
his hand on Hans's.

"Wait until you get home, Hans," Sebastian said with a wise
look and nod.

Hans knew by now to follow the old man's advice, so he placed the package in his bag with the others and boarded the carriage. He watched Sebastian as long as he could. Just as they were going out of sight, he waved one last time and pulled his head back into the carriage. He had not even noticed up until this time how many other passengers were on the trip with him. He looked to survey the inside of the carriage and quickly decided that this would be one of the more enjoyable carriage rides of his journey. Now, if he could just think of something to say.

Blinded

As the carriage lumbered along to Amicitia, his eyes focused immediately on the gregarious girl sitting across from him. She was about his age, dressed elegantly, and chatting gleefully with the two gentlemen on either side of her. As he took his seat, she glanced at him and gave a faint, courteous smile and quickly went back to talking.

Hans had not even noticed the young lady that he was sitting next to, who finally waved her hand in front of Hans's face to get his attention. With a slight frown at the interruption, Hans glanced at her, and she held out her hand, saying, "Hi, my name is Heidi."

Hans ignored her gesture of friendship and returned his eyes to the gregarious blonde on the other side of the carriage. He leaned over to Heidi and asked, "What's her name?" Heidi rolled her eyes and ignored his question, so he asked again, "What's her name?"

"Beatrice," Heidi replied curtly.

Heidi shrugged her shoulders and went back to reading the book she had brought for the trip. She assumed this young man had no real interest in a conversation with her, and she now had no interest in talking to him.

The carriage rocked along the dusty roads and would not stop until noon, so the passengers could eat and stretch their legs. Throughout the whole morning, the only one in the carriage to talk was Beatrice.

She spoke on and on about her favorite subject, herself.

As she rattled on endlessly, her curls bounced, and she fidgeted with her delicately embroidered handkerchief, which she would wave around with her hand when she got exceptionally animated with her stories.

The three men in the carriage were mesmerized by her stories, and she did not seem to mind that they were all fascinated with her. They would laugh at just the right time, and that would only encourage her to talk more. Occasionally, Heidi would glance up from her book at something outrageous Beatrice had said, raise her eyebrows in disbelief and then roll her eyes as the men laughed on cue.

By lunchtime, Heidi could not wait to get out of the carriage. She took the lunch provided and went to a quiet spot where she could not hear Beatrice droning on. The peace and quiet were so beautiful that Heidi lost track of time. Not only had she gone far enough that she could no longer hear Beatrice, but Heidi had also gone so far that she could not hear the driver calling for everyone to load up so they could continue their trip. The driver gave the three men instructions to help find Heidi, then he and the others all went in different directions to look for her. After about fifteen minutes of searching, Hans came across the small clearing where Heidi was sitting.

"Hey, you, we're ready to go," Hans said rudely, motioning for her to come and then turning around to head back to the carriage.

Heidi did not budge, and with as much indignation as she could muster, said, "I have a name, and it's not 'hey you'."

Hans turned back and asked, "What?"

"I have a name. Do you remember what it is, or is your brain numb from all that nonsensical chatter you have been drooling over all morning?" Heidi shot back.

"Well," Hans retorted mockingly, "to use your name, you would have to tell me what it is first."

Heidi snatched up her belongings and stormed back to the carriage. As she went by Hans, she said, "I told you my name this morning when you got on the carriage, but you were too interested in Miss Giggles to remember it."

The rest of that day and the whole of the next were pretty much the same. Heidi read her book, Beatrice talked, and the three men in the carriage listened. Heidi was happy when they finally rolled into Amicitia at the end of the second day of travel. She gathered her things and walked away as quickly as she could. Hans and the two salesmen fought over carrying Beatrice's bags to where a man was waiting in a small open carriage to take her away.

Hans found the directions to the shop where he would be working and started walking that way. He was unusually happy, and his step was brisk. During the trip, he learned that Beatrice was from Amicitia, so he was looking forward to seeing her again. Her family was wealthy and owned most of the forest land around the town. He got the feeling on the trip that she liked Hans very much, and he was anxious to get to know her even better.

At last, thinking as he walked away from the station, he didn't have to sit next to that grumpy girl with the book, whatever her name was. The stars were coming out bright, and the cool air seemed very fresh. He waved to each person that he saw, and he couldn't seem to get the smile on his face to go away. As he arrived at the shop and entered, a tall and broad-shouldered man walked over to him.

"You must be Frederick's son, Hans. I'm Henri," the man said as he offered his hand.

"Hello, sir, I am glad to meet you," Hans said as he shook hands.

The man almost broke Hans's hand as he squeezed it.

"Let's introduce you to the others," he said as he slapped Hans on the back, nearly knocking him down.

This was the biggest man that Hans had ever seen in his life. His hands were like the paws of a bear, and his chest like a bull. All of a sudden, Hans felt very small as he followed Henri through the shop to meet the other workers. He soon realized that Henri owned the shop, which was large, considering the town's size. Everyone gave him a wide berth as he lumbered through the shop and quickly answered when he spoke to them. Henri had a deep but gentle voice, and he spoke with respect to everyone. He had a tint of gray in his beard, which made him look very distinguished and wise.

"You'll work with me this month, Hans," Henri began. "I require a lot from my personal apprentice because I am often distracted by the affairs of the shop. Unfortunately, you'll have to sleep in the back corner of the shop because my five children take up all the room at my house. We put a bunk back there for you, and there is a well behind the shop."

"Thank you, sir," Hans said, nodding in appreciation. "I'm sure that it will be fine."

"We'll be closing in about an hour, so just familiarize yourself with the shop for tonight," Henri said with another slap on the back that made Hans lose his balance and stumble.

"Don't mind him," one of the workers said to Hans, laughing, "that's just how he says welcome."

Hans wished that he wasn't quite so welcome because one more slap like that was going to knock him on his face. He walked around the shop and looked at the different projects in various stages of completion. The shop turned out very elegant work, and he was going to enjoy working here. The hour passed quickly, and the workers began to leave. Henri saw to it that Hans was settled in and locked up the shop. As soon as Hans's head hit the pillow, he started thinking about Beatrice. He finally fell asleep that night, vowing to find her on his day off.

The next morning, Hans was eager to begin working with Henri, who arrived half an hour before everyone else.

"Hans," Henri said, "I have a job this month that I think will be perfect for you. In the village, there is a dress shop that belongs to my sister. She is out of town this month and has someone watching her shop. While she is gone, she has asked me to have some tables and shelving made and installed in the back room. I am going to let you do that job while you are here."

"Okay," Hans replied slowly. He had hoped to learn a new skill while he was here, but this seemed beneath him.

Henri continued. "I have a rough sketch of what she wants. Today, I would like you to go over there and begin taking measurements and creating some working plans. Most of it is a built-in cabinet, so once you have the plans completed, we can haul the lumber over there. You can work at the dress shop each day until it is done."

Hans tried not to show his disappointment in his new job as he gathered up the things he would need to draw up a set of plans. Henri told Hans how to get to the dress shop, and he was off to his new task before 8:00 a.m. Hans expected to have the plans completed by the end of the day and start building tomorrow. The dress shop was easy to find, and only a 15-minute walk from Henri's shop. The open sign was already hung in the window, so Hans walked right in. Hans had barely entered the shop when he heard a curt, "What are you doing here?"

"I could ask the same thing of you," Hans shot back.

"I work here," Heidi shot back, "but you still have not told me what you are doing here, and what is that you are carrying?"

"Well, I guess I am going to be working here, too," Hans said regrettably.

"So now you're a seamstress?"

"No, I'm a furniture maker, and your boss wants some shelving and tables built in the back room."

"Oh, great." Heidi said, rolling her eyes, "Now I have to spend every day with someone who doesn't even remember my name."

"I do too," Hans shot back.

"Then what is my name, furniture boy?" Heidi asked, crossing her arms.

"I know it, but I just can't remember it right now," Hans said as he wagged his head. Just then, all the papers, rulers, and pencils he was carrying began to slip, and the more he tried to hold them, the more they fell until they were all over the floor.

Heidi put her hand in front of her mouth, but it was clear she was laughing at him.

"Do you need some help?" she said, trying to stifle her laughter.

"No," Hans angrily said, "just show me where the back room is."

"It's in the back," She said as she walked away, waving her hand over her head. "If you can't find that, then I have little confidence in you as a craftsman."

Hans glared in her direction as he picked things up. He went through a small door into the back room and laid his papers down. Finding the rough sketch, he began to orient himself to the room. Hans worked quietly for the next two hours as people occasionally came and went from the shop. The little bell on the front door always alerted him that someone had come in. He would hear muffled voices, and then the bell would ring again as they left.

Just before noon, another customer came in, and Hans went to the doorway to listen to the conversation. It all seemed rather dull to him, so he went back to making his plans.

The next morning, Hans and Henri hauled the lumber they needed for the dress shop project to the alley just behind the store and stacked it there. By 9:00 a.m. Hans was ready to start building. He wasn't really sure how he was supposed to get anything done with all the dresses and bolts of material hanging and stacked in the back room. He found a spot and began to move everything out of his way. Just then, Heidi looked through the doorway to check on him.

"What are you doing?" she screamed.

"I'm making room so I can get some work done," Hans replied, a little unsure why she was so upset. He laid another handful of dresses on the pile.

"Do you realize those dresses are here for alteration, and they belong to our customers? You can't just throw them in a pile." Heidi said as she started picking up the dresses he had just thrown down.

"Listen, lady, I can't work in here if I can't move some things. I'm not hurting them. You're overreacting."

"You could have at least talked to me before you started throwing everything in a pile. Is that too much to ask?" Heidi asked, taking an armload of dresses into the front of the store to hang up.

As she walked back to get another load of clothes, she added, "And you had better do all your cutting outside. I don't want to have sawdust in here, too."

Nothing was said between the two the rest of the day. Heidi finished moving all the clothes from the back to the front, and Hans got busy on his first set of shelves. Hans had just about had it with this grumpy young lady.

When Hans got back to the shop, he asked Henri if they could talk for a few minutes.

Before Hans could say anything, Henri asked him how the job at the dress shop was going.

"Not very good," Hans said. "In fact, I'm not so sure I'm the right man for the job."

"Why's that? Surely a few shelves and work tables aren't beyond your skill level," Henri said.

"Oh," Hans replied, shaking his head, "I'm not having any trouble with the woodworking, it's that young lady who is filling in for your sister. She is the most irritating person I have ever met."

"Heidi?" Henri asked, raising his eyebrows.

"Is that her name?" Hans asked

"How did you work in a customer's store and not know their name?" Henri asked, a little surprised. "Anyway," he continued, "I have found Heidi to be a very hard-working young lady. Sure, she's not bashful to share her opinions, but there is nothing wrong with that, is there?"

"Not unless you have to work with her every day," Hans objected.

"A bit of a handful is she?" Henri asked with a wink. "To tell you the truth, Hans, I knew she would be a little tough to work with. That's why I assigned you to the job."

"To punish me?"

"No, so you would learn something valuable," Henri said with a slight chuckle in his voice.

"All I have learned so far is that she makes my life miserable," Hans said, feeling sorry for himself.

"Hans," Henri said, putting his hand on Hans's shoulder, "As I understand it, you want to be a craftsman one day and have your own shop or take over your father's shop. If you are going to be successful, you have to learn how to work with your customers."

"If I had a customer like that, I would tell her never to come back to my shop," Hans declared.

"Well then," Henri said calmly, "if you chase off every difficult customer you have, soon you will be a very poor furniture maker."

"So can someone else finish this job?" Hans asked.

"No, Hans," Henry said, shaking his head, "This is your job for the month. I not only want you to do it, but I also want you to have a delighted customer when you're finished. Understand?"

"Yes, sir," Hans replied, hanging his head like a sad puppy and walking away.

The next morning, Hans tried to have a better attitude. When he arrived at the dress shop, he made a point to go in and say good morning.

"Good morning, Heidi," he said with little enthusiasm.

"Well," Heidi said with a slight smile of satisfaction, "That's an improvement. You actually know my name."

Without saying a word, Hans just shook his head yes and got to work in the back room. Things were cordial over the next few days, and the week could not have ended soon enough for Hans. His one day off was welcomed, and he took the time to wash his clothes and take a nap after lunch. He didn't really look forward to Monday morning and returning to the dress shop, but at least he only had three more weeks to go before he traveled again.

On Tuesday, Hans was working steadily after lunch when he heard the familiar tinkle of the bell over the front door. He didn't think much of it until he heard a familiar voice talking to Heidi. It was Beatrice. He quickly put down his tools and made his way to the front of the store. He immediately thought of a ruse for going to the front.

By this time, Beatrice was standing on a short, round platform, while Heidi was on the floor, adjusting the hem of Beatrice's dress with some pins.

"I'm sorry for interrupting," he began, "but I have a question."

"What do you need?" Heidi asked.

"Beatrice," Hans said, totally ignoring Heidi, "How good to see you again."

Beatrice looked a bit puzzled, then her fake smile came back to her face. "Oh," she said, "you're that boy from the trip. Franz is it?"

"Hans, my name is Hans," Hans replied sheepishly.

"Oh, yes," Beatrice said as she turned her attention back to her dress and what Heidi was doing. "I just love this little platform I'm standing on. I would like one of these at home. Where did you get it?"

"It came from the local craftsman, Henri," Heidi said, still working on the hem.

"I can make one for you," Hans interrupted, moving towards Beatrice.

Beatrice looked Hans over, shrugged her shoulders, and said, "I want someone who knows what they are doing. You don't seem to be old enough to make something to my liking."

Hans was crushed and just looked down at the floor as Beatrice turned back to admire herself in the mirror. Heidi, for some reason, felt sorry for Hans and spoke up.

"Miss Beatrice," Heidi said very gently, not knowing how her suggestion would be taken, "I can assure you that Hans is an excellent furniture maker and he works in Henri's shop. He is in charge of the project here and doing an excellent job."

Hans looked up and tried to stand a little taller. He wanted Beatrice's approval so badly that he didn't even notice Heidi had given him a wonderful compliment and was trying to help him out.

Hans wanted to seize on Heidi's compliment as quickly as he could and said, "I know I can make a platform you will be proud to have in your home. If you would allow me to make one and you don't like it, you will owe me nothing, and you can keep it."

"Hum," Beatrice said as she fluffed the skirt of her dress, hitting Heidi in the face with the hem. "Well, I suppose that would be okay. I will expect the best, or I won't accept it. Will it be ready tomorrow?"

"No, ma'am," Hans said, trying not to lose the chance to impress Beatrice. "It will take me at least a week to make the kind of platform you want."

"Well, I might not even want it in a week, but go ahead, uh, Franz, was it?" Beatrice said as she climbed down and went to the dressing room, waving her hand over her shoulder as if dismissing Hans.

"Thank you, Beatrice," Hans called after her, "I won't let you down." Then he added softly, "It's Hans, my name is Hans."

Hans was walking on air; he was so excited. He went back to his work and could think of nothing except making and delivering the platform to Beatrice.

At the end of the day, Hans asked Heidi, "Does Beatrice come in here often?"

"I don't think so," Heidi replied, not looking up. "She is having a dress made for the annual town festival and dance her father sponsors every year in the village square."

"Oh," Hans said, rubbing his chin. "Can anyone go to this festival?"

"I suppose so," Heidi said.

"Would you mind if I run to Henri's and get a ruler and paper, then come back here and make a sketch of the platform Beatrice wants?" Hans asked.

Heidi said that it was okay because she had to wait for a delivery from the freight company and would be at the shop late.

As Hans was walking out the door, he stopped and asked Heidi, "Can you believe she didn't even remember my name? How can you spend all that time in a carriage with someone and not even remember their name?"

Heidi did not even answer. She just rolled her eyes and went back to her work. Hans hurried off, got his supplies, and returned to the shop as fast as he could.

As he came down the side street, he glanced down the alley that ran behind the dress shop and saw the freight wagon there with the back door of the shop open. Since it would save him a few steps to go in the back, he turned down the alley. As he walked past the team of horses at the front of the wagon, he could hear a commotion going on behind the wagon. As he rounded the back of the wagon, he could see the freight driver holding Heidi by her shoulders and trying to kiss her as she struggled to get away.

"Hey," Hans yelled as loud as he could, "let her go!"

The freight hauler turned around with a furious scowl on his face and said, "You better go away, boy, before I give you a thrashing." His teeth, the ones he had left anyway, were brown and black, his beard was covered in the spit from yelling at Hans, and he reeked of beer, sweat, and road dust.

Hans's initial confrontation was a reaction, but now the reality of the situation was settling in. The freight driver was three inches taller than Hans and outweighed him by seventy-five pounds. As Hans sized up the situation and what he was going to do, he saw the freight hauler's head snap to the left, and his eyes rolled back in his head.

Heidi had taken one of Han's boards in the alley and swung it as hard as she could, and caught the freight hauler on the side of his head.

This was Hans's chance, and he planted a solid right on the point of the driver's chin that sent him to the ground. He slowly got up, half limping, half crawling, to the front of the wagon and drove off.

"It's a good thing I showed up when I did," Hans said as he looked at his bruised knuckles with a sense of pride.

"Oh, please," Heidi shot back, "I was about to knee him when you showed up. I can take care of myself, Hans."

"Well, excuse me for trying to help," Hans said sharply.

"I'm sorry, I'm just a little rattled," Heidi said, her tone softer. "He's a brute every week when he comes in, and I hate how he acts towards me."

"Well, if he's got a brain, he won't bother you again," Hans said as they both started gathering their things and made their way inside.

Hans took his measurements and made a sketch of the platform, while Heidi put away the packages that had just arrived.

When Hans returned to the wood shop that evening, Henri was just finishing up and putting his tools away.

"Well, there you are," Henri said as Hans set his drawing down on a workbench. "What are those?" Henri asked as he picked up the drawing and looked at it.

Hans told Henri about Beatrice and how he had offered to make her a platform. Henri cringed slightly when Hans told him the part where she didn't have to pay for it if she didn't like it.

"Well," Henri began, "I am glad you are finding new customers, but if you offered to make it and she doesn't take it, then you will have to pay for the materials you used."

Hans thought about it for a second and then agreed. He was confident that Beatrice would like the platform he made. He and Henri discussed the plans for a few minutes, as well as the type of wood Hans should use.

Then Henri asked, "So why do you want to make this platform so badly? Are you sweet on this girl?"

Hans stammered and blushed just a little. "I came from a small village, and we didn't have people like Beatrice."

"What do you mean by 'people like Beatrice'?" Henri asked suspiciously.

"You know," Hans tried to explain, "she has a lot of money, dresses really nicely, and everyone wants to know and be around her."

"Including you?" Henri asked.

"Well, sure," Hans said proudly.

"You know, Hans," Henri said as he pulled up a stool and sat on it, "How someone looks, how popular they are, or how many people seem to want to be around them is not the real measure of a friend. Tell me what your impression of Heidi is."

"Well," Hans said and then paused a second, "she's just a normal person, I guess. Even though she works in a dress shop, she doesn't dress very fancy. She doesn't act sophisticated like Beatrice. She's an okay person, I guess."

"You seem to put a lot of emphasis on appearances, Hans," Henri said as he pulled up another stool and gestured for Hans to sit down.

Henri continued, "Do you know what the word superficial means, Hans?"

Hans tilted his head and looked upwards, "I think so. Just a thin covering of something?"

"That's a pretty good answer," Henri replied. "It's like the finishes we put on our furniture. It's just a shiny topcoat that makes something look good but has very little to do with what's underneath. Have you ever heard of a powder post beetle?"

"No."

"It's a tiny little bug that gets into the wood and bores tunnels through it underneath the surface. The first time you ever know you have them in a piece of furniture is when you see tiny little piles of sawdust on the floor. The holes they bore into the wood are so small that you might not even notice them. The furniture may still be shiny on the outside, but inside it has no strength or structural integrity."

"So the finish on the outside does nothing to make the wood strong and useful."

"That's right, Hans."

"So you're saying Beatrice has no integrity?" Hans asked.

"No," Henri replied, shaking his head. "What I am saying is that you cannot tell about something by how it looks. You have to look deeper than the surface to see what something is really made of. You have to watch for signs that something might be wrong on the inside. It's not what people or furniture look like, it's what's on the inside. Look at their actions and don't be fooled by what they say or how they look."

"That's easier said than done. How do I know what to look for?" Hans asked, puzzled.

"There are always little signs you need to look for in friendships. Like the little holes in the wood or the sawdust on the floor that let you know a piece of furniture is compromised. Watch for what people do, Hans. Most people listen to what is said and neglect what they see.

Friends are like furniture, you have to be able to depend on them."

"So I look beyond what's on the outside?" Hans asked.

"Yes," Henri shot back, "because if you don't watch for the obvious signs of what's on the inside, you will take a fall and get hurt."

"You mean like spending two days in a carriage with someone and not even remembering their name?" Hans asked, referring to Beatrice calling him Franz.

"Exactly, Hans. What does that say about you that you spent two days with Heidi and didn't even remember her name?" Henri said, placing his hand on Hans's shoulder.

Hans did not see that one coming, and it made him a little mad, so he just got up and went to the wood stack to pick out boards for the platform stool.

The rest of the week was spent working at the dress shop during the day and returning to Henri's to work on the platform in the evening. Hans was pleased with how the project was coming together. He was anxious to show it to Beatrice.

On Sunday afternoon, Hans applied the final coat of furniture polish to the platform. First thing Monday morning, he asked Henri to borrow the cart and horse so he could take the platform over to Beatrice.

The ride in the cart was short, and he soon arrived at an elegant home. He took his hat off and then knocked on the front door. A lady who looked a lot like Beatrice answered the door. Hans explained that he was delivering a platform for Beatrice and asked if she was in. The lady politely asked Hans to wait while she summoned Beatrice.

"What do you want?" Beatrice asked curtly as she came to the front door.

"I have your platform ready," Hans stated proudly.

"What are you talking about?" Beatrice asked.

"The platform you liked at the dress shop. Remember, I offered to make you one," Hans replied as politely as he knew how.

"I want to see it before you bring it in," Beatrice snapped.

"It's here in the back of the cart."

"You mean I have to come outside to see it?" Beatrice protested.

"Yes, I'm sorry," Hans said as he began walking to the cart and looking over his shoulder to see if she was following.

"Very well," Beatrice said as she followed in a huff.

When Beatrice got to the back of the cart, Hans pulled the blanket off the platform he had made, and Beatrice just stood there for a moment and then let out an ear-shattering scream. Hans jumped backward.

"Mother! Father! Come here!" Beatrice shrieked as her parents came running to the back of the cart.

"Beatrice, what's wrong?" her father asked as he reached her.

"Isn't it the most beautiful thing you have ever seen? Father, I want this in my room - NOW!" Beatrice said, clapping her hands while bouncing on her toes.

Beatrice's father looked at her mother with bewilderment and asked Hans how much he owed. Hans had already discussed with Henri what to charge and was promptly paid.

"I'm happy you like it," Hans said to Beatrice, who was still bouncing and giggling.

"Oh, it's absolutely wonderful, Franz," she said as she gave Hans a big hug.

By now, her father had summoned two men to unload the platform and take it up to Beatrice's room. She hugged Hans again and followed them into the house, squealing and giggling all the way.

Hans was on cloud nine as he returned the cart to Henri and went to the dress shop to work. He kept reliving the hugs that Beatrice had given him over and over again. As soon as he got to the shop, he had to tell Heidi all about it. It wasn't that she was a great friend; it was just that she was the only one to tell.

He finished his tale, looking up with a smile on his face and relishing it all. He asked, "Did I tell you Beatrice hugged me two times?"

"Oh yes, over and over again," Heidi replied, standing there with her arms crossed, neither interested nor amused by Hans's story.

The week flew by, and then on Thursday, Beatrice and two of her friends came into the dress shop to pick up her dress for the Village festival and dance. This was perfect because Hans was trying to think of a way he could talk to Beatrice before the festival that weekend.

Hans could not make out what they were saying from the back of the shop, even though he was trying very hard. He had put his ear against the door, trying to make it out when Heidi opened the door, and he almost fell into the room.

"Beatrice wants to talk to you," Heidi said very flatly.

"About what?" Hans asked.

"I don't know, just come out here," Heidi snapped, putting a smile on her face as she turned around to face Beatrice and her two girlfriends again. "Here he is," she announced.

"Oh, girls," Beatrice said as Hans walked into the front of the store, "this is Franz, and he made that wonderful dressing platform for my room."

"I'm glad you like it," Hans said, nodding slightly.

"Franz," Beatrice continued, "these girls may also want you to make them a platform, but you can't make it just like mine. Mine is to be one of a kind and special." Beatrice threw her head back and flipped her hair.

"Beatrice," Hans said, gathering all the courage he could, "I would like to ask you to go to the Festival and dance with me this Saturday."

Beatrice and her two friends gasped in unison as each one placed her hand over her mouth and looked at Hans. He knew Beatrice would be excited and surprised by his invitation.

"Oh, no," Heidi whispered under her breath as she closed her eyes, tilted her head down and put her hand on her forehead.

Heidi's gesture confused Hans, and as he looked back at Beatrice and her friends, they began to laugh uncontrollably, taking turns holding their stomachs. Hans could feel the blood running to his face, which felt very, very hot.

Just as one of Beatrice's friends caught her breath, she exclaimed, "I can't believe he thought you would actually go with him," and she began to laugh even harder.

"Franz, you silly boy, whatever gave you the idea that you could invite me to the festival. I wouldn't ever go with someone like you. You're, well, you're just a carpenter." Beatrice said as she shook her head and tried unsuccessfully to stifle her laughter.

"Shall we take care of the dress?" Heidi asked as she took Beatrice by the arm and led her back to the mannequin where the dress was displayed. She was trying very hard to change the subject for Hans, who was still standing in shock. "Why don't I have it wrapped up and delivered to your house this afternoon?" Heidi asked.

Beatrice nodded yes as Heidi escorted them to the front door of the store while they still laughed. The moment they were all outside, Heidi closed the door and turned to check on Hans. He was no longer in the front room of the store, so she went to check in the back. He was gone.

Henri was a little surprised when Hans walked in the door of the shop earlier than usual.

"What brings you back so soon today?" Henri asked.

"I'm finished with the job," Hans snapped.

Henri and a few of the other workers looked at each other as Hans stormed to his cot in the back of the shop. Henri put down his tools and went to Hans's room, where Hans had flopped down on his cot, crossed his arms, and was staring at the ceiling.

"What's up, Hans? Is everything okay?" Henri asked as he walked over to the cot.

"Nothing," Hans said without ever looking away from the ceiling.

Henri decided to take a different approach and change the subject.

"So, would you like to go with all of us to the festival this Saturday? It's a lot of fun and …"

"Not interested," Hans blurted out, interrupting Henri.

"It will be good for you," Henri argued, "you've been working really hard this month, and it will be something nice to do before you leave Monday."

"I SAID I'M NOT GOING," Hans screamed.

"Hans, what is wrong with you?"

"I don't want to talk about it," Hans snapped again as he turned over to face the wall so Henri could not see his tears.

"Hans, it seems like you are talking about it in the wrong way and taking it out on the wrong person," Henri said. Then he just waited through the silence until Hans began to tell the whole story of what happened in the dress shop with Beatrice and her friends.

"I'm sorry that happened to you, Hans," Henri said softly. "Is there anything I can do?"

"No," Hans said softly, feeling a strange sense of relief to get everything out in the open without being judged or lectured.

Henri let Hans have some time to himself that weekend, and on Monday morning, Henri took Hans to the station.

"So what did you learn here, Hans?" Henri asked as they drove along.

"I learned to be more careful in picking my friends," Hans replied.

"Hans, there are two kinds of skills you must have in life. The first one is your working skills. The second one is your ability to live with people. Both are equally important if you want to succeed."

As soon as they got to the station, Hans bought his ticket, and they were ready to load the carriage.

"Well, Henri, I guess this is goodbye," Hans said as he held out his hand. Looking up at this mountain of a man, he saw a tear in Henri's eye.

"I sure have enjoyed this time with you, Hans. I am really proud of how you handled things. Come here," and Henri picked Hans up off the ground and gave him a rib-breaking hug.

"Henri," Hans whispered.

"I know, Hans."

"Henri!"

"I'm gonna miss you too, little friend," Henri said as he hugged Hans even tighter. "Henri!" Hans whispered, "I can't breathe."

"Oh, I'm sorry," Henri said as he put Hans down. "You have a good trip now, and tell Frederick hello. Oh, and take this little gift I made for you," and Henri gave him a slap on the back that almost knocked Hans's shoulder out of joint.

Hans decided it was time to return the back-slapping. He reared back and hit Henri on the back with a slap as hard as he could. He only managed to get a solid thud, and Henri didn't move an inch.

Henri took off, and Hans walked over to the carriage and climbed in. He backed out of the carriage like a shot and ran back into the station.

"Sir, I need to exchange my ticket for a carriage tomorrow," Hans pleaded.

"Sorry, Son. The next carriage doesn't come through here until next week."

"But you don't understand, I cannot ride this carriage!"

A Trip To Remember

Hans just had to find a different way to get to Fidelium. He inquired about the next carriage, freight hauler, or any other means to make the trip. The station master said that if he were going, the only way would be on the carriage today. Fidelium was a five-day journey to the south, and there were no towns between here and there. The city sat at the base of the king's mountains on the border. The stops would be at a couple of farms and bunkhouses along the way. Hans knew that he and the other passenger would not be joined by anyone, nor would either of them get off until Fidelium. Begrudgingly, he walked back out to the carriage and climbed in.

"Hello, Hans," Heidi said quietly.

"I can't do this, Heidi, you'll have to ride back here by yourself," Hans said as he got out of the coach and climbed up by the driver.

"Boy, if it ain't asking too much, can we go now?" the old driver asked sarcastically.

"Fine with me!" Hans snapped back, "let's go 'cause the sooner we get this trip over with, the better."

It took Hans almost an hour to calm down and apologize to the driver for his rudeness. He wasn't enjoying the drive out of the forest, even though the trees were starting to bud. He just stared straight ahead and didn't say anything. It wasn't bad enough that Beatrice had totally humiliated him, but now he had to spend a week with the one person who had witnessed it.

When they stopped for lunch and to rest the horses, Hans kept his distance and did not even look at Heidi. It seemed to take forever before they headed out, and Hans climbed back up with the driver. The afternoon was long, and the air began to chill by late in the day as the trees hid the sun's warm rays. Hans was shivering, but he refused to give in to his discomfort and ride in the back. That night, they stopped at a lumberjack's house, which doubled as an inn for the carriage line. The lady of the house fixed an excellent meal, but Hans was seated right next to Heidi, so he only ate a few bites and then went to bed.

He was so angry about his embarrassment and having to face Heidi that he didn't sleep a wink that night. He tossed and turned all night, punching his pillow as sleep eluded him. The next morning, he skipped breakfast and climbed up next to the driver with a scowl on his face. He was tired, cold, and hungry, which did not help his mood. The whole day was spent in silence. About two o'clock, when the sun was gently warming them, Hans fell asleep and almost fell off the carriage. If it hadn't been for the quick reach of the driver to catch him, Hans would have had bodily bruises to go with his bruised ego and hurt feelings. He fought to stay awake until they got to the bunkhouse for the second night.

The only thing at the bunkhouse to eat was some dried beef and cheese. Hans was starved, but now he was too tired to eat, so he just went to his room and fell on the bed. He still couldn't sleep, and he thought he heard Heidi crying in the next room. Hans hoped that she was crying because he wanted her to be as miserable as he was. He decided that whatever her problem was, she deserved it. Finally, he fell asleep from sheer exhaustion. The next morning, the driver had to beat on his door for five minutes before Hans woke up.

Hans grumbled as he climbed up on the seat beside the driver.

"Boy, you don't look too good this morning," the old man said as he called to the horses and took off.

Hans scowled at him because he didn't think this scruffy-bearded, toothless old man looked good any day. He managed to catch a nap without falling off the carriage after lunch and felt a lot better. The driver spent the rest of the day telling stories from his forty years of being on the road. The stories weren't really interesting to anyone except the driver, but Hans listened out of a lack of anything better to do. That night, they were out of the forest and in the open farm country. They stopped at a large farm that also doubled as a freight depot. Hans continued to avoid Heidi and went to bed as soon as he could.

The next morning, Hans was in a little better mood because he was halfway through the trip. The driver was complaining about a bad back and asked Hans to help him hitch up the team. Hans gladly obliged since it got him out of the house and away from Heidi. She followed the two of them out and watched from the front of the barn. Hans had noticed her there, and it made him angry that she would not let him have a few minutes of peace. They were hooking up the second horse when they heard a commotion coming from inside the barn.

"Hey, boy," the driver said, "you better go check on that young lady. I think I just heard her scream."

Hans looked around and saw that she was no longer standing at the barn door and asked, "Why?"

"Well," the driver replied, "I think that the freight hauler that stayed here last night is bothering her."

"She can take care of herself."

"I don't think so; he's a pretty big fella."

"So?" Hans snapped.

"What have you got against that little girl? She could be in trouble."

"I just don't want to have anything to do with her."

"As I see it, boy, it don't matter what your beef with her is. The real question is what kind of person are you to let someone else be in trouble and do nothing?"

"Fine!" Hans said as he gave the old man a disgusting look and threw down the reins. He went in to see what all the fuss was about so he could get on the road.

As he walked into the barn, he saw the same freight hauler that had attacked Heidi before. He had Heidi backed into a corner and was groping all over her. Heidi was crying and futilely slapping at the big hands grabbing her. She was white with fear, and panic was in her eyes. Past differences aside, Hans was enraged, and he marched right over and stepped in between them.

"Leave her alone!" Hans barked.

"What did you say, little boy?" the freight hauler asked.

"Leave her alone. She's with me."

"I don't care who she's with," the hauler said as he moved right in front of Hans and got face to face. "Now get out of the way while you still can."

All expression went off of Hans's face. This man looked even bigger than the last time they met. It suddenly dawned on him that he was standing between a woman he resented and a large man with an angry, ugly, and foul-smelling face. Hans looked at the man's rotted, clenched teeth and froze.

"Well, boy, what's it gonna be?"

"This," Hans said as the anger came back to his face and he

brought his knee up as fast and hard as he could into the freight hauler's groin.

The big man's mouth dropped open, his eyes bulged out, and he let out a blast of his foul breath. Hans just stood his ground and waited for the hauler's legs to slowly give out. As the freight hauler toppled over, Hans grabbed Heidi, and they dashed to the carriage.

"Get in quick, kids," the driver yelled from his seat, "we're hooked up and ready to go." He called to the horses, and they sped away.

Hans was shaking inside and out. He couldn't believe what he had just done, but he was glad he did. He just closed his eyes and lay his head back, hoping to stop shaking. He was interrupted by Heidi.

"Thank you, Hans," she quietly said.

"You're welcome," Hans said without even opening his eyes to look at her.

"Hey, boy," the driver yelled back, "you really gave it to him. That skunk has been asking for it for years out here. It done me good to see him finally get his due."

"I really thought he was going to hurt me this time," Heidi said with her head held down.

Hans opened his eyes and looked at her. "I'm sorry I wasn't paying attention to where you were, Heidi." He could see the tears streaming from her eyes, and she started to cry harder and shake.

They sat in silence except for Heidi's sobbing. Just about the time Hans thought that she was getting over it, she would start again. Her eyes and nose were all puffy, and he was beginning to feel sorry for her. As Hans sat, waiting and unsure of what to say, his thoughts drifted back to Sebastian and his gentle ways. He remembered how Rafael had said that Sebastian's gentleness and love had helped him. He looked at Heidi, and for the first time, he saw her as a very kind person, and not just the witness to his humiliation.

"Would it help to talk?" Hans finally asked, not knowing he was going to get an earful.

"I don't understand why you are so mad at me, Hans," Heidi burst out, still crying, "I wasn't the one who treated you like dirt and humiliated you in front of everyone. I tried to help you every time Beatrice was rude to you. I changed the subject, and I stuck up for you. So why was I the bad person? I don't understand. Did you ever think that I might have liked to go to the festival?"

That last part Heidi didn't mean to say, and she put her hand over her mouth even though it was too late. Hans sat speechless. He thought she was going to talk about the attack by the freight driver, not their friendship. Things were getting very uncomfortable, but it was out in the open now. Heidi didn't wait for him to get his thoughts together or reply before she started again.

"You were so wrapped up in pleasing someone who didn't care about you that you missed everyone else. I don't even understand why you were mad at Beatrice. She never led you on. It was your own craving for approval that got you humiliated. You set yourself up, Hans, and you have no one to blame but yourself."

Heidi had stopped crying now. Her arms were crossed, and her brow wrinkled up. Hans thought the crying Heidi was much better than the mad Heidi.

"I'm sorry, but I ..." Hans began.

"Oh, don't even try to give me excuses, Hans," Heidi interrupted, "how could you not see that Beatrice didn't care about you at all? She hardly even knew you existed beyond what she wanted you to do for her. She never even cared enough to learn your name. I, on the other hand, was working in the same store as you every day for a month. I was new in town just like you, and it would have been nice to have a friend. Did you ever think about that?"

"No," was all Hans could say.

For the next hour, they sat in silence as the carriage bounced down the road and jostled them back and forth. Heidi stared out the window, and Hans just looked straight ahead at the other side of the carriage. Finally, Heidi spoke up.

"What did you see in her anyway? I mean, what was the attraction?" Heidi asked.

"I don't know …" Hans replied, shrugging his shoulders.

"Oh, come on, Hans, think about it. How are you ever going to learn if you don't think about what you did? You don't get away with this that easily." Heidi said, crossing her arms even tighter and raising her eyebrows.

Hans felt out-gunned at this point, but he tried to think about why it was so important to him that Beatrice liked him.

"I guess I just wanted to be accepted by her because it made me feel important and like I was an equal," he finally said.

"Equal to what?"

"Her and her friends."

"To what end?"

"So I could feel like someone."

"Hans, no one else can make you feel that way. Maybe temporarily, but if you depend on someone else to make you feel worthwhile, then it will only last as long as they keep feeding you approval. I saw your work, and you are a very talented person. Why would you need someone else to make you feel good about yourself?"

"You wouldn't understand," Hans said as he looked away.

"Try me, Hans. You might be surprised by what I understand."

Heidi said softly.

"This all started with my father and this trip. I thought he respected me, and then he had to send me away. Every shop I visit, I'm the new kid and have to prove myself. I just thought that if I could win Beatrice over, it might prove something. All I did was prove that everyone was right, and I am a loser." Hans said, looking down at the carriage floor.

"Wow," Heidi said, "That is some pity party. It's convenient to blame everyone else, isn't it?"

"I knew you wouldn't understand."

"I do understand, Hans. You want everyone else to give you the approval that you won't give yourself. It's your responsibility to find peace with who you are. No one can give it to you or do it for you."

"So I guess you have this all figured out for yourself?" Hans asked sarcastically.

"No, I'm afraid it's a day-to-day thing. Every day, you find reasons to doubt yourself and get tempted to seek the approval of others. Some days, you can believe in yourself, and other days, it's hard to do. The trick is to take life as it comes, forgive yourself when it's needed, and keep going, knowing that your life matters to others even when it doesn't appear so." Heidi said, desperately trying to get through to Hans. "You have to decide what you want in life, Hans. What is your dream? What is your passion?"

"I don't know what my dream is. I do realize I set myself up back there, and I'm just feeling sorry for myself and blaming you. You didn't deserve that." Hans said, looking at Heidi for the first time in a while.

"No, I didn't deserve it, but I'm your friend, and I forgive you."

"Why?"

"Because that's what friends do, Hans. They forgive each other when they act like jerks." Heidi said with a smile and a wink.

"Oh, so now I'm a jerk?"

"No, you acted like one. There's a difference."

"So we're friends?" Hans asked.

"I would like to think so. It's not that friends don't have arguments and stuff, but they work things out." Heidi replied.

The stop for lunch was much more relaxing after Hans and Heidi had talked. The carriage driver was relieved to see the tension gone for the first time on the trip. After lunch, watering the horses and a quick chance to stretch their legs, they climbed back in the carriage for the rest of the day.

"So if we're friends, I want to ask you something," Hans said cautiously. "Were you crying in your room last night?"

Heidi quickly turned and looked out the window, taken aback by the sudden shift in the conversation from Hans's problems to her own. After all she had said about friendship, she had little choice but to confess.

"Yes," Heidi finally said.

"About what? Are you okay?" Hans asked.

With a big sigh, Heidi decided to tell Hans just enough to satisfy him. "Two days before we left Amicitia, I received a letter from my mother which had some bad news in it. I'm not ready to share it all yet, and I want some time to process it myself. If you are patient, I'll try to tell you more when I can."

Hans let it go for the time being and didn't pry anymore.

As they arrived that night at their last stop, which was a vacant cabin and barn, Hans told Heidi to go inside, and he would get her bag. When he came in with the bags, she had already started looking for something for them to eat. He put the bags in the room and tried to help her. After a little while, they decided to go out and see what was keeping the driver. Just as Hans opened the door, the driver met him.

"Well, I got some bad news, kids. This morning, when we tore out of the station, we messed up one of the axles. I'm not sure that we can make it to Fidelium tomorrow, so we'd better sit tight until help comes."

"When will that be?" Hans asked.

"Well, let's see," he said as he rubbed his chin. "If we don't make it in tomorrow, they will send someone to look for us the next day. It will take them a day to get to us and then a day to take you on into town, so I guess three days."

"What will we do till then?" Heidi asked.

"Well," the driver answered, "I brought a month of supplies out to this cabin last week, so I guess we just wait."

Hans wanted to get to his next shop as soon as possible. He was only going to have three weeks, as it was due to the trip. Heidi didn't seem too happy about it either, but they all figured there wasn't anything they could do about it.

They decided that they might as well sleep late the next morning since they were exhausted from four days on the road. Hans didn't have any trouble sleeping that night, and he didn't wake until ten o'clock the next morning.

He stumbled out of his room to find the bunkhouse empty, so he decided to go outside and look around. As he walked out, he saw Heidi looking south. Since they were only a day north of Fidelium, they could see the mountains. It was the first time Hans had ever seen the mountains, and it almost took his breath away. They were topped with caps of pure white snow that towered to the heavens. He stood there in absolute silence, but Heidi must have sensed his presence because she turned around and spoke to him.

"Beautiful, aren't they?"

"I've never seen anything like it in my life. Do they always look like that?"

"Well, other than losing most of their snow in the summer, yes," she said as she giggled at his question.

Hans had an idea and hurried to his room to get his telescope. He brought it out and showed Heidi how to extend it to its full length. She smiled, winked, and scrunched up her shoulders at the thrill of getting to operate the telescope. She pointed it to the mountains and looked for several minutes. When she found what she was looking for, she handed it to Hans and pointed to a specific spot.

"Do you see it?" She asked.

"What am I looking for?" Hans asked as he looked towards the mountains.

"A great big building on top of that mountain right there. Do you see it?"

Hans looked for a few more moments, and then he spotted what she wanted him to see. "Wow, what is that place?"

"It's the King's summer castle."

"Really?!" Hans exclaimed. "I have never seen one of the King's castles before. It's magnificent! One day - one day…"

"One day, what, Hans?"

"That's my dream. One day, I will make furniture for the King, and it will be in a castle just like that. Maybe it will be in that very castle."

"I think I believe you, Hans. You're a good man, and I'll bet the King would love to have you make his furniture."

They spent the rest of the morning looking at the mountains

through the telescope. Heidi tried to point out to Hans where she lived, south of Fidelium in the foothills. It was much too far to see her house, but he did find the right spot.

They had to wake the driver up for lunch, and he wasn't pleased about it. They just ignored him and decided to spend the afternoon looking at the mountains again. As the day started to fade away, Heidi decided to go inside and find something they could fix for supper. The sunset had turned the sky into a brilliant firestorm. Hans looked at the castle until there was no light left.

That night, Hans heard Heidi crying in her room again. He decided to ask her about it again the next morning. He lay there, trying to think of what to do and how to help her. His thoughts turned to Father and what he had taught Hans. Hans thought back on a conversation he had with his father a year ago.

"Son," Frederick said, "people sometimes pull away or get angry when they are hurt. It can make them do desperate things they normally wouldn't do."

"Like when the neighbor's dog tried to bite me when it was hurt?"

"That's right, Hans. Do you remember what Father did to get that dog away from you?"

"Yes, you talked real nice and soft to him until he would let you pet him. But I'm still scared of that dog."

"I know, Son," Father said as he chuckled, "but sometimes people need a gentle voice until someone can help them out of a corner before they get hurt even worse."

Hans came back to the present and smiled as he thought of Father. He wished he could be here now to tell Hans what to do for Heidi. He could still hear her softly crying, and he hated to see anyone in that much pain. Hans had to figure out a way to coax Heidi out of her corner. He just felt so alone and inadequate to help anyone, especially Heidi.

The next morning, Hans could tell that things were getting harder for Heidi, and the telescope probably would not distract her anymore. He made small talk until about 10 o'clock and then asked her to come outside. As they went out front, they found the driver napping on a bale of hay and snoring. Hans held up his hand to stop her and put his finger to his lips to let her know to be really quiet. He took her hand, and they tiptoed past the driver and walked out across the prairie. When they were a safe distance from the bunkhouse, Hans spoke.

"I hope that you don't mind going for a walk. I can tell that the letter is bothering you because I heard you cry again last night."

"I'm sorry. I hope I didn't keep you awake."

"No, it's okay. When I was living at home, and I got upset about something, Father would take me for a walk, and it always seemed to help."

"I like to go for walks, Hans. I think it's a wonderful idea."

"Heidi, I don't mean to pry into your affairs, but if there is anything you want to talk about, I would be glad to listen."

Heidi just hung her head and said nothing. Hans had learned from Father that sometimes the best thing you can say to someone is nothing at all. He just walked beside her and waited in case she decided to talk.

Finally, after half an hour, she began. "I feel like I am being forced into something I don't want to do and can't get out of."

"I know that feeling," Hans said, nodding his head, "because that's how I felt when Father sent me away on this trip. I had a whole different idea about how my year would turn out."

"This is a little different," Heidi said, "because this won't be for just one year. It will be for the rest of my life."

Heidi began to tell Hans about her life. She had grown up in the mountains south of Fidelium, and her father was an evil man. She told stories of how she had watched him beat her mother and how she would cry herself to sleep each night. When Heidi was nine years old, her father left one day and never came back. She and her mother were left to care for themselves as best they could. Their life had been full of poverty and need, so her mother started making dresses for the women of Fidelium. She and Heidi would go to the market once a month and trade dresses and scarves for food, dress material, and thread. Life was very hard for them. Occasionally, Heidi would stop talking and cry.

Hans couldn't help but feel ashamed of himself. Heidi had had such a hard life, and the month he worked with her, he never asked or cared about her; only himself.

Heidi continued, "My mother informed me that she arranged my marriage while I was gone."

"What does that mean, arranged?" Hans asked, puzzled.

"Mother's health has been failing, and she's afraid she can't keep the shop open. We barely make enough money as it is. That's why I worked in Amicitia this last month: to earn more money. Mother made a deal for me to marry the butcher's son, whose shop is right next to our dress store, when I turn 18 in about two years. For my dowry, she agreed to sign over the dress store so he could expand his butchery."

"I've never heard of such a thing!" Hans exclaimed in disbelief. "Who does that anymore?"

"Hans," Heidi said, putting her hand on his arm, "my village is very old-fashioned. Mother was only trying to take care of me. I can't fault her for that. Parents might not always do the right thing, but I know she is trying. It's done, I just have to learn how to accept it."

"Do you like this butcher boy?" Hans asked, his voice growing louder.

"I hardly even know him," Heidi said, "but he is supposed to be a nice person."

"I saw the dress you made for Beatrice," Hans said now, making grand gestures as he talked, "and I know you could run your mother's dress store by yourself. You're very good at what you do, Heidi."

"I don't know, Hans," Heidi protested, "it's too late. The deal has been made."

"If I think I can make furniture for the King, then why can't you make dresses for the Queen?"

"You're a dreamer, Hans," she said, smiling and slapping his arm lightly, "but you're a good friend." She put her arm in his, and they headed back to the bunkhouse.

As they walked back, they laughed and joked about being the makers of furniture for the King and dresses for the Queen. They chatted about many things. Hans discovered that Heidi was only three months younger than he was. Heidi was glad that someone had listened to her story, and Hans was glad that he had been the one to do so. When they got back to the house, the carriage from Fidelium had arrived, and they would be leaving in the morning.

That night, he decided to write to Father before going to sleep. Hans excused himself early and went to his room to write.

Dear Father,

We had trouble with the carriage on the way to Fidelium, and my time there will be cut short. I will have to work
very hard to learn something there, but I will do it. I made

a friend on the trip. Her name is Heidi, and she is just a friend, but a very nice one. She is a young lady who has had a tough life, and I wish I could do something to help her. At first, we didn't get along, but once I got to know her better, she is a very special person. I hope that I can think of a way to help her, and I am glad for all the things that you have taught me. I miss you and Mother, and I am anxious to see you both again.
Love,
Hans

That night, Hans listened, but never heard Heidi cry. The next morning, they left for the final leg of the trip to Fidelium. The two of them talked and laughed, and Heidi seemed to be less worried about her future, or perhaps she just forgot it for a while.

She was reluctant and embarrassed, but Hans persuaded her to use his pen and paper to draw some dresses for him. He was impressed by the designs she came up with, and he continued to encourage her to make dresses for the queen one day. He wasn't sure that she would, but she enjoyed dreaming about it.

They arrived at the station in Fidelium late in the day. He helped Heidi get out and helped her with her bag. Her mother was there, and from the reunion, Hans could tell that they meant a lot to each other. He met Heidi's mother, and they said their goodbyes.

Hans looked through his bag to find his directions to the shop when his eye caught a fist coming straight at him with no time to duck.

Spinning Dreams

The same ugly freight hauler caught Hans right in the nose with a hard fist. The blow knocked Hans backwards onto the ground. He spun around and got up as quickly as he could, but it wasn't quick enough. His eyes were blurred because of the blow to his nose, but he could see enough to recognize another swing coming. He was stunned, and as hard as he tried, he could not make himself duck. Just when he thought that he was going to get hit again, a massive hand reached in and caught the freight hauler's fist in mid-air. Hans was dazed as he watched the figure pick up the freight hauler and throw him down the street.

Hans was shaking his head and trying to clear his mind when his rescuer turned around to face him.

"Are you all right, Hans?"

"Henri, what are you doing here? How did you get here before me?"

"Henri? I'm not Henri, I'm his twin brother, Alfred. Now you're not gonna tell me that I look like that ugly ole brute Henri, are you?"

Hans did not feel so good. His nose was starting to throb from the punch, and his head was spinning around him as he tried to figure out what was going on. He staggered, and Alfred caught him.

"I had better get you somewhere you can sit down," Alfred said as he walked Hans into the station. He found Hans a seat and went to get him a wet rag to put on his nose to stop the bleeding and ease the pain.

"I think he broke my nose and now it's gonna grow crooked," Hans complained as he held the rag gently on his nose.

"I don't know, Hans, let me see," Alfred said as he took Hans's face in his two giant hands. He placed his thumbs against Hans's nose and gave it a quick twitch.

"Ouch!" Hans exclaimed, "that hurt."

"I'm sorry, Hans," Alfred said, like he was surprised. "You're right about it being broken, but it won't grow crooked now."

"Thanks...I think," Hans said as he placed the rag back on his nose.

"So what was that all about anyway. How did you get involved with a scoundrel like him?"

"Oh, I had a run-in with him back up the road over a lady he insulted."

"Well, I think we've seen the last of him for a long time. If you think you can walk, let's go to the shop."

It was a beautiful spring evening. The warm April sun had begun melting some of the snow in the mountains, and the stream that ran through town was flowing swiftly. Many of the homes had flowers planted in their window boxes, which were just starting to push through the soil.

The pace of the town seemed rather slow considering its size. Hans thought he would like this wonderful town at the base of the mountains. Most of the homes were built from the cedar that grew nearby, and it gave a wonderful warmth to the town.

Everyone on the street seemed friendly, and Alfred pointed out to Hans the different places he had seen the king during his visits to the summer castle.

Alfred was very different from Henri in that he knew how to give a gentle pat on the back instead of the bone-jarring slaps that Henri gave. Despite his size, Alfred was one of the gentlest men Hans had ever met. He laughed a lot as they visited along the way. Everyone in town seemed to like Alfred. He stopped several times to talk to different people or lend a hand to the ladies.

When they reached the shop, Hans could tell it was just like Alfred, gentle and warm. The workers all stopped what they were doing and greeted Hans. The pieces they were working on were much more delicate than Hans was accustomed to, and he was fascinated as he walked from bench to bench to look over the projects.

"Hans, we are going to have to work really hard since we only have three weeks together. The trip from Amicitia was long enough without being broken down. Come back here and let me show you what you will be working on."

He led Hans to the side of the building that faced the stream. In front of each window were some of the strangest contraptions that Hans had ever seen. Fashioned out of steel, they stood just above waist high. Between the two ends, they had pieces of wood suspended so you could get all the way around them.

Above them on the ceiling was a large spring with a band attached to it, which ran around the piece of wood and down to a pedal on the floor. When the workers stepped on the pedal, it would pull down on the cord, causing the wood to spin very fast. When they let off, the spring would pull the cord back up, spinning the wood again in the opposite direction. As the wood spun, it looked like the workers were pressing chisels into it.

"What are these, Alfred?" Hans asked curiously.

"They are something called a lathe. We just got these machines a couple of months ago."

"What do they do?"

"Well, have you ever used a spokeshave to make a round column?"

"Oh, yes," Hans replied, raising his eyebrows, "Father made me carve a round cylinder by hand. I worked on it for three weeks before I got it perfectly symmetric."

"Well, these new machines do that for you. As the wood spins, you use a special chisel to cut the wood. Since the wood is spinning on centers, it automatically gives you a perfectly round piece. I even used it to make a set of soup bowls for my wife."

"Are they hard to use?"

"Not really, but it takes a steady hand and good coordination to get a nice turning."

"These are fascinating, Alfred," Hans said, wide-eyed like a child seeing a new toy.

"I'm glad you think so, Hans, because this is what you will be doing for the next three weeks."

"Really?" Hans exclaimed.

"Yes. So, I want you to take what's left of the day and watch the workers so that you can get an idea of how it works. Then tomorrow morning I will start you on one of the machines."

Hans watched with awe as the workers used the strange machines. He carefully observed how they would mount the square pieces of wood between the centers, and then effortlessly, they would shape them. He could not believe how fast the shavings were flying.

One of the workers was a journeyman, but the other two were craftsmen. Hans was greatly honored to be allowed to work on such a machine. As he watched, he felt like he would really excel at this because it looked so easy to do.

He could not quit talking as Alfred closed the shop and they walked home. Alfred had decided that, even though they had apprentice quarters, he wanted Hans to stay at his house so they could get to know each other better. The house was only a couple of blocks from the shop and they arrived to see four young children dashing about. As soon as they saw Alfred walk in, they attacked him. He allowed the children to drag him to the floor where they all started climbing on him. All at once, they started asking him questions and telling him stories of their day.

It was obvious by the attention he gave that Alfred loved his children very much.

Soon, the children were distracted by other things, and they left him to go play. Alfred was still chuckling when he got up to greet his wife.

"Do they play with you like that all day, dear?" he asked.

"Of course, Alfred, we just play all day," she answered sarcastically as she playfully slapped him on the arm and gave him a hug.

"Hans, this is my wife, Heather."

"A pleasure to meet you, ma'am," Hans said.

"Welcome to the circus," she said, looking at Alfred crossly. "We have made a room for you in the back. I think tht since spring is here you will be warm enough. We thought with you working every day, it was the quietest place for you to get some rest."

"I'm sure it will be fine," Hans said, nodding in thanks.

The supper table was a continuation of the ruckus on the floor. All the children vied for their father's attention, and in turn, he gave to each one. After the kids were put to bed for the night, Alfred invited

Hans to sit and visit for a while. Hans told about their home and the work Father did.

Alfred repaid by telling stories of when he and Father were apprentices. Hans had a hard time realizing that Father had been as young as he. They laughed as Alfred candidly told Hans of the escapades and messes they had gotten into while training under Sebastian.

Father would have many things to answer for after this night of tales.

"Speaking of your father, Hans," Alfred began to ask, "have you heard from him?"

"No, why?" Hans asked.

"I was just wondering how he was doing. We got a letter last month that said he had been real sick this winter. I wrote back, but we have not heard anything."

"I'm sure he is fine," Hans said. "He gets sick every winter because he goes to the woodshed without a coat and stays there for an hour trying to pick out just the right piece of wood."

The next morning, Hans awoke early. He was excited to get to the shop and try his hand at the new machine. He had visions of great turnings that he would soon be producing. It hadn't looked all that hard, and he was confident he would soon be on his own without instruction.

Hans had many questions for Alfred on their short walk to work that morning. He wanted to know more about the machines, where he could get one, how many other shops were using them, and a host of other questions. Alfred patiently answered all of the questions as they walked.

As soon as Alfred unlocked the door, Hans sprinted to the machines and waited for the others to arrive. He could not figure out what was taking everyone so long to get to the shop.

When they finally arrived, they didn't seem anxious to get started. After what seemed like an eternity, the men were at the machines and Hans was ready to start. Alfred placed Hans on a machine between the two craftsmen so they could both watch him and help him along. They were both very nice and appeared to be excited for Hans to learn, though they knew he was only an apprentice.

One of them helped him get the piece of wood mounted on the machine, but Hans was impatient with all the instructions on the proper way to do it. All he could think about was getting started and seeing all the wood shavings fly. Before he was allowed to begin, he was shown how he must carefully coordinate the movement of his foot on the pedal and the use of the special chisel. Hans tried to pay attention, but he was about to burst with anticipation of trying it.

The time came when the craftsman stood back and let Hans give it a try. He stepped firmly on the pedal and the piece of wood spun. Just as he placed the chisel against the wood, it stopped turning, and he looked with confusion at the craftsman.

"You must release your foot off the pedal, Hans," he gently said.

Now, Hans felt stupid because he had seen them do it, and he knew that it was to be a fluid movement of stepping on and off the pedal.

"Don't try to use the chisel. Just get used to the movement of your foot and see if you can get the piece spinning at a good and steady speed."

Hans did as he was instructed, but it didn't work as he had imagined. The piece would spin well for a time or two, and then it would stutter. He was immediately frustrated and embarrassed. With the craftsman's encouragement, he spent the entire morning trying to get the wood to spin correctly in the machine. Maybe this was not such a great invention after all. He imagined that the inventor was probably a blacksmith who knew nothing at all about building furniture. From lunch until quitting time, he practiced getting his foot to work just right. He had to keep switching feet because one would get tired. So every half hour or so, he would switch off, standing on one foot and running the pedal with the other.

He was exhausted as they walked home, and Alfred saw his discouragement, so he mentioned it to Hans. "The craftsmen said that you did very well today."

"I didn't think so," Hans replied.

"New things always take some time, Hans. You must be patient. I know tomorrow will be a better day for you."

Hans thought maybe he was right. He went to bed that night and lay awake, going through the motions of his feet over and over again. He knew that soon he would be good on the new lathe. The next morning, Alfred woke him early. Hans did not understand the reason why until he stepped out of bed. As soon as he tried to walk, pain shot from his calves all the way to his chest. Every time he tried to take a step, his feet refused to bend. He reached down to rub his calves, but they were so sore he could not stand to touch them.

"Come into the kitchen, Hans, Heather has what you need," Alfred said.

Hans sat down at the first chair he came to with great pain. Heather had hot, moist towels all ready for him to put on his legs.

"The other men and I learned that this is a very painful machine to use. We got so excited when they came, we spent sixteen hours trying to learn how to run them. We all found out how old we were the next morning. We discovered the hot towels help for the first few days until your muscles get used to it."

Hans had never felt anything so good in his life as those hot towels. When Alfred said it was time to go to work, he moaned at having to walk. The walk was a good thing, though, as it helped him work out some of the stiffness and he felt better by the time they arrived at the shop. He was glad to wait for the others to get there so he could rub his legs before they started. The craftsmen he was working with assured him that by the end of the week, he would no longer be sore.

Hans spent most of the day trying to persuade his legs to work for him. Each time he switched off, it took a while for the leg to loosen up. He was able to start making some cuts after lunch, but they were crude and sporadic. He had learned how to make the wood spin consistently, but when he started thinking about the chisel, his legs seemed to forget what they were supposed to be doing. By the end of the day, he was too tired and sore to worry about his progress. He just wanted to get back to Alfred's and sit down with some warm, moist towels. That night, it rained, and the gentle tapping on the roof helped Hans fall asleep quickly.

The next morning, he was still stiff and sore, but Heather's hot towel therapy came to his rescue again.

That morning, he started right in cutting on the wood and making the shavings he had dreamed about. His only assignment was to create a wooden cylinder the same size all the way across. He tried to concentrate, but every time he stopped the wood from spinning to check it, one end was bigger than the other. He kept trying to take just enough off, but would find he had taken too much and would have to make the other end smaller to match. Just when he thought that he had it right, the chisel cut through the cylinder and it snapped in two. One of the craftsmen saw it and came over to take a look.

"What happened, Hans?" he asked.

"I'm not sure. I had it just about right and the wood broke."

"That's because you got the wood too thin. You've worked very hard. This morning, you had a nice piece of wood, and tonight, you have a toothpick. It's all right, though. You have learned a lot. Tomorrow you can start with a new piece."

The next morning, Hans got a new piece of wood and put it in the machine. The craftsman asked him if he needed help, but he refused. He was sure he remembered how to put it in since it was the easiest step in the process. He soon had his wood in place and determined that this one would turn out right. He got his chisel in place and gave a firm step on the pedal. The wood came flying out of the machine and hit him in his already broken nose. He grabbed his face and jumped around while the others tried very hard not to laugh.

The second time, he accepted some help and learned what he had done wrong. It took about fifteen minutes to get his rhythm right, but soon he was making shavings. By the end of the day, he had produced a reasonably consistent cylinder. Alfred came over to look as he proudly displayed Hans's work to everyone. They all gave him a pat on the back, and he was sure he had finally mastered this awkward piece of machinery.

The next day, he was given a new piece of wood. After he had mounted it, he had one of the craftsmen check it to be sure it was secure. He again spent most of the day trying to get the cylinder perfectly round. After he had done this, Alfred produced a simple practice plan for a column.

Hans would now have to learn to make the various shapes on the wood using different kinds of chisels. He began to regain his dreams of making dozens of beautiful pieces on the machine. Since he had the basics down, he was sure that he would move along quickly.

The next Monday, he spent the day watching the craftsmen again. They showed him how to use the different chisels to produce the cuts he wanted. They also showed him how to use a measuring tool called calipers, which looked like odd tongs.

One of the craftsmen produced the practice piece in about an hour, so Hans felt it would be a breeze. He worked as hard as he could for the rest of the day. When his work was checked at quitting time, he had made several mistakes in the piece.

Hans only had two weeks left to learn this machine, and he was still struggling to make a practice piece. He was discouraged, but Alfred told him to relax on his day off and try again on Monday. Hans joined Alfred, Heather and the kids for lunch and then retired to his room for the afternoon. He had been thinking of a piece of furniture he wanted to build, so he took out his pen, ink, and paper and began to work on plans for it. It was a simple piece that he had helped Father build several times, and by evening, the plans were done.

After supper, he and Alfred reviewed the plans and double-checked the measurements. Alfred seemed impressed with the neatness and detail of Hans's drawings. He commented that Frederick was one of the finest draftsmen he had ever known.

Arrangements were made for Hans to work in the shop after quitting time, and Alfred furnished him with the wood at a very reasonable rate. Hans was pleased about building something on his own for a change, and it helped him get his excitement back for Monday.

"Hans," the craftsman said on Monday afternoon, "congratulations, you have made your first practice piece correctly." He removed the piece from the lathe and held it up high, "Look, everyone, Hans has done it!"

Hans was very proud of his work, but a little embarrassed at the attention. Now he felt he could move on to the more impressive pieces. Alfred came over to where he was and admired what Hans had done.

"What will I work on next?" Hans excitedly asked.

"Well, Hans, you must first make three of the practice pieces that are exactly alike in every detail, then you will practice on the test piece until you can make it in less than two hours."

"What is the test piece?" Hans asked.

"It is that one setting on the shelf. You will have no plans to go by. You must take that piece and use your calipers to reproduce it exactly."

The piece was small and elegant. It was a finial made of maple, a very hard wood. It was as pretty as Hans had ever seen. He knew that if he could make it, then he would truly have mastered this machine. He immediately set about getting ready to make another practice piece, and in two days, he had all three of his pieces ready for inspection. Alfred and the other craftsmen laid them out on the bench and carefully examined and measured them. They quietly talked among themselves while Hans eyed the test piece and thought of how he would make it. Finally, Alfred walked over to him.

"Hans, each piece is very nice and you did good work."

Hans was beaming with pride and ready to start on the test piece.

"There is only one problem, Hans, you have made three very unique turnings and they are to be exactly alike. Come here and let me show you."

Alfred took some time to show Hans the differences in the pieces and how they would show up badly if they were placed close together on a piece of furniture. He said that Hans had to start all over again with the practice turning before he could begin working on the test piece. Hans was heartbroken and discouraged, but he knew that Alfred and the other craftsmen were right.

By the end of the week, he still had not produced three like turnings. His work at night was a welcome refuge from the endless hours on the lathe. It felt good to do something he was good at to keep up his confidence, but he was getting very discouraged. Saturday night, while he was alone in the shop, he decided that he would ask to be taken off the lathe and work on other projects. He felt he was wasting Alfred's time and his own.

After lunch on Sunday, Hans asked to talk.

"Alfred, I'm just not getting what I should from the lathe. I have really tried hard, but I don't think I will get everything learned by the end of the week. Perhaps it would be better if I let someone else start using the machine."

After several minutes of silence, Alfred spoke up. "Hans, are you saying that you are willing to throw away two weeks of work and quit?"

"It's not throwing it away. I will at least know something if I ever have occasion to use a lathe again."

"But you can still become good at it if you just stay with it one more week."

"I'm never gonna get the test piece done, Alfred, I'm too far behind."

"Sure you can, Hans. It will just take a little more time. You are very close."

"How can you say I am close when I haven't even made my three practice pieces yet?"

"Because you have done the most difficult work. Whenever a person starts something new, getting the basic skills is the hardest part. You have those, so now all you need to do is refine them. I will not stop you if you want to quit, but quitting is always the easiest way out and the most expensive."

"How is it expensive? I'm costing you a lot of money by tying up that machine."

"Hans, do you ever look out the window of the shop at the stream which runs beside the shop?"

"Yes, sometimes. In fact, beside the stream is where I like to eat my lunch."

"And what is there beside the stream?"

"Well, trees and grass and the rock wall."

"Do you know what the wall is there for?"

"I guess to keep the stream in its banks and from washing away the foundation of the shop."

"That's right, Hans. You see, the stream is lazy and it goes wherever it's easiest to go. As it does, it washes away whatever is in its way and constantly gets wider. Have you ever noticed how gentle the water runs at the wide spots and how fast it is at the narrows?"

"Yes."

"That's how we are. The stream has the same ability to cut away the rock and soil, whether it goes straight or meanders. We have built a wall to direct it where it should go instead of where laziness will take it. I've found that people are like that. One must build their own walls of direction. Just like the stream, a person has the great ability to move and change things if they are faithful to their course, instead of taking the easy way. Many people take the easy way in life, and soon they are so wide that they have lost all their power to change things. You must decide if you want the easy way or to build yourself a wall of faithful direction."

Hans had no reply. He knew his frustration and disappointment were taking him away from the hopes he had two weeks earlier. He resolved he would give it two more days because he didn't want to lose face in front of Alfred. Hans respected him and had grown to like him very much. He decided he could not betray the trust and patience he had been shown.

On Monday morning, Hans decided that he would complete the three practice pieces, if nothing else. He worked carefully with each piece, taking the time for exact measurements. He was determined that this would be done, and he could not quit until he had made three identical pieces. He was amazed at how well he worked with this decision firmly planted in his mind.

Hans had been working with an attitude of maybe, but now it was an attitude of must do. Wednesday afternoon found him waiting for a decision from the two craftsmen and Alfred. They studied the pieces for a very long time, and Hans resolved to go ahead and mount another piece of wood to start over when Alfred approached him.

"Congratulations, Hans! You have made three identical pieces. We do not think that you have enough time to complete the test piece, but we would like for you to try."

"How long does it usually take?" Hans asked.

"The average is about a week of practice, but you only have three days. Would you like to try?"

"Yes," Hans said emphatically.

Now both of the craftsmen were working with him and encouraging him all the way. The test piece was smaller and much more delicate than the columns. Hans broke several pieces on the first day and had to start over. That night, after he had worked on his furniture project, he spent several hours at the lathe, trying to form the delicate shape. The next night found him spending many hours alone in the shop at his lathe.

Saturday after lunch, Alfred came to talk to the two lathe craftsmen. They decided it was now or never for Hans.

"You must try today if you are to complete your training on the lathe, Hans," Alfred said with hesitation.

"I have one request. Please let me make the test piece out of walnut instead of maple."

"The walnut is not quite as hard, but the wider grain makes it more difficult to turn, Hans. Are you sure of this?"

"Yes. Father works almost exclusively with walnut, and I know the wood well. If I must try, please let me do it in walnut."

Alfred and the two craftsmen looked at each other and raised their hands in surrender to his request. Hans waited for the signal of time and started. He had some difficulty with the walnut, as predicted, and had to be careful with the depth of the cuts he made. In spite of the challenge, he was able to keep from breaking the piece. He was feeling very confident and only had twenty minutes of work left when he felt Alfred's hand on his shoulder.

"Time's up, Hans. You have been working for two hours, and that was the limit, but you should be proud. If we had had more time, I'm sure you could have passed."

"No, Alfred, please. I have to finish."

"We have an hour and a half before quitting time. You can finish the piece you are on. It just won't count for the completion of the test."

"I know. What I mean is, let me do it again. If the others don't mind staying late, I know I can do it."

"Let the boy try, Alfred," one of the craftsmen said.

"O.k. I will give you ten minutes to get ready."

"I'll only need five," Hans said as he sprang into action for the next test.

Hans began with the deepest of concentration. All the noise and activity of the shop seemed to disappear as he focused on his lathe. He was now in his own world, and nothing would deprive him of his prize. The wood shavings flew as he gained confidence. The first time, he had been too cautious and hesitant with his cuts, and it cost him precious time.

Hans relied on the skills he had learned and worked briskly. He could feel the walnut through the handle of his chisel, and his hands didn't hesitate. He stepped back from his finished turning just moments before the two-hour limit was up.

He dismounted the piece from the lathe and handed it to Alfred, who walked over to a bench and laid it down to measure and inspect. Hans had been standing in one spot all day and had to find a stool to sit down. He waited patiently for the three men to discuss his work and make their decision. He felt at ease about things because he knew no matter what the outcome, he had done his best. He was glad he had not quit because he would have never known the pride of giving something his all.

"Well, Hans," Alfred began, "we knew time was running short, and you probably wouldn't be able to pass the test. I don't know how you did it, but you did. Congratulations!"

"Really?" Hans asked, "I passed the test?"

"You sure did. Everything your father said about you was true. I just thought that he was bragging, but you have his gift for woodworking."

Hans realized he had not accomplished this alone; his father had taught him many things. Had it not been for the years of Father's faithful teaching about walnut, Hans could not have done this. Everyone patted him on the back and gave him the turning as a memento of his hard work. He stayed for a little while and put the finishing touches on his furniture project. He was not sure he could get it done either, but he had managed to do so. When he got back to Alfred's, the kids were in bed, and the men sat down to talk.

"You really did well, Hans," Alfred said with a smile. "I have no idea how you got it done in three days, but I am very proud you did. Now that you are qualified to run it, maybe you can persuade your father to buy a lathe."

"Once you get the hang of it, it sure is easier than doing it all by hand."

"Hans, anything in life is better when you faithfully keep learning and growing. There are a host of craftsmen who never reach their full potential because they come to a point in their life where they just meander like the stream. It takes faithfulness to be good at anything. I hope you have learned that you can accomplish anything if you just keep trying and don't give up. You have something very beautiful to show your father when you get home."

"You know, Alfred, father was very faithful to me, too. He never did give up on me, even when I didn't like what he was teaching me. This trip was like the wood we work with on the lathe. It starts out just a square piece of wood, and we start spinning it back and forth and working with it until it is something beautiful. I started this trip with a lot of rough edges, and I felt like Father was just spinning me around for his own enjoyment. But he has applied many different kinds of chisels to my life to make me better."

"Hans, your father is a greater craftsman with men than he ever was with wood. I think you have learned more than he hoped for."

Since the carriage for Gaudium did not leave until Monday morning, Hans had Sunday afternoon free and one chore left to do.

"Alfred," Hans asked, "is there a freight hauler in this town?"

"Yes, there is," Alfred answered with a smile, "in fact, I think that you have met him a couple of times."

"Oh no, not him."

"Why, did you want something delivered tomorrow?"

"No, tonight."

"Sounds like a Sebastian delivery to me. Why don't you just use my cart and horse if you want. Do you need help?"

"No. I can manage by myself if you really don't mind me using the cart."

"It's all yours, Hans."

Hans got the key to the shop and drove down to load up. He was careful to secure the load since he wasn't sure what the roads were like where he was going. The sun was getting low in the sky as he left town, and he figured that it would be dark just as he got to where he was going. He enjoyed the ride and marveled at the towering pine trees that lined the road. He found his destination and waited for half an hour to be sure it was completely dark.

His getaway would be tricky. He decided it would be best to unload a ways from the house and then park the horse and cart down the hill. He would then carry the piece of furniture up to the house, knock, and run through the woods to his cart. When the time came, he quietly drove as close as he dared to unload. He found a spot on the road straight down from the house and tied up the horse. The walk back up the hill was harder than he thought and he had to stop several times to catch his breath. He picked up the furniture and carried it to a clearing in front of the house.

Quietly, he tiptoed up to the door and gave a sound knock. He turned and ran as fast as he could, hoping to get into the trees before someone answered the door. As soon as he reached the trees, the hill dropped off sharply, and he fell, stumbled, and slid down the hill to the road. He could hear someone calling out from the house, but he just kept going. He jumped on the cart and slapped the reins firmly against the back of the horse.

All the commotion of him running down the hill had unnerved the horse, and when Hans let him go, he bolted. Hans could hardly see a thing in the dark, but the horse could. Each time they came to a curve, he was caught off guard. It was all he could do to hang on and try to get the horse slowed down to a safe speed. Needless to say, most of the ride down the hill was very exciting, but they managed to emerge no worse for the wear.

As he headed back to town, Hans looked back and could see the full moon coming up behind the King's castle. It was the most beautiful sight he had ever seen as the moon completely surrounded the castle. He again dreamed of making beautiful furniture for the King with finely turned pieces from the lathe machine. Hans rode along and dreamed of the honor he would one day receive as the King's furniture maker.

Back on the mountain, Heidi and her mother stood at the door of their small house looking out. They could not see anyone there, and no one answered their calls. They were frightened and not sure whether to go out or bolt the door. They decided to go back inside and wait for the moon to rise higher in the sky before venturing out.

They really didn't own anything outside that someone could steal. They checked again in an hour and decided to venture out. Heidi insisted she would be the one to go.

She slowly and quietly walked outside and looked back and forth to see what had made the awful noise at their door. It had sounded like a knock, but who would come out there at night and then leave after knocking? As she walked away from the house further, she noticed something sitting alone in the moonlight.

"Mother?" she whispered, "I think I see something."

"What?" Her mother whispered back.

"I don't know, but it is straight out from the house a little ways."

"Is it an animal or what?"

"I'm not sure, but it isn't moving. I'm going to get a closer look."

"Be careful, Heidi."

"I will."

Heidi slowly walked out in front of the house until she could make out the object sitting in the clearing. The closer she got, the slower she walked. When she got right up to the object, she just stopped and looked. What was something like this doing out here? She looked around to see if she could spot anyone, but she couldn't. Then she began to realize how it had come to be here. Tears filled her eyes as she ran her hands over it.

The Last Step

Heidi had never seen anything more beautiful in her life. She knew exactly who had made this and left it for her; the best, the only real friend she had, Hans. She smiled as she gently sat down in the chair and ran her hands over the slanted top of the desk. She could see and feel the delicate wood turning for the ink well, and it was all made from the most beautiful walnut. A short note was attached.

Every great dressmaker needs a desk to draw her designs.
Use this desk often, and soon you will be making dresses
for the Queen!

The moonlight glimmered on the rich finish, and its touch was like glass. She called her mother out to help her carry it into the house. After they had set it in the middle of the room, she told her mother about her friend Hans.

The next morning, Hans and Alfred went to the station. Alfred had given Hans a package the night before and asked him to wait until he got home to open it. He also asked Hans not to tell Father who had told him all the stories of when they were apprentices. He agreed and was on his way to Gaudium. For once, the trip was uneventful and peaceful. Hans spent most of the trip wondering which town he would return to after Father gave him his journeyman's papers. He was still unsure, but knew that he would have a month or two to think about it when he got home.

Each time they stopped, Hans would get out his telescope and look back at the mountains for a glimpse of the King's castle, dreaming of filling it with his furniture. He had learned many valuable lessons on his journey, and his confidence was growing. He hoped to earn his craftsman's license within the next two or three years. That would make him the youngest craftsman in the country, and he was sure the king would take notice.

Even before he could see the ocean, he knew they were approaching the port city of Gaudium on the southern coast by the smell of salt water in the air. The sea held little fascination to Hans after spending three weeks under the majesty of the King's mountains, but he was glad to be at his last stop before home.

The city was medium-sized and situated on the plain, blending seamlessly into the ocean. Few ships came to Gaudium since it had no deep-water harbors. The ships all anchored out to sea, and things were ferried to them. Hans did not miss the docks and their dangers.

It was mid-afternoon on Tuesday when they arrived, and he followed his directions to the shop. Upon entering, he found himself in the smallest shop of his journey with only one craftsman, three journeymen, and five apprentices. No one had noticed his entry, so he made his way to a middle-aged man and introduced himself.

"Excuse me, sir, I am Hans, son of Frederick the craftsman."

"Oh, I'm sorry. I didn't see you come in. Welcome. I am Josef," the man kindly said. "I have been looking forward to your visit for such a long time. I understand that this is your last stop before home."

"Yes, sir," Hans replied.

"Well, I hope it is a joyous one. Let me introduce you to everyone."

Hans followed Josef around the small shop and met each of the workers. There was something about this shop that made it inviting and peaceful. He didn't mind the size of it and thought that a slower pace would be just the thing for him. He noticed the furniture was very ornate and just the kind a king would buy. He felt that he could learn a great deal about design here, which would serve him well in the future. Josef took him to a wall that was covered with the most incredible assortment of planes that he had ever seen. Josef took many of his prized ones down and showed them to Hans. He had made most of them himself and fancied himself a connoisseur of planes.

There was no place to stay in the shop, so Hans went home with Josef. The home itself was simple, but in it were many of the ornate pieces that were made at the shop. Josef's wife, Irma, was gentle and very hospitable. Their children were grown and moved away, so the house was quiet and peaceful. It was evident from the decorations that children seldom visited here. The next morning, Hans arrived at the shop full of anticipation. He had remembered to bring his pen and paper so he could keep a record of the things he learned. As soon as Josef got the rest of the workers started, he came over to Hans.

"I understand that you are beyond your years in ability and experience, Hans."

"Thank you, sir. I appreciate your confidence in me," Hans said as humbly as he could.

"I have a special project that must be done this month, and I am going to put you in charge of it. You will be responsible for the design, construction, and finishing of this project. It must be shipped by the end of the month," Josef emphasized.

"I am very honored, sir. I promise to do my very best even if

I have to work after hours and on my day off," Hans said excitedly.

"Wonderful, Hans, I knew that I could count on you. I have a bench in the back all ready. Come and I will show it to you."

Josef took Hans over to a large bench, and beside it lay a stack of rough oak. Hans could not imagine what project he would make in a month with such a large stack of wood. He began to feel nervous as he wondered about the project.

"I have made a small sketch of what I want you to build. It only has rough dimensions, but you can create the final plans and details as you like. Here, look at it and see if you can read my scribbles," Josef said as he handed the paper to Hans.

Hans tried to appear serious and knowledgeable as he took the sketch and examined it. On the paper was a rough drawing of a foot stool.

"It is a foot stool, sir," Hans said.

"Yes, it is. Take the morning and make your plans, and then proceed when you are ready. There is no need for me to approve your drawings," Josef said as he patted Hans on the back and went to look in on the other workers.

Hans looked at the stack of oak and then at the sketch. Surely this must be a test of some kind to find out if he can build something larger. He decided to make the nicest footstool he could, so he could get on to something more important. He carefully drew out his plans and checked them several times to ensure the dimensions were correct. He wished he had a lathe machine to make nicer legs, but still decided to round them by hand. It took him until Friday afternoon to finish building the stool, and he put a second coat of varnish on it just before quitting time.

The next morning, Hans polished the foot stool and took it to

Josef in the front of the shop.

"Oh, Hans, it is beautiful. I do believe that this is the finest stool I have ever seen. Everyone, look at the stool our Hans has made," he said as he held it up. Everyone seemed impressed, and Hans was glad that he had taken the project seriously. "I think that you are ready to move on now."

"Thank you, sir," Hans said. "I am grateful that you like it."

"Oh yes, Hans, it is perfect. Now, in the next three weeks, I need you to make fourteen more just like it for a total of fifteen stools," Josef said with a great big smile, expecting Hans to share his excitement.

"Excuse me, sir, did you say fourteen more?"

"Yes, Hans, just like this one," Josef said as he walked over to a shelf and put the foot stool on it.

Hans walked to the back of the shop and just looked at the pile of oak for fifteen minutes. This could not be true. He had traveled hundreds of miles across the country to find himself doing the same kind of menial work that he had done for Father. If he had kept his final turning instead of putting it on Heidi's desk as the inkwell, Josef would have known what kind of work he was capable of doing. He angrily picked up a board and began to plane it.

Sunday, after breakfast, he went to his room to avoid Josef and write Father. He just sat with his pen and paper and stewed about his situation for the longest time. Finally, he began his letter.

Dear Father,

I am now in Gaudium, making footstools for Josef. I cannot believe I have come so far to do the work of a second-year apprentice. I will be making the same style of stool for the whole month. I am very angry with him and ready to come home. I wish that my ticket were for today, but it cannot be exchanged or refunded. I cannot see wasting a whole month here.

I have thought a lot about coming to the city as a journeyman. I would like very much to talk to you about it when I get home. Perhaps I should wait until I have gotten my craftsman's license so I can open my own shop in the city and not have to work for anyone else. Could you let me stay on for several more years? Please think about it before I get home. With the things I have learned on my journey, we could make some great furniture together. Please give Mother my love, and I will see you in four weeks. I am not looking forward to seven days on the road, but it will be worth it to get home.

Love,

Hans

P.S. Have you ever heard of a machine called a lathe? I cannot wait to tell you about it.

Hans addressed his letter and took a nap for the rest of the day. The next morning found him at his bench making the stools that he had come to hate. He had learned enough to not let the quality of the stools slip. He tried to make each one better than the last without changing the design or style.

By the end of the week, he had added only three more stools to the shelf in the front of the shop. He figured at best he would only get eight more stools made in the next two weeks, leaving him three short. He decided to not worry about it until Monday.

Following lunch on Sunday, as Hans was retreating to his room, Josef asked him to go for a walk on the beach. Hans only accepted out of courtesy because he was still very angry with Josef. It was a beautiful day, and the two of them walked along in silence as the waves gently fell on the shore. After they had walked for a mile or so, Josef broke the silence.

"Hans, I'm not sure if you are anxious to get home or not, but you seem very unhappy here."

"No, sir, everything is fine."

"Now, Hans," Josef gently said, "I see your face every day as you work, and you wear a scowl. How can everything be all right with an expression like that? Please tell me what it is?"

"May I speak honestly?" Hans asked, not caring about the reply.

"Please. I want you to let me teach you, and that can only happen if we are honest with each other."

"I had hoped to be learning something important instead of making footstools all month."

"Oh," Josef said as they stopped to face each other, "I see that you do not like doing my job."

"Your job?" Hans asked.

"Yes, Hans. Every two years, we get an order for fifteen-foot stools, and I usually make them myself."

"Why would you do that? It is clearly a job for an apprentice."

"I do it for myself, Hans."

"I still don't understand."

"Well, as you have found out, making fifteen footstools is a very mundane job. Most furniture makers are looking for the grand jobs and want to get away from the mundane. Now, there is nothing wrong with doing a great piece of furniture as long as you have not forgotten how to enjoy it."

"How could one forget to enjoy it?" Hans asked.

"Whatever level you aspire to, it will one day become mundane. You must always remind yourself to find joy in the unimportant tasks so your work does not lose its wonder. Doing a simple task with joy reminds me of how far I have come and what the years have taught me. It makes me appreciate those under me who must do tasks like that every day. Hans, I count making the foot stools the greatest privilege in my shop. I hope that you will always remember to make foot stools so that the joy of furniture making does not leave you. Joy is the crowning achievement of your life."

"How do I find joy in something that I despise so much?"

"The happiness of most men's hearts lies in the task that they do. They let circumstances and accomplishments determine if they are happy or not. Real joy is in a man's heart, not in his hands. Lasting joy will never move from your hands to your heart; it must come from the heart to the hands."

"But is it wrong to find joy in your accomplishments? Don't you feel good when you complete a beautiful piece of furniture?"

"Why, of course. There is nothing wrong with the joy we get from accomplishments as long as we realize that it does not last. No one is successful at everything they do every time they do it. If it were not for my failures, I would have no wood for the stove in the winter. Have you ever found your failed pieces of furniture heating the shop in winter?"

"Yes. I remember a time when Father said that I was supplying most of his firewood because I had so many mistakes in the shop."

"Hans, I know from your father that you want to move to the city as soon as you complete your apprenticeship. I want you to think about something before you do that. If you cannot find joy in Crescere, you will never find it somewhere else. Men travel all over the world looking for joy when the only place they can ever find it is in their heart."

"I'm beginning to see that."

"I cannot take anyone else in the shop off what they are doing to complete the stools, so you must stay with them. The deadline is set and I must deliver them by the end of the month. You are a man now, Hans. Only you can decide whether it is a task of joy or drudgery. It will always be yours to decide."

Hans felt a bit humbled by Josef's wisdom as they walked back to the house. He sometimes did not understand his own impatience and anger. Josef was right. There were many things worse than building foot stools. He only had two weeks left before he went home, and he determined that somehow he would find joy in his work. It had to be better than the self-pity and arrogance that he had been swimming in.

Hans worked very hard that week and tried to quit scowling. Every time he caught himself doing it, he would try to replace it with a smile. He wondered what difference it made if he was making footstools or dressers; it was still wood. He realized he loved the smell of the wood as he planed it and watched it conform to his wishes.

The wood smelled as sweet as if it were going to be a leg for a stool or the front of a dresser. As hard as he tried to make the job enjoyable, the end of the week only produced four more stools. He had one week and seven stools left to make.

Monday, he and Josef sat down to work out the most efficient way to finish the job. For some reason, the work was no longer what mattered to Hans. He had found that his love and joy in life was working with wood, and he wanted to do the best he could. The lines of glory and shame were erased. He just wanted to let the work of his hands express what he knew was his calling in life.

Father had always told him that a piece of furniture should be a reflection of the man who made it. The little stools no longer looked like drab reminders of his work, but they danced on the shelf as each one was completed.

Hans worked sixteen and eighteen hours a day, and when Saturday came, he proudly placed the last stool on the shelf. Josef came over and stood by him as they admired the stools.

"They are kind of cute setting up there, aren't they, Josef?"

"You have done a fine job, Hans. In fact, I am going to have some trouble making as nice of ones in two years."

"That will just add to the joy of it," Hans replied.

Josef just laughed and ruffled Hans's hair. The two of them locked up the shop and headed for home. The next morning, Hans went with Josef to package up the stools and get them ready for the ship, which was anchored there. The ship was leaving at ten o'clock, and they would have to hurry to have them ready in time. They took them by cart to the beach where a boat was waiting to take them out. Josef struck up a conversation with a businessman who had come ashore while Hans helped the sailors.

"Hans," Josef called, "come over here!"

"Yes, Josef, what is it?" Hans asked.

"This man may have an interesting proposition for you. It seems that he has ship passage to Amare, but his plans have changed. He needs to travel overland so that he can conduct business along the way. Don't you have passage for tomorrow to Amare on the carriage?"

"Yes."

"This man is willing to trade you tickets if it is all right. You could be home in two days instead of seven."

"But Josef, they are ready to leave right now!"

"I will hold the boat if you run to the house and get your things. Hurry, Hans!"

Hans ran for the house as quick as he could while Josef and the other man tried to persuade the sailors to wait. Hans burst through the door and ran into the house. He startled Irma, but was too winded to explain what was going on. He went to his room and gathered his belongings into his bag as quickly as he could, along with a package that was on the bed.

Hans ran back down the stairs and quickly tried to explain what had happened so that Irma would not be worried about the commotion. He gave her a quick hug and thanked her for all that she had done.

The sailors were arguing with Josef when Hans got back to the beach. As he ran to get in the boat, Josef caught him by the arm.

"Hans, one last thing. Remember the stools. If you are going to work for the King one day, start now by making everything as though it were for him. Have a safe journey and tell Frederick hello." Josef gave him a quick hug, and Hans climbed into the boat as it shoved off.

"Hans, one more thing. Be sure the stools are picked up in Genus!" Josef shouted.

"How will I know who is picking them up?" Hans called back over the surf.

"They will be picked up by the King's soldiers."

"Why soldiers? Who is the customer?"

"The King, Hans, the King!"

"What King?" Hans asked.

"King Ivan of Valorem, who else! Every two years, he has us make all new step stools for his carriages. We can't have the King or Queen falling off of rotted old stools, can we?"

Hans just plopped down in the boat. All his life, he had dreamed of making something for the King, and he had done it. If he had only known sooner, he would have done a much better job. Now he understood why this job was so important to Josef and what an honor it was to be able to design and build the stools himself.

Hans just threw his head back and laughed at the thought of it all. As he looked back at the shore, he could see Josef laughing also as they waved goodbye.

That evening, they briefly docked in a small, remote port to deliver the stools and other freight for the King. Hans was very particular about how the stools were handled. He stood guard over them on the dock until three soldiers pulled up in a wagon.

Hans stood tall and proud as they drove up to him. He tried to act like it was an everyday occurrence as they loaded the stools into the wagon. As they drove off, he remembered how just a few months ago he had been dreaming of making things for the King.

The captain quickly set sail because a spring storm was brewing off the coast, and the seas were getting very rough. Hans spent the rest of the trip below deck. He had never been so sick in his life as the ship lunged to one side and then the other. He just kept thinking of the surprise his parents would have when he arrived home early. He kept trying to think of what he would say and how he would walk in to surprise them. After the longest trip of his life, they docked at Amare just before midnight.

Hans knew that there was no way to get home that night, so he rented a room in the Inn. He awoke with the sun and started looking for a ride home. Since there was no carriage to Crescere, he would have to find another way. It was not a scheduled day for Thomas to come to town, so he asked around until he found someone going his way.

A vendor Hans had heard about was just rolling out of town in his cart when Hans caught up to him. The man allowed him to ride along in the back of the cart. The ride was bumpy in the back, but he was just glad he wasn't walking. The vendor was going straight through, so Hans would be home by mid-afternoon.

By early afternoon, the scenery was looking very familiar, and Hans would occasionally look around to see how close they were getting. At two o'clock, they arrived at the road into Crescere, and Hans jumped off the cart, thanked the vendor, and started walking into town. He could not contain himself, so he sprinted home. It only took him half an hour to reach their village, and the covered bridge going into town was the sweetest sight he had ever seen. The village was quiet as he walked through, just as he remembered it. Suddenly, what he had remembered as boring was now peaceful.

As he reached the far edge of town, his house came into sight. It looked so wonderful tucked into the trees. Soon, he and Father would be working outside and telling endless stories of his journey. He couldn't wait for the right time to ask Father about his mischief as a young lad. He walked to the side of the road, hoping that his approach would not be noticed since the doors to the shop were open. He tiptoed up to the house and crept in the door.

What timing, he thought. A family was in the shop looking at a casket that Father had made. Since Frederick was the only woodworker in town, he had to make all the caskets. Often, the family would want something carved on the lid, and Father would have to complete it in a day. Then, like now, the family would come out to look at it and make changes.

Hans always hated it when Father had to make a casket because Hans would have to act really solemn when the family came out. How were they going to have their joyful reunion with these people in here?

He knew Father would not leave the grieving family no matter what, but Hans just had to let him know he was home. No one had heard him come in, so he quietly walked towards the people who all had their backs to him. He tried very hard to wipe the excitement off his face and look serious, but a slight grin kept coming back to his face. He decided to let Father see him and then go upstairs to greet Mother.

He slowly walked over to the people so as not to disturb them. Just as he got to them, they sensed his presence and moved aside just enough so Hans could see through. After all these months and great anticipation, Hans looked directly into his father's face.

The Letter

The stillness.

The quiet.

The emptiness.

No words can describe these things when you look at your father for the first time in months, and he is lying dead in a coffin. It is especially tragic when the last words you ever spoke to him were in anger. Hans tried to catch his breath as he stood there. Hans could not believe that this was happening or that it could be true. He never had a real chance to tell Father he was sorry for the things he said before he left. Never again could he hear Father's gentle voice as they worked beside one another in the little shop he had now come to love.

Hans shoved the people aside and looked at Father's face as Frederick's body lay in the casket. Hans could not believe that this was happening or that it could be true. Hans fell to his knees as his hands clung to the side of the casket, which held his father. He couldn't breathe. The room was spinning around as he tried to comprehend how this could be true. His heart felt as though it would burst inside him.

Hans's thoughts were numb as he knelt beside his father and felt the deepest pain of his life. In a moment of total despair, he cried out.

"Father!" he moaned as he hung his head and wept.

"Hans?"

"Father?"

"Hans."

"Father," Hans said as he looked up and saw his father leaning over the casket and looking at him.

"Hans, what are you doing here?" Father whispered.

"Father, what are you doing there?" Hans asked in amazement and confusion.

Father sheepishly climbed out of the casket and almost fell. He excused himself from the mourners and took Hans aside. Once in the corner, Father whispered to him.

"Hans, you weren't supposed to be home for four more days. What are you doing home today?"

"Father," Hans whispered back, "what were you doing in that casket? I thought that you were dead."

"I'm sorry, Son. Go upstairs and see your mother. I'll be up in a few minutes," Father said as he squeezed Hans's shoulder and went back to the family of the deceased.

Hans half stumbled up the stairs, looking back at Father and wondering what was going on. He was so drained that he couldn't say anything to Mother. He just hugged her and sat down at the table. In just a couple of minutes, Father came bounding up the stairs and gave Hans the biggest hug he had ever gotten. Hans was still in shock from the scare he had.

"Father, what were you doing lying in that casket? You scared me to death. I really thought you were dead."

"Frederick," Mother asked with a puzzled look, "you were in the casket? Why would you lie in another man's casket?"

"Well," Father started with an embarrassed grin on his face, "the family insisted the man who died would not fit in it. I tried to assure them that it was big enough, but they were getting hysterical about it. Since I am the same size as the deceased, I climbed in to show them that it was big enough. For some reason, I just closed my eyes and tried to look dead. That way, they could see how their loved one would look."

"Frederick," Mother scolded, "that's disrespectful of the dead."

They just stood there, looking at each other for a few moments, and then burst out laughing. Father and Hans felt very sheepish about the scene they had put on in front of the customers. Mother thought that they had both lost their minds, and she could not believe that her two men were still acting like boys.

They sat down and visited about how Hans had come to arrive home early. Father was very glad that it had worked out, but he felt bad that he had scared Hans so badly. Father finally had to excuse himself and go back to the shop. The deceased's family had wanted some carvings done on the lid of the casket. Hans followed Father down to help him.

Frederick had already drawn out the design on the lid, and he began at the top. Hans instinctively picked up a chisel and began to help as they talked about the amazing things Hans had seen, like the mountains and the ships. Father listened patiently as Hans rambled on and on. Hans was not really paying attention to his work as he told stories, but Father was.

"Hans," Father interrupted, "you have been practicing while you were gone. I have never seen you handle a chisel so well."

"I did a whole mantle for Sebastian while I was in Bonum. He and Millie are a sweet old couple. Did you ever make any night deliveries with him?"

"Oh, yes, many times. Does he still make furniture for the orphanage?"

"Yes. We made a table and benches for them while I was there. He always made me feel so good because he let me work by myself and didn't look over my shoulder."

"Like I do, Son?"

"Well, I didn't mean that."

"But it is true, isn't it?" Father asked. "You truly have made me proud, and I did not realize how good you were until the others started writing me."

"Who wrote you?" Hans asked.

"Everyone you worked with. They told me everything that went on while you were there."

"Everything?"

"Yes, Son. Like what you learned, how you progressed, and some girl named Beatrice."

"Uh oh," Hans said, "I can explain that, Father."

"No need to, Son."

"Father, speaking of learning about me, I learned a lot about you from Alfred. He had some very interesting stories of when you were an apprentice."

"Uh oh," Father said.

"There are several things that I would like to know more about."

"I'll make you a deal, Hans. I won't bring up your stories if you won't bring up mine. Deal?"

Hans had to think about that one for a while. He had been waiting for over a month to put Father on the spot about his escapades. Now, Father knew something about him that he did not really want to talk about. How was it that parents always seemed to be able to get out of telling on themselves? It wasn't fair to Hans, and he hated giving in, but he did. Beatrice was a story best forgotten.

With the two of them working, the casket lid was finished by supper. The evening was wonderful for Hans as they sat and visited more about the trip. He presented the silk handkerchief to Mother, and she almost cried in it. Hans told her not to because he had seen what crying could do to silk. He was most proud when he presented the plane to Father. Frederick could not quit looking at it and thanking Hans. Hans felt that he had received the greatest gift by being able to be with his parents again.

The next morning, he and Father loaded the casket so it could be delivered to the home of the family, which was five miles from town. Hans had planned on going with Father so that they could visit some more, but when he climbed up on the wagon, Father let him in on other plans.

"Hans, I want you to stay here because your trip is not over yet."

"What do you mean, Father?"

"Do you remember the packages that you were given? Each one of them has a special significance, and when I get home, we will see if you have learned what you were supposed to. I want you to clear off the workbench and set the packages out in order. This afternoon, we will look at each one."

"OK, Father," Hans said, a little confused.

He waited outside until Father was out of sight, and then he went inside. He had missed this little shop so very much. It did not have a lot of room or fancy tools like the big shops, but it was his and Father's shop. He realized that he was very proud of what they had done here and wondered why he had ever wanted to leave. There was only one thing on the workbench. It was covered with a blanket and set to the side.

"Mother?" Hans called up the stairs. Mother came down to see what he wanted. "What is this on the bench? Father asked me to clear it off, but I do not want to move it if it is something important."

"Oh, that," Mother answered. "Your father has been fretting over that project ever since you left. I think it would be all right to move it. Just hand me the blanket and put the piece wherever you want."

Hans walked over to the bench, took the blanket off the piece, and handed it to Mother. He then looked back at the bench, and his eyes widened. He looked at the bench, then at Mother, to the bench, and then back to Mother. She was smiling and waiting for Hans to say something, but he just kept looking back and forth.

"It's OK, Hans. Open it up and look at it," Mother finally said.

Hans smiled with wonder as he walked over and touched the toolbox on the bench. It was the very one that he had drawn before he left.

"Your father selected the finest wood he owned to make that. You would have thought that King Ivan himself was going to own it. I don't know how many times he asked me to come down here and look at it for him. I have never seen him worry so much over something before. That is why he didn't want to be here when you saw it. I think he was afraid of your reaction."

"Mother, it is beautiful," Hans said as he opened the lid and looked inside. He pulled out the top drawer, and a letter was inside. As he picked it up, Mother touched him on the shoulder and went back upstairs. Hans sat down on a stool and began to read.

Dear Son,
Well, I hope you like your new tool chest. I wanted to make

it for you while you were away so that I wouldn't miss you as much. I worked on it a little bit each night and felt like you were here with me. I was most impressed by your drawings of the chest, but I couldn't figure out what they were doing in the woodpile. I did not have to change a single thing because you thought of each detail. I hope that when you use this chest, whether here or in a city shop, you will remember the wonderful times we've had together. I never want to hold you back from your dreams, and I hope we can make them all come true. Thank you for being my son. I am very proud of you!

Love,

Father

A smile came across Hans's face as he thought of his father worrying about a project for him. It had to be the most magnificent tool chest in the world. He looked at it closely and found where his father had placed his craftsman's brand. Hans ran his fingers over the brand as he thought of Father.

He picked up the chest by the brass handles on the side and stood there looking about the shop for a place to put it. After several minutes, he set it back down because he did not know where Father would want it.

Finally, he spied a spot directly across the room from Father's chest. He thought this would be a good place since they worked on opposite sides of the workbench. He cleared the spot right next to the stairs and placed the chest there.

He stepped back to look at it and admire it. Then he went across the shop and looked at it. Next, he went to the back of the shop for a look and then from the front door. He looked around to see if anyone was there to admire it with him, even though he knew there wasn't.

"Mother!" he called, "can you come down here a minute, please?"

Mother walked down the stairs, trying to figure out what he needed, but couldn't.

"Do you think the chest looks all right where it is, or should I put it in the back?" Hans began. "Maybe I should put it by Father's... no, I already thought of that. What do you think?"

"I think it looks just fine where it is," she said with a smile. "I also think it has caused me more trips to the shop than anything else."

"Sorry, Mother," Hans said apologetically, realizing that she had work to do, too.

Hans followed her back upstairs, where he got his bag and took the packages down to the workbench, carefully laying them out. He gently placed what few tools he owned in the new chest and waited for Father to return. As Frederick drove up to the house, he could see Hans outside with a great big smile on his face. Father was glad to see that Hans was pleased with his tool chest.

After lunch, they went down to the shop. Father pulled up a stool and sat down as Hans prepared to open each package and explain its contents. The first one was from Peter. Inside was a straight plane and an oil stone. Hans looked at it as he remembered the month he had spent at the sharpening table. It seemed like it had happened in another lifetime, but he still remembered what he learned.

"Father, many times we are called upon to do things that are not fun. In Pax, I spent a whole month at the sharpening bench, taking care of all the planes in the shop. At first, I was very angry, but then I learned that the only way to make it through difficult situations was to make peace with them. Anger, many times, just makes a job harder."

"Very good, Hans, continue."

Next was the package from Johann. Inside was cloth with sand glued to it. This confused Hans until he read the note, which explained that this was an invention of Johann's, born out of an accident. It seems that he had walked out back to rinse a cloth full of glue and dropped it in the sand around the well. He wanted to try this instead of the dogfish skins to smooth the furniture. He called his invention a "sand-cloth."

"Father, I have not eaten any fish since I left Johann. I have never spent so long smoothing a piece of furniture as I did there. I resented that we did not do something more important until I saw it finished. You would not believe how beautiful the piece turned out. Learning to be patient was very hard for me until I realized the great reward that came with it. So many people are like me and just want to rush through the boring parts of things, but it is the small things that make all the difference."

Third was the telescope, which Rafael had given him. He showed it to Father and proudly pulled it out until it clicked twice. He took Father outside and let him look all the way through town to the covered bridge. Father laughed when he got over the shock of the bridge looking so close.

"So what does it mean, Hans?" Father asked.

"That sometimes we have to see beyond other people's faults and not treat them as we think they deserve. There was another apprentice named Franz, and I wasn't very nice to him. He was rude and obnoxious, so I treated him the same way. I felt so foolish when I realized he had a reason for being the way he was. I have to learn to treat people the way I know I should and not just the way they treat me. Kindness is to be a gift from us and not just a repayment to those who treat us nicely."

The fourth gift was from Sebastian. Hans just held it for a moment as he remembered the cheerful smile that Sebastian always had. He opened it up and found a jar with a coin in it.

"This is special, Father. This jar sat on the table at Sebastian's. He said that he regularly put some money in it so that he could buy lumber for his special projects. I can't believe that he gave it to me. He said that if he always put a little bit in here, then he would never have an excuse not to do something nice for others. I think he wants me to follow in his footsteps and start now to give back what I have. He said that no matter what our talents were, we should share them with those in need as a way of showing kindness and goodness. Father, have you ever seen him drive a cart at night?"

Father threw his head back and laughed. "Many times, Son, many times. It's a wonder he has lived this long the way he drives that cart."

They both laughed together, and then Hans picked up the fifth package, which was from Henri. This was a large package that had been an inconvenience to carry around. He opened it, and inside was the curved front of a dresser drawer. Hans thoughtfully looked at it, realizing exactly what it meant.

"Father, many times life will give us curves in our pathway. It is not always easy to determine which way we should go. Sometimes the curves take us away from where we should be going, and we lose our way. A person must have self-control in their life to stay on the proper path. Self-control is knowing the difference between what we WANT to do and what we NEED to do. I almost got off the path in Amicitia. Henri told me that the real problem was not taking a wrong turn as I did, it was being too proud or too stupid to go back and get on the right path."

The sixth package was from Alfred. Hans was pleasantly surprised to see his three identical practice turnings inside. He gasped when he saw them and started telling Father all about the lathe and how hard it was to learn. Frederick was very impressed to see how the lathe turned out identical pieces in such a short time.

"But, Hans," Father said, "I have not seen the beautiful test piece you made."

"I gave it away."

"Oh, I so wanted to see it."

"If you buy a lathe machine, Father, I will make you another one!" Hans said excitedly.

"That's OK, Son, Alfred described it quite well. So what do these three turnings, as you called them, mean?"

"I had given up on being able to learn the machine, Father. It looked easy, but in reality it was very hard. I wanted to quit several times, but Alfred kept encouraging me. I learned that the only way to succeed in anything is to be faithful to it, even when it looks like you will not accomplish your task. It was tough to keep working with the machine, but I now know that it is always worth it to finish what you start."

"Now, Hans, open the last one and let's see what is in it."

Hans opened the package from Josef and laughed. It was a miniature stool exact in every detail to the ones Hans had made.

"Look, Father," Hans said as he handed it to Frederick, "this is exactly like the stools I made in Gaudium."

"They must have very tiny people there, Hans."

"No, Father, mine were bigger."

"Oh, I see. Well, what could you learn from making a stool?"

"I didn't make just one, Father. I made fifteen of them. You are not going to believe this, but they were for the King! I know because I gave them to his soldiers myself on the way home."

"Really, Hans? I am impressed, but what did it teach you?"

"That it doesn't make any difference what you are building as long as you learn to find joy in it. I have to make everything with the same joy as if I were making it for the King. I must find enjoyment in my work if I am to excel at it. Josef said that everything you do will eventually become mundane if you forget why you are doing it. I found that when I started enjoying what I did, my results were much better."

"Excellent, Hans. You have learned well," Father said with a smile.

"Father, there are two more things I learned while I was gone that I would like to tell you about."

"I would like very much to hear."

"I traveled to Fidelium with a person whom I was very angry with. I remembered the telescope and tried to see beyond my own problems. I found out she had challenges in life, too, and needed encouragement just like I do sometimes. I have come to realize that my problems are because of the wrong choices I have made. And that sometimes bad things just happen to us. We are all struggling in life, and I should be more gentle in how I treat others. There is not much gentleness in the world, is there, Father?"

"No, Son. Life can be very hard sometimes."

"I don't want to be hard, Father. I want to be more gentle to people. I used to think gentle people were weak, but it takes a lot of strength to be gentle to others when they need it, and even more to ask for it when I need it."

"You're right, Hans. What was the other thing you learned?"

"I learned it the day I left for my trip. You and Mother have been good to me, but I only appreciated you when you did what I thought was best. I didn't love you right because I was being so selfish in it. I now realize that love doesn't always do what we want, but it always has our best interests at heart. I have come to love you and Mother for who you are, and not for who I want you to be. Will you forgive me for leaving the way I did?"

Frederick stood up and put his arms around Hans. They held each other and had no need for words. Frederick finally stood back and held Hans by the shoulders. He knew that he was looking into the eyes of a man now, and not a boy. It was all Father could do to keep the tears back. Before either one of them could say anything, Mother called out to them from upstairs.

"Frederick and Hans, could you please come up here?"

They looked at each other and headed up the stairs as quick as they could. It must be something very important, or bad, for Mother to interrupt them in the shop. They found her standing in the kitchen.

"What is it, Elsa?" Father asked very concerned.

"Look," she said.

They both looked around but saw nothing.

"What are we looking for?" Father inquired.

"I cleaned the kitchen. Doesn't it look nice?"

"What?" Father asked. "You called us out of the shop to look at the kitchen? Elsa, we have things to do down there. I cannot come upstairs every time you clean a room."

"My point exactly, boys. This is how it feels to be interrupted just to see your work all day long," she said as she smiled and hit Father with a dish cloth.

Father grabbed her around the waist and tickled her as Mother shrieked and beat him with her dustrag. The three of them laughed at how Mother had finally gotten even with them. Hans was so glad to be home with his family again. He didn't even mind the time he had to finish his apprenticeship.

That night, Mother had a wonderful meal for them. It was the kind of meal she fixed on birthdays and Christmas. Hans thought that it was very special for her to have this celebration for him. After supper, Mother cleared the table and sat back down. Hans wondered what was going on because she had never done this before. Father got up and left the room. Hans and Mother sat in silence while they waited for Frederick to return. When he did, he sat down and just looked at Mother.

"What's going on?" Hans asked.

"Well, Son, I have a package I would like to give you to go along with the others."

"But, Father, you already gave me my tool chest."

"I know, but this is something you have earned," Father said as he handed the package to Hans.

He took the package and carefully opened it. Inside was a parchment with writing on it. Hans took it out and read it.

This certifies that Hans Von Zelditch has successfully completed the apprentice training and is qualified as a furniture-making journeyman.

Frederick Von Zelditch
Supervising Craftsman

Hans could not believe it. Father had given him his journeyman's certification. He looked at Father and then back down at the certificate.

"Father, I don't know what to say."

"You have earned it, Hans. I am very proud of you."

That night, Hans went down to the shop and selected some wood to make a frame like the one Father had for his craftsman's certificate. He carefully shaped it so they were the same. He liked going to "his" tool chest to remove his tools and put them back again. Father just smiled as he watched Hans work.

When the frame was completed, the next challenge was to find a place in the shop to hang it. It was a tradition of respect in Valorem that only the craftsman's certificate hung on the front wall for all to see. All others were hung on the back wall, if at all. Hans looked at the back wall and tried to find the perfect spot. His eyes kept going back to the front of the shop where Father's Craftsman Certificate hung. Finally, he got up the courage to ask.

"Father, do you think that it would be possible to hang my certificate under yours?"

"No, Hans," Father said as Hans hung his head, "but I would be very proud if you hang yours NEXT to mine."

With great joy, Father and Hans hung the new certificate. They stepped back, and Father put his arm around Hans as they admired it. Once again, they had to interrupt Mother to come down and look at it, only this time she did not mind. She was proud and happy to see her two men standing together in the shop they both loved.

The next several weeks went very well as Father allowed Hans to take on several projects. Each time they built something that had legs, Hans would again mention the lathe machine. Father continued to refuse, saying that it would cost far too much, considering the amount of work they had done. Hans did not give up, though, and kept looking for a chance to bring it up. Frederick never became annoyed because he was just glad that Hans was planning for the future in "their" shop.

On Friday of the third week after Hans had come home, Father answered a knock at the door of the shop. There was a messenger there who handed a letter to Father.

Frederick looked at the letter for a few moments and then walked over to Hans. "This came for you, Son. I think you should open it."

Hans took the letter and looked at it. His hands trembled as he tried to get up the courage to open it.

the end

of the beginning ...

Find out what's in the letter as Hans's journey continues in Book Two of the trilogy:

The Journeyman

The journey continues, with harder lessons, deeper consequences, and the pursuit of a dream that
may cost more than he ever imagined.

About The Author

Midwestern author and master woodworker Timothy Buchanan crafts both furniture and fiction with patience and care. A husband, father, and grandfather, he often writes with his Border Collie at his side and credits his wife, his muse and best friend, for inspiring his work.